I0785032

# CRACK of DAWN

# CRACK of DAWN
## PART ONE: GONE to HELL

MICHAEL GLENZEL

To my amazing wife. When she says the story is good...it's good.

And for my Mom and Dad who I miss tremendously.

# Contents

# RAISING KANE

*Thirty Years Ago*

"Get up."

Kane Garner stirred. An empty beer can fell off the couch and rolled away across the hardwood floor. He glanced at his phone to see the time, but the charge was dead.

In the kitchen, his younger brother was banging cabinet doors and clanking dishes.

"Time is it?" Kane asked groggily.

"Time for you to get a life," Avery said.

"What the fuck is your problem?"

Avery spread his arms. "Look around, Kane."

Kane didn't need to look. He knew. His empty beer cans and spent vape pens littered the coffee table. Sweaty socks filled mud-caked boots. Half-eaten containers of food were discarded on the floor, spilled and reeking. On the countertop was a spoiled quart of milk, more food. Dirty dishes filled the sink, and the refrigerator door, which had been left ajar, emitted a sour smell like bad cheese. Avery slammed the refrigerator door closed.

"I just got off a double shift. It sucks to come home to find you like this. On top of the fact, the house is a mess and I'm the one stuck cleaning it." Avery shook his head. "You're the older brother. Take care of shit."

Kane whipped his long, dark hair out of his face. He tried a few vape pens until he found one that still had some juice left. He took a long drag and exhaled. "I got to get to work."

"You're already late, Kane. Don't lose this job too."

Kane pulled on his socks and boots. "Wow, little brother. You're channeling the old lady this morning."

"And you're channeling the old man."

Kane stood abruptly. "Watch it. I'm nothing like that son of a bitch."

Another beer can bounced loose from the couch, coming to a stop at Avery's toe. He looked down at it, then back up at Kane.

"I don't have time for this." Kane pocketed his dead phone, snatched his truck keys, and brushed past Avery.

"I'm moving out," Avery announced before Kane reached the side door.

Kane stopped cold without turning around.

"You can keep the house," his brother added.

Without a word, Kane shrugged and exited.

*"Today's weather is your pick of the week with clear skies throughout the day and into the evening. No need for a jacket either. The temperature right now is 66 degrees with highs reaching 74. After 5 p.m., things will cool down a bit. Overnight, temperatures fall to 58 degrees in most regions. Tomorrow, clouds roll in by midday, and we can expect some storminess during the afternoon commute. Temperatures will be in the low 60s. We will have another look at your weather at the top of the hour.*

*In other news, NASA unveils its first tactically integrated and artificial intelligence suit. Demonstration exercises of the manned device will be conducted in Arizona to best simulate the geography of Mars—"*

Kane switched off the radio and parked his 4x4 outside Reynolds & Sons Manufacturing. His phone had chimed repeatedly during the ride after reaching enough charge to turn on. He had missed a text from Avery yesterday afternoon saying that he was working an overnight shift. It was easy to let himself think his night would have ended differently had he received it. Five texts and two missed calls from Becky. She was going to be pissed to learn he had fallen asleep instead of meeting her last night. He ignored the two late payment notifications from God-knew-who this month. And Roger, a co-worker, had messaged to say he'd punched his timecard for him this morning. That, at least, was something worth seeing.

As he walked across the parking lot, he received a text from his boss, Mr. Reynolds himself. He hesitated a second, anticipating it might be about his tardiness—he already had one warning—then looked at it. Reynolds needed him on the boring machine, and to see Lester.

That had Kane evading the main employee entrance and entering the factory warehouse through the loading docks. A delivery last night of twenty plastic-wrapped pallets of raw materials stood on the receiving floor. Most of them he should have had moved by now. He hopped onto a forklift and started staging the materials. He'd stocked several pallets before Reynolds found him.

His boss was a man in his fifties, partially bald, mustached, and round. He was old-school when it came to technology. Although he knew how to use a smartphone, he didn't use a computer, never turned one on. He carried with him at all times a clipboard stuffed with papers curled at the corners. The office staff was regularly printing inventory reports and shipping orders for him. He always had a pen in his mouth and a habit of chewing the end.

"Hey Garner!" he said. He switched the blue-colored pen to the other side of his mouth.

Kane slowed the forklift.

"Did you get my text?" Reynolds didn't trust technology either. "I need you on the boring machine. Lester says it's catching on the molds and throwing off the drill points."

"I'll finish this, then go see him," Kane said.

Reynolds looked at the remaining pallets in the receiving area and then at his watch. "This should have been done already. Go see him now; you can catch up on your break."

Kane nodded.

"You're a good worker, Garner—when you're here. Consider this your last warning," Reynolds said, then hustled away toward the office.

"Shit." Kane watched the fat ass walk away. His mood turned grim. People either attacked him or wanted something from him. Why couldn't everyone just leave him alone?

Still, Mr. Reynolds's mood of late was more forgiving since winning the government bid to build a rock pulverizing device that would see use in outer space. Reynolds & Sons manufactured precise machine parts for automobile and aerospace companies, and the bid required they build a fully assembled and functioning arm piece for the mechanical suits to be used on the surface of Mars. Tough and reliable in the harshest conditions, the mechanical arm would break rock with either a retractable hammerhead or an intense light beam depending on the hardness of the rock.

"Fucking finally," Reynolds had said when the United States announced its partnership with China and India to man a mission to Mars.

Kane could not have cared less.

A few moments later, he found Lester trying to fix the boring machine himself.

"Look who decided to show up today," Lester said. He had a slight whistle when pronouncing certain words on account of him missing half his teeth. Lester was one of the old-timers who'd worked for Reynolds their entire life. He couldn't pass up a chance to bust on the newer employees.

Kane only smiled as he took a glance at the machine. "You break every machine you touch, Lester."

"Screw you, you little peckerhead," Lester said, but he was grinning too. "It's not necessary to have machines do all the work. They break more often than they work."

"Really?" Kane straightened. "Weren't you in the Vietnam War? Tanks were quite handy back then."

"War is different, but your entitled generation wouldn't know a thing about it," Lester said.

"Easy now. That's getting a little personal."

"Can you fix it, or should I get one of those pretty girls in the front office to help?"

"Christ, Lester. Who shit in your Cheerios this morning?"

Lester burst out laughing and nearly killed himself as it turned into a coughing fit. "Good one, kid. Good one."

Kane opened his toolbox and set to work on the machine. Lester eventually wandered off to have a smoke. The assembly floor was a wide-open space with thirty machines. Half were manned and monitored by workers, the other half automated. Parts moved from one station to another either by conveyer belt or floor jack. It was deafening when everything was in full production. The fact that he heard his phone ring was dumb luck. It was Becky; he let it go to voicemail. Phones for personal usage were strongly discouraged during production, but Kane stole a glance. She'd sent him a text.

'where r u? im worried sick,' she wrote.

Kane sent a quick text back. 'im at work im sorry talk later'.

A loud bang sounded next to his ear, making him jump.

"Ha ha!" Douglas Reynolds slammed a wrench against the boring machine once more, acting like it was the funniest thing ever. Douglas was the teenage son of Mr. Reynolds—and heir to the business. The kid abused every perk that came with it too.

"No phones on the floor, Lame Brain Kane," Douglas said, grinning. "Unless you're arranging for a tug and jerk at the break, then count me in."

"Speaking of jerks, go beat off to your Porsche, Dougie," Kane said.

The smile fell from his face. "Don't call me that, or maybe my Dad finds out that Roger Dodger has been clocking you in every time you're late. I believe you're on your last warning for tardiness. It would suck to see Roger fired too."

"Oh my God, Dougie. What would I ever do without this job?" Kane said. "Go do nothing somewhere else."

Dougie flipped him the middle finger as he walked away, almost bumping into Lester as he left. "Get to work, Lester Molester."

For the next hour, Kane and Lester worked together on the boring machine. Kane made adjustments to the longitude and latitude slides, while Lester re-measured the drill placement on the mold template. After several test runs, they'd fixed the problem, the boring holes now realigned within specifications. Kane finished packing the tools as the 10 a.m. break buzzer sounded.

He was now back on the forklift, skipping break to stage pallets and try to catch up. He was driving the forklift up and down the aisles to make room for the new shipments among the storage racks by pulling and shifting other pallets when he noticed Dougie in the adjacent aisle walking with a woman. He couldn't hear over the forklift engine, but it appeared they were engaged in a disagreement.

During his next load, the two were still in the same place. Dougie was doing most of the talking, arms gesturing wide and wild. This time Kane recognized the woman from Quality Control. Dark hair, dark complexion. Jalanda was her name.

On Kane's way back, they had moved farther down the aisle. Dougie had his arms around her now and was talking in her ear. Jalanda, stiff, pulled back, not showing the same fondness.

Kane wasn't certain if they were dating and fighting, or if Dougie was being inappropriate. Either way, something wasn't right between them. He raced the forklift to the receiving area to pick up his next load, watching all the while. Dougie's hands wandered down Jalanda's back and hips. She tried to wriggle away from his advances, but Dougie held her close. His hands slid to the front of her hips. She slapped them off and abruptly walked away. Dougie's face twisted and turned red. He grabbed her by the arm and yanked her back with force. His other hand came around and slapped her across the face.

What Kane saw was the hand of his father striking his mother.

He braked and leaped off the forklift before it came to a complete stop. He didn't consider the circumstances or the consequences of his actions for a second. So many times as a boy, he felt he couldn't do much to stop his dad. As an adult, nothing stood in his way of stopping Dougie.

Dougie released Jalanda's arm as soon as he saw Kane coming. Kane didn't slow. He shoved Dougie hard against the storage racks and punched him in the jaw. Dougie's eyes rolled around in his head and his knees buckled. Kane lifted him by the shirt and readied to deliver another beating.

Jalanda shoved in between the two men. "Stop! Stop!" she said to Kane.

Kane met her eyes. This was her fight. He could help. But she didn't want it.

He let go of Dougie's shirt. The prick slid unsteadily to the floor. Blood pooled in his mouth.

Jalanda pushed Kane away, then dropped down to sit at Dougie's side. "Why'd you do that?" she yelled up at Kane.

He didn't answer. He exited the warehouse to cool off outside.

It was like his mother all over again. A woman who excused the abuse of a man desperate to dominate her to control his insecurities. It made no sense.

Several moments later, Mr. Reynolds found Kane sitting in his truck puffing on a vape pen. Papers clamped to the man's clipboard fluttered as he approached Kane.

"If it was up to my son, he'd press charges," Reynolds started. "His girlfriend backs his version of the story that you attacked him."

Kane scoffed. "How romantic."

"I reviewed the security video. You did that young lady a favor, even if she doesn't know it yet."

"You're still firing me," Kane concluded.

"My son is an ass, but he's still my son," Reynolds said. "His behavior is on me to correct. Not you."

Kane shook his head. There was no point in arguing the facts.

Reynolds handed Kane an envelope. "Two weeks' pay. You're a good man, Kane. Surely destined for a greater purpose than manning a forklift. Good luck."

Kane sat at a bar with his head hung over a half-empty beer. He had already emptied two others. The two weeks of pay in cash that Reynolds had given him was fanned out in front of him on the bar top.

He shared the barroom with very few patrons, not entirely surprising since it was 11 a.m. on a Tuesday. He'd been in this bar once before with Becky to watch a local band play. Besides the occasional live performance, the place served primarily as a sports bar and a regular hangout for college students. Big television screens hung from every wall, surrounding the bar. Not much was playing today except college baseball and golf. Kane couldn't decide which sport was more boring to watch.

He downed the rest of his beer and waved to the bartender for another. As he took a sip from his fourth beer, his phone chimed with a text. It was Becky again. Instead of responding, he called her. It could help to hear her voice.

No hello. Becky got right into it. "I couldn't reach you all night. You don't answer your texts. I thought something happened—"

"Becky, Becky," Kane interrupted. "I lost my job today."

There was a long pause on the other end. "What happened?" There, at least, was some concern.

"I punched a guy at work."

She paused longer this time, her next words not so understanding. "Kane, I don't think I can continue like this."

"It's not what you think," he said.

"Sure, Kane. I bet there are a thousand reasons why this guy deserved it. The results are always the same. Wait—are you calling me from jail?"

"Of course not," Kane said.

"Are you getting arrested?"

"Jesus Christ with the condescension."

"Well, when does this end, Kane?"

"When does what end? What are you talking about?"

"I'm talking about you're twenty-three years old. Most guys have their shit worked out by now. A steady job. No reason to go around punching people." A pause. "Were you drinking last night? Is that why you didn't call?"

"I don't need to answer that. You were completely wasted and throwing up in my bathroom three weeks ago," Kane said.

"Right. Three weeks ago. Because I don't drink every day. And if I remember correctly, no one got punched, no property got damaged, and no one got arrested that night either. Where are you now?"

It was Kane's turn for a long pause. "I'm at Ray's."

"You see, Kane. This is what I mean."

"What the hell do you want from me?" Kane's voice drew glances from other customers.

"You have no clue, do you?" Becky said.

"If you're going to talk to me in riddles—"

"Only because you can't puzzle out how to be grown-ass man."

"Are you done? Because I have a cold beer that's getting warm."

"Go to hell, Kane." Click.

Kane put down his phone and waved to the bartender. He pointed at the line of shot glasses behind him. "Anything."

When the bartender passed the full shot over, Kane poured it down his throat in one gulp, then winced. "Shit. What was that?"

The bartender shrugged. "Beam."

"Nice." Kane slid five dollars to him from his pile of cash.

"The guy over there took care of it." The bartender thumbed over his shoulder.

A large, broad shouldered man in fatigues sitting at the corner of the bar raised his glass in Kane's direction.

Kane nodded. "Thank you."

"Break-ups are a bitch," the big man said in a rumbling baritone.

The room rotated slightly as his words fell loosely out of his mouth. "Yeah, I'm pretty sure she's done with me."

"Mine got tired of my bullshit too," the big man said.

"Well, it's not bullshit," Kane said, speaking slowly.

The man laughed. "Oh, it's bullshit, bro. Look where you are. It's before noon in the middle of the week. It's definitely bullshit."

Kane smiled, then shook his head. "You might be right."

The big man laughed again. "I'll drink to that."

"Get a drink for my friend," Kane asked the bartender.

"Just a coke. I'm on duty in a little while." The big man flipped the lapel of his uniform jacket. "I'm Ben."

"Kane. People ever call you Big Ben?"

"Damn. Big Ben. Now that's original. Can't say I've heard that one before."

"Oh, you'd think people would associate—"

Ben broke out in laughter again. "I'm just busting you, bro. I get called that all the time. Don't mind at all."

"You're a funny guy, Ben." Kane took a sip of his beer. "Where you stationed?"

"Kansas City. I finished boot camp last month. Hoping to get into Special Forces in the fall," Ben said.

"What's happening in Kansas City until fall?"

"Recruitment."

"You don't look like a recruiter," Kane said.

"I go where and do what my country says. Besides, I have to drop fifty pounds to qualify for the Special Forces program. I'll train all summer," Ben said.

Kane pointed at the coke and plate of leftover hamburger and French fries in front of Ben. "Last meal then?"

"Something like that," Ben chuckled. "What about you? Ever think about a future in the service? I get a little commission if I recruit anyone."

Of course his friendliness had a motive. "I'm here to enjoy my beer, not join the military. But thanks for the drink." He picked up his beer and cash, and moved toward the other end of the bar.

"Maybe you'll reconsider," Ben called after him.

"I doubt it. I don't follow orders very well."


More customers arrived for a quick lunch or a drink. Kane's buzz subsided after he ate a sandwich. He switched over to drinking water and ordered a coffee as he watched golf.

"Is there anything else on?" he asked the bartender.

"Not on a Tuesday afternoon. It's this or soap operas," the bartender said as he took Kane's lunch plate away and wiped down the bar.

Watching golf was like watching paint dry. He never understood the amount of time invested or why it was imperative to play all the time. He and Avery had played once with their father as teenagers. His father had criticized them the whole time. After losing interest and realizing their father wanted to golf alone, they had searched for lost golf balls instead.

He sipped his coffee, reflecting. Ever since Avery started working as an EMT, the brothers hardly saw each other. Why would Avery want to move out? No mortgage to pay—the house was a gift from their mother after her passing. The bare few chores, groceries, household repairs—all of that could be divided up between them. It wasn't all of Kane's responsibility, but it wasn't all Avery's either. What the hell was his problem?

His leaving would change very little at least. He could sell the house now. Maybe move to New York or California. There certainly wasn't anything keeping him here. But if he did stay, he knew a commercial farm out in the plains that was always looking for help.

He scrolled through Becky's texts. As he read the old messages, he realized how often they fought. He couldn't find a recent text that was purely complimentary or that reflected any attraction toward one another. Perhaps Avery was right. As much as he despised his father's behavior, Kane acted a lot like him, especially toward Becky. Adding disappointment to misery, he placed his phone down and continued watching golf.

A news break rolled across the bottom of the television screen about an earthquake in California. *Forget moving to California.*

Another report followed about an earthquake hitting Japan. Imagine. Two earthquakes in one day, and on opposite sides of the Pacific. He hoped absently they didn't cause immense destruction.

Then the golf game disappeared entirely, replaced by the Emergency Alert System. It blared on every one of the televisions and on every phone in the bar.

"*Earthquake. Earthquake. Earthquake. Duck. Cover. And hold on.*" A siren from every TV followed the announcement.

Everyone in the bar looked at each other in disbelief. Some people laughed.

"*Earthquake. Earthquake. Earthquake. Duck. Cover. And hold on.*" The siren repeated.

"This is a mistake, right?" a woman said from across the bar. She held up her phone. The screen was red with a clock ticking down from twenty.

Kane grabbed his phone. The screen displayed the same countdown. This had to be a test. It couldn't possibly be real. Earthquakes didn't happen in Plattsburg, Missouri.

Five.

Becky sent him a text. 'OMG is this real'.

Avery sent him a text. 'where r u'.

Four.

The roar sounded like a freight train approaching at Mach speed.

The remainder of Kane's buzz washed away as adrenaline flooded his system. His focus narrowed.

The barroom sat on the first floor of an old three-story building. The second and third floors housed residential apartments. Overhead, thick wooden beams held up the ceiling. Some had been reinforced with steel plates at the joints. The only posts in the entire open space surrounded the horseshoe-shaped center bar.

Three.

He jumped out of his stool. "Everyone, behind the bar!"

"We've got a wasted one," a man chuckled.

Two.

The shock wave got louder and louder. People were laughing, ignoring the warnings. Could they not hear it? Kane leaped over the bar. "Take cover!"

One.

Air vacuumed out of the barroom and pumped back in within the same half-second. The windows imploded. The glass detonated at lethal speeds. The building shook with violence and screams. Televisions fell from the walls. Drinkware and plates vibrated off every surface and exploded on the floor. Tables and chairs tipped over. Wood creaked and snapped, sounding like gunfire. Ceiling beams twisted like spent matchsticks and fell from above. A couple of guys who were trying to keep their beers from spilling looked up too late to see a busted joist drop part of the ceiling on them. Then the lights exploded as electricity surged, killing the power.

Kane curled into a ball behind the bar and covered his head. He heard a loud boom from above followed by a second louder boom, and then the entire ceiling gave out and collapsed on top of him.

The shaking stopped seconds, maybe minutes later. Water dripped onto Kane's face. He coughed and spit dust. He shifted his arms and legs. Not pinned. As his eyes adjusted to the darkness, the small space behind the bar came into view, looking relatively intact. The posts had held the brunt of the weight above. He'd gotten lucky. The bartender, however, had not.

A few feet away, the man stared at Kane with absent eyes, a copper pipe speared through his chest.

"Can anyone hear me?" Kane yelled.

Except for the sound of running water, everything was deathly quiet. No one responded to his cries. Surprisingly, he had maintained a death grip on his phone, but its signal was dead too.

Kane pressed the phone's flashlight on and peeked over the bar top. Wood and debris from the upper floors filled the room. He could see no one. And more pertinently, he saw that he was trapped behind the bar by the fallen beams and concrete.

"Hello? Anyone?" he said with a quaver in his voice.

His initial shock wore off, and so too the adrenaline. Kane took a few deep breaths. He needed to think. He searched behind the bar and found a case of bottled water. He opened one and drank the whole thing down.

If this building had collapsed, what did the rest of the town look like? What if the fire department never found him? It could be days before they came. He could make the water last him, but for how long? He had no food except some cut lemons and cocktail cherries. He'd be sharing a tight space with a decomposing body a few feet away.

Kane breathed faster and faster. He grabbed another bottle of water and gulped it down. After the last swallow, he inhaled deeply and held his breath a moment, two, three. He finally exhaled, slowly, trying to calm down. "Get a grip, asshole."

The darkness of the ruined bar slowly paled. Sunlight filtered through the crisscross of broken beams and wallboard as the dust settled. He shined his flashlight, pushing back the shadows. There. A space. With some maneuvering, he might be able to crawl through it.

"I am getting out of here," he said to the deceased bartender with conviction, then quickly realized that other people were not. He reached over and closed the bartender's eyes.

Once he pulled himself onto the bar top, he squeezed under a beam, then dropped onto the other side. A refrigerator had fallen through the ceiling and crushed the chair where he'd sat several moments ago. He flattened low to the floor and slid under a nearby table, the only thing that had kept a tower of timber from blocking this path. He placed his hands and knees delicately as he moved beneath it. If he brushed one of the legs, he'd surely be crushed.

Feeling like a rat in a maze, he progressed toward the only light source he could see. But no sooner did escape feel certain than his way out end abruptly. The light was coming from a gap in the outer wall that was too small for him. Made of stone and brick, the gap couldn't be widened by hand.

"Damn it." Sirens sounded in the far distance. "Help!" he yelled through the hole in the wall, but no one replied.

Kane shimmied backward the way he came. Dust fell occasionally into his face and mouth. He breathed in short bursts again. The collapsed building was highly unstable and could shift at any moment. The devastation around him was like a cage. He hadn't known he had an issue with tight spaces, but he had never been in a situation quite like this before.

His feet and legs hit a mass of cable and wire, tangling up with them. He couldn't see past his chest to free them, and the space was too narrow to turn around. Sweat beaded on his brow and rolled into his eyes. Frustrated and exhausted, he rolled onto his back. He wiped sweat and dirt from his eyes, and when he finally opened them again, he saw the blue sky above, and a clear path up and out of the collapsed building.

His eyes welled, and a tear leaked down the side of his face. "Son of a bitch," he sighed with relief.

Kane found a couple of solid holds above his head and pulled himself to a seated position. Heavy gauge wires hooked his pant leg and boot laces. He freed them quickly. Begging his arms to accept the task, he pulled his entire body up until he could get his legs under him.

Within moments, he emerged from the pile of rubble. He climbed down into the middle of the street, fell to his hands and knees, and threw up.

Downtown Main Street looked as if a bomb had hit. Every building on the half-mile stretch was leveled. Not one structure remained standing. Parked cars were crumpled and the street a mess. Smoke rose from the rubble at several locations. Natural gas tainted the air.

Other people who had emerged from the wreckage stood in the middle of the street with the same look of bewilderment and disbelief as Kane knew he had.

"Help!" The call to his left sounded weak and muffled.

Kane snapped out of his daze. Glass crunched under his feet as he searched for the person who had pleaded for help.

"I hear you," he yelled as he approached the dry cleaning business across the street from the bar. The roof of the single-story building had folded in the middle. On each side of the entranceway, two large glass windows had blown out. He stepped through one of them and ducked under the leaning ceiling. "Where are you?"

"Here." A pudgy hand with painted nails waved from under a pile of clothing and twisted metal.

"I got you," he said touching the person's hand. The hand gripped his tightly and wouldn't let go. Kane shoved pants, jackets, blouses, and suits aside until he uncovered the woman's head and shoulders. She started crying as soon as they locked eyes.

"You're OK," Kane said. "You're going to be OK. What's your name?"

"Katie." Thick mascara streaked down her plump cheeks.

"Can you move your other arm and legs, Katie?"

She nodded and sobbed.

Kane pulled more clothes away. Katie was pinned under the rack that normally wound around the shop as a conveyer for customers' garments.

"I'm going to lift the rack, and you're going to pull yourself out. Can you do that?"

Katie nodded.

Kane gripped the rack and lifted with every bit of strength he had. The rack shifted an inch. For a frazzled person, Katie maneuvered quite nimbly out from under the clothing rack. As soon as she was clear, he released the rack and helped her out of the store.

Except for a cut on her leg and some bruising, Katie appeared to be fine. About a foot shorter than Kane, she threw her arms around his neck and nearly pulled him over with her hug. "Thank you so much. Thank you. I thought I was going to die," she managed through uncontrolled sobs.

A police cruiser turned slowly onto Main Street with its blue lights flashing, and weaved around the rubble and destruction.

"You're safe now, Katie," he said. "The police will direct you where to go."

Katie wiped her tears, causing her makeup to smear more. "You're a hero," she said, sniffling.

Kane thought immediately of Avery. If only this woman knew the truth of the life he had been leading, she wouldn't be saying a thing like that. "Unlikely," Kane said.

The cruiser slowed alongside them. Kane had gotten to know many of the local police over the last several years, often from the backseat of a police car. He recognized this officer rolling up to them, a real tough guy behind the badge, but that wasn't the person who stared at them now.

"Judgment day is here," Officer Burl Murphy said with a crackling voice and dry mouth. His eyes were wide in what was likely shock and disbelief.

"There are people trapped inside," Kane pointed to the bar.

"Sinners will pay for their wrongdoings. And I am God's vessel." Officer Murphy pointed his gun at Kane and Katie.

"Oh shit!" Kane dove and pulled Katie down with him.

Murphy shot twice, then continued his calm way down Main Street before detouring down a side road.

Kane rolled off Katie as soon as the cruiser disappeared.

"He just shot at us," Katie said in disbelief.

"That bastard! Are you OK?"

She didn't answer. She was staring the way Murphy had gone.

Kane gripped her by the shoulders. "Do you have a way to get home?"

Katie nodded. "My car is over there." Hers was a blue compact car parked across the street, one spared by the collapsed hardware store.

"Go home. Stay off the main roads if you can."

The two parted ways. Kane's truck was parked behind the bar where he had left it earlier in the day. Thankfully, it wasn't damaged, but debris had fallen everywhere around it. He moved what materials he could, then got in, shifted it into four-wheel drive, and navigated carefully out of the parking lot.

The damage from the earthquake extended far beyond Main Street. Along his route, he detoured several times. Powerlines were ripped from toppled utility poles, trees lay uprooted, and in a few neighborhoods fires had ignited. A tipped tanker truck sat in a pool of yellowish liquid that was still pouring from the top of its payload. People stood outside their destroyed homes clutching onto one another.

A half-mile before his house, the paved road looked like a roller coaster of ribbon. Kane steered his truck off-road and cut across the adjacent cornfield. With the growing season only beginning, the bottom of his truck easily cleared the newly sprouted stalks. If they had been any taller, Kane would have never seen the chasm in the earth.

He slammed on the brakes. His tires locked and plowed through the soft soil before coming to stop. A rift had opened in the middle of the cornfield, easily twenty yards wide and ripped the full length of the cornfield far out of sight.

Kane exited his truck for a closer look. He stepped gingerly toward the edge. Across the gap, loose earth fell into its depths, which only confirmed his fear of the unstable ground. The hole went deep. How far, he couldn't tell. The shadows of the day obscured the bottom, and he didn't dare get any nearer to inspect. He returned to his truck and backed away from the crack in the earth.

It was mid-afternoon by the time he found a way around the chasm and finally arrived home. Kane threw his truck into park before leaping out of the cab.

"Shit." The massive tree that he and Avery had climbed thousands of times as kids had fallen on the house. The old oak had torn the roof off of the porch. Its wide span of branches speared the windows on the second floor and obscured the front door. One of the thickest of them had snapped free and landed on Avery's car.

"Avery!" Kane ran around to the back of the house. "Avery!"

A whistle came from the garage.

Kane sighed in relief. As a kid, Kane had been loud, animated, antsy, and had dominated every conversation. His mouth moved so fast that it often got him in trouble at home and school. The only way for Avery to get a word in around Kane was to whistle. The technique still seized his attention to this day.

Avery waved from where he was kneeling over a chainsaw by the garage. He had ditched his EMT uniform for regular jeans and a green t-shirt. The white patch of hair above his right eyebrow stood out amongst the rest of his brown hair. Avery's poliosis bothered him, and he had tried hair dyes to cover it up over the years to no avail.

Kane never paid much attention, except for today.

"I've been trying to reach you, you son of a bitch," Avery said.

"I would have been home sooner, brother, but a building fell on top of me," Kane said.

"You look it. You should clean that cut on your head. There's antiseptic in the bathroom. I'm fine, by the way."

Kane nodded, then spun on his heel. He could leave Avery alone if that's what he needed.

"Hey."

Kane turned in time to see Avery's glossed eyes and opens arms before his brother enveloped him in a hug. "I thought you were dead, Kane."

Kane came back outside after changing his clothes and cleaning a few of the cuts he hadn't noticed. Avery was shutting off the chainsaw and removing the last of the large branch from his car. "I have to go to work," he said.

"I can't reach Becky." Kane waved his phone. "Do you have a signal?"

"I see. Let's make this about you again. I checked on our neighbors already. You know them, right? Mrs. Wilcox. Alan and Gale. They're OK, in case you were worried."

"I'm glad we have an EMT in the family," Kane said, shooting down his brother's sarcasm. "I was going to offer you a ride—Baker Road is torn up—but maybe you should walk instead."

"You saw the branch on my car and the chainsaw in my hands. Do you think you could have told me that before I did all this work?"

"I thought you were working on the tree that landed on the house. That seemed like the higher priority to me."

"If it's such a high priority, why are you worried about Becky?"

Kane's brow furrowed. "Because she's my girlfriend, jackass."

"Are you sure about that?"

"What do you know?"

"I know you lost your job today. You're lucky if they don't press charges, Kane."

"She told you?"

"She texted me."

"Why would she do that, brother? Do you two have something going on?"

Avery scoffed. "Who's being the jackass now? Take me to work, or let me use your truck."

"I'll drive. But we're checking on Becky first."

The two brothers rode in relative silence except for their reactions to the extensive damage from the earthquake. Tucker's Farm was the largest commercial farm in the area. Rows and rows of heaved ground like frozen waves contorted the crop fields. Hundreds of cattle outside their pens ran panicked. Employees riding ATVs tried desperately to herd them back toward their enclosures.

They detoured down Clay Street. Every other house on it had collapsed. Neighbors helped neighbors search for missing people in the ruins of their homes.

"I should be helping," Avery said.

"This is too big for one person," Kane responded, keeping the truck steadily moving through the ravaged neighborhood.

Maple Street was flooded. A geyser of water bubbled in the middle of the street and poured water into the broken basement windows of every house. A lone city worker operated a backhoe in an attempt to locate the massive break and divert the water.

They turned onto Frost Road. The asphalt and sidewalks looked like shattered glassware. Smoke choked the air. Two of the houses were on fire. With no fire trucks in sight or sound, the homeowners sadly and powerlessly watched their homes burn.

Frost Road adjoined with Fourth Street. Becky lived in the second house on the right with her elderly father. Kane jammed the brakes at the intersection. A large elm tree blocked the way. With no way around it, he shut off the engine.

"Let's go."

She lived in a single-family ranch with a detached garage. Becky's father, Mr. Kirkland, took great pride in his home. The house and lawn were well-maintained, even now, and early summer perennials blossomed. What Kane noticed before all that, though, was that Becky's car wasn't in the driveway.

"She's at work," Kane said, then started to turn back.

Avery grabbed him. "We're here. We can at least make sure Mr. Kirkland is OK."

Kane hesitated. "I don't want to."

Avery rolled his eyes and knocked on the front door. "Mr. Kirkland?"

"Perhaps he's dead," Kane quipped.

A grainy voice came from the other side of the door. "Who's there?"

"It's Avery Garner."

"I have a shotgun. No funny business, ya hear?" Mr. Kirkland said.

"No, sir."

The front door cracked open an inch, and the barrel of a shotgun poked through. "Who is it?"

"Avery Garner, sir. Are you alright?"

The door slammed, a chain latch jingled, and then the door swung wide open. Short and sinewy, strands of grey hair combed over and greased to his scalp, Mr. Kirkland wore a white tank top over his hunched body, a permanent scowl on his face, and a shotgun across his chest.

"The Garner brothers." He nodded. "Avery, you're welcome here. Your brother is not. If you're about to say something, speak up."

"We wanted to make sure you were OK," Avery said loudly.

"Is that so? I bet that one was hoping the house had fallen on my head." Kirkland jutted his chin toward Kane.

"Actually," Kane started, but Avery cut him off.

"What he'd say?" Kirkland asked.

"He said hello," Avery covered.

"Bullshit. I heard what he said."

Avery ignored the grief between them. "Are you hurt, Mr. Kirkland?"

"Am I hurt? No. I'm fine, young man. Some pictures fell off the wall, Marit's ashes fell off the mantel. Luckily, the urn held strong. Even in death, she's as tough as always."

"I'm sorry that happened," Avery said solemnly.

"Sure, kid," Kirkland said, then leaned around Avery and spoke to Kane. "Maybe you could take your damn hands out of your pockets, Garner, and go find my baby girl."

"I intend to, Mr. Kirkland, but we're spending too much time listening to your tired ass," Kane shot back.

Kirkland's eyes narrowed on Kane. "The actions of man speak louder than his word."

"And sometimes the old never wise up," Kane retorted.

"Alright," Avery interrupted. "Let's . . . um. We're going. I'm glad you're OK, Mr. Kirkland."

Kirkland nodded. "Bring my Becky back. She's at her work."

With a final wave, the two brothers were back in Kane's truck and reversing up Frost Road.

"I never understood why you two hate each other so much," Avery said.

"I'd rather not get into it now," Kane said while turning the truck around.

The two brothers again rode in silence and awe as they rounded more devastation from the earthquake. Street after street seemed worse than the last. They cut through the high school parking lot, where a large section of brick had fallen off the face of the school and exposed a few of the classrooms on the top floor. They drove instead across the football field, leaving behind tire ruts on the manicured grass, and exited onto Birch Street.

Three-story Victorian houses, most converted for commercial spaces, lined the street. All of them had suffered the same fate as houses in other neighborhoods. The dental office where Becky worked was no exception. The entire structure had toppled like a house of cards. The walls were fanned on the ground around the roof, which had caved into the second floor. That the building wasn't flattened to the ground was a miracle.

A dozen people stood outside, and a few sat on the ground with various injuries. Kane and Avery jumped out of the truck and hurried toward the group. Avery split off to attend to the injured. Kane spotted Becky amongst the crowd, and his fear and anxiety fled. She was kneeling over a person who had their arm in a makeshift sling and an open gash on their forehead.

"Becky!"

Kane rushed to her; Becky met him halfway. Tears flowed from both as they embraced.

"Are you OK?" Kane asked.

She nodded and buried her face in Kane's neck. Her sobs continued as he held onto her. He picked bits of dirt and paper from her long black hair and brushed some of the dust off her pink scrubs.

"Everything shook," she said, catching her breath. "We all ran out, then . . . then the roof fell."

"You did the right thing. Everyone's safe now," Kane consoled.

"No." She leaned off his chest. Her brown eyes glossed over again, and more tears ran down her cheeks. "Dr. Ryan was upstairs in his office. He didn't . . . he's still . . ."

Kane followed Becky's gaze. The roof had turned the second floor into scrap and pulverized plaster. There was little chance Dr. Ryan survived.

"I'll go," he said, seeing how upset Becky was. "Maybe he's trapped."

"Shouldn't we wait for the fire department?" Becky said.

"Becky, the town—everything—is ruined. They won't be coming anytime soon. We should at least know. OK?"

Becky wiped her teary cheeks and nodded.

Kane shoved his way into the building. The office had maintained the original layout of the old Victorian home with all original moldings and reproduction wallpaper. Now, it would need to be rebuilt. He entered the reception area that had once served as a foyer; behind a reception counter consistent with the historical style was a set of stairs that normally led to the second floor but that Kane wouldn't get far by taking. Debris filled half the staircase, and part of the wrecked roof was jutting into the stairwell at its top near the second floor.

This wasn't working.

Kane hurried back outside. A large section of an upper wall leaned against the building like a ramp. He scaled it and soon found a narrow opening between the floor of the second level and the collapsed roof. He peered into the cramped space.

"Dr. Ryan!" Kane yelled, then muttered to himself, "This is dumb."

Kane slipped between the floor and rafters with care to prevent getting stabbed by a nail or electrocuted by an exposed wire. Once inside, he hesitated until his eyesight adjusted to the dimness. The space was high enough to continue on his hands and knees. Dental and medical supplies littered the floor. Metal shelves suspended this section of the roof, giving an occasional unsettling creak.

He left the storage room, crossing over disintegrated paneling, fragmented wall studs, fallen rafters, and torn insulation in the hallway. There was no way through to the other side. To his left, a door wedged askew inside its casing led to another room; the thin metal placard hanging by a single nail on it indicated that Dr. Ryan's office was on the other side.

"Dr. Ryan?"

A moan and movement came from the adjacent room.

"Can you hear me?" Kane called more loudly.

The door opening was too narrow for him to squeeze through, and he feared the header might crash down on him if he tried prying the door any wider. Kane pressed on his phone flashlight.

The entire ceiling had buckled into a tangle of beams and tiles. An old oak desk had taken the brunt of the collapse and splintered apart. Shattered picture frames, a contorted desk lamp, a demolished keyboard, and a fractured computer monitor were among the wreckage.

Kane's light revealed a bloody hand, then found a pair of eyes staring back at him from beneath the rubble. "Dr. Ryan!"

Dr. Ryan groaned and winced in pain. His eyes slowly closed, then reopened. Red spittle leaked out of his mouth and coated his white goatee as he tried to speak. "I . . . I can't move."

"I'm going to get some help," Kane said. "We'll get you out." But as he scanned the rest of the room, he quickly calculated the futile enormity of the task to dig out Dr. Ryan.

Dr. Ryan's eyes rolled as he forced them to stay open. "Tell my staff . . . I'm sorry . . ." He coughed, and more blood shot out of his mouth. "Tell them—"

"I'll remind you when we're both out what you wanted to say." Kane swallowed down his anxiety. "What else?"

"Becky . . . that I . . . I loved her . . ."

Dr. Ryan exhaled his last breath, the choked air releasing as though from a deflating balloon. His head rolled slightly, and he closed his eyes for the final time.

It was the first time Kane had witnessed someone die other than his parents. His father had died of heart disease when Kane was ten years old, and his mother of cancer last year. Maybe because he anticipated their passing, both deaths had felt peaceful. Dr. Ryan's passing felt immediately traumatic. He hadn't even known Dr. Ryan except through what Becky shared about her work.

What had he meant—that he loved her?

Kane's grief warped with distress. He didn't want to understand it. He swallowed his sorrow and returned to where Dr. Ryan's staff, Becky included, waited for him.

"I'm sorry. He didn't . . . um . . ." He couldn't finish delivering the bad news, but they understood.

The sun dipped low on the horizon. Within a couple of hours, darkness would shroud the town, complicating rescue and disaster relief. Avery finished administering first aid to a few of Dr. Ryan's staff and clients. Rides were arranged for everyone. Kane tried to convince

Becky to come back to their house with him and Avery, but she insisted they drive her home so she could see her father.

"What do we do about Dr. Ryan?" Becky asked after the silence in the truck had gone on for a period.

"I'll call dispatch as soon as I get a signal," Avery said. He wrapped an arm around her shoulders. "It's OK. There's nothing more we can do."

The three of them rode shoulder to shoulder with Becky sitting in the middle of the cramped cab. She reacted with a series of gasps as Kane traversed town.

"How far does this go?" Becky asked, eyes roaming the destruction.

Kane shrugged. Avery did not contradict him.

Becky reached across the dashboard and turned on the radio. The unpleasant yet familiar signal of the Emergency Broadcast System buzzed three times over the speakers.

"*An earthquake has occurred. Expect aftershocks. For your safety, evacuate all buildings. Remain outside for further information. Additional news and information will follow this broadcast. This is not a test.*"

A long tone followed, and then a man spoke authoritatively.

"*This is a news and information update from the Federal Emergency Management Agency. Several catastrophic earthquakes struck many cities across our nation today. Subsequently, coastal states on both the East and West Coasts experienced significant tsunami events and flooding in addition to seismic damage. Allies and other nations have reported similar events around the world. The cause of these global events is unknown at this time.*

*The National Guard is mobilizing in every state. Troops from all branches of the military have been ordered to support rescue and humanitarian efforts domestically and abroad. All reservists are expected to report for duty. Local law enforcement, fire services, and first responders ask that communities extend their full cooperation. Triage units will be established at every functioning hospital and care center. Anyone who needs aid will receive aid, and citizens are asked to understand the number of anticipated causalities. Please stay tuned to this broadcast for more news and information in your area.*"

The radio fell silent for a moment, then the Emergency Broadcast System buzzed three more times and the same report repeated.

Becky turned off the radio and cried. Avery stared out the window at nothing, his fingers digging into a callus in his palm. Kane felt numb and nauseous. He twisted his hands around the steering wheel until his knuckles turned white.

"You done good, boys. Thank you for bringing my baby home," Kirkland said through tears of joy, his permanent scowl turned up as he gazed upon his daughter and squeezed her hands.

"You're welcome, Mr. Kirkland," Avery said.

"What about you?" Kirkland chinned at Kane. "Do ya have anything to say? Speak up if ya do."

Kane rolled his eyes.

"Dad," Becky interrupted. "I'm going with the boys. Come with us. It's not safe to be here alone."

"Bah!" Kirkland flipped his hand.

Avery didn't hesitate for a second. "We have plenty of room, a generator, and running water. It'll be a long time before things get back to normal."

Kane stiffened. "Ah, wait a minute. I didn't—"

Avery raised his hand, delivering a not-the-time side-eye.

"Ah, don't like the idea too much, do ya, Garner?" Kirkland scowled. "Just because ya did one good deed today don't make ya a hero. I'll go. Someone has to take care of my daughter."

"Here we go," Kane said exasperatedly.

"Dad, let's go pack some things," Becky said, and gently ushered her father back toward the house. She turned back to Kane before following her father. "You could try a little harder."

Kane threw up his arms, dispirited. "You've got to be kidding."

Becky and her father each filled a couple of suitcases with clothes and toiletries. They emptied the freezer and refrigerator, packing as much as they could into two large coolers. Their pantry of dry and canned goods filled three trash bags. It was Avery's idea they bring the food, and Kane had to admit it wasn't a bad one. Necessities would likely be hard to acquire over the next several days.

Kane and Avery piled everything into the back of Mr. Kirkland's pickup truck for them, and Becky jumped up behind the wheel.

"You can't follow us out of here because of the elm," Kane said. "Meet us on Maple. It gets dicey after that, so you can follow my route back to the house."

"We know where ya live, Garner," Kirkland barked. He had come out of the house carrying one last item and was passing it to Avery so he could climb into the passenger seat. Kane saw after a moment that it was an urn—his wife's. Once Kirkland was settled, Avery wordlessly and tenderly passed the urn back to him, which the man hugged to his chest with two arms.

Kane desperately held back his tongue. "Meet us on Maple. You'll see what I mean, old man."

Kane could have easily avoided driving by the large crack in the earth, but he wanted to shut the old man up for once. Kirkland's craned neck hung out the window so he could gawk at the wide chasm in the middle of the cornfield. That was enough satisfaction for Kane.

They arrived at Kane and Avery's house moments later. Avery helped Becky and Kirkland bring in the food and suitcases. Kane went to work on the generator since it hadn't run in some years. He cleaned the filter, checked the plug and oil, and filled the fuel tank. As soon as night fell, the generator begrudgingly but obediently restored power to the house.

Avery and Becky slapped together sandwiches for everyone, but no one was particularly hungry except for Mr. Kirkland. Instead of eating, Kane hunted down the portable radio they stored in his mother's room. She called it a boombox, which made Kane smile given the radio's capsule aesthetic and tinny speakers. He tuned into every frequency in turns, but every news station within range was broadcasting the same emergency message they had heard earlier. Disappointed, Kane shut it off.

"Leave the damn thing on and bring it closer, will ya?" Kirkland yelled from the living room. Becky's father had quickly made himself right at home. He was slouched in a chair, shoes and socks off, feet propped on the coffee table. A book he'd somehow found in the house lay open in his lap. His wife's urn rested on the floor beside him.

Kane brought the boombox over to Kirkland. "It's not technically news if it repeats, you know."

"I'd rather listen to the radio than listen to you," Kirkland scowled.

"Believe me, the feeling's mutual, old man," Kane said.

Becky glared at Kane when he returned to the dining table. "I don't like when you talk to him like that," she said.

"Are you serious? You don't hear the stabs at me every chance he gets?"

"He's my father."

"Is that supposed to excuse his nastiness?"

"Can you two not do this right now?" Avery interjected. "We got bigger problems coming in the days and probably weeks ahead."

Kane watched Avery rub his tired eyes and run his hands through his brown hair. The patch of white strands above his brow bounced back into place as if magnetized together.

Becky seemed to notice how tired he was and rubbed his shoulder. "Avery, I never thanked you for helping my patients and co-workers. You were amazing today."

Avery grinned politely. He had other matters on his mind, apparently. "Look, it's going to get harder to buy food, water, gas—any basic necessity. If this has global impacts, imagine the effect on manufacturing and distribution. We won't be buying groceries in a grocery store for a long time. Paper money might not even be worth much to anyone."

"The stores are open," Becky said with a bit of panic in her voice. "We can stock up with as much as we can buy."

Avery put up his hand. "The store shelves are probably empty by now. I think we should—"

"Weapons," Kane interrupted.

Becky huffed. "You're not serious."

"We're not the only ones thinking this right now," Kane explained. "We're going to need to protect ourselves."

"That wasn't what I was going to suggest," Avery said. "We have the means to start growing food ourselves. It's the beginning of summer. If we plant right away, we'll have food by July."

Becky paled. "You're—that's long-term."

"People will start looting soon," Kane said. "In a few days, people will get desperate and do anything to feed their own. They won't wait a couple of months."

"So your idea is to shoot people," Avery said exasperatedly.

"If we grow food, we need to protect it. That's all I'm saying, brother."

Avery rubbed his face and yawned. "I can't talk about this anymore. I have to go to bed. I've been awake for two days." He avoided eye contact with Kane as he cleared the dishes from the table and put away the leftovers. He closed and locked a few of the windows too before disappearing up the stairs.

"Can my father take your mom's room?" Becky asked. "I'm going to help him to bed."

Kane nodded. "Yeah, of course."

As Becky assisted her father into the back bedroom, Kane exhaled into his clasped hands. His leg bounced unconsciously, a jackhammer under the dining table, as he sat alone, a thousand thoughts racing through his mind. What if they ran out of gas for the generator and couldn't buy anymore? How would they get food and clean water? Were they safe in this house? Were they safe anywhere? What if they needed medicine? What medications did Becky's father take regularly? What if people started coming around looking for food?

Avery was right. What the hell were they supposed to do?

Too anxious, he got up, looking for something to do. He shut off the radio and lamp in the living room. The downed oak completely blocked the front door, but he locked it anyway. He checked the windows; a couple had been broken and branches poked through, but it looked like Avery had latched them anyway. Kane pulled the shades on them closed.

Back in the kitchen, he tested a flashlight from a cabinet. The beam was strong, but for how long? He couldn't find any spare batteries in the junk drawer.

The stove, the microwave, the refrigerator—all ran on electricity. How long before the electricity got repaired? The fireplace in the living room hadn't functioned in fifteen years. The chimney was plugged at the base and capped at the top of the flue to prevent animals from entering the house and nesting in the chimney. They could light a fire outside if needed for cooking, but would that put a target on them?

He opened cabinet doors and inventoried the dry goods in the pantry. He and Avery were not good shoppers or regular cooks. For four adults, he guessed they had enough food for a week, maybe two weeks if they rationed. The supplies the Kirklands had brought added three weeks at the most to that.

Kane grabbed the flashlight and headed to the basement next. The boxes and storage bins stacked everywhere mostly contained their father's and mother's things. Their mother never dared to get rid of their father's belongings, and Kane and Avery had felt the same way after her passing.

He hadn't been down here in months, but he knew right where to find what he was looking for, and went straight to a long crate tucked away in the corner of the basement. He moved a few boxes clear of its lid and pried it open.

He shined the flashlight on the contents inside: his father's guns. His mother had hated guns and had told her boys that she'd sold them. But when Kane turned eighteen, she surprised him with them for his birthday. He hadn't opened the crate in the five years since.

Two hunting rifles wrapped in brown wool blankets lay inside the crate. One had a scope. A double-barrel shotgun, a compound bow, and two handguns were among the cache, each meticulously cleaned and properly stored. At the bottom of the crate were several boxes of ammunition for each firearm.

Kane picked up one of the handguns, Glock 19 imprinted on its side. It weighed more than he'd expected and was cold to the touch. It also smelled like mixed oil and metal. It had an empty magazine in the handle, which took him a moment to figure out how to slide open. He slapped the empty magazine back into place and aimed the gun at a stack of boxes.

What was he thinking? He had no experience with such things. The thought of shooting another person twisted his stomach. Bar fights and swinging fists were a lot different, meant to make a statement not to kill. He put the handgun back and closed the crate.

On his return upstairs, the flashlight beam flashed across a cardboard box with KANE written in block letters in his mother's handwriting. A wooden baseball bat he recognized immediately stuck out of the box. He grasped the handle, instantly nostalgic for his days in high school as a first baseman. He had hit many home runs with this bat, several of them game-winning and even championship-clinching plays. His grip found home in the handle, and the barrel swung with perfect weight and balance. He took the bat with him and headed upstairs.

"Expecting a ball game to break out?"

"Geez, Becky." Kane jumped as he entered the kitchen. "I thought you went to bed."

"I can't sleep with everything . . . I mean, you know," Becky said, picking at the label on the beer bottle in front of her. She slid a second beer across the table. "Thought you might like one."

"You know it, babe," Kane said. He popped the cap and chugged a quarter of the beer. The cool malts slid easily down his throat and warmed him inside. Beer would be hard to come by soon too. He smacked his lips. "That's real good."

Becky smiled while continuing to pick at the beer label. Without looking up, she said, "What's the bat for?"

Kane shrugged. "Protection. Maybe. If we need it."

"Kane, half the population east of Kansas City carries a gun."

Kane's brow furrowed, surprised at her response. "Could you do it, Bec? Shoot someone?"

"If it meant protecting me or my family, yes. I think I could."

"That goes without saying. What if someone stole from you. Broke into your house looking for something to eat. Could you still pull the trigger?"

"I wouldn't have to. You'd be there to take care of them," Becky said. "Right?"

A wisp of her long dark hair fell into her face. She pulled it back, tucking it behind her ear. Kane's eyes caught on the cluster of freckles dotted high on her cheeks and across the bridge of her nose. Her brown eyes sparkled, as they always did when she smiled, and she quickly looked away. It was this shyness about her more than her looks that Kane found attractive. He reached across the table and rubbed her hand, gently intertwining their fingers.

"We're going to be OK," he assured her.

Becky slid her hand back to lift her beer and took a few swallows. Avoiding. Something was on her mind.

"What's wrong?" he asked. "Is it about this morning?"

Becky shook her head. She took a deep breath. "Kane—"

The lights in the kitchen went dark.

"Damn it, the generator must have run out of gas." Kane stood from his chair and snatched the flashlight off the kitchen counter. He was headed to the door but quickly backtracked and grabbed the baseball bat before proceeding outside.

"I'm coming," Becky said anxiously, following him out of the house before he could protest.

The night air carried to them the burning scent from the houses that had sparked into flames after the earthquake. Sirens echoed somewhere miles away. Otherwise, the evening was quiet, the usual chirping crickets and croaking frogs voiceless.

Kane led Becky to the garage to retrieve a gas can and then around the rear of the house toward the generator.

"Where is it?" Becky asked.

"Gone."

The generator had been ripped clear of its concrete pad. Kane's flashlight beam followed the frayed, thick gauge wires that now hung limply from the house. Broken white plastic housing lay scattered in the grass. The beam tracked patches of missing grass leading toward the destroyed generator a few yards away. The cover had been completely ripped off. The fan, exhaust system, fuel tank, and battery were gutted and cast aside.

"Who did this?" Becky asked, a quaver in her tone.

"No person did this," Kane said trying to ease her fear. "There's nothing to be gained destroying something they could use or barter." He turned a circle, searching. "Cattle were roaming everywhere after the quake. It could have been a bull drawn to the sound."

A loud shriek pierced the night. It sounded close.

The hair on the back of Kane's neck stood up. He quickly spun the flashlight around, searching for the source, and raised the bat onto his shoulder, grip tightened.

"Kane?" Becky squeezed his arm, digging in her nails.

"I've never heard anything like that."

Kane started toward the opposite side of the house, but Becky yanked him right back. "Can we go back inside? Please."

"Wait inside if you want," Kane said. "I'd like to know what destroyed the generator."

"I'm not leaving without you," Becky said.

Kane proceeded cautiously around the back with Becky close behind. The flashlight beam bounced off the house, cut through the dark spaces between the bushes, and illuminated some of the trees and branches overhead. He swept the area back and forth as they rounded the corner. He searched the side lawn for hoof prints or any other clue as to what could have wrecked the generator.

At the front of the house, the downed oak tree obscured most of the front lawn. He probed the branches leading up to the second floor and lit every dark shadow.

Becky sniffed. "Do you smell that?"

Kane breathed deep. "Ammonia?"

"More like rotten eggs."

"Sulfur."

"Gross. It stinks," she said.

Kane hushed her. "Listen. Can you hear that?"

Labored breathing came from the roadside on the other side of the downed tree.

Kane followed the tree trunk toward the upended roots. He firmed his grip on the bat handle and took a wide path around the roots. He felt ready for anything, but for what they discovered, nothing could have prepared him.

The beam of light illuminated a cow's face. She rested on the ground with her head hanging low and breathing heavily. She belonged to Tucker's Farm going by the green tag pierced through her ear. A wet smacking sound had Kane putting the flashlight back into motion down the cow's body. Her back was wet with blood. A large flap of hide had been peeled back and hung from a massive wound, exposing muscle and ribs. Several bite marks punctured her haunches and oozed crimson. And something still feasted on the other side of the cow.

Kane whistled to get its attention.

"Kane!" Becky whispered.

The wet smacking stopped. A hairless and bulbous head rose from the other side of the dying cow. Two short horns protruded from each side of its forehead; one had a broken, jagged end. Black eyes like orbs of pure evil crested the cow's back and narrowed slightly in the piercing beam of Kane's flashlight. A mouthful of stained teeth pointed unevenly as if sharpened by an unsteady hand. Blood discolored its mouth and ran down its small chin. Its skin stretched paper-thin, almost transparent, showing black veins in places across its head and neck.

It hissed at them, the tendons in its neck pulled taut, baring teeth above its kill.

"Oh my God!" Becky screamed.

Its long, sinewy limbs flexed and sprung the creature effortlessly on top of the dying cow.

He didn't have time to think or weigh options but would later wonder if, had he made an alternate choice, the outcome would have been different. "Run!" Kane pushed Becky into motion.

They ran back around the tree and behind the house. Kane shined the light ahead of them as they rounded the corner. Though not daring to look back, he felt certain the creature was in pursuit and only a couple of steps behind him. He pumped his legs harder.

They cut between the house and the garage. Ahead, Becky rushed inside the house through the side door. Kane stopped, spun, and swung the bat blindly, striking nothing but air. He fumbled with the flashlight. His hands shook uncontrollably.

Nothing was there. The creature hadn't followed.

"Get the fuck inside, Kane!" Becky yelled. "Kane!

Kane walked the few steps to the side door backward. He swung the flashlight back and forth, shining it across the driveway and lawn.

Instead, a hiss came from above.

Kane angled the flashlight directly above him and found those evil eyes peering down at him from the rooftop. The creature leaped. Kane was suddenly ripped backward by his collar. He stumbled over the threshold. Becky slammed and locked the door as he fell onto the kitchen floor.

Kane breathed heavily as sweat rolled off his brow. "What the hell was that?"

Becky threw her arms around Kane. "I don't understand. What's going on?"

A heavy bang struck the side door, startling them both.

Kane scrambled to his feet, holding the bat with both hands as if waiting for a pitch to come through the door.

After a moment, a series of knocks pounded the outside of the house, each one higher than the next.

"It's climbing up the side!" Becky yelled.

Glass shattered upstairs.

"Avery!" Kane threw Becky the truck keys before running upstairs. "Get your father up. Run for it if I'm not back by the time you're both in the truck."

Kane charged upstairs two and three steps at a time and burst into Avery's bedroom.

The creature had entered through the bedroom window and was leaning over Avery's sleeping form.

"Avery, get up!"

The creature stepped backward, assessing this new threat. At the same moment, Avery sat upright, cursing at his older brother before opening his eyes to the present danger prowling in his bedroom.

At its full height, the creature likely stood a head taller than Kane, but its rounded shoulders and slight hunch had it at eye level. Humanoid in appearance, the creature was hairless and oily. It appraised Kane for a moment longer, then lunged at Avery.

Through a flurry of blankets and bedsheets, Avery kicked and fended off the attack and fell out of his bed. Sheets ripped as the creature raked at its new prey.

Kane swung the bat, hitting the creature on the upper arm. He didn't stop to see if it would react. He swung again; it glanced off the shoulder, striking its neck and rocking the creature. It rubbed its neck and hissed, revealing those crooked teeth and spraying saliva, more discontent than hurt.

"Come on!" Kane pulled his brother off the floor by the arm.

The two brothers backed out of Avery's bedroom. Kane scrambled with the doorknob and pulled the door closed. They rushed toward the stairs while eyeing the closed door.

Guttural clicks echoed inside the bedroom, then pounding shook the door. The panels cracked from the force. A bit more pressure, and the door would break in half.

"Go, go!" Kane yelled.

They were halfway down the stairs when the bedroom door split open. The creature barreled through without pause. It shredded the wallpaper as it ricocheted down the short hall to the top of the stairs.

Kane and Avery landed at the bottom and met Becky, who was emerging from the back bedroom with her father in tow.

"In the basement!" Kane said, knowing even in his reeling mind that, outside, they would never outrun it. His heart was ready to slam out of his chest.

They hastily filed down into the basement. Kane shut the basement door right before the creature crashed into the living room. Luckily, the basement door locked from both sides. Kane turned the deadbolt, and Avery reinforced the door by wedging scrap lumber between the door and jamb.

"Grab some rags off the workbench and douse them with turpentine or something," Kane said to Avery.

"Why?" Avery furrowed.

"To stuff them at the base of the door," Kane replied. "I don't know for sure, but I think it can smell us."

Avery returned a moment later with the putrid rags and stuffed them into the gap between the door and floor. The brothers moved back and waited quietly in the dark stairwell.

The creature did not attempt to be discreet. It hissed and clicked and screeched as it searched the house. Glass broke. Objects thunked in every room as the creature hunted them.

"Mom's bedroom," Avery whispered.

The creature stayed in the bedroom for several moments. All they could hear was the faint sound of ripping fabric. It returned to the living room and knocked something heavy over.

"TV," Kane guessed.

Its footfalls approached the basement door and stopped.

Kane and Avery readied themselves.

The creature snorted, then continued into the bathroom. The shower curtain rings sang across their rod several times before what must have been the dislodged rod clattered against the ceramic of the tub. More items fell, smashed, or bounced on the tile floor. A wet slapping sound followed.

"I think it's drinking from the toilet," Avery said softly.

After several moments of slurping, it moved into the kitchen. Pots clanged and dishes shattered. Once it discovered the food in the cabinets and refrigerator, that's where it stayed.

For more than an hour, Kane and Avery listened at the top of the steps as the creature ate.

"I have to get some rest, brother," Avery said wiping his brow.

Kane nodded. "I don't think it's interested in us anymore. I'll be down in a few minutes."

While Avery joined the others downstairs, Kane stayed by the door, still in disbelief. The thing in their kitchen looked like a being straight out of *Lord of the Rings*—the movies; Kane had never read the books. Where had it come from? Was it a diseased person that had escaped from a secret government facility? Was it an alien? Did the earthquake awaken something from below? He rubbed his hands through his stubbly beard. No. That was all fantasy and nonsense. There had to be a logical explanation.

"Kane." Becky waved him down from the bottom of the stairs.

He rose slowly and stepped down on each tread on his toes. He leaned the bat at the bottom of the stairs before joining Becky.

Becky lowered her voice to a whisper. "I think Avery's sick."

Kane followed Becky to Avery's side. He was flat on his back on the concrete floor. He shivered with his arms wrapped around himself. His brow felt damp and warm.

"You feeling OK, little brother?"

"I'll be fine. I'm sure it's because I worked a double shift," Avery explained.

"Do you have blankets down here?" Becky asked.

Kane pointed at the boxes labeled MOM. "Check any of those."

"I'm sorry for yelling at you this morning," Avery said chattering. "It's none of my business what you do. We're not kids anymore."

Kane shook his head. "I deserved it. Mom was on my case for years to contribute. It felt poignant coming from you."

"I miss her," Avery said sadly.

Kane didn't respond at first. This was the first they'd talked about her together in a way other than accusations and insults. "I've felt . . . empty since Mom passed. I don't know what I should be doing anymore."

"I wonder what she'd say if she was here now."

"'Get off your asses and do something.'" Kane mimicked his mother's voice, which made Avery smile.

Becky returned with a plain comforter and floral-print bedsheets. She quickly folded the sheets into a pillow and spread the comforter over Avery.

"What is that thing anyway?" Avery asked.

"God only knows," Kane replied. "Hopefully, it'll leave the house on its own."

"We should stop it so it doesn't hurt someone else," Avery said.

"It took down one of Tucker's cows with its bare hands and scaled the side of the house. We're not trapping something like that," Kane said.

"I didn't say trap it. I said stop it," Avery corrected. "And a baseball bat isn't going to do the job."

"Shoot the damn bear between the eyes already," Kirkland said from the shadows behind them. His gruff tone knew only one pitch: loud.

"Dad!" Becky hushed him.

"It's not a bear," Kane said harshly. "It has no hair."

"Bears get diseases and lose their hair all the time," Kirkland said.

"It walked like a human," Kane said.

"Bears walk on their hind legs if they're injured," Kirkland said.

"Mr. Kirkland, it's not a bear. You didn't see it."

"You should stop hiding in the basement and take care of it like a man."

"Dad! It will hear you," Becky said. "I saw it too. I know what bears look like."

"Keep any guns, Garner? I'll take care of it myself since there are no men left in this house," Kirkland said coarsely.

"Why do you hate my brother so much, Mr. Kirkland?" Avery asked wearily.

"Oh, I can't wait for the answer to that," Kane said cynically.

Kirkland was quiet for a moment. His feet shifted in the dark. They couldn't see the snarl forming across his face as he spoke, but Kane could hear it. "I don't like a womanizer."

The old man wrapped an arm around the urn sitting next to him. "Once I met my Marit, we were inseparable. I never looked at another woman again. He's not good enough for my daughter. He has no job, no direction, and doesn't care much for himself as evidenced by that long damn hair. Makes him look like a girl for Christ's sake. There's a time when a boy becomes a man. Garner, you are long past overdue, and I don't like you near my daughter."

"Mr. Kirkland, I have never been unfaithful to your daughter," Kane said, surprised by Kirkland's reasons. He had pegged Kirkland as a mean old man who had nowhere to direct his nastiness except him. He was still mean, and judgmental, but he at least wanted the best for his daughter. He could understand that, but he was beyond worrying about what people thought of him. "I don't really—"

"Stop it," Becky interrupted them. Her voice shook. "Just stop. It's me. I'm the one. I was cheating. You should be mad at me."

The room fell silent as she broke down and cried.

"Dr. Ryan," Kane concluded. When Becky looked up shocked, Kane went on. "Before Dr. Ryan died, he said that he loved you."

Becky buried her face in her hands. "I'm so sorry, Kane. I should have—"

"I'm the one who should be sorry," Kane said. Things hadn't been right between them for a long time. He was so wrapped up in his junk that he couldn't give her the attention she needed. He touched her on the arm. "I haven't been good to you, and you deserve much better. We've been on different paths for a long time. You've started your career. I'm still figuring out what I want to do . . ." Maybe he was jealous of her, but he wasn't mad at her. "It's OK."

"Oh, Kane." Becky threw her arms around his neck and sobbed.

"Well la-di-da. Aren't ya the sensitive type," Kirkland grumbled.

"Were you born prickly, or are you intentionally choosing the wrong time to be this way?" Kane said.

"I don't care what my daughter has or hasn't done. I still don't like you, Garner," Kirkland said.

"Tell me how you really feel," Kane said scornfully.

"Big night for reveals," Avery deadpanned.

One by one, sleep fell upon each of them as they waited out the night. Kane checked on Avery one more time before settling himself. His brother was still warm, but Kane hoped his fever would break by morning. Kane finally closed his eyes while sitting at the bottom of the stairs, bat resting across his lap.

Kane bolted awake. He punched at the air, still half in a dream. The creature was inches from his face and fire erupting all around them. He could almost smell the creature's rank breath while his flesh blistered and burned.

He shook the lingering dream from his mind and noticed early dawn peeking through the small basement windows on the east side of the house. Becky and Kirkland still slept, leaned against one another in the corner and surrounded by boxes. In his spot on the floor, Avery had worked the covers over his head. His arms and legs shifted restlessly under the comforter.

Kane knelt beside him and placed a hand on his chest. Avery jerked again and fell still.

"How you feeling, brother?" Kane pulled back the comforter and couldn't believe the horror cast upon his little brother. "Avery!"

His brother's face was deathly white and drenched in sweat. His damp hair plastered his scalp. Clumps of it had fallen out and coated the pillow. His skin had thinned; black and blue veins popped out of his neck, jaw, and forehead. During the night, he had ripped off his t-shirt. The left side of his upper chest and shoulder had turned shades of green and yellow spotted with black. But worst of all, Avery's eyes had changed color. Both were black, and the whites were webs of thin red lines.

"What—what's happening?" Kane stuttered over his own words.

"It hurts so much," Avery gulped. He held his breath, making his neck bulge unnaturally.

"What does?"

"Everywhere!" He breathed again, but it was rapid and shallow.

Becky scurried over next to Avery. "Oh my God!"

"My head is pounding like a mother fucker," Avery said.

Becky touched his forehead. "Holy shit, you're boiling." She looked at Kane. "He's too hot. We have to cool him off fast. Otherwise, he's going to die."

Kane bit his lower lip. "The tub. We can fill it with cold water."

Becky spoke to Avery. "Can you move? We're going upstairs."

"We can't. The creature . . ." Avery said weakly. His eyes closed.

"Stay with me. Avery, stay awake," Kane pleaded.

"I got him," Becky said. "You make sure that thing isn't around. Dad, stay down here!"

On one-two-three, they lifted Avery to his feet. The comforter fell away. The shades of green and yellow and the speckles of black across his skin covered his torso front and back. The outline of his ribcage was stark, every joint enlarged and looking painfully inflamed.

"His arm," Kane pointed.

An open wound about two inches long marred his left forearm. The edges were cherry red with infection. Pus and discolored blood encrusted his arm.

"Did the creature scratch you?" Kane asked.

"I don't know," Avery slurred, and rolled his head.

"We have to do this now, Kane," Becky ordered.

They each grabbed an arm and part-carried, part-dragged Avery up the stairs, Kane with the bat under his armpit. Kane knocked away the wooden barricade with his foot. The pieces made an awful sound as they clattered down the stairs.

"Head to the bathroom straight across the hall," Kane said as he undid the deadbolt. "Water is from the well, so it should work. You stay with Avery and get the tub filled. I'll check the rest of the house. Ready?"

Becky nodded, seeming more determined than ever.

"Here we go."

Kane kicked open the basement door. They rushed Avery across the hall and into the bathroom. Glass, toothbrushes, soap, tissues, shampoo, shaving cream, and all the contents from the medicine cabinet covered the floor. Kane threw the shower curtain and rod out of the tub. Becky was running the cold water by the time he'd placed Avery, unconscious and breathing rapidly, inside the tub.

"Hang in there, brother," Kane said. Then, to Becky, "Lock the door behind me."

Kane quickly shut the bathroom door. He heard Becky lock it as instructed but tested the doorknob to be sure. He stood quietly in the hallway facing the kitchen. Except for the running bath water, the house felt eerily stagnant.

A floorboard creaked as he took his first step. He cringed as the board groaned back into place when he lifted his foot. Why was he being so quiet anyway? The creature would have to be deaf to have not heard the commotion they made.

He entered the kitchen with his bat ready, looking left, right, up, and down. The refrigerator had been tipped onto its side. The freezer had thawed into a big puddle. Food lay spoiling on the floor. Meats and dairy were partially consumed. Most of the cabinet doors were wide open, some hanging by a single hinge. Bits of glass and ceramic crackled underfoot as he moved through the kitchen, scanning the living room, dining room, and outside through the windows for any sign of the creature.

He was deciding what to do next when the hair on the back of his neck stood on end. Chills washed over him, sending goosebumps running down his arms. The smell of rotten eggs choked the air.

Kane spun around but not soon enough. The creature rushed him from behind, emerging from the guest bedroom at the end of the hallway. Kane stumbled and caught his foot on the refrigerator door. His blunder saved his life.

He fell backward right as the creature pounced. Its claws missed by inches. Kane landed on his back but regained his footing fast. The creature, however, matched his pace, somersaulting gracefully to recover and face Kane again on its hands and knees.

With the bat firmly in his hands, Kane swung upward and struck the creature under the chin. Its head snapped back with a smack, then rolled slowly forward again, cold evil eyes leveling onto its target. It snarled and spat out a broken tooth.

"Let's go, you son of a bitch!" Kane's heartbeat echoed in his ears. Adrenaline coursed through his veins. His muscles tensed. Every sensory input became increasingly acute as time slowed down.

The creature exhaled in short bursts. Its narrow chest expanded and contracted rapidly. The scent of rot and decay, either from its bleeding gums or something it had consumed, and the sulfuric smell of its pasty body wafted toward Kane. He wanted to lift his shirt over his face, but he would not let go of the bat.

The creature swayed back and forth on the balls of its taloned feet. Its muscles twitched randomly as if reacting to some invisible sharp prod. The creature was afraid but surely not of Kane. It struggled with some unseen demons. The literal meaning of that statement would become all too true.

With Kane still studying the beast, it didn't hesitate a moment longer to attack the human with the big stick. It raked the air with its claws to disarm him, but failed; Kane had easily predicted the creature's movement and intent, and had shuffled out of reach. He waited for the creature to open itself up again, and again it grabbed and missed. Kane did not. Like swinging for the fence, Kane stepped inside and drove through. The bat slammed against the side of its face in a perfect sweet spot. A crack sounded, but he wasn't sure whether it came from the bat or the creature's skull.

It crumpled to the kitchen floor among the spoiling food and broken glass. Black blood oozed from its pointed ear and serrated mouth.

Kane waited for it to stir again, but it remained sprawled on the floor. It was breathing, if its rising and falling chest was any indication, but not as rapidly as before. Kane kicked its clawed foot. He poked it in the leg with the end of the bat. He tapped its stomach. The creature didn't budge.

That's when Kane noticed the stained and tattered loincloth tied around its small waist.

"What the hell?"

He rested the end of the bat on its chest and held it there. Should he kill it? Bash in its brain or crush its neck?

"Kane!" Becky yelled from the bathroom.

Kane's head snapped toward the bathroom door; something was wrong.

Below Kane, the creature swiped at the bat, stealing it from him. It leaped to its feet and shoved Kane hard in the chest. He flew backward, tripping over the refrigerator and sliding across the milk-soaked tile. His back struck the kitchen counter, and he slumped to the floor, winded.

The creature was upon him instantly.

Kane threw his arms up to protect his face when the gunshots boomed—two shots, fired swiftly, one after the other—deafening him within the confined space.

The creature took one shot in the chest and the second one in the neck. The shotgun pellets ripped through its thin skin as though it were wet tissue, destroying muscle, bone, and organ. The creature screeched as its blood poured onto the floor and the life drained from its eyes.

"That's how you kill a bear," Kirkland said. He lowered the shotgun only when the creature stopped twitching.

Kane's ears rang as he climbed back onto his feet. "Christ, Kirkland."

"You're welcome," Kirkland said, popping the spent cartridges from the shotgun with a smug look across his face.

A loud bang resounded against the bathroom wall.

"Avery, no!" Becky's voice sounded muffled.

Kane slipped as he pushed by Kirkland, and nearly fell in the hallway. He grabbed the doorknob to the bathroom.

"Becky! Unlock the door! Becky!" Kane tried turning the knob back and forth. He took one step back and kicked the door inward with all of his weight. The door gave. Splinters flew from the door jamb.

Another creature stood over Becky. She cowered in the corner between the wall and the toilet, defending herself with the shower rod.

"Hey!" Kane yelled.

The second creature spun its head.

"Avery! My God!"

He looked more identical to the creature lying dead in the kitchen than his former brother. His dark eyes were cold and foul. His skin tone had completely transformed into shades of greens and yellows. His ears were smaller and pointed at the tips. Black veins protruded through paper-thin skin from the surface of his shockingly emaciated body. His hair had fallen out, all except for the white patch above his brow.

He hissed, looking at Kane, then back at Becky.

"We got us another bear I see," Kirkland said from behind Kane.

"No!" Kane knocked the shotgun from Kirkland's hands. It fired, missing its target but shooting a hole in the adjacent wall.

The thing that was Avery reacted to the sudden noise and bolted out of the bathroom. It rushed past Kane and Kirkland, knocking them both off their feet, and hissed again from the kitchen.

"Avery!" Kane stumbled out of the bathroom, sprinted through the empty kitchen, and bolted out the side door, but his brother was nowhere to be seen.

"Avery!"

The morning sun rose above the horizon. Kane knelt in the driveway with tears streaking down his cheeks. Before his mother had passed, she had told her two sons to take care of each other. She had said those words while staring at her oldest. If he hadn't been such a fuck-up, if he hadn't been such a loser, things would have turned out different. He could have done better to protect his only family. Avery, Becky, and Kirkland had tried to tell him. They'd expected more of him. His mother had expected more of him. He had failed when it mattered most.

He dug his fingers into the gravel, letting the small bits of sand and stone bite under his fingernails.

Never again.

He lifted his head and let the early sun warm his face and dry the tears.

Never again.

When they could finally hold each other, Kane and Becky did.

Becky sniffed, watching the rising sun. "He never touched me. It was still Avery. He knew I was trying to help him."

"I'm going to find him," Kane said.

"I know," Becky replied. "Do you think there are more of those things?"

Kane took in a deep breath, wondering the same thing.

As if to squash their doubts, from the far distance came a long, drawn-out screech. A moment later, another screech farther away in the opposite direction answered the call.

# TRANSCRIPT

## SUBJECT
Clinton County, Missouri Earthquake and Risk
Assessment; Telephone Correspondence

## PARTICIPANTS
Sergeant Benjamin Pavlov (newly appointed) and
Major Daniel Edward Hunt

## DATE, TIME, PLACE
05-04-2035, 0413, Plattsburg, Missouri


[BEGIN CALL]

HUNT:    Corporal Bennet, give me some good news.

PAVLOV: Sir, Corporal Bennet is dead. Sir.

HUNT:    Identify yourself.

PAVLOV: Corporal Benjamin Pavlov, sir.

HUNT:    What happened, Corporal?

PAVLOV: We were rescuing civilians from an office
        building. Bennet, two servicemen, and one
        civilian were caught inside when it
        collapsed. No one survived. We were able to
        recover the bodies, sir.

HUNT:    Who's in command there?

PAVLOV: No one, sir. That's why I called.

HUNT:     Shit. *[Long pause.]*

PAVLOV: Major? Hello? Can you hear me?

HUNT:     Private, we got ourselves in a real clusterfuck.

PAVLOV: Sir?

HUNT:     Earthquakes, God's wrath. It's everywhere. The whole country. The whole world for all I know.

PAVLOV: What should we do, sir?

HUNT:     How many servicemen do you have there, Private?

PAVLOV: Including myself, 23.

HUNT:     I'm not waiting for our incompetent governor to decide whether to declare a state of emergency. We need to act now. Are you familiar with our emergency procedures?

PAVLOV: Sir, yes, sir.

HUNT:     Start up the triage center like at a hospital.

PAVLOV: The hospital is completely gone, sir. It was the first place we checked last night.

HUNT:     Any building and space large enough to process hundreds, thousands of people. Start directing displaced people there. Assume everything is at your disposal. Do you understand?

PAVLOV: Sir, yes, sir.

HUNT:     Let me know what you need. I'll do what I can, although every town and city in the state is likely in the same shit can. Get resourceful. Start collecting food, medicines, clothing. OK? Recruit any civilian, police, first responder, doctor, nurse, put them to work. Deal with looters swiftly. Can I count on you?

PAVLOV: Sir, yes, sir!

HUNT: Good. I'm promoting you to Sergeant and placing you in charge of the Plattsburg region.

PAVLOV: Thank you, sir.

HUNT: Make sure your men are well armed. Take good care of them and they'll follow your lead.

PAVLOV: Yes, sir. We took down a local police officer last night. He was indiscriminately shooting civilians and screaming Bible verses.

HUNT: You're already thinking like a leader. You did the right thing, Sergeant.

PAVLOV: Sir, there's something else.

HUNT: Let's have it.

PAVLOV: We received dozens of reports of people being attacked by wild animals. We're not sure. A rancher reported several of his cattle slaughtered, eaten.

HUNT: Could be some locals taking advantage of a crisis. There are always a few assholes. You'll have to root them out quickly so they don't create unnecessary panic. Civilians need to feel safe.

PAVLOV: Understood, sir.

HUNT:     All    communication    comes    through    me,
          Sergeant.  I  expect  an  update  within  24
          hours.

                     [END CALL]

# RECKONING

Kane Garner was trying not to rehash the events from last night and failing miserably.

He pulled the top of his shirt over his nose as he entered his house. The stench of ammonia and sulfur stung his eyes, burned his lungs. The creature that Mr. Kirkland had killed had putrefied into a pool of thick, dark liquid that was slowly seeping between the kitchen floorboards, a reminder of the nightmare that had raided his and Avery's home. With his free hand, Kane grabbed clothing, blankets, and the little remaining food the creature hadn't devoured or spoiled. Each trip from the house to the truck became more frantic, more frenzied, the images of the creature that terrorized them overnight and the cold look in his brother Avery's eyes before he fled stuck in his mind, playing and rewinding and playing again.

Kane hadn't any idea that the creature laying on his kitchen floor had scratched his brother across the arm. He could have done something if he had known.

*I'm not a doctor. What could I have done?*

He ran to the garage, grabbed two gas cans, and cut a length of hose. He forced the hose into the gas tank of Avery's car, transferred as much fuel into his truck as it would accept, then filled the gas cans with the rest. Back to the garage; he loaded a shovel, an axe, toolbox, rope, plastic sheets, a tarp.

Avery had transformed so violently. Over the span of eight hours, his skin thinned and discolored; his hair fell out except for the white patch of his poliosis; his hands, their nails overgrown, warped into knotted claws. In the last moment Kane had seen him, his brother had been more creature than human. The look in his eyes though? Kane had seen it. His brother was still in there, fighting back.

*Was that even possible?*

The supplies in his truck clanged and banged as Kane threw more stuff into the bed.

He darted one last time into the house and down into the basement, returning with the long wooden crate packed with his father's more useful weapons: two hunting rifles, two handguns, and several boxes of bullets for both firearms as well as bullets for the double-barrel shotgun Mr. Kirkland continued to keep in his possession.

Kane threw the tarp over the truck bed and tied it down securely.

"Let's get the fuck out of here," he said to Becky Kirkland and her father.


Grey clouds blocked the mid-morning sun. Rain was forecasted.

"We have to call the police," Becky Kirkland said exasperatedly after a few moments riding in the silence. She gripped the dashboard from the middle seat between Kane and her father as Kane maneuvered the truck around trees that had fallen during the earthquake the previous day.

Mr. Kirkland sat in the passenger seat looking stoic and unfazed, his late wife's urn held between his legs. The old man still maintained that he'd shot a hairless bear last night. Nothing more. They could not convince him otherwise.

"Are we going to tell someone what happened back there?" she asked, annoyed after no one had answered her the first time.

Kane wrested a hand off the steering wheel, now realizing how tight he gripped it, fingers and palms curled as if glued to the thing. "Who's going to believe us, Becky?" He rubbed his stubbly beard and the back of his neck. "Some creature attacked us and then transformed my brother into—into a goblin or something. It sounds crazy when I say it aloud. We don't have any evidence to back it up either. Once we find Avery, we can go to the police."

"What really was that thing?" Becky asked. "Where did it come from?"

Kane sighed. "I don't know."

"A bear," Kirkland said, tapping the lid of his wife's urn and nodding once, resolute.

The clouds released a fine, steady mist. The town needed the rain to squelch the many fires that had erupted after the earthquake.

Kane drove close to the passable roads, giving the gas pedal even and steady pressure. A few times the wheels spun in the thickening mud, causing the rear of the truck to drift. Each time, Kane turned into the slide to regain control while Becky dug her nails deeper and deeper into his arm.

They were a quarter-mile from town when they met their first roadblock. Blue and yellow lights flashed ahead.

A few dozen vehicles lined bumper to bumper formed two lanes. Some people were out of their cars wondering over the holdup. The National Guard had arrived overnight and set up barriers. They motioned cars through a choke point and directed them to follow the barricade markers. Randomly selected drivers pulled to the side where officials searched their entire vehicles.

"Hide your gun, Garner," Mr. Kirkland said coarsely. He cleared his throat of phlegm and spat out the window.

Kane watched the chaos ahead. Sure enough, Kirkland was right. The soldiers confiscated weapons and food from a rusted blue sedan, heedless of the owner's protest.

"Fuck that," Kane said, concluding he had seen enough. He shifted the truck into reverse and backed out of line.

"What are you doing, Kane? They can help us. We need to tell them what happened."

"I'm not risking our stuff with these assholes, Bec," Kane said.

Kane doubled back and turned onto Maple Street. A main break flooded the road. A backhoe sat dormant in the middle of the expanding pool. He drove slowly through where the water deepened to the top of the oversized tires and got the pickup to the end of the street where the water subsided.

Maple Street intersected Main Street. The air here still reeked. The earthquake had leveled every business building along the road. A wave of claustrophobia hit Kane when he spotted the barroom that had fallen on top of him a day ago.

*Was it only a day ago?*

Becky placed a warm, comforting hand on his lap. "It's a miracle you got out of there."

"A bunch of people didn't though," he said solemnly, thinking of the bartender and the other patrons still buried under the rubble.

At each end of the half-mile stretch of Main Street, more blue and yellow lights pulsed. National Guard Humvees had formed barricades at both ends.

Kane's frustration boiled over. "Why is the entire town blocked in?"

"Do you think this is a good idea?" Becky asked gently. "Avery could be anywhere by now."

Kane whipped his head around and glared. "It's fine with me if you don't want to help, Becky. But he's my little brother. I'm supposed to take care of him. If things were reversed, he'd do the same for me." He bowed his head until it touched the steering wheel, already regretful for barking at Becky.

Avery had been right. He was sounding increasingly like his father.

But Becky only placed her hand on his back. "Hey, I didn't say I wouldn't help. I meant maybe there is a better way instead of driving around town."

"What're ya going to do now, Garner?" Kirkland challenged grouchily.

"I like it better when you don't talk, old man. It helps me forget you're here." Kane's emotional bandwidth was at zero. Anything could set him off right now.

Kirkland gripped his wife's urn a little more tightly. "Maybe I shouldn't be here anymore."

Becky frowned at this. "I don't like it when you talk to my father like that," she said to Kane. She seemed emotionally torn between him and her father. They both needed her help in separate ways, and Kane knew she was under pressure to choose whether to help him find Avery or ensure her father's safety.

"We got company," Kirkland said, glancing at the side mirror.

A sudden tap on the driver's side window startled them. A broad and imposing figure dressed in green camouflage rain gear tapped again on Kane's window with the knuckle of a large, gloved hand.

They hadn't noticed the Humvee that had pulled up behind them.

Kane rolled down the window. The rain turned to heavier drops that splashed inside the truck. Water dripped off the narrow visor of the man's hood as he stooped slightly to peer inside. The uniformed man, in his mid-twenties, not much older than Kane, was the soldier he'd met at Ray's before the bar had collapsed. Big Ben was his name.

"This area is unsafe," Ben said authoritatively in his low baritone. He didn't seem to recognize Kane, and now wasn't the moment to broach the subject. "We're asking residents to return to their homes."

Becky spoke first. "We can't."

"Our house was destroyed in the earthquake." Kane's stretched truth was not technically inaccurate. The oak tree that fell on the porch had only broken a few windows. But the creature that invaded his house might have been a result of the earthquake.

"I'm sorry to hear that. Was anyone hurt?" Ben asked.

"Yes," Becky said.

"No," Kane said at the same time.

"Pardon?"

"We're looking for my brother," Kane replied quickly. He placed a hand on Becky's lap and squeezed. They couldn't afford the full details complicating things. "He might be injured. We're not sure."

Ben hesitated a moment, looking between Kane and Becky. "What does your brother look like?" he finally asked.

"Oh, that's not necessary. I'm sure you're busy helping with bigger issues. He's not technically missing. Besides, he is extremely sick," Kane said.

The soldier leaned forward, taking a renewed interest. "He's sick? Can you describe his symptoms?"

*Shit.* He had said too much. This wasn't going well. Kane still had his foot on the brake, the truck idling in gear. Even though the National Guard had Main Street blocked, the McDonald's parking lot connected to the next street. He knew this town better than anyone. He felt confident he could lose them if they chased him.

Becky elbowed him in the ribs. And not very kindly.

"You wouldn't understand," Kane said, frustrated with the conversation and irritated at Becky.

"I've seen some weird shit in the last twelve hours," Ben insisted. "Try me."

"Weird how?" Becky asked.

"Miss, I—"

Static from a walkie-talkie hidden under the soldier's raincoat interrupted him. "Unit 6, be advised," said a female voice, "gollums sighted near 9th and Elm. Proceed with caution. Terminate with extreme prejudice. Over."

The soldier retrieved his walkie and spoke. "Roger. Unit 6 proceeding to location. Over." He slid the walkie back under his coat.

"What did that mean?" Kane asked, brow furrowing.

Ben pointed. "Sir, drive to this roadblock. Someone will escort you to the high school, where we've set up emergency services." He left them and quickly jumped back into the Humvee. The military vehicle accelerated around them, crossed Main Street, and disappeared behind the McDonald's in a hurry.

"Gollums . . ." Kane repeated the word softly, thinking to himself. What if Avery was among them?

"What are gollums?" Becky asked.

He ignored her question. Everyone who was a fan of *The Hobbit* knew Gollum. Kane took his foot off the brake and let his truck roll forward onto Main Street. His decision was made.

"We're going to follow them," he said, and floored the gas pedal.

"Bad idea, Kane," Becky warned. "Kane!"

But Kane wasn't listening. The soldiers had orders to kill. If Avery was there, he had to stop them.

He steered the truck hard into the McDonald's parking lot, fishtailing on the wet pavement. He quickly took back control, regaining traction in the debris and broken glass from the collapsed restaurant. He couldn't find the Humvee ahead, but he knew 9th and Elm. It was near where he worked.

*Used to work.*

"You're making me nervous the way you're driving, Kane." Becky's fingers tightened on the dashboard as the truck bumped over debris spread over the torn-up pavement.

Kane wasn't going fast enough. The damage from the earthquake made it impossible to speed. The wiper blades worked overtime as the pelting rain obscured all vision. He swerved, braked, accelerated, avoiding only the worst of the obstacles and rolling over the rest. His truck handled it easily.

He detoured through someone's backyard, tearing up grass and mud, then turned onto Elm Street, truck tires spinning off dirt as they jumped back onto the road. Ahead of them, the Humvee was stopped in the middle of the street, its four doors left wide open.

The soldiers were gone.

"Where'd they go?" Kane asked.

Kane rolled down his window to get a better view of the houses to his left. No sooner did he do that than someone screamed. It sounded like a child pretending, but today, they were far from needing to fake monsters.

"Oh my God!" Becky pointed to the right.

Two elementary school–aged children, a boy and a girl, materialized between two houses sprinting at full tilt. They shrieked as they ran into the street, heading straight toward Kane's truck. In pursuit a short distance behind them was a half-naked creature like the one that had raided Kane's house last night.

*Avery?*

But the creature was completely devoid of any hair. No chance this was his brother.

Kane had no way to reach his handgun in time. He had stashed it with the others under and behind the seat. Even so, without any practice handling the gun, he'd risk shooting one of the kids by accident. He was left with only one choice.

"Hold on to something," he said.

He floored the accelerator, the tires spinning momentarily until they found their purchase, and sped the truck down Elm.

The two children saw Kane coming and waved him down, but he wasn't slowing. He drove past them, continuing to gain speed. He aimed straight for the creature.

The thing stayed its course and never veered from the center of the street. The truck struck true. The sudden impact knocked the trio forward. Becky yelped. Kirkland grunted and mumbled something about incapable drivers.

The awful beast was shrieking, undoubtedly from pain but more from frustration at missing its prey. The creature's spotted head and greenish arms had slapped hard on the hood of the truck, leaving a big dent. But it held on to the front grill. It howled again as its dark eyes found the driver and passengers.

It had new prey.

Kane held the gas pedal down and continued down the street toward the Humvee, waiting in vain for the creature to release its hold and fall under the tires. "Damn it, why are these fuckers so hard to kill!"

The distance between the truck and the rear of the Humvee was closing fast. Kane had a new idea, and Becky read his mind.

"You can't be serious!" she said, but she gripped his shoulder and threw her other arm across her father's chest.

Kane had no idea at what speed he struck the back of the Humvee, but it hurt just the same. His nose bounced off the top of the steering wheel a split second before the airbag punched him in the face and threw him back in his seat. The passenger's side airbag deployed, saving Becky and Kirkland from flying through the windshield.

Kane sat for a few moments waiting for his vision to clear and the stars to stop dancing around his head. A childhood memory surfaced like a remembered dream. A traumatic incident he had forgotten until now. He and Avery were playing with a lighter and gasoline in their father's garage. Ants had built a nest in a crack in the concrete. Avery poured a little gas on the nest and Kane lit it. The fire ignited quickly. They laughed, watching the ants scurry away, tiny bodies shriveling in the flames. Their father suddenly appeared with a half-empty beer in his hand and a look of unfiltered rage on his face. He swayed slightly in the light of the open garage door. He carefully put his beer down. Then he forcefully lifted Kane by the front of his shirt and slapped him hard across the face. The stars around his head had looked similar then, even at nine years old.

He shook away the ones distracting him now. "You OK?" he asked Becky and Kirkland. He tasted a little blood in his mouth.

Becky nodded, rubbing her head.

"You're the worst driver I've seen, Garner," Kirkland grumbled. He clutched his deceased wife's urn tighter between his spindly legs.

Kane couldn't get out of his door and climbed out the window instead.

The creature was dead, crushed between the truck and the Humvee. Tainted blood like used oil had sprayed out of its mouth and small nose. Its body steamed as rain fell on it. The stink of sulfur and ammonia wafted off the creature.

How many more of these things were out there? He felt finding his brother getting a lot harder.

Making matters worse, radiator fluid and oil were spilling from underneath his truck. The front end was sandwiched like an accordion, the windshield cracked. The front axle looked broken and one of the front struts was snapped off its post, causing the front wheel to rest inside its well. His truck wasn't going anywhere except to the junkyard.

Becky had climbed out of the truck and was kneeling next to the children the creature had chased. Both were crying and clutching each other as she tried consoling them.

Kids were not Kane's thing for a number of reasons that he didn't care to think about right now. He turned his attention to other pressing issues. They were going to need another vehicle. He had owned the Nissan Titan for a long time, had put a lot of miles on it, dependable and tough. He wasn't sure if he'd own another one like it given the state of the country right now.

He eyed Mr. Kirkland through the cracked windshield. "You OK?" Kane asked. "Mr. Kirkland?"

Kirkland sat staring straight ahead, unmoving, urn held tight. His cheeks were wet. "It's time, young man. It's time for me to be with Marit."

It was the first time the old man had spoken to him without a series of insults. He rushed to the truck and forced the passenger door open, eyeing the man up and down. Kirkland wasn't physically hurt as far as Garner could tell. His face held all his pain. Kane had never seen Kirkland with his spirit squashed. He felt at a loss to say something. Fortunately, he didn't have to.

A screech cut through the misty air somewhere in the small neighborhood. Somewhere close.

The young girl and boy yelped and flew into Becky's arms, nearly knocking her over.

Another shriek, then another, and a third answered the call, each response farther away and from various locations surrounding them.

Automatic gunfire echoed a street or two away.

*The soldiers.*

"Becky! We have to get out of here!" Kane exclaimed. "Kirkland, pull your shit together. We're moving."

Kane peered inside the bed of the truck, piled full with food and supplies. It pained him to leave so much behind. He grabbed two backpacks he'd filled with necessities, tossing one of them to Becky. He clipped one handgun to his waist and stuffed the other in his backpack. The two rifles, he slung over his shoulder. Kirkland carried the shotgun and his wife's urn.

Kane nodded at the two frightened children holding Becky around her waist. "They're coming with us."

They abandoned Kane's truck and hustled in the opposite direction from the gunfire. They heard occasional weapon fire as they cut through a well-manicured backyard. A couple of dogs barked from inside the small ranch-style house. They sounded little. Kane saw a window curtain move.

He quickly turned and started pounding on the back door. "Hello? Hello!"

The dogs went berserk on the other side of the door. Inside, someone tried hushing them.

"Can you let us in, please?" Kane asked.

"Go away, or I call the police," snapped a muffled voice.

Kane found himself getting louder. "You really think the police—"

"Please," Becky interrupted, trying her own plea through the door. "We have children with us. "They're frightened."

A shriek echoed even closer than before. The dogs started barking again, now even more determined.

Becky's eyes were wide with terror. "Kane, something moved by the truck." She motioned the kids to lead the way behind the house.

"Fuck this. I know a place we can go," Kane said.

The rain transformed to mist as they left the house with the yapping dogs and rushed between a couple of two-family homes. The houses on this street had suffered a lot of damage from the earthquake. Kane's group continued down the sidewalk to the gas station on the corner and waited for Mr. Kirkland to catch up.

"Dad! You have to hurry," Becky said, waving him forward with a bit of panic in her voice.

Kane motioned silently for her to wait on the sidewalk while he checked out the gas station. The steel canopy over the gas pumps had toppled like a house of cards on top of the tiny convenience store, pinning a car under one of the posts. Kane checked the car first. Blood stains ran down the passenger door, and a bigger pool of dried blood coated the front seat. He didn't find a body, but someone had been severely injured.

Seeing nothing to take, he put eyes back on Becky to be sure she was OK. Down the road, Kirkland was still taking his sweet time catching up.

Kane ducked inside the convenience store. Ceiling panels had fallen, and fluorescent lights dangled from electrical wires like hanged men. Once he decided it was safe, he strode quickly to the coolers. Other people had gotten the same idea; the coolers were empty.

"Kane!" Becky screamed. A shotgun blast followed.

Kane ran out of the convenience store and found evil. For someone who wasn't used to holding a gun in his hand, he couldn't remember at what point he had unclipped the one from his belt. He held the weapon firm in his grip, pointing at the three creatures that hissed at Becky, Kirkland, and the kids.

One of the goblin-esque creatures looked identical to the one they hit with the truck and the one that ransacked his house. The other two were slightly smaller, both bare-chested and hairless, but one wore ripped jeans, the other stained underwear. Had these two transformed like Avery?

Kirkland fired his shotgun again and startled Kane out of his moment of hesitation. The three creatures were unfazed. They hadn't been hit by either bullet; Kirkland missed both of his shots. And now the shotgun was out of ammo.

Kane's hand shook as he fired his handgun. He missed. "Fuck!"

He hustled to Becky, Kirkland, and the kids and led them quickly across the street while aiming the handgun and keeping himself between them and the goblins.

The tall goblin calmly watched Kane and the group as they retreated. The other two bobbed on the balls of their feet and glanced at the larger one occasionally as if waiting for some impending command.

A car appeared then, driving slowly down the street, its interior packed to the windows with the occupants' shit. The driver turned into the gas station and stepped out of his car, oblivious to the waiting goblins until it was too late.

The taller goblin signaled, a *tick* snapping from its throat, and its minions pounced. Blood sprayed and splattered. A woman in the car screamed. The man overpowered, the two goblins silenced the woman in a matter of seconds.

Kane urged his group across a large employee parking lot toward a brick factory building. A large sign that read Reynolds & Sons Manufacturing hung from the side.

He tried the employee entrance but wasn't surprised to find it locked. He knew another way in. All those mornings he'd gotten into work late was paying off after all.

"This way," he said pointing at the end of the building.

A series of shrieks and clicks echoed across the employee parking lot behind them. The two goblins that had attacked the couple in the car were bounding toward them. Fast.

Becky and the kids raced ahead. Kane followed right behind Mr. Kirkland, who was struggling to keep up and breathing heavily.

"We have to hurry," Kane said to Kirkland, trying to hide his panic. Leaving the old bastard behind crossed his mind. He was endangering all of their lives. Could he actually do it? Becky would never forgive him, but could he forgive himself?

*Damn it!* He gritted his teeth. He'd carry the old-timer if he had to.

"Reload that fucking shotgun while you're at it."

"I am, God blast it!" Kirkland barked. "I can only do one thing at a time."

They rounded the corner of the factory at the same time the two goblins closed half their distance. Three empty loading docks framed the rear of the building. Kane ran up to the service entry door to the right of the docks, approaching the keypad that kept the steel door magnetically locked. He punched in the four-digit code.

Nothing happened. The door handle wouldn't turn.

The two goblins careened around the corner of the factory as Kane tried entering the passcode a second time. They hissed and brandished their jagged, blood-stained teeth.

The two children screeched, which only seemed to excite the two goblins.

Kane took a deep breath and pressed the same four buttons a third time, forcing himself not to rush, making sure he depressed each completely. The magnetic lock clicked; the handle turned.

The goblins rushed them.

Kane threw open the steel door and everyone shoved inside. He ripped the reloaded shotgun out of Kirkland's hands as the man passed him.

"Chew on this, motherfuckers!" Kane fired. Once. Twice.

Each creature took a full round to the chest. Kane slammed the door against their flinching forms only to feel the blast of the pair ramming the steel at the same moment the magnetic lock reengaged. They clawed frantically at the door, their razored fingers a hundred nails squealing across a chalkboard.

Kane thought they might break down the door, but the ear-splitting screeching and slashing subsided after several moments. He sighed relief, then turned around, meeting the barrel of a rifle and the smiling douchebag at the other end.

"Hello, Lame Brain Kane," Douglas Reynolds said, pushing the rifle an inch closer to Kane's face.

"Move that thing out of my face, Dougie," Kane said stoically.

"Nobody calls me that anymore. Not around here," Dougie said unwaveringly and through gritted teeth. He held the rifle firmly pointed at Kane. "Check them," he said over his shoulder.

Behind him was a group of a half-dozen people. Kane recognized the employees of Reynolds & Sons. A couple of the older men drove delivery trucks. One woman worked in the front office answering the phone. Roxanne was her name. Two of the younger men, Chad and Duane, worked on the assembly floor—classmates of Dougie's. They purposely broke their machines at least once a week so they could scam an extra break and get high with Dougie. The other woman was Jalanda Woods, Dougie's girlfriend, and the reason Kane was fired a day ago from Reynolds & Sons. Dougie's lower lip still showed a little fullness where Kane had punched him, unable to standby and mind his own damn business after Dougie slapped Jalanda across the face.

Dougie's high school buddies started for Kane, grabbing at his shotgun, his handgun, his backpack.

"Hey!" Kane elbowed Chad in the neck and shoved Duane off.

Dougie leapt closer to Kane, shoving the rifle barrel into the center of his chest. "I will shoot you, mother fucker! I will shoot you!" he barked, spittle flying out of his mouth.

Becky yelled. Kane tensed to see her struggling under the hold of one of the truckers. The children, untouched but cowering to the side, started crying again. The other trucker, who was holding Mr. Kirkland, was on the receiving end of the old man's best insults.

"*STOP!*" A male voice echoed over the intercom system, freezing everyone in place. Mr. Reynolds, a balding and grey-mustached man in his fifties wearing a sports jacket over a white t-shirt stretched too tightly over his round belly, entered the loading area. He lowered the walkie talkie he'd bellowed into. "Douglas, put down the rifle," he said firmly to his son as he approached the group.

Dougie's eyes narrowed and his mouth pursed. A wave of anger and humiliation washed over his face. Reluctantly obeying his father, he lowered the rifle but glared at Kane a moment longer. "We said we weren't allowing anyone else inside," he complained.

"No, boy. You said that. I did not agree. These people are more than welcome here," Reynolds said, then glared with unchallenged authority at the rest of the group. "Get back to your posts. We have more work to finish before dark."

One by one, the group dispersed, vacating the loading dock.

Dougie was the last to leave. Before he left, he whispered to Kane, almost spitting his words.

"Me and you? We're not finished yet."

Kane grinned, finding the idle threat amusing. "Get back to work, Dougie. Like Daddy said."

Dougie pointed at Kane as he backward-stepped, then turned, strolling down one of the storage aisles with the rifle casually slung over his shoulder, whistling a non-descript tune as he left.

Mr. Reynolds shook Kane's hand. "It's good to see you again, Garner. I apologize for . . ." He thumbed over his shoulder. "You *are* all welcome here." He placed a reassuring hand on Becky's shoulder and shook Mr. Kirkland's hand too. Then he stooped down to eye level of the two children. "And who do we have here?" he asked.

The boy spoke for both of them. "I'm Mason. She's Olivia. Our mommy and daddy, they—they changed . . ." Mason's eyes watered.

Dread rose in the pit of his stomach and lodged in his throat. What these kids witnessed mirrored Kane's own experience with Avery. He related to the boy in a way, observing something that could never be undone and a burden likely to be carried for a long time. Kane cursed under his breath.

"I understand, young man," Mr. Reynolds said consolingly. "You and your sister are very brave." Reynolds straightened and took a sorrowing breath. "You can place your things in the break room. There are cots set up there if you'd like to rest. Garner, I could use your help once you're settled, yes? Find me in my office." He smiled, then spun on his heel and walked away.

"Are you OK?" Kane asked Becky.

She nodded, pulling Mason and Olivia close to her. The two children wrapped their arms around her waist. It was like they'd known her for years.

"I'm fine, thank you for inquiring," Mr. Kirkland huffed.

Kane guided them through the warehouse and into the main building. Reynolds & Sons manufactured and assembled thousands of machine parts for appliances, medical and electrical devices, and robotics and other assembly equipment. For such a small company in a small Midwestern town, Mr. Reynolds was a brilliant engineer and an equally intelligent businessman who had negotiated domestic and foreign deals, landing in each market both private and government contracts.

"There are drinks and food," Kane said pointing to the vending machines and refrigerators as soon as they entered the break room. The scent of brewed coffee had him immediately craving a cup of his own. He handed Becky his backpack. "There's food in here too."

"Where are you going?" she asked.

"To see how secure this place is. Looks like we're spending the night," he said.

"Looks like you got us out of boiling water and into the fryer to me, Garner," Kirkland interjected.

"Into the *fire*, it's into the—never mind." Kane shook his head as he prepared himself a cup of coffee.

"I don't like those guys," Becky added, referring to Dougie and his friends.

"They're bratty teenagers. Nothing more. Reynolds keeps them in check. You let me know if they bother you though." He touched her arm, hoping it might comfort her. He wasn't exactly sure where their relationship stood at the moment. Their feelings for each other had been more than awkward since she admitted to her relationship with her boss. The last twenty-four hours hadn't allowed much time to be alone and talk. But Becky surprised him by closing the awkwardness between them and throwing her arms around his neck.

"Be safe," she said in his ear, and kissed him there, right below his temple.

"I'm always safe," he said wittingly.

Her pasted smile failed at hiding her worry. "Your definition of safe might be different from mine," she said.


A few moments later, Kane entered the front office in search of Mr. Reynolds. The small office space had three metal desks and three wide filing cabinets buried under the office equipment and supplies. Stacks of blue softbound product manuals and loose papers covered every surface. Purchase orders and invoices overflowed from plastic inboxes next to boxy and dusty computer monitors. Reynolds preferred to run his office old-school. If asked to modernize his office, he'd explain his method prevented hacking and secured his product designs. In all his irony, Reynolds was a little intimidated by smartphones and innovative technology even though his company manufactured the equipment pivotal to creating such high-end electronics.

Roxanne stood by the employee entrance guarding the door, at watch for any activity across the employee parking lot. She wheeled herself on her office chair between the side glass panel next to the door and the large office window, both taped top to bottom with paper except for a couple of small peep holes.

She was a long-term employee and worked in the office answering the phone, fulfilling orders, checking shipments, and taking messages for Mr. Reynolds. Roxanne was in her early forties, single, and hippy from regular consumption of assorted sweets and from never leaving her rolling chair. She snubbed Kane as soon as he entered the office.

"You saw us running from those creatures," Kane said reproachfully. "You didn't open the door."

"I didn't see nothing," Roxanne said, avoiding eye contact and peering more intently out a peep hole.

Kane held his gaze upon her, but she never turned to face him. Instead, she spoke while looking above her.

"'Blessed is he who reads and those who hear the words of this prophecy and keep those things which are written in it; for the time is near.'"

"Roxanne, shut your goddamn mouth," Mr. Reynolds interrupted, entering the front office. "You never stepped one foot in a church your entire life. Now you're quoting nonsense that you have no idea what it means."

Roxanne scowled. "The day of reckoning is upon us."

"Keep watch, please. Thank you." He waved Kane inside his office. "Come in, Garner."

Kane eyed Roxanne a moment longer, then followed.

Mr. Reynolds had his own office space across the small hallway from the front reception area. A timeclock and employee timecards hung outside his door. A worn, oversized oak desk sat centered in the room covered in an array of disorganized papers. More blue bound product guides and manuals filled open shelves and spilled onto the floor in several piles. Photos of Mr. Reynolds posing with local politicians, business leaders, and some celebrities decorated the walls. Among the photos were a few of his sports conquests; in one, Reynolds held a golf ball from an improbable hole-in-one shot. The golf ball itself sat in a glass case on a matching oak credenza behind the executive desk.

On the adjacent wall hung a large paper schematic of what could best be described as a robot. To Garner, it looked like a trashcan with two arms and two legs. One of the arms was highlighted more prominently than the rest of the diagram with a red circle around it and *Congratulations!* written beside it along with the mayor's signature underneath.

A year ago, Reynolds had won a government bid to build one of the appendages of the mechanical suit to be worn during the first crewed Mars exploration, one as yet unscheduled. The attachment pulverized rock, then extracted and identified the minerals. Kane had joined Reynolds & Sons right before the company won the contract. There was a big celebration on the factory floor with cake and balloons and the town's mayor in attendance. The contract was a big win for the company and the Missouri town.

Mr. Reynolds sat in a high-backed leather chair chewing on the end of a pen and looking as if sleep might overtake him at any moment.

"Please have a seat," he said, gesturing to one of the two guest chairs.

"The shop held up from the quake," Kane noted, feeling awkward. It wasn't that Reynolds thought his son didn't deserve the punch he'd fired Kane for delivering. Family was a hard bond to break. Kane understood that now more than ever.

"A few of the machines snapped off their footpads, east side brick wall cracked all the way up the middle," Reynolds said. "We got lucky. No one was hurt."

"Those kids? What they said? They weren't off the truth. My brother, he um. . . ." Kane fought back a sudden swell of unexpected emotions. He cleared his throat. "He turned into one of them. Those . . . goblins. I wouldn't have believed them if I hadn't seen it with my own eyes."

Still, telling Reynolds was less about convincing his former boss and more about confirming he wasn't crazy. That everything he witnessed in the last twenty-four hours was real. Perhaps there was a rational explanation.

Reynolds tossed his gnawed pen on the desk and pushed himself out of his chair. "Come with me," he said.

The two men left the office. Reynolds led Kane across the assembly floor where the impact of the earthquake had been more prominent. A few of the machines had indeed snapped off their bolted anchors and vibrated across the concrete floor. Fallen molds and raw materials littered the dusty floor. But this wasn't what Reynolds wanted to show him.

They continued into another section of the factory down a wide hallway where under normal circumstances most workers were not permitted. On both sides of the hall were air-controlled rooms. In them, the more intricate electronics and microchips were assembled and tested. Authorized Personnel Only signs hung on the walls alongside other signs that read Proper Gear Required.

At the end of the hallway was a set of restrooms and an entry door to the boiler room. Chad and Duane stood by the door huddled together and snickering over something on their phones. As soon as they noticed Reynolds, they stashed the phones and dropped the laughs. They subserviently acknowledged Mr. Reynolds but gave Kane the side-eye.

Not much got past Reynolds, however. He glared at both of them. "Go check the loading docks and ensure the doors are secure," he ordered the two teenagers.

Chad and Duane hurried away to do as they were told.

Reynolds waited until the two young teens were out of sight before turning to Kane. "I'm sorry about your brother, Garner. He was a first responder, a paramedic, yes? I hope I'm remembering correctly."

"He was."

"How did it happen? The transformation, I mean."

"A goblin broke into the house, got into Avery's bedroom. Scratched him on the arm," Kane explained.

Reynolds's eyes widened. "We thought whatever sickness they carry only spreads if they bite. Scratching makes sense. Damn. How long did the transformation take?"

Kane stared at Reynolds a moment. He was talking as if this was already a world where these creatures belonged. Talking as if his brother was one data point in the science of understanding them. "I— I don't know. I didn't time the goddamn thing. He was one of them by morning. Eight hours at most?"

Reynolds lifted his clipboard, flipped a page, and nodded. "Sounds about right." Reynolds rubbed the stubble on his face, one knuckle pausing between his nose and upper lip. "Goblin, you say? That's a better moniker." He took a note on his clipboard.

Kane might have yelled then, but a loud thud struck the boiler room door, causing him to flinch. Reynolds appeared unfazed.

The door had its usual red lettering warning KEEP OUT across its face, but now its window, a single pane of tempered glass at eye-level, was shielded with cardboard. He became transfixed by whatever waited unseen on the other side.

"After the earthquake," Reynolds began, "I sent our people home. Some stayed to assess the damage, help clean up. As soon as it got dark, we heard screeching in the parking lot. An awful sound like someone was dying. Several of us went outside to investigate. One of those things—your goblins—was squatting in the back of Lester's truck. It was eating a dog.

Kane cursed.

"It didn't care much about us yelling at it. Lester sneaked his rifle from the cab. But it was quick and leaped on top of Lester before he could get in a single shot. The wound, after it bit him on the leg? Looked like a shark bite, I tell you. It wouldn't stop bleeding either. The thing left him alive, but Ole Lester went feverish and pale. We took turns watching him overnight. So we noticed when his skin started changing color. First by the bite mark, then all up his body. His blood turned black."

Kane nodded his head, remembering the black spider veins that had spread underneath Avery's skin.

Reynolds sighed as if second-guessing the actions that had led him to this moment. "There was no one to call, nowhere to take him. Half the hospital collapsed in the quake."

Another thud sounded on the opposite side of the boiler room door.

"Lester's in there," Kane said stoically.

Reynolds removed the cardboard that shielded the windowpane.

Lester was an old-timer, had worked for Reynolds for years, a veteran from a war waged before Kane was born. Kane had worked with Lester and enjoyed the back-and-forth banter they shared. The distorted face that filled the square glass didn't resemble the old man's wizened one save for the mouth missing half its teeth. Its blackened tongue slid and slobbered all over the glass. Its eyes had drained of all color and stayed on the two men, two circles of darkness surrounded by a sickly, muddy, mustard color. Patches of a once long full beard hung for dear life from its jaw.

The Lester-goblin banged its forehead on the door vehemently, hissing at the sight of the two men.

"Christ."

"I doubt our Lord had much of a hand in this mess," Reynolds said sadly, replacing the piece of cardboard over the window with a calm hand.

The two men walked back toward the wide-open assembly floor. Reynolds took a detour off the main floor through another door with an Authorized Personnel Only sign slapped on it. Reynolds produced a key card from his breast pocket and waved it over a square pad. An indicator light on the pad turned from red to green and a magnetic lock sprang free. Reynolds opened the door and waved Kane inside.

Task lighting illuminated three workstations around the perimeter of the small, air-conditioned room. Computer monitors, microscopes, and other intricate equipment crowded desks and work surfaces. A mild odor of lubricant and epoxy tinted with charring suffused the air.

At the center of the room sat Mr. Reynolds's greatest engineering achievement. The blueprint in his office was an exact representation of the large object resting on the worktable before Kane.

"This was supposed to travel to Mars with the rest of the suit next year," Reynolds said sadly. "But I doubt we'll explore the Red Planet anytime soon."

The appendage had the form of an arm twice as long as a human one and two feet at its widest point, with an articulating elbow and wrist. A dozen wires and tubes connected to multiple ports at one end. A hole at the same end allowed for a person's arm to fit inside. The other end of the device, its outer casing blackened with soot, looked all business, a lethal conglomerate of tools capable of boring, piercing, cutting, heating, and clutching. It looked excessive, and Kane said so.

Reynolds scoffed. "You need a durable and capable suit if you're working over two hundred million kilometers from the nearest Home Depot."

Kane stared blankly. He wasn't sure why Mr. Reynolds was showing it to him.

Reynolds smiled proudly and rubbed a hand across the sheened surface. "NASA commissioned us to manufacture six of these puppies. Add this arm to the rest of the suit, and you've got a one-man wrecking machine. It has its own power source, plenty of other redundancies. We started testing two days ago. No major issues. Pick it up. It's exceptionally light."

Kane shook his head. "I don't want to break it." Truly, he didn't care if it broke. Reynolds couldn't fire him a second time.

But Reynolds was laughing. "You could drive a truck over it. The truck would break before the gauntlet did. Go ahead."

"Hey Rey! We have an issue in the break room." It was Roxanne shouting through the walkie-talkie on Reynolds's belt.

Reynolds's face went flat. "What was I saying about no issues?" He unclipped the talkie. "We'll be right there."

Kane rushed out of the room first with Mr. Reynolds close behind him. Immediately they heard the shouting from the break room on the other side of the assembly floor. They hurried across the floor, arriving to find guns pointed at one another among shouts and chaos.

Kirkland had his back against a wall, his shotgun pointed squarely at Chad and Duane. The two teenagers held rifles aimed right back.

"Lower the gun, old man," Chad threatened.

Becky, pressed against the small refrigerator with Mason and Olivia squished behind her, was yelling back at all of them.

"Take the shot, chicken shits," Dougie shouted.

Jalanda and Roxanne added to the commotion, their shouts combining with Becky's for the men to give up their stalemate.

Kane never slowed as he entered the break room, shoving between Kirkland and the two teenagers. But the shouting didn't settle until Mr. Reynolds hollered over the entire group.

"What in hell is going on here?"

Chad and Duane held their rifles tighter, higher. Both barrels now pointed at Kane's chest. "Everything gets shared equally. Those are the rules," Chad said this last through clenched teeth. He rocked back and forth from his heels to his toes, repeatedly adjusted his grip on the rifle. "Someone's got to teach these people the *rules*."

Kane looked to Becky for her piece.

"He sucker punched my father in the face," she shouted over the continuing commotion.

"That's nice you wanted to inform our guests of the rules," Reynolds said firmly. "But that's not your job, son. Is it?"

Chad pursed his lips and, quickly glancing at Reynolds, took a deep breath. "No, sir."

"You'll take first shift tonight," Reynolds said as he pushed the end of Chad's rifle down. "Duane?"

Duane lowered his rifle automatically.

"You'll take the shift right after your idiot friend. Do I make myself clear, boys?"

The two teenagers nodded.

Dougie snorted behind his father.

"Since this is entertaining to you," Reynolds said to his son, "you will take roof duty all night."

Dougie burst into the likes of a tantrum. "What did I do?"

"Before you go, Chad." Kane swiftly grabbed the teen by the collar and jabbed him in the nose.

Chad fell back cupping his nose. "You mother!" Blood leaked into his mouth, coating his teeth crimson.

Duane and Dougie jumped at Kane, but Mr. Reynolds stepped into their path. For a seemingly unfit man in his fifties, he held the two young men back effortlessly.

"Get back to your posts," Reynolds ordered. "The fight is out there!"

One by one the young men left the break room, each eyeballing Kane as they left. Kane waved them off with the middle finger. "Enjoy your night."

Reynolds spun on his heel to face Kane. "I don't agree with the young man's methods, but he is correct about our rules. We don't know how long this catastrophe will last or when we'll see relief. Your presence may be making a tense situation worse, Garner. Earn your keep. That includes sharing food and, by all damn means, keeping the peace." He looked at Kane, then to Becky, and finally to Kirkland. "Are you alright, Mr. Kirkland?"

"Right as rain," Kirkland grumbled.

"Very well," Reynolds said. "Garner, I can use you down in receiving. The locking mechanism is not engaging with one of the overhead doors when it's closed. I'll need it working before dark. The rest of you can take a watch. We're going to need all eyes available."

Reynolds turned and left the break room.

"What an ass," Becky broke the awkward silence. "Was he like that before too?"

Kane nodded. "Pretty much."

"I don't want to stay here, Kane. They creep me out, especially Dougie and his friends."

"Reynolds keeps them in check," Kane said.

"And if something happens to him?"

How could he possibly argue with her about that? Dougie's behavior was becoming more erratic and unpredictable. What if Reynolds couldn't keep his kid in check? But where could they go? Could they even get anywhere safely?

"Look, it's shit, but this is probably the safest place to be right now."

Becky sighed and shook her head.

"Another fine mess you go us into, Garner," Kirkland said from the corner of the break room. His wife's urn sat comfortably on the chair next to him. The shotgun lay on the table within arm's reach.

"You forgot to load the shotgun, didn't you?" Kane asked him.

"I would have shot the little bastard otherwise," Kirkland muttered.

Kane went to his pack, retrieved a handgun, and handed it to Becky.

"I don't want this," she said. "I wouldn't have—"

"For those creatures. In case any come around," Kane said. "Please. I'll feel better knowing you can protect yourself."

Becky reluctantly took the handgun but looked uncertain about where to put it.

"Here," Kane said. He reached along her waist, past Mason and Olivia, who were still glued to her leg, and clipped the holster at her side slowly so she could see how to adjust it herself.

For a brief moment, their hands touched, the scent of her perfume rising strong from her neck where he'd leaned in. Their eyes met, and Kane wanted to take her in his arms, to steal her away from this horrible nightmare and never let go. Was she thinking the same thing? But he couldn't find the words to bridge the pain they had caused each other. Not especially in this moment. Mason and Olivia were attached to her. Kirkland was eyeing him from the other side of the break room. And who knew what hell was coming their way when darkness fell. Instead, he stepped back, gave her an approving nod and a half-smile, and parted to fix Reynolds's overhead door.

The receiving area was on the opposite end of the manufacturing building. All special orders arrived at the factory through a single garage door. Boxes of varying colors and shapes stacked on top of one another sat along one side of the space. A tablet and scanning wand rested on a high-top workstation for inventorying incoming shipments and matching them to their original orders. Typically, two workers were in here always, hustling to open boxes, scan the contents' barcodes, and deliver the items to the proper departments. Within the last forty-eight hours, things had changed from standard receiving operations to two armed men guarding the entrance from aggressive monsters.

Manuel and Antonio welcomed Kane as he entered the receiving area. Both held semi-automatic rifles across their laps where they sat in folding chairs, sharing a smoke and sipping coffee. They guarded the overhead door that had clearly malfunctioned based on the one-foot gap below it. Either someone had pulled the emergency cord, or there had been a temporary loss of power. Or both. Reengaging the clutch was an easy fix, and one that would stick so long as Reynolds kept the back-up generators powering the factory.

Kane retrieved a step ladder and climbed up to the gearbox. He pushed the sprocket back into place, which allowed the chain to follow suit.

"All fixed," he said as he returned the step ladder. He pressed the button. The door went up several inches. He pressed another button. The door closed and remained so.

"Thank you so much, Señor Kane," Manuel said, shaking his hand. Kane didn't miss the tremor in it; the man was petrified.

"We don't need no Devil's children in here tonight. They're coming for sure," Antonio added.

Someone behind the men began clapping. "Kane the Fix-It Man does it again," Dougie mocked, appearing from behind a stack of boxes near the entrance. Jalanda followed close behind, an unsure puppy. "Hey, Super Mario Bros. You have roof duty tonight." He thumbed for Manuel and Antonio to leave.

The two truck drivers grabbed their gear quickly and left without another word.

"Roof duty was your job," Kane said, folding his arms.

Both men stared at each other in silence, testing each other's resolve. Dougie pretended to lunge at Kane.

"Ha! Made you flinch," Dougie laughed.

Kane's blood began to boil. "Why are you such a tool? This isn't how you'll finally win Daddy's approval."

Dougie grabbed his chest dramatically and leaned backward. "Oh, how you've hurt my tender heart."

"You really like hanging around this ass?" Kane asked Jalanda, who stood timidly off to the side. She avoided eye contact once she realized he was addressing her.

Dougie went ramrod straight, a serious scowl overtaking his face. "Don't talk to my woman." He stepped in close, expecting to intimidate Kane despite his shorter stature. "I don't like you, Lame Brain Kane."

"I don't give a shit, Dougie."

*Do something stupid,* he silently dared. He had destroyed guys bigger than himself. This would be over before it started.

Dougie went red in the face. "Don't. Call. Me. That."

Jalanda covered up a smile, but Dougie saw. "You dare disrespect me?" He pointed and waved his finger. "You will pay for that, woman."

"If you put your hand on her or anyone, there will be no one stopping me from stopping you. Not your daddy and not your stupid friends." Kane leaned in close to Dougie and let his eyes slowly travel up and down the kid. "What the fuck's actually the matter with you, I wonder?"

"You! I'm in charge here, and you'll listen to me if you want to stay here!" The more Dougie yelled and stomped, the redder his face became, the more spittle flew out of his mouth.

"No one wants to listen to a punk ass bitch, especially not a spoiled and entitled one like you. You got a lot to learn, junior."

Kane braced against the attack.

Dougie threw down his rifle and came for Kane like a rabid dog. Jalanda yelped, the only one surprised by Dougie's reaction. The kid had been looking for a fight the moment he entered the receiving area. Kane was more than happy to oblige.

Dougie wielded his fists like an angry chimpanzee. Kane sidestepped and shoved Dougie away. The teen dramatically fell into a stack of boxes, an almost comical display. Was he being for real? Dougie bounced back onto his feet, fists back in Kane's direction. Kane again easily deflected them, enraging Dougie further.

Desperate to land a punch, Dougie kicked his feet erratically instead, one after the other, after the other, missing its mark each time. Kane grabbed the last kick, trapping Dougie's foot and ankle and twisting. This time, Dougie's flounder to the ground was genuine.

"Stay down, Dougie, or you're going to get hurt." Kane released Dougie's leg and backed up.

"How about fuck you, fuck you, and fuck you!" Dougie clambered back onto his feet, lunged for his rifle, and took aim. "Look what I got, you mother fucker! I'm gonna shoot you right in the fucking gut, then feed you bleeding and alive to Ole Lester the Molester." Dougie's eyes were wild. His teeth showed behind a smile plastered too wide. "Then, I'm gonna eat your food, take your gear, and fuck your bitch. Hell, I'll have her worshipping me by the end of the week. I'll have her begging."

Kane rolled his eyes. "I'm getting tired of people pointing guns in my face."

Dougie licked his lips. "Yeah? You gonna do anything about it, Lame Brain K—"

Kane snatched the barrel of the rifle and yanked it downward. His swift action took Dougie off-balance and pitched him forward into the receiving end of Kane's fist. Kane's other hand grabbed the butt of the rifle and twisted it easily out of the teen's hands before he could pull the trigger.

Kane popped open the rifle and saw the bullet in the chamber. Not completely comfortable around guns, it took another moment for him to figure out how to eject the live round. It pinged and bounced again and again on the concrete floor. Once it settled for good, Kane kicked it out of sight.

Dougie spit out something white and red. "You broke my tooth!"

"This isn't Thunderdome, Dougie." Kane rammed the butt of the rifle between Dougie's eyes, right across the bridge of his nose. The kid's eyes rolled inside his head, then he dropped to the floor, a bag of bones. Kane stood over him to check he was still breathing. He turned to Jalanda. "If he touches you again, you'll tell me."

Kane found Becky and her father on watch by the shipping docks where they had entered the factory earlier that day. A tiny oval window through the industrial overhead doors gave the perfect eye-level view of the wide trucking lot. The rainy weather had drifted away, but a blanket of clouds lingered in the early evening sky. It was going to be dark soon. Kane shivered at the thought of what the night might bring.

Mason and Olivia had eventually detached themselves from Becky's legs. They had devised some sort of game using broken and spare parts from the defect bin. They waved when Kane approached.

"Hi, Mr. Garner," Mason said.

"Hi, Mr. Garner," Olivia repeated her brother.

"Hello." Kane quickly skirted by the children, largely uncomfortable over what else he should say. Should he be encouraging and offer hope? Honest and instill despondence?
He said nothing.

Becky chuckled lightly. "You really don't like kids, do you?"

"I like kids," Kane defended himself. "Maybe I don't relate so well."

"Maybe?"

Kane shrugged and redirected the subject. "How are things here?"

"Boring as shit," Becky said. "Did you fix the door Reynolds mentioned?"

"Yes, among other things." Kane wouldn't expound any further. "You were right about those kids. We should leave by morning. We'll go to the high school first. If it's shit there too, we'll hole up in your dad's house until things are safe."

Becky's smile broadened her face, causing a twinkle in her welling eyes. "That sounds"—her words caught in her throat for a moment—"good, Kane."

Silence fell between them, causing Kane to look down at his feet. Kirkland caught his eye. The old man had been glowering at him since the moment he had arrived.

"Is the shotgun loaded this time, old-timer?" Kane asked him.

"Go suck an egg," Kirkland growled.

"Suck an egg," Mason said in a low mimicking voice.

"No, you suck an egg," Olivia said. Then they both lost themselves in a fit of giggles.

The three adults couldn't resist the urge to join in the laughter, a sound that had been so rare in the last forty-eight hours.

It was short-lived. An alarm blasted over the intercom system, silencing them. The walkie-talkies Becky and Kirkland had been given came alive.

*"Breach! East—"* Static.

*"Say again. Repeat, say again!"*

Static. *"—those fucking creatures in the—"* Static.

*"Where?"*

*"Rey!"*

*"East side of the building. East side!"*

*"Receiving! They're coming in!"*

Gunfire blasted over the walkies.

*"Manuel, Anto—"* Static.

*"We see 'em."* More gunfire.

*"Chad, Duane, Doug—"* Static.

*"Where's Garner?"* Static.

"Stay here with the kids and your dad," Kane said to Becky. "If things go sideways, get to the high school. Got it?"

Becky nodded automatically as fear flooded her face. She put on a false bravado as Kane parted and left her alone with the two children and her elder father.

Kane sprinted across the warehouse through the aisles of machine parts. He detoured through the break room and grabbed one of the teen's abandoned rifles and a box of ammo for it. Already he could already hear gunfire echoing throughout the factory. He loaded the rifle as he sprinted across the assembly floor.

His heart raced. Sweat beaded on his forehead. Kane had no time to think, only to act, and yet he had time enough to hope he wouldn't freeze in the heat of battle. The shouts and weapon fire grew louder as he got closer. The sound became deafening, chaotic. It wasn't until he entered the receiving area where he and Dougie had tried working out their differences mere minutes ago that he saw how much worse things were.

The overheard door stood wide open, welcoming the darkening dusk. Shrouded by the shadows, large shapes flitted at the edge of illumination from the factory's fluorescent floodlights. Screeches and hissing resounded between the intervals of guns blasting and reloading. It was hard to tell how many were out there. At least one had dared to enter. Bullet holes riddled the nearby creature's dead body. Grey fluid marred the concrete floor. Steam emitted from the body, ammonia astringent in the air.

Kane spotted Roxanne standing in the doorway, shaking and holding the butt of her rifle painfully high. She likely hadn't fired a shot yet; the kickback would have bucked her in the face.

His sudden appearance startled her, and she fumbled with the rifle. Kane clasped his hands on it and shoved it into an actually serviceable position. "Hold the butt against your shoulder and line up the two pins with your target. Only fire when you're sure," he said. "And breathe."

Dougie, Chad, and Duane stood shoulder to shoulder in the middle of the receiving area spraying bullets blindly into the night from the semi-automatics at their hips.

"Stop shooting, you idiots!" Mr. Reynolds yelled as the three teenagers emptied one clip and started blasting through another. He was kneeling behind a large wooden crate with Jalanda crouched next to him, her head between her knees. "Douglas!"

Kane aimed his rifle, aligning the pins down the barrel, and searched for anything that might move in the darkness or dare to cross into the light. Nothing.

He quickly approached the three teens from behind and tapped them each on the shoulder.

"You're wasting bullets!" he yelled over the clatter; then he addressed Duane. "Help me with the door. You two keep watch. Shoot only if you see something."

The three teens stared at Kane distrustfully; Dougie, with a swollen nose and bruised eyes, held a slight smirk across his face. The spiteful shit had disengaged the overhead door; Kane knew it with every fiber in his body. He needed the boys split up to keep himself from getting hurt. Or worse.

Mr. Reynolds appeared from behind the crate to join them. "Listen to Garner, or you can find your way home tonight," Reynolds ordered.

Kane strapped his rifle and grabbed the nearby step ladder. "I have to get the clutch back into gear," he said to Duane, pointing to the gearbox. "Hold the ladder so we can make this quick."

Kane set up the ladder feet from the overhead door opening. Everything outside seemed blacker than before. The factory lights pushed the darkness back only so far. In it, an invisible army of creatures stirred. They hadn't come close enough to be fully seen, but their ever-present hisses, shrieks, and clicks conjured fearsome images. At any moment, it felt like the milling horde might rush through the open door. He took a deep breath. It did nothing to calm him.

It was a mad scramble to the top of the ladder. Duane gripped it to stop it from swaying. Kane had his hand on the clutch, but it didn't budge.

A quick burst from one then the other of the semi-automatic rifles fired into the night. He should have expected it, but it startled Kane all the same, and he nearly toppled the ladder.

"Hold it tight," he screamed. He slapped the clutch again.

"They're coming!"

Kane wiggled the clutch back and forth. It wouldn't give. "Damn it!"

Dougie, Chad, and Reynolds opened fire. So, too, did Duane. Kane swayed on the ladder again.

"Hurry up, son!" Reynolds yelled at Kane.

"It won't—" He had an idea. Kane swung his rifle off his shoulder and used the butt to hammer the clutch. Once, twice, and finally the third time he hit it, the clutch slipped back into the place. "Yes!"

Then the ladder tipped, and Kane fell.

He landed hard on his back. The air in his lungs escaped in a rush. His ears rang from the deafening automatic fire and his head cracking off the concrete floor. Feet away lay the dead and already decomposing creature. He sucked in a breath, and it was full of that familiar pungent stench. Gagging, he struggled to his feet, praying nothing was broken.

Outside, a wall of creatures was fast approaching the entrance. Their eyes, hundreds of them, glowed eerily as they approached the light.

Kane stumbled over to the electric door opener and punched the red button to close it. The overhead door engaged and started to progress along its track. But it was too late.

Two creatures broke through the entrance. They tackled Duane and dragged him outside amidst a flurry of bullets. Most missed their targets, but the few that struck the creatures didn't slow their attack. Duane screamed as the horde swallowed him. It was a horrifying cry, one that Kane would hear repeatedly for many years to come. And always, as now, it was accompanied by the sickening feeling of complete defenselessness to stop it. Of nothing to do except fight the next fight and stop this terror from spreading.

Kane took aim at the next creature that entered the receiving area. It wore a shredded and stained dress shirt and a tie that swayed loosely from its neck. It hissed at him, revealing a mouth full of blackened teeth and stringy saliva. Kane squeezed the trigger. The force of the kickback surprised him even though he was expecting it.

"Nice shot!" Reynolds yelled.

Kane had closed his eyes, something he'd known since he was a kid he shouldn't have done. When he opened them, he saw the creature, dead on the floor with a bullet hole between its eyes. Thick, black blood oozed out of the fatal wound.

*I can do this*, he thought.

The overhead door continued to narrow the gap between ceiling and floor inch by inch.

Kane took a shot at another creature, this one completely nude except for a pair of dirty and torn pink fluffy slippers. He didn't close his eyes this time and witnessed the hole suddenly open in its cheek as he squeezed the trigger. Black and bits of gore sprayed the closing overhead door a millisecond before the creature crumpled to the floor.

They held the horde back. The door was almost closed. No more dared enter the receiving area, somehow cognizant of their dying brethren. Dougie, Chad, and Reynolds continued to fire bursts into the darkness. The door was at waist height and still closing.

Kane relaxed his stance to check how many bullets he had left in his rifle. The night would be a night of many hard lessons that cost lives. He would not spend one on running out of ammo.

When he looked up, the overhead door was splitting in half. Metal screeched and tore as if a battering ram was punching through the steel.

Through the center came what truly was a live battering ram: an infected bull, spurred along by the creatures.

The diseased and disoriented animal plowed into the receiving area, catching everyone off guard. Its heavy momentum after destroying the overhead door sent everyone diving out of the way. It narrowly missed trampling Kane. Boxes and crates flew up in its wake, parts and wood splinters soaring in every direction.

"Get out!" Kane yelled at the scattered men and women.

Reynolds nodded, understanding Kane's logic. "Retreat," he supported. "Let's go!"

The bull circled. It stood between the group and their only escape.

"Hey, over here!" Kane waved his arms at the confused bull. "That's right. Look at me." Kane raised his rifle and shot, hitting the deranged animal in the shoulder.

The bull went berserk. It snorted, blackish mucus shooting from its wet nose, then charged.

Kane dove out of the way of the big animal, not knowing if he was leaping far enough. But he had. The bull's hooves slid on the smooth concrete as if on ice, sending it careening into a wall.

The distraction had worked. Reynolds, Roxanne, and the teens were already on the other side of the receiving area. Kane was back on his feet in a flash and running to join them.

Dougie's eyes suddenly went wide. "Oh my God! Jalanda!"

"You *idiot*." Kane spun around searching. The crate she had hid behind was a pile of splinters. He searched again. There! Under a pile of cardboard boxes.

Kane and Dougie reached her at the same time, grabbing and pulling and throwing boxes aside. She was conscious. They had her on her feet and hurried out of the receiving area before the bull had another chance at them.

Reynolds shut and bolted the double doors fast behind them all. Roxanne wheeled a six-foot crate in front of the doors for added measure.

Kane leaned against a cutting machine trying to catch his breath. He panicked for a moment when he felt a bead of liquid roll down the side of his temple. Instead of seeing red when he looked at the fingers he touched to it, he saw that it was sweat moistening his brow and dampening his shirt.

"Check for any scratches," he said to the group.

Reynolds and Chad shook their heads after patting their arms and legs and chests.

Dougie knelt over Jalanda. She had an egg-sized bump on her head as far as Kane could see. The look in Dougie's eyes, however, spoke of a worse injury with unspeakable consequences. Kane shoved him aside and saw the blood on the arm of Jalanda's shirt.

The bull's horn must have gouged her during its rampage.

Dougie's accusing glare upon Kane was unmissable, but Reynolds acted first. He stood in front of his son at the same moment Dougie squeezed the trigger on his automatic rifle. A rattle of several bullets chewed into the factory floor, but the last one caught Reynolds in the stomach. The impact surprised both father and son.

Reynolds dropped to one knee, one arm finding his son's shoulder. Dougie fell with him. A well of tears streaked down his cheeks.

Roxanne bawled. "What did you do?" She dropped down beside Reynolds, urging him to keep his eyes open.

Kane, after a moment of stunned motionlessness, kicked the automatic weapon out of Dougie's hands. He hadn't thought the kid would have it in him to shoot at anyone, but he had become a ticking time bomb waiting for the right fuse.

Heavy pounding shook the steel double doors behind them. Gunfire echoed above them on the rooftop where Manuel and Antonio were keeping watch.

He needed to get back to Becky.

"We're moving," Kane announced. "Chad, Roxanne—help Jalanda. I've got Reynolds." He grabbed a nearby hand truck. "Let's get you out of here, Mr. Reynolds."

Reynolds held a hand over his stomach. His shirt was saturated with blood that seeped through his pressing fingers in rivulets. "It's pointless, Garner."

"Bullshit. I'll cart you out of here myself." Kane helped Reynolds onto the hand truck. To the rest of the group, he said, "Follow me."

Kane wheeled Reynolds ahead of the group with Chad and Roxanne supporting Jalanda. The gunfire from the roof had died down; Kane hoped that Manuel and Antonio had escaped. Dougie refused to move. He remained despondent, kneeling in the middle of the factory floor. They were left with no choice but to leave him behind.

They'd gotten across the assembly floor when they heard the double doors finally fail and burst open with an incredible crash. Screeches echoed across the open space.

The creatures were inside the factory.

A large sliding fire door separated the assembly floor from the warehouse and the offices. Kane smacked the emergency button. A little luck was on their side; the door slid quickly along its greased rails, sealing off their side of the factory with a resounding thud.

Kane pushed Reynolds hastily into the break room. Blood spilled over the cart, leaving red tracks behind on the concrete floor. Together with

Chad and Roxanne, he transferred Reynolds and Jalanda to the cots as carefully as possible.

"Go find Becky," Kane ordered Roxanne. "Bring them here."

Roxanne hurried out of the break room as if wanting to be anywhere else but here.

"Chad. Chad!"

Tears ran down the teenager's cheeks. His chin quivered and his hands shook.

"Look at me, Chad." Kane snapped his fingers. "I need you to bandage Jalanda's arm."

"My friends are—are—" Chad tried to get the words out, but his grief was too overwhelming.

"Focus on me, Chad. I need you to do as I say, or more people are going to die. Can you do that?"

Chad cleared his throat while rubbing his eyes and carefully wiping his swollen nose. He nodded and set to work on Jalanda's arm.

Kane turned his attention to Reynolds. The man's eyes hung heavy and his skin had paled. The lower half of his shirt was scarlet. Kane grabbed a roll of gauze from one of the first-aid kits hanging on the wall and started wrapping the bullet wound. The gauze bled through immediately. Kane applied more pressure; Reynolds groaned sickeningly. The man was fading.

Where was Becky? She would know what to do.

A moment later, Roxanne returned unaccompanied. "I can't find them," she said.

Kane's stomach leaped into his throat. "Was there any—do you think—fuck!"

"They left their post if you ask me," Roxanne accused. "No blood or sign of struggle at all."

"I hope to hell they left. I told them to head to the high school if they heard any fighting. That's where we'll go," Kane announced.

"How do you suppose we do that with those creatures everywhere and Rey like this?" Roxanne motioned to Reynolds and then pointed at Jalanda. "And this one's gonna change before dawn. We might as well start repenting now."

"You really know how to express optimism at a time of crisis, Roxanne," Kane said.

"We were doing fine until you showed up," Roxanne glared. "Rey would want us to defend his place."

"He'll die if we stay," Kane said.

"He'll die if we try moving him," Roxanne countered.

"I'm not dead yet." Reynolds spoke weakly, each breath a gasp. His eyes were half-closed and glossy. He gripped Kane's forearm. "Don't bother with me. Take the gauntlet. There's a portable power pack in my office. Send them all back to Hell, son."

"You're serious?"

Reynolds's hand fell off Kane's arm. His eyes closed, exhausted for the moment. Every breath he took rattled in his lungs. He wasn't dead, but he was dying.

Kane's mind reeled and filled with doubt. Their options were limited. Reynolds would surely bleed out if they stayed. Jalanda rested on the cot beside Reynolds with an ice pack on her head. Chad had done a decent job bandaging her arm. They had to watch her closely. He had no idea if the infection acted differently from person to person. He lost his brother Avery within eight hours. Would she have more time? Less?

Kane prayed that Becky, Kirkland, and the kids were safe. What would he do if he learned they were lost? He needed to get his shit together.

If they left for the high school, they might cause the creatures to follow them and put more people in danger.

But if they stayed, they could keep the fight here. Perhaps by morning, there could be a greater chance for reinforcements or escape.

Chad sat despairingly next to Jalanda. How much more could the teen take? Roxanne appeared emotionless but had a lot of fight in her. Instead of fighting against him, perhaps he could redirect her resentment.

Kane faced Chad, who wouldn't make eye contact, and Roxanne, who remained cross-armed and stubborn as she could be.

What in hell was he doing?

"We'll hold them off for the night. Chad, you're on the forklift. Roxanne, help me move Reynolds and Jalanda into the front offices. We end this fight tonight."

Within minutes, they each had their assignments. In the warehouse, Chad would drive the forklift, positioning metal shelving units and box pallets to create a maze with several choke points. Roxanne was moving Reynolds and Jalanda into the front offices as instructed. They'd be separated to be safe, but Roxanne insisted on staying with Reynolds and keeping pressure on his bullet wound.

In Reynolds's office, Kane found the power pack. It was the size and weight of a typical car battery. A set of cables was clipped to the leads on two sides of the battery case. He wrapped them up and took the power pack with him.

The shortest way to the prototype room was through the assembly floor, but they had closed that off. Kane took an alternate route down a long, carpeted corridor. The overhead fluorescent lights flickered.

Power was failing at this end of the factory.

He followed the corridor, pausing at every corner. Ahead, the door on the left led to the prototype room. Kane twisted the door handle, then waited a moment to see if anything inside reacted. Instead, he heard something stir farther down the hall.

But what? All that was here were the sterile rooms where intricate chips and gold-plated electronics were stored and assembled. After that, the corridor looped around to the restrooms and the boiler room.

Thoughts of Lester trapped in the boiler room entered his mind. If they left, who would ever let him out? But that was crazy thinking. The creature down there wasn't Lester anymore.

Kane shook his head as if clearing brain fog. "Stay focused," he whispered to himself.

The lights flickered on and off in the test room as he entered. A dim emergency light above the entrance supplied enough illumination for Kane to tackle his task.

The gauntlet sat on the center table as it had when Reynolds had showcased it earlier. Kane quickly pulled the various cables from their posts and wrapped the lengths around the wrist of the gauntlet. The device was surprisingly light for its size but too bulky to tuck under his arm and carry the power pack too.

He found an empty canvas bag on one of the workstations. The bag had straps that made it good for travel. He stuffed the gauntlet and its connector cables inside.

Kane returned to the corridor, rifle strapped over one shoulder, shopping bag on the other, power pack in hand. He swiftly spun on his heels. Had something moved down by the restrooms? A moment later, one of the hall doors closed, echoing loud enough up the hallway to rip away any doubt he might have had. *Damn it!* Who was down there? Dougie?

He quietly put down the power pack and gauntlet, then unslung his rifle as he hurried down the corridor toward the restrooms, keeping close to the wall. Rifle pressed snug to his shoulder, he stopped at the end of the hallway. The restrooms were across the hall. The boiler room was farther to the right. It appeared locked.

"Just pick one," Kane mumbled. He rushed into the men's restroom, quickly scanned the open area of sinks and urinals, and kicked open the two stalls. Nothing.

Kane pivoted back out, pointing his rifle in both directions before exiting the men's room. He kicked in the ladies' restroom door. The door banged wide open, slamming into the metal wastebasket behind it with an incredible clatter. He heard a whimper come from the other side of the partition ahead of him. Within a heartbeat, he searched for the source of the noise. Three stalls on the left, three sinks on the right. Sweat rolled down his temple as his finger rubbed the trigger.

He fully expected to find one of those goblins, but nothing prepared him for what he discovered rummaging through the trash in the last stall of the bathroom.

From behind, it looked like any family dog, a Golden Retriever perhaps. Furry long tail wagging, golden hair covering its hind legs, back, and belly, but the similarities ended there. Its front legs, chest, neck, and head were devoid of fur. Its bare skin was blotched black as if the pink was rotting away. One of its ears had been chewed off, leaving a hardened mass of dried blood caked on its neck. It plowed through the overturned trash with its nose, overly moist and dripping with infection. Its lips were stretched thin around its mouth, revealing black gums and grey teeth as it chewed through used tissue paper, its black tongue probing the meager findings.

The creatures that had invaded the Earth weren't bound to infecting only humans.

The canid picked up its head, noticing Kane's presence. Its eyes glowed unnaturally. It snarled, curling up its lip as it turned fully to face him.

Kane didn't risk another second; he dropped the dog where it stood. The rifle shot was quick and painless.

A loud bang drew Kane back out into the hall. The boiler room door was now wide open.

*What the fuck?*

The Lester-creature was loose. But how? From what he could see, the door hadn't been forced open from the inside. So what had done it?

Kane doubled back down the hall, rifle poised. He snatched the gauntlet and power pack up again along the way. Within a few moments, he was inside the administrative office.

Kane heard Roxanne before seeing her. She was crying, draped over Reynolds, face buried in his chest. She lifted her head when Kane entered but wouldn't look at him. He already knew.

"He worked all the time. He never stopped, you know?" Roxanne's voice was watery. "He asked me to stay sometimes, on nights and weekends. Just to help. After a while, we got close. I—I loved him," she said softly.

Kane knew Reynolds was married. The situation sounded complicated. But he nodded, giving Roxanne room to mourn, and checked on Jalanda in the opposite office. She was asleep. Her breathing was elevated, and her brow glistened with sweat. Blood had soaked through her bandages, and the infection had started to spread down her arm, her fingers and fingernails already greying.

It was Avery all over again.

He couldn't stop the infection or prevent her from transforming like his brother.

This office door didn't have a lock. Instead, he dragged one of the chairs out with him and wedged it under the doorknob. He wasn't sure how long it would hold. Perhaps long enough. He rejoined Roxanne once he had convinced himself Jalanda was sufficiently barricaded.

"We have to go, Roxanne," he said.

She nodded and slowly rose to her feet. With one last look over her shoulder at the man she adored, Roxanne followed Kane back to the warehouse.

Chad had finished the maze. Walls of shelving and pallets formed three narrow choke points only wide enough for the creatures to file in one behind another. The three aisles spit out in front of a tall barricade with an opening at chest height. Behind it, Kane, Chad, and Roxanne would wait and pick off the creatures one at a time. If they became overwhelmed, they had an escape route through the loading docks.

God save their souls if all failed.

"What do we have?" Kane asked Chad.

"Three semi-automatics, two handguns, two rifles including yours, and Roxanne's shotgun." Chad pointed at each in turn, then at a pile of boxes. "We have enough bullets for a couple reloads. I'd feel better if we had ten times that amount."

Kane sighed. "Pick your shots carefully. Headshots or two at most to the chest. Drop them in the choke points; it will be harder for the next one to follow. Yell if you're out of ammo."

"What's that?" Chad asked as Kane pulled the gauntlet out of its bag.

"Mr. Reynolds seemed to think it could help, but I'm not quite so certain." Kane did not plan to let the creatures get close enough for it to be of any use.

They loaded the guns and placed extra ammo within easy reach. They took their positions behind the barricade and waited. The creatures screeched and hissed behind the large fire door. No telling how many there were.

Chad was looking down the scope of his semi-automatic. He was sweating, hands shaking.

"Take a few deep breaths," Kane said to Chad. "Control your shots. Squeeze nice and easy."

"Got it."

Kane then made eye contact with Roxanne, who was wincing.

"I know what I'm doing," she snapped irritably. "I hate hearing them is all."

Chad at once pulled out his smartphone from his back pocket. "We backdoored Mr. Reynolds's speaker system with Doug Jr.'s help. Give me some musical requests."

Kane, for the first time in what felt ages, smiled. "Immigrant Song, Led Zeppelin. Paranoid, Black Sabbath. Sabotage, Beastie Boys. Crank it and loop 'em for as long as the power lasts."

"Rock classics. Good choices." Chad tapped his phone, then the music echoed throughout the factory.

The fire door, although massive and heavy, hung on a set of rails. With enough leverage and strength, the door could easily be taken out by lifting it off the rails and letting gravity take over. No sooner did he think this than it happened. They couldn't see much, but the loud thuds, screech of twisting metal, and the uprising sound of the creatures approaching made clear they had breached the fire door.

Zeppelin's staccato riff ripped through the noise. On cue, the horde appeared like a black mass, filling every void and open space. They knocked out the lights as they came, as if expecting the standoff waiting for them. It was hard to see where one ended and the other began as they poured into the warehouse and the funnel of shelving and crates. They fought amongst themselves for the front of the rush, clawing and crawling over each other. As soon as one took the lead, another tore it backward and took its place. The horde slowed as the walls narrowed and forced them into one of three aisles. The funnel was working perfectly.

"Got 'im," Kane called as soon as the first creature entered his aisle. He tapped his foot to the frenetic beat of the music. He enjoyed squeezing the trigger.

Kane's shot ripped through the first creature's neck. He was aiming for its forehead. It screeched and clasped its throat as black blood spurted forth. It didn't stand for long. The creature behind it forced it down, stepping on its back and head to get by. Kane took his next shot. He missed the creature in front but struck the one behind it. Even a bad shot was as productive as a good one. Still, he adjusted the aiming pin on the rifle by a quarter turn, then took another shot. Bullseye! A bullet hole ripped through the forehead of the creature in front, dropping it.

Next to Kane, Chad was rapidly shooting three rounds at a time.

"Slow down!" Kane yelled. He grabbed Chad by the arm. "You're using up ammo. One shot at a time. Take a breath."

Roxanne handled her shotgun like a pro, taking down one, two, sometimes three creatures in succession.

Time seemed to speed up as the body count grew and narrowed the aisles. There were more creatures still coming, but they weren't leaping over the piles of bodies as quickly as before.

Kane reloaded his rifle. He had lost count of the number of times he had done so but now realized he was down to his last bullets. The second rifle was useless without them. He had two loaded handguns within reach. Surely, though, they didn't have the same stopping power as the rifle. Roxanne had run out of shotgun shells and switched to one of the semi-automatics. Chad's own semi had jammed, and he'd replaced it with the last of them.

"What are they doing?" Chad asked after a round of firing.

Kane peeked over the barricade. Creatures crowded the other end of the warehouse, except they weren't advancing down the aisles of carnage anymore. The shelving units at the end soon started swaying.

"Shit!"

The creatures had changed their tactical approach and now climbed the makeshift walls, turning them top heavy. The metal shelves twisted and buckled under the added weight and stress. Once the first section collapsed, the rest cascaded down like a set of dominoes, hitting the floor with a horrendous cacophony of screeching metal and splintering wood. An acrid cloud of air rushed into the barricade, along with some of the crashing units. Yet the barrier held.

Unfortunately, nothing prevented the mob of horror from advancing anymore. And all at once they came, climbing and leaping over warped metal, broken plywood, and rotting goblins. A tidal wave of creatures rolled right at Kane and his group.

Kane, Chad, and Roxanne fired everything they had. Their success rate dropped considerably. The creatures bobbed and weaved as they quickly closed the distance to the barricade.

"I'm out!" Roxanne shouted and threw the semi-automatic aside. Kane tossed her a handgun.

"I'm out too!" Chad yelled. Kane gave him the last handgun.

The creatures were nearly on top of them.

"There's too many of them," Roxanne yelled between shots. She screamed as one of the creatures threw itself against the barricade, startling her. She gritted her teeth and shot the creature at close range through the head.

"Shit!" Kane yelled again, taking down another creature as its arm reached through the barricade. "Go! I'll hold them off!" he said to Chad and Roxanne.

They both hesitated, knowing exactly what he meant.

"We go together," Roxanne countered.

Chad nodded.

"They'll chase us down. We won't make it," Kane said.

"They'll cut you down and get us anyway," Roxanne replied.

Last resort time. He tossed the rifle with its last remaining bullets to Roxanne. "Hold them off."

Kane grabbed the gauntlet. Several colored cables hung from the device. The power pack also had a set of colored cables secured to the terminals. Kane had no clue which cable was hot and which was ground. He looked at the colors again, noticing the matching ones. Was it that easy? He quickly connected the matching color cables. As soon as the last pair connected, the gauntlet lit up. Thin lines of blue and white illuminated the arm in some kind of useless stylistic design. He shoved his entire arm into the portlet. It fit like a sleeve. The inside was cold. A number of electrodes contacted his skin from fingertip to his bicep and tricep. He tried bending his arm. The device bent at the elbow and flexed at the wrist naturally.

The business end of the gauntlet hung down to his knees. It had every possible interchangeable tool, but how did he use them? Kane moved his wrist, flexed his fist, bent his elbow.

"Hurry up, Kane! They're getting closer!" Roxanne yelled.

She was right. The creatures were up against the barrier, fighting to come through. Only Roxanne's and Chad's last remaining bullets prevented them from crossing.

Frustration and panic mounted. How did this thing work?

He flicked his fingers. A wide drill sprang from a hidden receptacle, spun for a moment, then stopped.

How'd he do that?

He tried moving his fingers again. This time the drill protruded about six inches and spun at a high speed.

A creature entered the lookout through the barricade. Kane instinctively rammed the drill into its head. The bit chewed and spit flesh, bone, and brain as if all were butter. The creature's eyes rolled up, and it crumpled to the floor. Kane didn't have time to process before he did the same to another creature, then another.

"I'm out," Roxanne yelled and threw down the rifle.

"Same," Chad yelled back.

The creatures crowded against the barricade, piling on top of each other to reach its top.

"Can't that thing do anything else?"

"I'm trying!" Kane maneuvered his fingers. A pair of large cutters replaced the drill bit. With a flick of his thumb and forefinger they opened and closed rapidly. He punched through the line of creatures. The cutters sliced through throats like a hedge trimmer. Black blood sprayed. But as creatures fell away, more took their place. The barricade of box crates and shelving swayed. The weight of the horde pressed harder.

"Come on, Kane!" Roxanne screamed. She and Chad had their backs against the wall opposite the barricade.

Inside the gauntlet, Kane tried another hand gesture as if grasping a gun. The cutters slid back, and a narrow cylinder appeared. He aimed at the center of the writhing demons and pulled the imaginary trigger. A red beam buzzed from the barrel. Three creatures fell away, a burning line slashed through the middle of their bodies.

"Yeah!" Chad cheered from behind Kane.

Kane kept firing. The short bursts mowed down the creatures as though blades of tall grass, but he was too unpracticed with the monstrous weapon to keep his rogue shots from burning through the wooden pallets. The barricade rocked violently. The stacked crates would collapse at any moment.

"Now!" Chad called, enacting some impromptu plan with Roxanne.

The pair rushed to the barricade and used all their strength to topple the whole structure onto the remaining creatures. Kane took several more careful shots at the base of the barricade. His last started a chain reaction. Metal screamed and wood cracked. Crates, pallets, and shelves fell like a house of cards on top of the surviving creatures.

The power to the factory finally failed. The lights and rock music shut off at once.

In the deafening silence, as the structure and dust settled, several creatures that had survived the collapse screeched and hissed. Pinned, their anger and frustration echoed from beneath the pile.

Kane climbed carefully through the wreckage and finished them off.

Shelving shifted in the back. A bony hand reached through a void in the tangle of debris, followed by the rest of the bloodied goblin. Its skin, shades of greens and yellows, was paper thin, a roadmap of black veins traveling beneath it. Its ears were small and pointed at the tips. It had no hair except for a white patch above its brow.

Kane froze. *Avery.*

The creature's dark eyes fixed on Kane.

"I got him," Chad called. He pointed his handgun.

"No, don't!" Kane threw up his hand, stopping Chad in time.

Avery snarled and bared his teeth at Kane. Then he jumped down from the debris and disappeared into the depths of the factory.

Morning light gushed into the dim factory warehouse. The rain had stopped at some point during the evening. Behind the rush of fresh air flowing into the loading dock came a squad of National Guards soldiers with weapons at the ready. All took different positions throughout the warehouse.

A broad man parted from the squad and approached the exhausted trio. "From the bar, yesterday, before the quake. I knew it."

So the soldier had finally recognized him. "Ben, right?"

The big man yelled over his shoulder. "Yo! Let her through!"

Becky ran into the warehouse and didn't slow until she was in Kane's arms. "My God, Kane. I thought I lost you."

"Your father, the kids," Kane started.

"They're fine," Becky said through her tears. "We made it to the high school."

"Becky, Avery was here."

"Are you sure?"

"I'm certain."

She nodded, then looked at the debris pile, aghast. "Is he . . . ?"

"No." Kane swallowed. "He got away."

Ben yelled over them. "How many we got?"

A few soldiers climbed over the pile and shined flashlights through the remains of the maze.

"I count twelve."

"Eight over here."

"I got fourteen, Sergeant."

"Damn. Thirty-four gollums. Largest group by far," Ben reacted. "How the hell did the three of you take down all these Middle Earth sons-of-bitches?"

Kane leveled a stony gaze at the destruction around him. "By losing several people."

Ben eyed Kane very carefully.

"Sir!" Another soldier approached the Sergeant to report. "We found casualties: a male in the front office, two males on the rooftop."

"One in the office is Douglas Reynolds Sr.," Kane explained. "He owned this place. The other men were employees. Was there a woman in the other office?"

"No, sir. The door had been forced open," the solder said.

"She'd been infected. Likely she took off."

"Is there anyone else we should be looking for?" Sergeant Ben asked Kane.

"Duane and Douglas Jr. Male teenagers. Although, if you didn't find their bodies, they likely suffered the same fate as the woman."

"Keep looking," Ben said to his men without taking his eyes off Kane.

"Are we free to go, Sergeant?" Kane asked, uncomfortable with how the Sergeant continued staring at him.

Ben nodded. "A Humvee will take you back to the high school. Get some rest there. We'll be talking again soon."

A new chain-link fence, its top coiled with barbwire, surrounded the entire school as if a strange reverse prison. National Guard, Red Cross, local fire and rescue, and thousands of townspeople filled the gymnasium. Armed soldiers stood guard everywhere; many more chipped in setting up cots, handing out blankets, serving meals, and attending to the wounded and sick. It looked like organized chaos.

Kane turned to Chad at the entrance to the gym and shook his hand. "I'm not sorry for punching you."

Chad's eyes watered. "I'm certain I'd be dead if you hadn't." He looked at Becky. "I'm sorry about . . . well, you know." He spun on his heels and hurried away into the school.

When Kane faced Roxanne, she snorted. "I'm not shaking your damn hand. Am I supposed to be grateful? You can go sit on a stick. Rey would still be alive if none of you had shown up." She spat at their feet, then walked away, disappearing into the bustle.

"Come on," Becky said, pulling Kane away. "Let's get you some food and a bed."

Becky led him inside the gymnasium. The old basketball court was wall to wall cots. She escorted him to an empty one with a set of folded blankets at the foot and asked him to wait until she returned with some food.

He wasn't aware of Kirkland sitting nearby until the old man spoke to him. "You look like shit," Kirkland said. Amazingly, the old man still held his deceased wife's urn.

"Yeah, I suppose," Kane responded tiredly. He caught a whiff of his own sweat and the faint odor of ammonia clinging to him. Stains of blood dotted his shirt and arms. Blood that wasn't his own. "Any chance of a shower in this place?"

"Only if you like a cold one," Kirkland said gruffly. He paused for a moment, then added, "I honestly didn't think you'd make it out of there."

"That makes two of us," Kane said. "Hey, we finally agree on something. See? We can get along."

"Don't get your hopes up, Garner."

"Right. Why would I ever do that, old man?"

The cot was rigid but surprisingly comfortable. He unfolded one blanket and tossed the other one under his head. He didn't remember Becky returning with a sandwich or her adjusting the blanket or pulling off his boots or planting a kiss on his forehead.

Kane slept an entire day and woke the following morning to the call over the intercom system that breakfast was underway. Becky, her father, and the two children were nowhere in sight, likely already in line.

Still in the same stained and sweaty clothes, Kane slipped into the boys' locker room for a quick shower. The warm water lasted a minute at best until icy needles stung his body. He endured the chill, scrubbing the dried blood out of his hair and off his skin.

When he exited the shower, his old clothes were gone. In their place was a fresh towel and new clothing. Government-issued, of course. He dried off and pulled on the pants and shirt. He didn't care who brought him the clothes. He felt refreshed just the same.

As Kane exited the boy's locker room, he found Becky holding a plate of scrambled eggs, toast, and coffee.

"Just the way you like them," she said, smiling and handing him the paper plate and cup.

The smell of cooked eggs and hot coffee hit him with a surprising ferocity. He hadn't realized how hungry he was until now. "You know me well." They took a table nearby, and Kane gobbled the meal in short order. Satisfied, Kane sat back in his chair and sipped his coffee.

"I am so sorry, Becky."

"For what?"

"I put you and your father in danger. I should have listened to you when you first wanted to leave."

"How could you have known?" She smiled. "Besides, when have you been one to listen to anyone?"

Kane rubbed his hand through his damp hair. "Look, I'm done with that. I'll take you and your father wherever you want to go."

Becky shifted uncomfortably in her chair and clasped her hands in front of her. "About that."

Two soldiers dressed in full military fatigues and carrying automatic weapons across their chests approached their table. "Kane Garner. You're needed. Follow us," one of the soldiers said firmly.

Kane slurped his coffee, smirking. "You didn't say please."

The soldiers were not amused.

"Kane, go with them. Please," Becky added as she reached a hand across the table to touch his. Her eyes turned glossy.

She knew something.

"OK." Kane nodded at her, then faced the soldiers. "See what please gets you? Lead on."

The two soldiers led him out of the crowded gymnasium and into the hallway. Kane was a student years ago in this fine establishment and remembered triumphs and defeats in these halls too well. They passed several military personnel along the way, some standing guard outside certain classrooms, each with its small glass window covered. They crossed through the cafeteria next. Half of it was set up for eating, while the other half had more occupied cots. Back into an adjacent hallway, they turned left toward a pair of double doors leading into the auditorium.

"Ah, guys? Principal's office is that way," Kane said, thumbing over his shoulder.

They kept walking.

"Boy, I can't get a smile out of you two at all."

They opened the double doors and ushered him inside. At the opposite end of the auditorium in front of the stage were a number of soldiers in green camouflage uniforms standing around a lengthy line of tables. Sergeant Ben was among the group. All conversation ceased and all eyes turned to Kane as the soldiers escorted him down the middle aisle. The gauntlet Kane had used in the goblin skirmish lay on the center table, the apparent subject of the suddenly hushed conversation.

Sergeant Ben broke from the group. "Thank you, Privates. You're excused." He waited a few moments for the two soldiers to exit the auditorium before addressing his new guest. "Garner, welcome to the Ready Room." Ben stuck out his hand.

Kane's hand was lost in the big man's meaty mitt. He hadn't realized how imposing Ben could be. He was a head taller than Kane and easily outweighed him by fifty pounds of pure muscle. He was broad in the shoulders and chest with thick arms and legs. His uniform fit tightly. Kane was feeling a little at a loss for words among the group. What did they want from him?

"Did you sleep well?" Ben asked.

"Yeah." Kane rubbed his arm nervously. "Hey, um, I—ah, I didn't thank you for coming to help us at the factory."

"Ha! You're the one who helped us. Before today, you held the record for taking down the largest horde in the area. You taught us how to be more effective against those things."

"Well, that thing on the table is what made the difference," Kane pointed. "Not me."

"You're splitting hairs," Ben said. He motioned Kane forward. "Please, a demonstration."

"As in, actually use it?"

"Please," Ben repeated.

Kane walked up to the center table. Two men and two women who didn't bother introducing themselves stood around it. Everyone including Ben stared at the gauntlet with bated anticipation. He slid his arm inside the device until it was snug.

"It has interchangeable tools at the end." Kane lifted the device to show them. "I got the drill bit to work, the cutters, a laser. It's a simple motion of the fingers is all." Kane flexed his hand. When the thick drill bit emerged, he drilled a hole through the table. He flexed his hand again. The drill disappeared, and the cutters took their place. He cut through one of the metal folding chairs as if it were paper. He flexed his hand a third time and shot a red laser beam into the floor. It burned through the carpet, subfloor, and concrete foundation like butter, leaving behind a tendril of smoke.

"Sure wonder how far that went," commented the woman closest to Kane as she peered into the inch-wide hole.

Ben wasn't smiling, but his entire being glistened with hope. "Does Reynolds have any more of these?"

"It was a prototype for an unscheduled Mars mission," Kane explained.

"Damn. NASA gets all the good shit," Ben said. He turned to the panel of men and women standing around the table. "Fly this back to HQ along with the blueprints. Tell them to reverse engineer this puppy. We're going to need a whole bunch of 'em."

Kane placed the device back on the table.

"I have a job for you," Ben said to Kane.

"I told you back at the bar that authority and I don't get along so well."

"Given the circumstances, we need that kind of unconventional thinking out there," Ben said. He threw his hands up as Kane opened his mouth to reject the offer. "Before you answer, think about it."

"You should know, I've been fired from every job I've ever had for insubordination," Kane replied.

"Me too," Ben shot back smiling.

Kane returned to the gymnasium hours later. The lunch line had formed. He found Becky playing ball with Mason and Olivia. Other children had joined the absurd game of bounce-n-catch. Mason and Olivia broke from the circle and raced to greet Kane. They threw their arms around his legs and held on tight.

"Hi, Mr. Garner," Mason said, squinting his eyes.

"Hi, Mr. Garner," Olivia copied her brother.

"Hi," he replied in as neutral a tone he could manage.

"Are the monsters coming back?" Mason asked. Olivia repeated him.

Kane took a deep breath, searching for the words that would ease their worry without frightening them. He knelt to their height. "Nope."

He heard Becky suppress laughter behind him.

Mason, however, didn't seem like he'd have reacted different to any response. "My friend Carl said the soldiers here aren't real soldiers and they sneak out at night and leave and they don't have bullets in their guns and they're scared too." The words fell out of the boy's mouth like a waterfall.

"Yeah, not real soldiers," Olivia followed.

Becky intervened. "Mason, Olivia, let's play with the other kids and let Mr. Garner eat his lunch."

Kane watched the siblings run back to the play circle. Becky took a seat next to him. "They really like you," she said. "Who would have known that tough guy Kane Garner would actually be good with kids?"

"I said two words to them," Kane retorted, but he knew she'd caught his half-smile.

After a moment of silence, he added, "We can go any time you and your dad are ready. We can get a ride back to your dad's house. I'll salvage what I can from my truck when it's safe."

"We're staying here," Becky blurted. "Sorry. I mean, this is where we part ways. I have the kids to watch along with my dad. Besides, the Red Cross can use all the help they can get. It feels right for me here, Kane."

"What about parting ways is right?" Kane asked, but he already knew the answer.

"You can't sit still for a moment, and I don't want you feeling responsible for me." Becky placed a reassuring hand on his knee. "Go find Avery. Or help these guys fight those creatures. Or both. You want to, and they can use actual help."

"You knew they were going to ask me?"

Becky scoffed. "They've been asking everyone who walks into the gym, even my father."

Kane chuckled. "How quickly did he sign up?"

"Immediately." Becky laughed. "You should have heard his list of demands." She fell silent, watching Mason and Olivia negotiate a new game and assign team members. "Kane, you were meant to be something greater—that's what attracted me to you in the first place—but I realized I wouldn't be able to keep up with you. This might be your opportunity."

He didn't know what to say to that. What did anyone say to something like that? To someone hitting the truth square in its chest?

Becky patted his hand before leaving to referee a disagreement between Mason and another boy that was quickly escalating.

Kane finished the rest of his lunch, then took a walk outside. Although he hadn't expected Becky's admission, he couldn't say he was entirely surprised either. He and Becky had fallen out of their relationship a long time ago. He felt obligated to stay with her given the circumstances, and he'd do it if she asked, but his thoughts were occupied with locating Avery. His brother was out there somewhere. Maybe, just maybe, there was a cure for him.

Vehicles and soldiers rushed around the high school parking lot. Three vehicles left the perimeter at the same time that three vehicles returned with supplies or distraught residents. He suddenly wanted to leave to grab the rest of the supplies in his truck he had crashed yesterday. It would be a decent walk, and the supplies could help. More than that, it would give him something to do. But at the exit, a fresh recruit stopped him.

"No one leaves without authorization," the soldier said to Kane. He gripped the semi-automatic across his chest tighter.

"Fuck authorization. I'll leave if I want," Kane argued, continuing toward the exit.

The soldier firmly held his ground. Kane wasn't looking for a fight, but he'd throw some fists to get what he wanted.

"Private, I'll handle this." It was Big Ben, calling to the soldier from across the parking lot.

Kane glowered at the soldier blocking his way until Ben slipped between them.

"You're crazy, Garner, I'll give you that much. My men have orders to stop anyone approaching the gate. You're lucky he didn't shoot you."

"I didn't realize I was a prisoner," Kane said, letting his discomfort with this show clearly.

"Obviously that's not what this is. We can't have people coming and going as they please. Resources are spread thin. Look, we're trying to contain this thing. It's a lot easier to protect people if we know where they are."

"I'll join your band of brothers under a few conditions," Kane said, surprising even himself. Becky was right. He had to be out there.

"Name them," Ben said without blinking.

"I'm searching for my brother. I'd like time to look for him and a no-kill order should anyone else find him."

"Those creatures all look alike. How would we know?" Ben asked.

"I'll provide a description."

"We'll do our best," Ben agreed.

"Second, I answer only to you," Kane said, thumbing at the soldier behind him. "Don't stick me under some eighteen-year-old greenie."

"Agreed. Anything else?"

"Yeah." Kane grinned. "I want a truck. One with a radio and a set of dope speakers."

# TRANSCRIPT

## SUBJECT
Clinton County, Missouri Crisis and Threat
Assessment; Telephone Correspondence

## PARTICIPANTS
Major Daniel Edward Hunt and Sergeant Benjamin
Pavlov

## DATE, TIME, PLACE
05-05-2035, 1719, Plattsburg, Missouri

[BEGIN CALL]

HUNT:    Sergeant, don't sugarcoat. Give it to me
         plain.

PAVLOV: Major, we are under attack. Repeat, under
         attack. They're monsters—actual monsters.
         Gangly, yellow, green skin, claws, pointed
         teeth. Tough as nails to kill. My vehicle was
         attacked, and we lost three men this morning.

HUNT:    Get a hold of yourself, soldier! (*sighs*) I
         wouldn't believe you if I hadn't seen them
         with my own eyes. You're not the only squad
         encountering these . . . things.

PAVLOV: How bad is it, sir?

HUNT:    On a scale of shit hitting the fan, we got
         splatter everywhere  across  the  country.
         Reports  indicate  they  appeared  from  quake

centers as if woken from dormancy. I'm not buying it. I'd bet foreign involvement.

PAVLOV: Who would do such a thing?

HUNT:   Who wouldn't? But that's above my pay grade. We'll find out, that you can count on. When we do, all hell will break loose.

PAVLOV: It looks like it's already broken.

HUNT:   Sergeant, we are at war. Conduct yourself durably and lead your men as such. Establish a perimeter, then expand from there. Search every house, turn over every rock, flush them out, and eliminate on sight. Do you get me?

PAVLOV: Yes, sir. We're set up and fenced in at the local high school and receiving civilians.

HUNT:   Good work. How about recruitment?

PAVLOV: Plenty of volunteers in medical and food prep. Many are willing to pick up arms. Others need a little more convincing. We could use more weapons and ammunition.

HUNT:   I'll see what I can do. Anything else, Sergeant?

PAVLOV: Sir, I'm flying to you a prototype device we recovered this morning. I think it can help us against the creatures.

HUNT:   I'll have our engineers look at it. Keep up the good work.

PAVLOV: Thank you, sir.

[END CALL]

# TRAINING DAY

*Six Months Later*

Kane Garner whipped the steering wheel right, then hard to the left. The airless rear tires flexed and spun, leaving behind dual ruts. Clumps of brown grass shot out like a rooster's tail. Garner pressed the gas pedal and squeezed the steering wheel, knuckles white. The rear of the truck swung to the side. He controlled the drift, holding the right amount of speed, a smile plastered across his face as the thrill coursed through his veins. Ram Jam's "Black Betty" blasted over six speakers, vibrating the entire cab.

"Garrrnerrr!" Private Casie 'Wonderboy' Edwards yelled from the passenger seat, his eyes wide, knees braced against the dashboard, and both hands clutching the overhead grip handle for dear life.

The end of the fairway approached fast, dropping off into a bunker wide enough to roll the customized Titan pickup truck.

"I'm gonna die! I'm gonna die!"

"Hold on, Wonderboy." Garner shifted gears. The rear wheels slowed as the back end swung into alignment with the front. He braked, steered easily around the sunken bunker, then floored the gas again. The truck hit a small rise, catching a little air before landing inside the putting green on the other side. He whipped the steering wheel to the right, to the left. The rear end swung around once more. The truck ripped up the overgrown turf, carving several circles around the hole.

"Woo! That's what I call a hole-in-one!" Garner laughed. He hadn't enjoyed a moment like this since before the quake. Since Hell's scum spilled out from below ground six months ago.

"That makes no sense," Wonderboy said, his face pale. "I think I'm going to be sick."

"Where's your sense of fun?" Garner asked joyfully, turning down the radio.

"Do you know how hard it'll be to repair that green?" Wonderboy asked.

"No one is playing golf anymore."

"Yeah, like a lot of things," Wonderboy said gloomily.

"I have an idea." Garner shifted the truck into first gear. It rolled slowly off the torn putting green and crawled over the sand trap, two rows of trampled ground in its wake. Following a narrow track meant for golf carts and lawn mowers, he drove the truck at a steady speed across the ninth hole fairway and around the putting green until he found his destination. A snack shack sat between the ninth hole and tenth tee. He parked and leaped out of the truck.

"What are you doing?" Wonderboy asked, exiting from the other side.

Garner smiled. "You'll see. Keep an eye out for . . . you know."

The shack's serving window was boarded with a sheet of plywood, the entrance door padlocked. Garner returned to the pickup and grabbed a hammer from the bench toolbox in the back. He took several swings at the padlock before the metal finally gave up.

"You're making too much noise," Wonderboy said as he watched the tree line bordering the course.

Garner tossed the hammer aside, then kicked in the door. He disappeared inside for several moments. When he emerged, he held up two beers and two bags of potato chips as if they were the largest catch of the day. "Happy birthday, Wonderboy!"

"It's not my birthday." Nevertheless, Wonderboy welcomed the unexpected gift.

The two men sat on a nearby picnic table quietly munching chips and sipping warm beer. Several large modern-style homes opposite the golf course broadened their view from between the ninth and tenth greens. A cool, light breeze carried up the fairway, a sign of a potentially early winter. The skies had been grey for months, but today, the sun's rays poked through the fleeting clouds. Garner closed his eyes. For several moments, as the afternoon sun warmed his face, everything felt normal.

Throughout the summer and into late fall, fighting had been nonstop. Ben Pavlov, now a staff sergeant, had branched out the little army he'd established at the high school in Garner's hometown. Squads of mixed military personnel, National Guard, and citizens formed the tip of the spear. They'd begun by searching one house at a time, eliminating the enemy and rescuing civilians. Within a month, the perimeter had expanded from a few blocks to the entire town of Plattsburg. Neighboring towns capable of organizing had done the same. Within two months, many towns had merged, creating a safe zone against the creatures. By the end of the summer, Kansas City, Topeka, St. Joseph, and all towns in between formed the largest safe zone in the Midwest. Combat operations centralized around Kansas City, with dozens of additional squadrons pushing the boundaries fifty to sixty miles in multiple directions around the city like a hub and spoke.

For the last month, expansion had slowed to a standstill as supply lines failed to stabilize. Not only were they fighting creatures from Hell that had an insatiable appetite for any kind of flesh and the ability to spread a transformative disease, but the human population, those who had survived, were reeling from devastating earthquakes that had topped the Richter scale, shifted entire continents, and shook the ground with unrelenting tremors that continued to this day. Day-to-day living had become life-or-death, catching many people unprepared. The slow disaster recovery coupled with the lack of resources meant the greater good was weighed and compromised every day among government, communities, and families.

After months of fighting, these food, weapons, and ammunition shortages didn't sit well with those who agreed to defend their country. Eliminating the enemy and rescuing citizens was becoming secondary to replenishing munitions and finding food for the region's many squads.

Garner's squad was no exception. A few days ago, they had observed a sizeable horde moving east. Easy pickings, but the staff sergeant's orders were to search for food and ammo instead. The squad was now divided into two-person teams; they'd been scouring the region for days.

"Blackwell's not going to be happy we ate all the food we found," Wonderboy said.

Garner opened his eyes, the moment of peace dashed. "Why'd you join the Army, Wonderboy?"

"I was getting my ass kicked every day in high school and figured college would be the same, so I joined to learn how to defend myself," Wonderboy said practically. He didn't express any bitterness or vengeance or hatred about his experience. It seemed he had grown a thick skin during his youth.

Garner looked at him in disbelief. "Seriously? Geez, you could have saved yourself a lot of aggravation by taking karate or something."

"Perhaps, but I took care of that in my first week of boot camp."

"What do you mean?"

"I dropped the biggest recruit in my unit as soon as the hazing started. That's how I got my nickname," Wonderboy said. "Because it was a wonder that boy didn't whoop my ass back."

Garner laughed. "No shit. I didn't know." He leaned back, clasping his hands behind his head. "Good for you, bro."

He closed his eyes again, letting the last gleaming rays warm him and hoping for another quiet moment's reprieve. Birds sang near and far. The air was cool across his skin and carried only a slight trace of burning oil. The world was always on fire nowadays, carrying pollutants in from the west. For months, smoke and smog drifted in and out, thick like fog. The blue sky poking through from time to time today was a rarity; perhaps a shift in air currents had redirected the cloud cover. Who the fuck knew? Garner wanted to enjoy this little bit of comfort even if it only lasted a few more moments.

"Did you know that golf started in the United States in the 1730s?" Wonderboy asked.

"Mmm."

"Although, it's disputed that it started eighty years earlier in the 1650s in New York." Wonderboy sat silently for several moments, then added, "Tiger Woods played on this course once."

"Who cares?"

"I never played golf."

"Why would you want to?" Garner asked. "Buncha fat-asses chasing a ball into a hole."

"I probably won't get a chance to do a lot of things anymore." Wonderboy picked at a callus in the palm of his hand.

Garner sat up and draped an arm over Wonderboy's shoulder. "See those houses over there? Every homeowner loved golf so much, they had a house built next to a course. Now that sounds like the dumbest thing to do."

"A lot of people build homes next to the things they like to do. Campers or fishermen live on their boats, or business owners live above their stores," Wonderboy retorted.

"You're missing the point—"

Both Garner and Wonderboy froze for a second. They heard the noise again, a revving car engine accelerating and decelerating, and immediately lowered themselves below the picnic table. Wonderboy unshouldered his semi-automatic and Garner unclipped his handgun.

Garner pointed across the fairway. A black and green car sped along the residential street behind the houses. "Binoculars," he said, snapping his fingers.

Wonderboy retrieved a black pair from his waist belt and handed them to Garner.

It took a moment to locate the car again. It had stopped at the end of the street in front of the largest mansion. Two men dressed in black quickly exited the car; one stayed outside holding an automatic rifle across his chest, the other man kicked in the mansion's front door. The sedan and the men looked too familiar.

"Stay here," he said to Wonderboy, handing him back the binoculars. "Watch for my signal."

Garner ran low across the overgrown fairway, keeping houses between his approach and the two men. He was across in moments, leaping the fence and sprinting between two mansions. He curved toward the street, moving until the man waiting outside entered his line of sight. As soon as the man turned his back, Garner hustled across the blacktop and toward the backyard of the house opposite the largest one. He dropped to his stomach along the side of the house, then stopped.

Garner cursed. He knew this car. It belonged to his unit. No plate, and it had been painted over in shades of green and black camouflage, but he knew it. His stomach sank.

The man leaning against the car's hood was short, his dark hairline receding, and was dressed in full combat garb.

"Turn around so I can see your face," Garner whispered to himself. He feared he already knew.

As if the man had heard him, he turned, looking up and down the abandoned street. He paced the driveway before settling back into his former position against the car.

*Damn it!*

Specialist Marco Reed was a member of the squad. The funny guy. What was he doing here, and who was he with? Both questions were abruptly answered.

A scream came from inside the house followed by a gunshot, both of which startled Garner. Staff Sergeant Rick Blackwell, their squad leader, exited the house in no particular hurry, an orange backpack slung over his shoulder. Reed met him with his weapon aimed at the front door, covering Blackwell's retreat. The two men returned to the car. Blackwell threw the backpack into the back seat. A woman with disheveled grey hair and wearing a knee-length cotton dress emerged screaming from the house, something wooden held in her hands.

"You took everything! You murderers!" she yelled.

"Reed," Blackwell ordered with a dismissive wave.

Reed raised his automatic rifle and shot the woman in the chest, stopping her dead. The old woman face-planted to the driveway and never moved again.

Garner buried his face in the ground. *Shit! Shit!* He stayed flattened to the grass as Blackwell reversed the car and then sped away in the direction they'd come.

As soon as they were out of sight, he sprinted across the lawn, across the street. Garner knelt next to the woman and rolled her over. Her eyes stared lifelessly into the forever void. A rolling pin lay next to her, soaking in her pooling blood. He left her, unclipping his handgun as he entered the house. He didn't have much time. Goblins had a nose for fresh blood from long distances; he didn't need to come back outside facing a horde.

The interior was exquisitely furnished, and decorated with many fine antiques. Paintings and original artwork covered the plaster walls; none of it Garner recognized, but it smelled of wealth and over-exuberance. He searched the first floor, moving quietly from room to room, and found no one. He paused at the bottom of the curved mahogany staircase, listening.

"Hello?" he called, before sprinting up the flight of stairs.

At the top, a hallway branched in three directions. He took each one in turn, searching a total of five bedrooms and three bathrooms. All were empty. Then he entered the last room, which appeared to be a study.

A large mahogany desk sat in the middle of the room facing a wide picture window that overlooked the golf course and the low-lying hills on the horizon. Built-in shelves held old and current books, framed photographs, a variety of sports memorabilia, and golf trophies.

The desk was a mess of papers, with many more strewn on the floor. Books had been pulled seemingly haphazardly off the shelves. On the opposite side of the study, a painting had been ripped off the wall. A square safe had hid behind it, its door now open and contents emptied. He moved behind the desk to take a closer look and stepped into a lake of blood. Lying face down in the saturated carpet was an older man. He'd been shot in the back of his head.

Garner gagged at the sight of the man's skull, peeled open and emptying itself. The beer and chips he had eaten threatened to escape. He swallowed hard.

Among the papers on the desk were insurance policies, a will, trust documents, and certificates. "Jonathan and Patricia Westcott," he read aloud from one of the documents.

What did Blackwell take from this couple? None of it made sense. There had to be an explanation.

The communicator chirped in his ear, startling him. After a second taken to recover, he spoke. "Garner here."

"Hey, recall came over the box. Blackwell wants everyone back at base ASAP," Wonderboy reported. "I heard a screecher, maybe a quarter-mile away."

"Understood. Pick me up," Garner said.

He looked around the study one more time. *What were you doing here that required the murder of two innocent people, Blackwell?* He had to find out what was in the orange backpack.

A moment later, Wonderboy pulled up in front of the house as Garner exited.

"Who did this?" Wonderboy asked as he motioned to the body in the driveway.

Garner climbed into the passenger side. "Looters. Let's go," he said sullenly.

Wonderboy perked up. "Are you really going to let me drive her back to base?"

"It is your birthday, isn't it?"

Wonderboy bounced the truck into the parking lot of JayJoe's Country Store and Eatery, a former truck stop at the intersection of Interstates 70 and 41 sitting five miles west of Columbia, MO, and now base operations and outpost for the squad of eight who called themselves the Unstoppables. At one-hundred twenty miles from Kansas City, they were the farthest squad from Central Ops, the round-trip a somniferous six hours. They drew cards from a freshly wrapped deck every seven days—the country store had an unopened box of souvenirs in storage full of cheap landmark-themed playing cards— and whoever pulled the lowest card drove to Central for new orders and rationed supplies. Each week, the supplies became less and less, the orders always forthcoming.

Wonderboy ripped through the parking lot across cracked pavement and into the dirt secondary lot that the big rigs once used as a turnabout. The aggressive tire treads tore into the packed gravel, whipping up grit and stone as they gripped the earth for traction. He turned the wheel left, then right, like Garner had done at the golf course, while pressing the gas for all its worth. The rear of the truck whipped around in a perfect circle until he finally let off the gas and slammed the brakes.

"Yeah!" he cheered.

"That's what I'm talking about. Nice, Wonderboy," Garner high-fived the young soldier.

Wonderboy parked Garner's truck next to the other vehicles closer to the diner's entrance. They were the last to arrive.

"Hey, let's keep where we were today to ourselves," Garner said.

"No one'll care we were doing donuts on the golf course," Wonderboy said.

"It's not that. I saw something that I'd like to understand a little better before worrying everyone for nothing."

"Oh? Let me drive your truck again, and we have a deal," he said with a shrug and a smile.

Garner took a deep breath, then pushed open the door. As they entered the former diner, some members of the squad looked their way. A couple of the men called Wonderboy's name in jest. Except for some rogue glances, no one acknowledged Garner's entrance.

Staff Sergeant Rick Blackwell had a leg propped on one of the bench seats and stared coolly as Garner dropped into the nearest booth. Blackwell was ten years his senior with dark crew-cut hair and even darker eyes staring down a crooked nose. He wore a vest jacket that allowed him to vaunt his chiseled arms and tattoos.

"You're late," Blackwell said to Garner, his demeanor easy, as though he hadn't murdered two people only minutes ago.

Another car pulled into the parking lot—the reason they had gathered, and the distraction Garner needed to keep from confronting Blackwell.

"I believe I'm right on time," Garner remarked.

Corporal Tyrone 'Gelly' Gelloti sprung from his car and burst into the diner yelling. "We got new orders!"

Everyone shouted and hooted excitedly as Gelly ran up and down the aisle slapping everyone.

"Alright now," Blackwell said above the celebratory cheering. He did not shout. Still, after a moment, the squad quieted down. Blackwell was not a man who repeated himself.

"Before we get into that, we have a new member joining us. Angelina Dorsey." He gestured to the woman, who had quietly followed Gelly from the car and stood respectfully by the entrance. Dressed in Army-issued black fatigues, she held her stance in a way that exhibited confidence. Her blonde hair was tied back in a small bun. Her blue eyes connected intentionally with everyone in the room in turn.

Blackwell continued. "She's our new field doctor and, I hear, an excellent markswoman."

"Thank you, Staff Sergeant, but I'm actually a nurse," Angelina said, holding her head high.

"No matter to us, and no need for titles out here. We work as a unit. You'll get the idea soon enough." Blackwell proceeded to introduce the entire team. "You met Gelly already. The jokester next to him is Mayor."

Mayor stood and bowed. "Don't listen to him. I am Specialist Marco Reed."

Garner frowned. The two were acting like nothing had happened. Had they killed before?

"Sit down, Mayor. She don't like you."

"That loudmouth back there is Sticks," Blackwell pressed on. "The big man eating over there is Ox. Mags is there."

"Finally got us some girl power going on," Mags said, pumping the air with her fist.

"And Wonderboy and Garner are behind you," Blackwell finished, clearly annoyed by the shouts and comments. "Alright, Corporal, let's have them. I know it's been tearing a new hole in your ass."

"They want us in Columbia to secure the Army National Guard base," Gelly said.

More cheers from around the cramped room.

"Wait, wait, there's more," Gelly teased. "They want us to catch one of those creatures," he continued, adding a little suspense to his tone. "Alive."

"Alive?" Sticks repeated from the back.

Gelly nodded. Shouting and groaning followed.

"That's impossible."

"Enough," Blackwell commanded. "Do we have any supplies coming?"

"No, sir. The staff sergeant at Central said there would be enough supplies at the base to outfit a battalion."

Sticks scoffed. "How does he know?"

"Yeah, that Russian doesn't know a fucking thing," Mags sounded off.

"He's Ukrainian," Garner corrected. Probably wasn't a good time to do so, but why should he give a shit?

Mags flipped him her middle finger with the hand draped over her knee, the foot up on a bench seat. She chomped gum insatiably, and wore a red handkerchief as a headband like Private Vasquez in *Aliens*. Acted just as cocky and vulgar too, as if to overcompensate for being the only woman on the team. Correction: now one of two on the team.

Blackwell ignored the snide reactions. "Be ready tomorrow at sunrise. That means you too, Ox."

The unit erupted in amusement.

"What did I do?" Ox asked, shoving another spoonful of grub into his cheeky mouth.

Dismissed, the squad split in different directions. Garner slid out of the booth and introduced himself to Angelina. He extended his hand, smiling. "Let the posturing begin."

She returned the handshake without a smile or warmth. "You're Kane Garner," she said factually. "Corporal Gelloti said you're dangerous and a bit of an ass."

He rocked on the back of his feet as if he had been slapped. Not that Garner felt she was attractive—she really wasn't his type—but he had a flair for charm. She wasn't impressed.

"Gelly said that? That's great. Well, enjoy the ride while it lasts." Garner sidestepped and left the diner, bruised ego in hand.

The dim afternoon gave way to thickening smoke clouds, which brought early darkness and a sharp decline in temperature. Gollum activity increased during evening hours. Though they hadn't had an encounter in weeks, Blackwell insisted they stick to standard night rotations. "We start getting careless, people start dying," he grunted.

At 1 a.m., Garner was awakened by Gelly. He bolted upright, startling the corporal.

"Take it easy, amigo," Gelly said reassuringly. "Everything's real quiet."

Garner's feet hit the floor, dispelling a dream of his brother drifting away on a raft taken by the tide. "Hey," he said to Gelly before the corporal slipped into his own bed. "Did you really tell the doctor that I was dangerous?"

"And that you're an ass." Gelly denied nothing.

"That's real nice." Garner knew he was the only civilian among the squad of soldiers and not a favorite with the staff sergeant, but over time, he thought relationships were improving with some of the other soldiers. It . . . hurt.

"I'm messing with you, man. I need to knock out the competition if I'm gonna score with the sweet doctor."

Garner snorted. "You son of a bitch."

Gelly slid into bed chuckling.

Garner grabbed his gear and stepped outside into the cold evening, his breath visible like puffs of smoke. With his assault rifle slung over one shoulder, he unwrapped a dried meatstick and ate while he started the rounds. He held a mini flashlight in the other hand but used it sparingly. His eyesight adjusted to the shadows and his hearing tuned into the surrounding sounds.

His boots crunched in the hard dirt as he circled the diner and weaved between the parked vehicles. He selected his footfalls more carefully, silently, as he tracked wider circles around the diner. At the fuel pumps, he stopped and leaned against their cool metal, listening to a horned owl in the far distance. The patrol tiresome, he let his thoughts drift, mulling over the shooting at the golf course.

Should he confront Blackwell and Reed? Report them? It was his word against theirs. Blackwell had served in the military for ten years, Reed for five. Being the newest member and the least experienced, he might lose that argument or, worse, his life. Since the beginning of the war, he felt fear for the first time. He was serving with a couple of cold-blooded killers. He'd never figured for one second that the most immediate threat to him and his squad would come from inside it.

He sighed.

Garner pushed away from the fuel pumps, crossed the highway, and marched a quarter-mile before turning back. He hopped the guardrails and cut along the edge of the parking lot, which bordered a thicket of trees and underbrush. A raccoon digging for grubs scampered away.

He returned to the diner and climbed the ladder to the flat roof. There he stayed, watching, listening, troubled. His eyes kept dropping down to look at the black and green sedan parked below. They weren't so stupid that they'd have left evidence in the car, right? His shift was nearly over when he decided to find out for sure.

Garner climbed quietly down from the roof. He flashed his light through the window of Blackwell's car; the front and rear seats sat empty. He opened the driver's side door slowly and peered inside the center console, under the seats, within the glovebox. When he opened the trunk, he was surprised to find the orange backpack sitting there in plain sight as if it'd been begging to be found. He lifted the pack. It had some weight to it. He unzipped the top.

"Oh shit." Gold and silver gleamed back at him—sleeves of silver coins wrapped in plastic, six gold bars of maybe an ounce each, and a zip-top bag of assorted jewelry that included gold rings, diamond earrings, gemstone necklaces.

Garner quickly put everything back and shut the trunk. He slouched against the car.

Were other members of the squad part of this? He didn't think so. What was he going to do about it?

"Hey, everything cool?"

Garner spun. His stomach leaped into his throat at the sight of Reed approaching.

The specialist chuckled. "You look like you saw a ghost. Or worse." His eyes scanned the area for gollums despite the joking tone.

"No, man, you startled me." He glanced at his watch. "I wasn't expecting you for another fifteen."

"Yeah, well, can't sleep before a mission," Reed explained coolly.

Even though the temperature had fallen below freezing, sweat rolled down the center of Garner's back.

"Get some rest. I'll finish your shift," Reed said. "Look like you could use it."

Garner nodded and headed straight inside to his cot. Reed hadn't seen him in the car. If he had, Garner's brains would be splashed all over the parking lot. His stomach churned, agitated by what he should do.

Garner woke, ate, and geared up for the day before the crack of dawn. Duty, day-to-day survival, life-and-death decisions—these new realities had changed his ethic in recent months. His leg jackhammered under the diner table as the rest of the squad prepared for the mission.

Ox was last to join the unit. Blackwell quietly regarded the heavyset man, watching him plod down the aisle to an empty booth while fishing his arms through a dirty sweatshirt one size too small for him. Clearly, Garner wasn't the only one Blackwell disdained.

"Listen up," he scowled. "We'll split into two teams and take both JVs." The joint light tactical vehicles, a cross between a Hummer and a tank, each had a turret mounted on its roof and enough payload to carry six men and their gear. Basically, battering rams on wheels. Garner loved them.

"Garner, Sticks, Mags, and Ox will take the lead in JV1; everyone else is with me in JV2. We stay together until we reach our target destination. When encountering gollums, spare your ammunition unless it's absolute. Civilians are not our mission. Comms open at all times. Report what you see. All orders through me. Am I clear?"

"Yes, sir!" everyone in the diner replied.

"We move out in fifteen. Garner, a word."

Garner remained with Blackwell as the other members departed to prepare for the mission.

"Sir, may I ask how we're going in?" Angelina interrupted before Blackwell started in on Garner. "I grew up in Columbia and may advise."

"Straight over on 70 and then north on 63. Four lane highway," Blackwell mused.

"Due respect, 70 runs dead center of Columbia. If the city is overrun by gollums, we could be facing tens of thousands. We'd have a better chance coming in from the north. Cut northeast and join Route 63 by the town of Hinton," Angelina said.

"That's solid thinking," Garner offered. "There's nothing on the old country roads. Even if we had to detour, it's pasture out there."

Blackwell glared at Garner, then at Angelina. "Is that your professional opinion as a doctor?"

She opened her mouth to reply, then chose it'd be best to keep it closed.

"Keep your opinion to yourself about my operations, and I promise I won't express my opinion about your healthcare practices," Blackwell pressed. "Dismissed."

"Yes, sir." Angelina quickly departed, leaving Garner alone with Blackwell.

"Wow, you're a badass with your intimidation glare," Garner delivered. "Is that part of your training, or are you naturally an ass?"

"The only reason you're here, Garner, is chain of command believes you belong here." Chain of command. Meaning Pavlov. He'd taken a liking to Garner, for reasons he still didn't understand but didn't yet desire to question. It seemed Big Ben was yet another name on Blackwell's shit list. "If it were up to me, I would have sent you back to Central Ops a long time ago. You're rogue, undisciplined, and lack training. That gets people killed. Orders keep people alive."

"Yeah, yeah, I get the orders part. It's your delivery that sucks."

"Can you do better, Garner? Can you lead these men and women?" he said.

"Better than you? Anybody here could lead better than you," Garner said into the eyes of a murderer. He wanted to question the contents of the orange backpack, but the other members of the unit, though scattered as they prepared for the mission, were well within earshot. He didn't think anyone else was part of Blackwell and Reed's scheme, but if he was wrong, it could mean a quick death covered up as a casualty of the mission. No one would ever question the report.

Blackwell stiffened and pulled on the bottom of his jacket.

Garner grinned. "You want to hit me? Teach me a lesson?"

Blackwell looked like a bull ready to charge and stomp on Garner's face. Instead, he leaned in. "Here's your chance to lead. Don't fuck this up. If you do, you and I are going to have an exchange, and it won't be with our words."

"There it is again. It's that delivery you need work on, Rick," Garner provoked. "By the way, you may want to cut back on that cheap liquor you have stashed under your rack. Try brushing. I'll let you borrow my toothbrush if you need one." He walked away and slipped out of the diner.

*Orders keep people alive.* It was bullshit.

It wasn't. The events over the next six hours bared truth to those exact words.


They cruised east on Interstate 70. Months of neglect and decay had the highway crumbling in many places, but the military trucks rolled over the potholes, cracks, and debris as if the road had been paved yesterday. Abandoned vehicles, rusted and useless, also did nothing to slow the lead JV as Garner weaved around them.

*"Check your speed, JV1,"* Blackwell said over comms.

Garner eased off the gas, bringing the speedometer down from sixty to forty-five miles per hour. The JV had no rearview or side mirrors; instead, a video feed on the center console showed everything surrounding the vehicle.

Mags swiped a finger across the screen, which showed JV2 about a quarter-mile behind them. She glanced at Garner, realizing he wasn't going to answer. She touched two fingers to her earpiece. "Roger that, JV2. Adjusting speed."

*"Coming up on the river. Drop speed to twenty-five once you cross,"* Blackwell said.

"Understood," Mags replied. Off-mic, she said to Garner, "Are you going to add anything?"

Garner gave her the side-eye and gripped the steering wheel tighter. "Pay attention, everyone," he said over comms. "We got a couple gollums coming up on the right."

*"Save your ammo and stay your course,"* Blackwell ordered.

Garner huffed and shook his head. He veered the JV toward the two naked gollums bouncing and flailing around a tiny smoking fire inside a tin can on the side of the road as if conducting some ritual dance.

"What are we doing?" Sticks shouted from the turret. "Am I taking them?"

"Hold your fire," Garner shouted back.

Mags stiffened her arm on the dashboard as the JV steered into the path of the two gollums. "What are you doing, Garner?"

"Saving our ammo." Garner clipped the first gollum. The front of the vehicle struck the creature in the chest, sending it along with the can of fire into the other creature. Both gollums toppled over one another in a tangle of spindly arms and legs. Whatever was in the tin can sprayed them, igniting their bodies if their skin was flash paper.

"Holy Christ!"

Garner grinned. "Two for one."

"You're a badass, Garner. I'll give ya that much," Ox said.

"More like a dumbass," Mags corrected.

A few moments later, they crossed over the Missouri River. Three miles from Columbia, flat pasture spread as far as the eye could see on both sides of the highway. Patches of bare trees broke up the dull scenery. The highway gently dipped and rose. Garner's speed started to increase only for him to be reminded again to keep it low by JV2 and his navigator to his right.

As they crested the next rise, Garner slammed hard on the brakes. On the opposite side of the highway, a yellow school bus crawled along the road, thick black smoke belching from its exhaust. A crowd of gollums leaped and bounded alongside it, trying to latch on. Mechanical issues overwhelmed the bus as it struggled to keep ahead of the amassing creatures.

A lump formed in Garner's throat. Pressed against every window were faces—young and old, hopeful and grim—staring back at him.

"*Keep moving, JV1,*" Blackwell said over comms, voice hollow and detached. "*Stay on mission.*"

A wave of frustration and anger snapped inside Garner. Why should he listen to a murderer? These people could be saved. Everything else should be secondary.

"Fuck your mission."

Garner floored the gas pedal. He maneuvered the JV across the highway divide in pursuit of the foundering bus.

"*Mags, relieve Garner!*" Blackwell barked. "*Any means possible! That's an order!*"

Garner flung his earpiece down, eyes on Mags.

She retrieved her sidearm and pointed it at him.

"Are you really going to let a bus full of people die?" he asked.

The comms lit up as Blackwell continued yelling orders, but he couldn't hear him anymore.

"Don't you want to light these fuckers up?" Garner pressed. "That's all you've been talking about for weeks. Or was all that talk bullshit?"

"Yeah!" Sticks yelled from above, slapping the roof of the vehicle. "Let's do this! Come on, you mother fuckas!"

Mags's eyes narrowed. She looked at Ox in the backseat for some support, but the big man was wide-eyed with fear; beads of sweat rolled down his doughy forehead. She cursed, holstered her sidearm, and nodded. "Let's do this."

The school bus finally succumbed to its fate. Something metallic dropped from its undercarriage, leaving a trail of smoking oil. Black smoke plumed, briefly obscuring the mob of bloodthirsty creatures. Then the bus lurched and came to a final stop.

The mass of creatures, a hundred or more, rushed the disabled bus, climbing and crawling over one another. They were up the sides prying at the windows and on top clawing at the roof. Most were naked while some wore the tattered remains of clothing from their former human selves. Their toad-colored skin glistened wetly in the yellow morning light. With temperatures close to freezing, they appeared impervious to the cold, driven purely by the warm blood inside the bus.

"What's the plan?" Mags asked.

"Take 'em out!" Garner said as they rapidly approached the hamstrung bus. He pounded on the roof. "Go, Sticks!"

Rapid artillery fire burst from the roof of JV1. A torrent of red-hot slugs ripped into the riot of gollums. Bodies tore apart and dark blood sprayed, but for every creature that fell, several more took its place.

"Hold tight!" Garner plowed into the horde, working to dislodge their hold on the bus. Creatures disappeared under the JV as the wheels pulled their bodies down and grinded bones to pebbles.

A few creatures managed to leap onto the hood of the JV. Mags rolled down her window, sat on its edge, and shot the bastards off. As Garner drove alongside the bus, each passenger's expression of fear or desperation etched itself forever in his head as if everything were moving in slow motion. He diverted his gaze to the rear video feed, which showed a pile of broken bodies. Some creatures surfaced from the mound of blood and guts only to resume their attack on the bus. He banked the JV around for another pass.

"Let's do that again!" he yelled, and pounded the roof.

Sticks swung the turret around and made quick work of the surviving creatures.

"Yeah!" Mags sat inside her window taking aim at any creature who got too close. She leaned back into the JV with a scowl across her face. "Get in the game, fat ass!" she said to Ox.

At that moment, though, things turned for the worse.

Those creatures not attacking the bus launched an assault on the JV. Mags never saw the two creatures who rushed the vehicle from behind. She dropped her sidearm. Long nails dug into her arms and lower back, threatening to topple her from the vehicle. The woman screamed and yelled, trying to fight them off.

Garner reached across, snatching one of her ankles while keeping the JV on a course to sideswipe the bus on his side. A gun fired inside the cab next to Garner's ear, the noise deafening. Blood and guts splashed inside the cab. The two creatures fell back; Mags, completely limp, fell backward out of the vehicle with them, her leg slipping from Garner's grasp.

"Oh my God! Oh my God! I didn't . . ." Ox held his smoking handgun in a shaking hand. "It went off . . . I wasn't . . ." Eyes and mouth wide with shock, Ox panicked and fumbled with his seatbelt.

"Ox! Ox!" Garner yelled. "This fight isn't over. Stay in your seat!"

Above, Sticks pumped the second mass full of lead as the JV plowed the creatures, they and the bus's rub rails squealing from the impact. The JV rocked over the bodies, then abruptly stopped.

Garner pressed the gas, but the tires spun in place. Broken bodies, limbs, and gore packed tighter under the vehicle. He tried reversing, then rumbling forward, rocking the vehicle back and forth.

Sticks, still firing, stomped on the roof. "We got to move, man!"

The rear door opened, and Ox jumped out the back.

"What are you doing?" Garner called.

The big man started firing his weapon at random as if his finger had been glued to the trigger. Creatures closed in on him from all sides; a bloodcurdling scream rang out, and the gunfire ended.

Glass broke and people screamed. The creatures had taken advantage of the unit's position, entering the school bus from the JV's hood.

"Shit. Come on! Come on!" Garner continued his frantic attempt to free the JV.

Sticks swore. "They're too close!" The turret stopped firing. A handgun took its place. "Get us out of here, Garner!"

One of the windows of the bus slid open next to Garner. A woman thrust an infant out of the opening, holding him in midair. Her pleading eyes met Garner's. Her end was near—but perhaps there was still a chance for her child.

Cursing, Garner rolled down his window and grabbed the child.

Tears streamed down the woman's cheeks. Relief spread across her face as she lipped "Thank you" to him.

The JV finally found traction and steamrolled several creatures still attempting to scale the hood. Garner escaped the massacre and turned around again. Most of the creatures were dead, crushed, or blown apart, but many more had survived and entered the school bus. The people inside were trapped with nowhere to go.

The infant in his arm wailed. The realization and gravity of what just happened hit Garner like a sucker punch. He floored the JV back to base camp.

Garner arrived at base in a cloud of dust. He exited the vehicle while holding the baby in his bouncing arms, which did little to comfort the crying child.

Sticks jumped down off the turret cradling his bloody arm. "I'm bit."

Any possible words choked to a stop in Garner's dry throat.

JV2 roared into the truck stop a moment later, and all of its occupants leaped out, including Blackwell.

Angelina met Garner first. She took the wailing child out of his arms and disappeared into the diner.

Blackwell was on Garner in a flash, gripping him by the collar. "Orders!"

He punched Garner in the nose.

"Keep!"

He slammed him in the nose again. Blood showered his face.

"People!"

He punched him across the temple.

"Alive!"

He struck him on the jaw.

Garner's every muscle went rigid. His knees buckled. The late morning faded into darkness.

Garner groggily peeled open his eyes. One didn't want to open as wide as the other. Everything hurt. His teeth throbbed as if they had been rearranged. His nose was blocked and bandaged, forcing him to breathe heavily through his mouth over severely chapped lips. A sharp pain stretching from his chin to his earlobes flared every time his mouth moved.

He stared at his arm with some confusion. A tube led from it to a bag of liquid hanging from a pole. Around him, blurred shapes moved among rows of beds. A hospital.

*What . . .*

How had he gotten here?

"Awake at last," said a rumbling baritone.

Garner hadn't noticed the big man sitting at his left until he spoke. Staff Sergeant Benjamin Pavlov, built like a powerlifter and surely as strong as one, rose to his six-foot, five-inch height. His combat uniform pulled snug around his broad chest and round shoulders, giving him an even more imposing look.

"The baby?" Garner mumbled.

"Safe." Ben said empathically.

Garner looked away sadly, remembering.

Ben leaned in close, inspecting Garner's cuts and bruises. "Did you try at all to defend yourself?"

"Fuck off." He winced as pain shot along his jawline. "Why are you here anyway?"

Ben pulled back and crossed his thick arms across his chest. "Under normal circumstances, there would be an investigation while you all sat in jail cells, statements drafted, lawyers assigned, a presentation before a judge. You'd try to defend your case, but in the end, you'd be found guilty and tossed in prison. Fortunately, these days are not normal circumstances, are they? Even for warfare."

Garner waved a hand in front of his face. It weighed like lead. "I caused their deaths. I deserved this . . ."

"There were plenty of mistakes to hand around, including my own." Ben let out a long sigh. "Ultimately, I'm responsible for the individuals under my command. And their actions."

"Don't try to soften what happened," Garner said, mashing some of his words.

"Oh, you definitely fucked up. The deaths of those three soldiers will weigh on your conscience for a long time."

"Sticks is dead?" Garner cursed.

"On the other hand, the people on the bus were already dead. You just happened to save one of them," Ben added.

"Is that supposed to make me feel better?"

"This is war, Kane Garner, and war is ugly. The sooner you realize that, the more you can make a difference. We can't save everyone."

"I don't want to be a part of this anymore," Garner said intently.

Ben chuckled. "The enemy is all around us. It could reveal itself unannounced right here in this hospital." His eyes narrowed. "What are you thinking? That you can quit, find yourself a little farmhouse, pretend none of this is happening? Sooner or later, the war comes to you."

"You should leave," Garner said angrily.

Pavlov sighed. "I don't believe for one second you're a quitter. Defeated, yes, but not down. Rest up—"

"I already told you—"

"I need you back on the frontline," Pavlov interjected.

It was Garner's turn to sigh. "Unstoppables?"

"The Unstoppables squad is no more. As a matter of fact, all squads are being split into smaller tactical units. I need you to lead one of them."

Garner's scoff sounded more like a snort. Pain rocketed through his nose.

"You'll receive a full briefing shortly. Until then, get some rest." Ben turned to leave, then hesitated. "For what it's worth, I also came by to see how my friend was doing."

"You're full of surprises today," Garner said, though inwardly, he cursed. He often felt mistrusting of others, authority figures especially, the wake of relationships he had abandoned evidence to the fact. If he was going to survive, if the human race was going to survive, he needed to start trusting others.

"Staff Sergeant, there's something else you should know."

A week later, Garner was feeling better. His bruised left eye looked worse than it felt. He ate comfortably without much jaw pain and could finally breathe through his nose. His mental injuries, however, would never heal. Those scars he'd carry for the rest of his life. When he was alone, he replayed the botched rescue. He'd done that. He'd caused the deaths of three good soldiers. He spent a second week exercising and running, trying to clear his mind and plan the details of his next assignment while wondering how receptive the new team would be. Telling Ben about Blackwell had likely put a target on his back, especially once the man's expulsion had unofficially filtered back to him.

Garner held his breath as he approached his team outside Central Ops near the deployment station. Wonderboy, Gelly, and Angelina waited together next to a refrigeration truck.

Gelly saw him first. "You've got to be shitting me."

"Garner!" Wonderboy yelled. The young man greeted him halfway, full of smiles and excitement. "Damn, I thought you were dead. Staff Sergeant gave you a beating like I've never seen. He hit you a dozen times, then after you dropped, he continued to pound on you. Took four of us to pull him off you."

"Thanks, Wonderboy. I was there," Garner said.

"Probably not how I would have done it, but I thought you did the right thing back there." Gelly shook Garner's hand.

Angelina stood cross-armed. "You saved that infant's life, but if we had worked as a team, we could have saved more."

"Damn, girl. Do you have to say it like that?" Gelly asked.

"Best we know where we all stand on the matter," she responded firmly.

"It's OK," Garner said openly. "I made a mistake that got people killed. I can't fix it, and I regret it. I hope I'm able to earn your trust."

"We'll see," Angelina said.

Gelly knocked on the refrigeration truck. It and one of the JVs had been modified courtesy of one of Gelly's many talents. He had removed the insulated panels off the diesel truck and replaced them with a steel bar cage; the repurposed panels he'd used to reinforce the utility vehicle's windows and tires. "Where's the ice cream run?"

Garner smiled uncomfortably. "Columbia is showing the most gollum activity."

"Right back into the fire," Angelina grumbled.

"No one has been able to capture one alive," Wonderboy said. "They tear themselves apart in isolation. Go berserk when cornered. They don't react to sedation either." He started chewing his thumbnail.

"Ops has provisioned the supplies we need. This could be a turning point in how to defeat them. We use the cooler truck to find a way, trial and error."

"Let's hope the error part doesn't kill one of us," Angelina said coldly.

Garner grimaced. "We'll have each other's backs, best we can."

"And if we find civilians?" Her arms remained folded, and now she tapped her foot.

"We rescue as many as we can. As a team," Garner replied, then looked at his watch. "We leave in four hours. If you need other supplies, now is the time to gather them."

He left his new team behind to finish his own arrangements. The meeting could have gone a lot worse, but he had his work cut out for himself if he wanted to earn their trust.

He turned his face toward the overcast sky, realizing it had turned brisk. Kansas City wasn't known for much snowfall during the winter months—ice mostly—but lately it felt like something worse was brewing on the horizon.

Two days later, they caught their first gollum.

"Wonderboy! Get the cage ready!"

Garner, Gelly, and Angelina yanked and pulled a small hostile gollum toward the cage. It gripped a dirty teddy bear with a missing eye and arm in its filthy hand. No one wanted to openly admit that the creature used to be a young child. They wrangled it wordlessly with long aluminum control poles. It hissed, spittle flying from a mouth of yellowed needle teeth, arms and legs flailing. It pulled unsuccessfully at the steel cables looped around its thin, sinewy neck. Realizing defeat, it went boneless and dropped to the ground, forcing its captors to work a lot harder. The three were dressed in thick leather jackets, gloves, and leggings, along with plastic face shields. Although the clothing restricted their movement, Garner insisted on every precaution to stay alive. He wouldn't lose anyone else.

They angled the control poles and pushed the creature toward the cage like a mop head. Its destination looming, the gollum sprung to its feet once more and thrashed wildly. The sudden bolt of energy nearly pulled Angelina off her feet.

"Hold steady!"

The creature locked arms and legs against the cage opening, stopping all progress. The teddy bear fell to the ground.

"Push!"

Deformed bones cracked and a leathery shoulder dislocated before they finally lodged the creature into the cage. One by one, they uncorded the control poles. Garner held the last one with Gelly as his aid.

Garner nodded at Wonderboy. "Ready? As soon as we let go, shut the gate. One, two, three!"

The last control pole detached from the creature's neck and the gate slammed shut.

"We did it!" Wonderboy cheered, looking for anyone to high-five or fist-bump, but no one felt celebratory quite yet. They watched through the bars as the creature's thrashing became increasingly violent. It threw itself against the steel repeatedly, hissing and screeching like a rabid animal. Its black eyes regarded them with madness. Another charge at the bars split the thin skin down the center of its forehead. Thick, poisonous blood ran freely down its face and into its mouth, coating bared teeth before dripping back out down its chin and bare chest. It raked at its eyes over and over until both orbs ruptured.

"Dear God!" Angeline gasped.

Both hands clasped its neck. Nails penetrated the thin skin, finding soft veins and arteries. With a sudden rip, the creature tore out its own neck. The stink of ammonia filtered through the air as the creature bled out. Within moments, only a smoldering stink of fleshy goo remained.

Angelina covered her nose and mouth. "I've seen it dozens of times but can never get used to the melting."

"Check yourself for scratches or cuts," Garner said disappointedly.

"Sir, I'd like to have a word," Gelly said formally. He'd been acting strangely since they left Central Ops by maintaining rank and requiring Wonderboy to do the same as if Garner was their superior officer.

"Cut the shit with the sir crap, Gelly, OK? I'm not in the military. Never was. I see it as if I was hired to do a job. For the last time, call me Garner. I'm actually preferring it these days."

"Garner, sir. I thought we could brainstorm some ideas before our next catch, sir. I mean . . ."

Garner shook his head, smiling, and slapped Gelly on the shoulder. "Let's call it a day. We got some planning to do."

Five miles outside Columbia, a few miles from the bus incident and Interstate 70, they found a beer and wine store. It had been cleared out by looters but, situated off the main roads, worked well for their camping needs.

They ate before convening around a high table once used for wine tasting and cheese dipping and now serving simply as a flat surface to stabilize their map. The 3D digital representation of the region, projected by three round image pods, hovered in midair an inch above the surface.

"Go ahead, Gelly. What do you got?" Garner asked.

The corporal had tied his long, dark hair back to keep the long strands away from his face. His trimmed dark beard outlined his square jaw and highlighted a scar that ran partially around one side of his neck. His dark eyes met each of them before he spoke, ensuring he had their attention.

"What do we know about these things?" Gelly started.

"There are two types, the originals and the people they transformed," Wonderboy answered.

"No, no. What do we know about their behavior?" Gelly clarified.

"They bite people and eat everything else," Wonderboy stated simply.

"They don't sleep from what we can tell," Angelina added.

"They travel in groups," Garner said.

"Afraid when alone," Wonderboy said. "And go insane to the point of death when captured."

"Exactly," Gelly said, his eyes wide. "But I don't think they're afraid, certainly not of us. It's more like off-the-charts separation anxiety."

Wonderboy snorted. "Yeah, well, separate a cub from its mother and see how desperate the cub becomes."

Gelly pointed at him. "But keep them together, and—"

"—and they succumb," Angelina finished.

"We capture two," Garner stated, putting Gelly's thoughts to words.

"More perhaps. I don't know what their minimum threshold is before they self-mutilate," Gelly said. "We need to figure that out."

"That might actually work," Angelina said. "How did you come up with this?" she asked Gelly.

Gelly cast his gaze down to his feet. "Let's just say I can relate."

"So where do we try next?" Wonderboy asked.

Gelly moved one of the image pods halfway across the table. The digital map zoomed onto a large neighborhood of cookie-cutter houses. He pointed as the image slowly turned on its axis. "Hundred houses, maybe more. Several access points. No chance of getting backed into a corner. It's about a quarter-mile from here."

"Good work, Gelly. Any objections? OK, let's get some rest. We'll start first thing in the morning," Garner said as he dimmed the light over the high table.

Garner flew out of his rack at the distant sound of gunshots. At a quick glance, his watch displayed 2:30 a.m., and the dark forms of neither Gelly nor Angelina had stirred. He rushed quietly to the front of the beer and wine store, handgun at the ready, and met Wonderboy at the doors.

The young private swiped through each remote camera feed on his tablet, quickly adjusting angles and visual spectrums from night vision to infrared to standard with precise turns of his hands and pinch gestures of his fingers. Without looking up at Garner's approach, he said, "I don't see anything, sir."

"How close do you think?"

Wonderboy shrugged. "A mile, maybe less. The south camera recorded car headlights moving slowly along the back road about an hour ago."

"What's your assessment?" Garner prodded, still shaken from the sudden snap out of a dead sleep.

"No hostiles coming this way, sir. Creature or human. I'm guessing a local coming home from a searcher ran into a gollum or two."

Garner holstered his handgun. "Thanks, Casie. Why don't you turn in? I'll take the rest of the shift."

Wonderboy handed Garner the tablet, saluted, and then hesitated a moment.

"Is there something else?"

"Sir, I'd prefer if you called me Wonderboy. My real name doesn't suit me anymore."

Garner smirked. "Sure. As long as you stop saluting and calling me sir. Deal?"

"Deal, sir. I mean, yes." Wonderboy spun on his heel and slipped quietly into the dark depths of the looted store.

Temperatures fell near single digits overnight. Winds howled in from the west at daybreak. Garner had their two vehicles idling and warming as the crew readied for the day. The refrigeration truck he'd used to charge the battery cells of the electric utility vehicle.

A short time later, both vehicles rolled into the target neighborhood. A tall metal fence separated it from the main road. A section had been ripped from its posts, likely a result of the quakes. The rusted, twisted metal lay on the side of the road with a small sedan trapped beneath the distorted fence as if pinned by a claw.

After passing a few houses, they stopped the vehicles and stepped outside into the brisk morning air.

"Wonderboy saw a car last night. Be aware of local residents with nervous trigger fingers." Garner strapped his semi-automatic rifle to his back and grabbed the control stick from the back of the utility vehicle. "Let's head out, two by two."

The houses were spaced with a fair amount of yard between them, their backyards expansive. Several variations of styles repeated, with colors, window sizes, front door placement, and garage size the largest differences. The houses were eerily dormant.

They checked each house by testing the front door. If it was locked, they moved on to the next one. They had no interest in busting down doors and taking the risk of getting shot by a holed-up homeowner.

The first three houses proved empty and abandoned months ago, the next several locked. The house they tried next was full of mystery.

As they approached, flanking the door, they saw it was left partially open. Windows had been boarded from the inside.

"Survivalists," Gelly said quietly.

"Hello, anyone home?" Garner shouted, and rapped on the door. The house was as silent as a prayer.

"Ready? You know the drill."

Gelly and Angelina entered first and steered to the right; Garner and Wonderboy followed and veered to the left.

The first floor was a large open-concept combination that included the kitchen and living and dining rooms, as well as a pantry, closets, bathroom, and a large guest room, this at the back of the house. Much of the furniture had been rearranged to fit a stockpile of boxes, stacked three and four high, and full of various goods and household supplies. Both teams met at the foot of the stairs leading to the second floor.

"So this is where all the toilet paper went," Gelly said softly, nodding to a pile of Charmin stacked to the ceiling.

"There's bags of trash piled in the backyard next to a handmade smoker," Wonderboy said. "I don't like this."

Angelina crunched her nose. "It smells like spoils in here."

They hustled up the stairs in the same formation, splitting right and left at the top. Garner and Wonderboy approached two closed doors at the start of the hall; he motioned for Wonderboy to take the first door as he proceeded to open the second.

"Anyone home?" he asked as he opened the door to a master bedroom. The king bed was unmade, the sheets and blankets draped over onto the floor. A neat stack of folded clothes sat on a chair nearby, a shotgun and handgun lying on top.

Wonderboy stumbled into him then, white as a sheet of paper. "Bedroom. Body in the bed. Male. About my age, I'd guess. Looks like he was shot in his sleep."

Garner turned to leave—there was nothing to see in here—and the smell drifting in from the adjoining bedroom churned his stomach. At the same time, he noticed a red stain on the hallway carpet, another stain a few feet away, another. The trail led them down the hallway and past both bedrooms.

"Blood?" Wonderboy asked.

Garner didn't bother to confirm what Wonderboy already knew.

"Garner, sir. We got something you should see," Gelly called from the opposite end of the hall, holding the collar of his shirt over his nose. The stink grew stronger as Garner joined Gelly in an office, Wonderboy following behind.

Two bodies lay face down, a male and female. Their hands were bound behind their backs with plastic zip ties. Blood had splattered the walls, windows, and carpet.

"Both shot in the back of head," Angelina said, pointing to the entry wound on the male victim. "This is recent—like, a day ago."

Garner surveyed the room. The home office had two desks with dead computers against opposite walls. Shelving, full of collectibles and family photos, decorated the room. To the right of one of the desks sat a tall wooden cabinet with its four drawers wide open. Tossed on the floor beside it lay a metal lockbox.

Garner picked up a slip of paper with wording that caught his eye. It was an authentication certificate for registered gold coins, but nowhere in the room were any coins to be found.

"Find anything else?" Garner asked.

Angelina shook her head. "We inspected the bodies. Nothing. But their fingers are broken. Probably after they were shot."

"Someone breaks in, kills them, takes the valuables, but leaves the weapons and the food," Gelly said with confusion.

"Unless they're all coming back to take the rest of it," Wonderboy said.

"All? You think it's a group?" Gelly said.

"How else do you overpower three armed adults?"

Gelly frowned. "No one hears them enter?"

Wonderboy shrugged.

"What do you want to do, Garner?" Angelina asked with a slight edge to her tone, as if any answer he gave would fall short of her expectations.

"The ground is too hard to bury them. Wrap them up in sheets. We'll place them in the bedrooms and lock up the house," he said distantly.

The murders were too familiar to ignore. He kept his thoughts to himself as he helped carry the bodies to the bedrooms. The four of them stood quietly for a moment over the wrapped dead.

Wonderboy's wristwatch chirped. As he glanced at it, the blood drained from his face. He quickly swung his pack off his shoulders to retrieve the tablet.

"What is it?"

He swiped furiously through the images. "Three of the cameras were tripped back at camp."

"Gollums?"

Wonderboy flipped the tablet around to show the rest of the team. A dozen or more of the spindly, pasty creatures had breached the former beer and wine store and now tore through their only supplies like a whirlwind. They consumed the food, including the packaging. They shredded clothing with their teeth and trashed the rest of their gear.

"Oh, damn," Gelly complained. "And I was so looking forward to powdered chicken pot pie tonight."

"Looks like they're coming this way," Wonderboy said. "The south camera just tripped."

"What do we do, boss? Are we going to take them out?" Gelly asked, bouncing on his toes. "I wouldn't mind a little payback."

"No," Garner said firmly before anyone else had a chance to speak. "I want lookouts posted in here and across the street. We'll wait them out and let them pass."

"If we pick several of them off, we might be able to capture a couple," Gelly suggested.

"Let's see what we're up against first," Garner countered. "Gelly, Doc, you're here. Wonderboy and I will take the house across. Keep on comms. Report only what you see."

"I count twelve," Wonderboy reported over comms minutes later.

*"Roger that,"* Gelly said.

*"Two young ones breaking from the tree line,"* Angelina said.

"Got them," Garner acknowledged.

*"Are you seeing this, boss?"* Gelly asked.

He was. The pack of creatures followed a single creature, an alpha. It walked apart from the trailing and bobbing group wearing only a torn, loose-fitting sports jacket and carrying a long stick wrapped in fabric, a tattered strand flapping in the wind. The pack crossed through a backyard three houses from their position, then disappeared between neighboring homes.

"Anyone see them?"

*"Negative."*

A moment later, the pack reappeared in the street.

*"I still count fourteen including the little ones,"* Angelina said.

The alpha stopped in the middle of the street, its nose pointed in the air. The rest of the pack stopped and mimicked their lead. The two smaller creatures found an interest in licking a fire hydrant.

"Can they smell us?" Wonderboy whispered from beside Garner.

The alpha took a few more cautious steps along the street. It sniffed the air repeatedly.

"Doc, do you have a sight on that one?" Garner asked.

*"All lined up and waiting for your order,"* she said.

A bead of sweat rolled down Garner's temple. They must have been smelling the dead bodies or the stored food in the house or the rotting trash in the backyard. Either way, Gelly and Doc were in trouble if the pack became frenzied, but he couldn't be sure what the creatures were tracking.

A shriek echoed from the other end of the street.

"Everyone hold. Can anyone see where that came from?" Garner asked.

*"I got it,"* Gelly reported. *"Your nine o'clock."*

Garner adjusted his binoculars to expand his view until he found the new target. "Acknowledged."

The lone creature scrambled up the street running sideways on its arms and legs like a wounded crab. A broken ankle flopped uselessly while its arms and other leg compensated. Deep scratches marred its face, and patches of missing skin on its scalp suggested it had pulled out what little hair it once possessed.

It approached the pack carefully, now appearing less agitated. The alpha sniffed the wounded creature. After another moment, the alpha nodded to the pack, and the wounded creature calmly joined the compliant group.

The younger creatures interrupted the reunion. The two tumbled into the street in a tangle of lanky arms and legs as they fought over a dashing mouse. The alpha hissed and slapped them both with the stick. They scurried to hide behind the rest of the group. Back in control, the alpha led the pack across the street, where they disappeared into a grove of trees.

Garner let out a rush of air, now aware he'd been holding his breath. He stored the binoculars back in their case and sat back. "Tell me you recorded all of that," he said to Wonderboy.

"Every minute."

*"Me and the Doc have an idea,"* Gelly said over comms. *"For capturing the alpha."*

Garner, Doc, and Gelly met in the living room of the second house, which had large windows that facilitated a clear view of the street and one side of the neighboring home. Wonderboy remained upstairs on lookout.

Garner sat silently, catching his thoughts. The alphas, as they'd come to be known, had been the first to emerge from the depths of Hell. He and his brother encountered one the first night after the quake. It scratched his brother, Avery, turning him into one of those things. Although he maintained that he would one day find his brother, in an unexpected way, he was relieved Avery was not part of this group.

Even though intelligence reports listed the alphas as special, this was the first time anyone had witnessed their behavior as exhibiting a social structure, one that seemed similar to a wolf pack. Capturing an alpha would gain them invaluable intel, but it'd be too dangerous for their unit.

"Hear me out before you say it's too dangerous," Gelly said, reading the thought surely plain on Garner's face. "We lure the alpha by capturing the two little ones. We'll draw them into a funnel down this street, separate the alpha, and pick off the others. The houses are close enough that we can effectively cut off any avenues of escape."

"You're assuming the alpha will follow, don't you think?"

"After what we saw, it'll come," Gelly said confidently.

Garner leveled eyes on Gelly. He wouldn't tell him how this could end horrifically. It wasn't his job as leader of this team to tell them what they knew. It was his job to ensure they knew all they should know. "The rest of the pack will be in pursuit, not just the alpha."

"We pick them off as soon as they enter the kill zone," Gelly said.

"Anything could go wrong," Angelina said, reconsidering her position.

"Best case, we capture an alpha and two little ones. Worst case, we capture just the little ones," Gelly answered her. "If your aim is as good as I've heard, we have a real chance."

Angelina cursed. "OK, I'm in."

Garner looked at his watch. "Six hours until dark. Let's make this happen."


Each two-person team started preparations. Gelly and Wonderboy stripped down their packs to allow for quick and quiet travel. They screwed silencers on their rifles and armed themselves with the long control sticks as well. As soon as they departed, Garner and Angelina got to work on forming a funnel and the choke point.

Over the next four hours, they chained several abandoned vehicles, plucked from neighboring streets and hidden in garages, to the JV and towed them into the street, maneuvering each to form an elongated V-shaped string of cars and trucks. Farther down the street, a construction site offered plenty of plywood, planks, and nails. They built several eight-foot fences, using them to close off open areas between the houses surrounding the funnel. It was late afternoon by the time they finished. Low clouds thickened, dropping temperatures even lower. Snow began to fall.

"Gelly, do you read?"

No response.

Garner and Angelina sat in the utility vehicle at the entrance of the improvised funnel waiting for any response from Gelly or Wonderboy. An inch of fresh snow had fallen within the last hour. The wind swirled the accumulation around them.

"The guys said you lost your brother," Angelina said, both breaking and worsening the awkward silence between them.

Garner glanced up, catching her warm blue eyes. Her usual hard stare had softened.

"Lost but not gone," Garner said, remaining guarded.

"What did he do before?"

"He was an EMT, and a really good one," Garner said.

"You're proud of your brother," she observed.

He nodded. "Your fiancé and mother-in-law were taken from you?"

"How did you know?"

"I read your profile when I was recovering," he said.

"I never told anyone," she said with a bit of sadness as if she'd been taken back in time. "After he changed into . . . um, he ate his mother. I hid in a closet thinking it was only a matter of time before he found me next. I was so scared. After hours of waiting, I finally talked myself into doing something about it. He kept a gun in his bedroom, and I put a bullet in his head."

The guts that such a devastation would have required gave him pause, but only for a moment. "I couldn't do the same for my brother. I believe he can be cured. I'll find him again," Garner said.

A look of concern crossed Angelina's face. "How much do you know about these creatures?"

"I don't pretend to know more than what I've experienced and observed with my own eyes. There are smarter people than me studying them I hope."

"Garner, it's not curable, not by a long shot," Angelina said carefully. "I worked in a trauma hospital after I lost my fiancé and his mother. I saw people who had been bitten and scratched. We watched many of them transform. None of us knew what was happening—not doctors, nurses, the CDC. We couldn't stop or slow the transformation no matter what drugs we administered. It was unfamiliar territory. Still is. The change occurs at the DNA level. We don't have that kind of science. Your brother, if you ever find him, would be best served by doing him the ultimate favor."

Garner turned away from her. Surely he had thought about what he'd do if he ever found his brother. But would he really have the courage to follow through?

Angelina's hand fell on his arm. "I apologize, sir. I didn't mean . . ."

"Please stop with the sir thing. I told these guys it doesn't suit me. Garner is fine."

"Fair enough. I'm warming to Doc myself."

"*Garner, do you read? Over.*" Wonderboy was breathing heavily.

Garner quickly tapped the mic on his earpiece. "We hear you."

Quite a bit of white noise came through as he replied. "*We captured the two small gollums, and it pissed off the rest of the pack. Gelly's plan worked.*"

"Good. What's your 20?"

Gelly, also panting loudly, joined the communication. "*We're on the run. Fifteen minutes out.*"

"We'll be ready," Garner replied, then turned to Doc. "You're up."

Doc nodded once, intense focus on her face. She hopped out of the vehicle, shielding herself against a squall as she hiked along the barrier of cars and took her position inside a van at the opposite end of the funnel.

Yet another few inches of snow had already fallen. Garner wiped fog from the inside of the windshield and side window. He sparingly used the wipers to clear the outside. He had a line of sight up and down the street, and he waited for Gelly and Wonderboy, who should appear any minute, but the snow was steadily worsening all visibility.

Two beams of light suddenly appeared, approaching fast from an adjacent street. Headlights.

"*What do we got coming at us?*" Doc asked over comms.

"Not sure. Residents perhaps." Garner rolled down the window to get a better look.

"*If they turn our way, it'll ruin our trap,*" Doc said.

"Understood." Garner leaped out of the vehicle. The snow whipped his exposed face. He crouched low as he exited the funnel, hoping not to be seen until absolutely necessary. He was two houses away from the approaching vehicle.

The car fishtailed in the snow as it entered a cross street. The rear slid, the taillights illuminating Garner's face. The spinning tires threw snow as they fought for traction to speed the car in the opposite direction, but not before Garner got a good look at the painted shades of green and black camouflage.

Garner swore under his breath.

*"What do you see, Garner?"* Doc asked.

"Bad company."

*"Five minutes. We're in sight. Pack is gaining,"* Wonderboy reported, still breathless. Their transmission was coming in much clearer despite the weather.

Over the howl of the wind came a god-awful shrieking and screaming. Garner ran back to the vehicle, slipping in the snow several times. Blackwell and Reed would have to wait. If they interfered, things were going to get messy.

No sooner did Garner climb back into the utility vehicle than Gelly and Wonderboy appear on the snow-covered street with two young gollums thrashing at the end of their control sticks. On their tail was the alpha, and behind it, the pack—all as angry as the two young ones.

The two men slipped in the deepening snow, thrown off balance by the wiry gollums. They passed Garner and spilled into the narrowing street. As soon as the alpha passed, Garner rushed the utility vehicle forward, cutting off the rest of the pack.

"Take down any that get through, Doc," Garner ordered as he left the vehicle and grabbed another control stick.

The gollums started climbing the barricade. Doc's high-powered sniper rifle had a silencer screwed onto the barrel, but the bullets could still be heard whistling through the cold, blowing snow as they found their marks.

Before Garner, the alpha spun around angrily, realizing it had been separated from its pack. It raked the air, narrowly missing Garner's face. He fended off the attack with the control pole, shooting the lasso out from its end. It landed perfectly over the alpha's head. He quickly tightened the cord and held the creature, keeping at bay its thrashing claws.

Ahead, Gelly and Wonderboy hurried far down the narrowing funnel of cars and plywood. The cage door stood wide open at the end.

Everything was noise. The pack screamed every time one of its own dropped dead from Doc's precision shots. The alpha hissed and spit, knowing it was trapped.

*"Bad company incoming on your six,"* Doc said over comms.

Blackwell's high beams sliced through the blinding snow as it drove too fast toward them, giving no indication of slowing down. He wasn't expecting the barricade of vehicles blockading most of the street. The car slid uncontrollably into a plywood barrier and mowed down a number of creatures. Then it continued barreling through the snow straight toward Garner. He dove away as the car careened into a parked vehicle, launched off another, and landed on its side in the middle of the street.

Garner landed on his back, saved from significant injury by the thick snow. His relief was short lived, however. He no longer held the control stick. The alpha was gone.

He scrambled to his feet, handgun drawn. A lot of good it would do against an alpha.

*"Jesus Christ, you OK, Garner?"* Doc asked.

"The alpha slipped through my hands," he said over comms.

*"I don't see it,"* Doc replied. *"You're exposed. Come to me, sir."*

Garner crouched low, sweeping for possible targets and moving toward the barrier of cars for cover while working his way toward Doc's position. "Gelly, Wonderboy: status!"

*"Almost got them in the cage. Fuck, they're strong!"*

"Watch your back. Alpha is loose with some of the pack," Garner warned while weighing the risks. "Doc, if you have the shot, take the alpha down."

*"Roger that,"* she replied.

"Once the young ones are secured, we leave," Garner said to all of them.

Between the blinding snow and the diminishing light, Garner couldn't see but a few feet around him. The creatures' shrieks echoed near and far, but he couldn't get a bead on their whereabouts. Nor could he see where Blackwell and Reed had gotten to. He hurried through the snow along the barrier until Gelly and Wonderboy came into sight, shoving the second young gollum into the cage. The cage door slammed shut and latched automatically.

Shots fired from somewhere in the snowstorm, followed by a man screaming in agony. More shots echoed throughout the neighborhood.

Gelly and Wonderboy joined Garner near Doc's van. Her sniper rifle poked out of the back window.

"Someone needs our help," Gelly said.

Garner searched for any movement in the whipping snow, giving no indication he had heard Gelly.

"Boss?"

"Be ready for anything," Garner muttered.

Gelly and Wonderboy looked at each other, bewildered.

"Blackwell and Reed are out there," Doc said from inside the van.

"Then let's go help our brothers." Gelly checked his rifle and swapped the spent clip for a full one. "Are we doing this?" he asked, puzzled.

Another shot echoed, this one not far from their location. A gollum appeared from behind the shroud of falling snow, running frantically toward them. Doc placed a perfectly round hole in its head. The creature spasmed and jerked as it crumpled and fell into the fine powder, the clean white now a putrid black smudge.

The air split near Garner's head before he heard the gunshot. Behind him, Wonderboy yelped and jerked backward, clasping an arm.

"Put down your weapons!" a voice echoed from beyond their sight. "Do it. I don't intend to miss the next shot."

Garner nodded for them to comply. As they dropped their weapons, a man materialized as he approached them. He wore a black jacket and thin tech-goggles over his eyes, the kind that allowed him to see clearly through the driving snow and dimming daylight. He pointed his automatic rifle steadily at them.

Gelly recognized the man immediately. "Staff Sergeant, it's Gelly. Tyrone Gelloti."

"Hello, Gelly. Angelina. Wonderboy. Sorry about the arm." Blackwell pulled his goggles down off his eyes and let them hang around his neck. "Kane Garner, you son of a bitch. You healed up nicely. Don't tell me they put you in charge of my squad?"

Garner's mind reeled to find a way out of this mess without anyone getting seriously hurt. Wonderboy had taken his jacket off to examine his arm; the bullet grazed him good but hadn't been life-threatening.

"What's the matter? Nothing witty to say?" Blackwell asked as he pointed his rifle directly at Garner's chest. "I plan to take back what was taken from me."

Garner scoffed. "They threw you out."

"No thanks to you," Blackwell said coldly. "The old brass was sold a story from a smart-mouthed, punk-ass bitch over a ten-year war veteran with six tours under his belt."

"You must have left out the part where you murdered people in cold blood," Garner tested.

Blackwell smirked.

"What are you talking about?" Gelly asked.

"They should know, don't you think, if you want what was taken?" Garner said. "Maybe you'll convince them what you and Reed were doing was right."

Blackwell rolled his jaw. Garner was certain the man was deciding whether or not to shoot him on the spot.

"What were you going to do with the gold and silver you killed for anyway? It can't possibly be worth anything to anyone," Garner said.

"Oh, you'd be surprised," Blackwell said.

"This is crazy talk," Gelly said, frowning.

"You're absolutely right, Gelly," Blackwell ridiculed.

"Interestingly enough, we found three more dead civilians about a block from here. I bet I'll find their missing jewelry in the backseat of your car," Garner added.

"You seem to know a lot about what happened. So much that the brass might even believe you killed those people," Blackwell said.

"Garner didn't kill anyone," Wonderboy said, sniffing, his nose red and running in the cold air.

"Are you sure about that, son?" Blackwell asked. "You have no evidence, so I guess it comes down to whose word you believe. The rest of you can either stay with this liar and die, or you can come with me. What's it going to be?"

"Central should have buried you in the deepest, darkest cell they had available. Instead, they expelled you. Probably not the best decision," Garner said. He stared defiantly into Blackwell's eyes like he had learned to do to his father when a leather belt was imminent.

"Probably not." Blackwell scowled and flipped the safety off on his rifle. "You always did talk too much."

Garner's stomach sank. Blackwell had lost his mind.

Appearing from the falling snow, two jagged claws wrapped around Blackwell's throat and yanked him off his feet as if a gust of wind had airlifted him.

Blackwell screamed. He pulled the trigger of his automatic rifle reflexively, spraying a line of bullets that narrowly missed Gelly and Garner. The alpha threw him down into the powdery snow and pounced.

Doc recovered her sniper rifle and put several bullets in the alpha's back. Gelly scooped up his weapon and joined her, filling the alpha with lead. The alpha jerked and spasmed as a hail of bullets punched through its thin skin. It fell dead on top of Blackwell.

Blackwell scrambled and flailed under the dead creature until finally pushing it off. Garner rushed over, kicked Blackwell's gun away, and pressed a boot to his chest, keeping him down. He aimed his handgun between Blackwell's eyes.

Blackwell slowly raised his arms over his head. He winced, and his eyes followed the pain to a tear in his jacket. The creature's teeth had sunk through the fabric and penetrated his skin. Blood soaked through his clothing and stained the snow.

"This might be the best justice after all," Garner said.

"Fuck you!" Blackwell spat and gritted his teeth. "I know you're a man of mercy, so go ahead and shoot me already."

Garner scoffed. "Mercy? Like the mercy you showed all the people you and Reed murdered?"

Blackwell shook his head. "Do what you want, peckerhead. I'll roam this Hell on Earth as one of those fucking mindless creatures. I don't give a fuck. You can watch me transform. Maybe that'll get you off."

Garner smirked. "Doc, Gelly. Grab the control sticks. Put him in the cage with the others."

"They'll tear him apart," Gelly said.

"I don't think so," Garner said, gaze hard on Blackwell. "He's one of them now."


By morning, the snowstorm had cleared after dropping more than two feet of fresh powder across the region—more snow in one storm than in the last ten years combined, a record for Missouri. Gelly and Doc took turns driving the converted refrigerated truck with Garner taking lead in the JV back to Central Ops during the night. Wonderboy, whose arm Doc had stitched and mobilized during the trip, rested. Doctor's orders. The ride was slow going, the highway an endless stretch of untouched snow. As they approached Kansas City, modified pickup trucks and heavy equipment worked to clear the city streets.

Garner's team maneuvered their vehicles over the plowed roads and rolled into Central on their last volt and drop of fuel. As soon as they crossed the gated checkpoint, they were directed to a large maintenance garage. The door closed behind them after they parked and killed the engines.

Staff Sergeant Ben Pavlov, accompanied by an assortment of officials dressed in military fatigues and white lab coats, met Garner and his unit. Gelly and Wonderboy stood rigid and saluted. Garner, not in the saluting mood, folded his arms across his chest and leaned against the truck.

Pavlov knew the unit had been through a lot. He puffed his chest and raised his chin. "Show me," he said, cutting right to business.

Garner nodded to his unit. Gelly and Doc immediately loosened the straps of the canvas tarp that shrouded their cargo. As they rolled it back, three gollums stood panting behind the bars, two young ones and one large one. They stared with a menace in their black eyes.

"They're alive!" one of the white lab coats said.

"We've been underestimating our enemy," Garner explained. "We have video to prove it."

"Alpha?" Big Ben asked, thumbing at the big one.

"No," Garner said flatly.

Ben looked closer at the larger creature—the bite scar on the shoulder, the sleeve of tattoos inking one arm. "Thank you all. You've done a great service to this country and to the world," he said. Many of the white coats behind him nodded approvingly. "Get some rest. You've earned it."

As the unit dispersed, Pavlov leaned in so only Garner could hear. "How'd you find him?"

"Let's say we found each other," Garner reacted.

Ben raised an eyebrow. "I'd like to hear about it. Drink?"

Declassified by order of the<br>
Governor of the West North Central Territory<br>
Declass No.: 0626

# TRANSCRIPT

### SUBJECT
Defending Rights & Dissent(DRAD) Investigation;
Audio File, Intercepted; Length: 9m 43s

### PARTICIPANTS
Major Daniel Edward Hunt, Staff Sergeant Benjamin
Pavlov, Unknown

### DATE, TIME, PLACE
11-10-2035, 0811, National Guard Central
Operations, Kansas City, Missouri


[BEGIN AUDIO]

HUNT:   What's this I hear you have a ten-year veteran in custody?

PAVLOV: *[Pause.]* Two in custody. Blackwell and Reed, sir.

HUNT:   Tell me more.

PAVLOV: Murdered at least two civilians while stealing their valuables.

HUNT:   Any witnesses?

PAVLOV: A member from the same squad. Garner.

HUNT:   Isn't this the same Garner that cost the lives of three good soldiers and a bus full of civilians?

PAVLOV: Yes, sir.

HUNT:   Is he in custody?

PAVLOV: He's recovering in the hospital.

HUNT:   Well, Staff Sergeant, it's simple math. You have a couple field-trained, battle-ready veterans responsible for two deaths. And an untrained, undisciplined, inexperienced civilian responsible for . . . I'm not sure I have enough fingers and toes to count that high. Who do you want fighting beside you?

We're at war, Pavlov. If you want to put a label on it, go ahead. My soldiers kill. It's unfortunate that some people get caught in the crossfire. Collateral damage.

I like you, Pavlov. You have the added respect of everyone on the base. Our job may be the hardest of all. Making the tough decisions and putting good people in harm's way.

I expect Blackwell and Reed to be released immediately. Send them to my office for reassignment.

PAVLOV: *[Pause.]* What about Garner?

HUNT:   *(sighs)* I don't care much for non-enlisted personnel sharing the battlefield with my soldiers. He's a liability as far as I'm concerned.

PAVLOV: Perhaps. But pointed in the right direction, he's effective.

HUNT:   He's under your command, Staff Sergeant. Do as you wish. I hope I never hear his name again.

PAVLOV: Thank you, sir.

*[A drawer opens.]*

HUNT:  We have a problem. *[Pause.]* No, nothing that I can't handle. *[Pause.]* A civilian thinks he saw something. *[Pause.]* I need a little more time. My guys will make up the shortage. *[Pause.]* Killing him would only raise more suspicion. *[Pause.]* I don't know. A few days *[Pause.]* I don't need a fucking lecture. You do your job, and I'll do mine. You'll have the gold like we agreed. *[Pause.]* For Christ's sake, are we done here?

[END AUDIO]

*INVESTIGATOR'S NOTE: After Staff Sergeant Pavlov left his office, Major Hunt retrieved a burner phone from his desk drawer to make the phone call transcribed above. At the time of the compilation of this transcript, it is unknown with whom Major Hunt spoke.*

# SECOND WAVE

*One Year Later*

The HX Harpy helicopter lifted out of Columbia, Missouri thirty minutes earlier under the cover of darkness. The pilot and copilot spoke with each other over headsets, relaying instrument levels, adjusting their heading based on radar, and reporting back to Central Operations. Their green-tinged visors peeled back the shroud of night, allowing both to see as clear as day the landscape rushing by. They flew low along a grove of trees that stretched for miles across Illinois toward their destination. Anyone directly underneath the helicopter would have felt a slight breeze but heard nothing as the Harpy sliced through the air at its top speed, silent as a bird of prey.

Sitting with his crew in the rear cabin of the Harpy, a fatigued Kane Garner dozed, the motion of the aircraft having rocked him into a light slumber. Desperate men, women, and children screamed inside a yellow school bus. Hundreds of goblins swarmed, crawled, and attacked. Wails trailed off one by one. An infant pressed against a window, an expression of agony on his face. His mouth opened wide, too wide, and he screeched, echoing the shrieks of the creatures storming the bus.

Garner jerked awake. Sucked in a deep breath. Remembered where he was. He stole a glance at his crew, wondering if anyone had noticed.

He closed his eyes to calm his anxiety and shake away the nightmare. What he wouldn't give for a solid night's sleep. The endless assignments, the high-stakes missions, the ache of wanting for normal—it all weighed on him, wore him down.

His crew was feeling it too. Next to Garner, Corporal Tyrone 'Gelly' Gelloti sat with legs stretched out. A couple of spent jerky beef wrappers lay on his lap. With a bud in one ear, he slouched over a handheld device watching a news report and occasionally commenting to no one in particular.

"These two asshats in neckties are reporting the war's a hoax. No creatures roaming in North Dakota, so the whole thing must be made up to scare people." He laughed. "Who listens to this crazy shit?"

"Other asshats," Private Casie 'Wonderboy' Edwards said out of the corner of his mouth, pretending to be busy with the straps crisscrossing his shoulders.

Gelly scowled at Wonderboy and kicked his foot. "Was I talking to you?"

"Hey!"

Angelina 'Doc' Dorsey sat next to Wonderboy, trying in vain to ignore her team members' childish behavior and peering out the small window beside her. She had confessed before lift-off that this was her first helicopter ride. Even though the night concealed their surroundings, she watched the shadows pass below, seemingly lost in her own thoughts.

"Incoming communication from Central," the pilot said to Garner's crew over his shoulder.

Garner perked up. He circled the air with his finger and nudged Gelly to put on his headset. Garner nodded back at the pilot once they were ready to receive the message.

The red-tinted hologram flickered at the center of the cabin, then the bust of Sergeant First Class Benjamin Pavlov materialized. His deep voice and confidence demanded immediate respect; though not many people knew his age, he postured and spoke like a man twice his twenty-five years. He quickly got to the point.

*"Garner, I wish I could have seen you before your flight. Unfortunately, as you and your crew know too well, duty often calls at the most inconvenient of times.*

*"You're headed to Springfield, Illinois. This is strictly reconnaissance. Satellite images captured unusually large gatherings of civilians in the vicinity of an equally large number of creatures, and their numbers grow daily. We need boots on the ground to learn what's*

*happening. You have twenty-four hours to assess and report back to Central. Your pilots will provide pick-up coordinates once you land.*

*"And Garner? Do not engage with the enemy. I expect your team will ensure you don't. Good luck."*

The hologram flickered off.

"That," Gelly said, with a begrudging sigh, "would explain the minimal supplies they gave—"

"Think they're aiming for Chicago next?" Wonderboy asked, talking over Gelly.

Gelly threw his arms up and pointed to his ear. "Can you hear? Don't interrupt me when I'm speaking."

Wonderboy purposefully ignored Gelly's outburst. "Can't say that I miss Chicago. Tough growing up there."

"Tough my ass. You grew up in Aurora. Big difference from the inner city."

"Try getting your ass kicked every week from sixth through eleventh grade. I was a punching bag," Wonderboy leveled with Gelly.

"What happened in the twelfth grade?" Doc asked.

"Struck down the biggest bully in the school and got suspended," Wonderboy shared boastfully.

Gelly glared. "I lived on the streets out of the backseat of my mother's car. She was too strung out on meth to care much about what her two sons did with their free time. I'd have welcomed the occasional beating if it'd meant a roof over my head and food on my plate. You have no idea."

Wonderboy shrugged and returned to fiddling with his shoulder strap.

Garner's team was coming apart, the tentacles of a malignant tumor spreading, growing, slowly destroying its host from the inside out. For the past several weeks, Gelly had a bone to pick with Wonderboy no matter what the kid said or did. Wonderboy was wound so tight Garner feared the kid would tear out of his own skin if he could. He couldn't blame Doc for putting in for a transfer even if he felt a pang of sadness thinking about it.

He felt more loner than leader. Early in the first year, he'd been eager to take on each new mission, already looking forward to the one after that. The last few months had been a struggle to jump back into the fight. Every day it got harder and harder to wake up and get moving. Back at Central, he knew a runner who, for the right price, searched neighboring towns for alcohol and drugs. A golden fifth of

Jim Beam regularly waited for him upon his return. Plenty to drown his misery until the next mission. His mouth watered imagining that first shot of diesel rolling down his throat.

"Five minutes," the copilot said over the headsets. "We're dropping you three miles west of your target. I uploaded the relevant files to your field tablet."

Garner retrieved the device from his kit and tapped the screen. The priority folder opened instantly. He swiped through the various radar and satellite images. Figures in the images were color-coded: friendlies and not-so-friendlies. There were so many of them!

"When were these taken, Commander?" Gelly asked the copilot while looking over Garner's shoulder.

"As close to real-time as we can get from this distance."

Garner handed the tablet to Doc.

The blood drained from her face as she scanned the images. "What's happening here?"

"We're about to find out," Gelly said grinning.

"One minute out." The helicopter entered a quick descent over an open field. The side doors slid open and cool night air rushed into the cabin. The crew clipped on their packs and readied their weapons. "Three, two, one, go!"

Garner and Doc jumped out one side and Gelly and Wonderboy leaped out the other. Boots hit ground, and the helicopter shot straight up, slipping silently away into the night and leaving a round patch of tall grass briefly swaying in the diminishing air current.

The crew of four knelt motionless for several moments, eyeing through night scopes down the barrels of their automatic rifles. After a few moments, crickets resumed chirping.

"Clear," Garner said over comms even though his team was within speaking distance.

"Clear," the other three members reported quietly.

"Set your watches. We're back here in twenty-four hours." Garner set his own timer. "Let's move."

They rotated running point and guard along a stretch of deserted country road. After a mile, the landscape transformed from overgrown farmland to sparce commercial properties. A building with large windows the full height of the structure appeared on their right like an enormous carcass. Someone had spray painted in bold red letters a scraggly *NO* amid the Church of Hope signage.

They rushed by a car dealership, silently noting that none of the new cars had been removed or damaged. It was like everyone had picked up and left. Movie theatre, auto repair shop, financial services, plumbing and heating, apartments—the buildings became more and more dense as they approached the city.

Wonderboy, on point, signaled to stop.

"We should get off this road and travel cross-country." He pointed the field tablet at a grove of trees that had overgrown a former park. "We can pick up the train tracks in a quarter-mile. Our destination is about another mile down the tracks."

Doc and Gelly both nodded in agreement.

"Let's hope we can find some high ground," Garner said.

They split away from the road, ran behind a cluster of small businesses, and plunged into several acres of trees and undergrowth. Wonderboy's keen spatial senses brought them through the brush within a short time, and they emerged onto a set of rails.

Without a word exchanged, Wonderboy fell back to the rear and Doc took point, picking up their pace. They made good time running along the tracks for another mile. Garner stopped them to catch their breath once they reached the branch point. The night sky was aglow to the southeast and the smell of burned wood tainted the air.

"About five hundred yards in that direction and we should be able to see them." Wonderboy pointed toward where the sky glowed.

"Any high ground if we skirt north?" Garner asked.

"No. It's flat terrain around here. If anything, they'll have the high ground. There are low wetland areas here and here." Wonderboy swiped over one of the satellite images given to them by the pilots.

Gelly stepped in for a closer look at the images. "I don't want to get wet crawling through a marsh tonight. What's over here?"

"Shopping center or something like it. Several buildings on the northeast side could give us a better vantage point, but we'd have to cross two open roads and a large parking lot to get there. Chances are high we'd be seen."

"We stay on the tracks, then cut back to the shopping center and come in from the north," Gelly suggested without much indication in his voice that he'd accept an alternative.

Wonderboy huffed. "That's two hours more travel."

Garner's mind reeled. A mild headache already stabbed repeatedly at the base of his skull. He hated serving as referee for Gelly and Wonderboy. Both men had their valid points. Playing tiebreaker between them meant siding with one of them in the eyes of the other, when in fact he only ever sided with the best interest of the mission. He rubbed his palms against his temples as the two men continued reasoning through why his idea was right and the other was wrong.

"We got company," Doc said, her back toward the rest of them while looking down the sight of her night scope. "Three—no—four coming our way. Hundred yards."

The crew of four sprung into high-ready automatically, dropping arguments and disputes. Weapons drawn and comms live, they stepped off the tracks and slipped silently into the cover of the underbrush.

"I got a line," Doc said softly. "What are we doing, Garner?"

"Observing," he said firmly. "Hold your fire."

Three gollums stumbled along the tracks, vocalizing in some cackling gibberish that echoed down the steel. They carried spears, staying close to the fourth individual as if escorting it.

"I'm observing three gollums and one human," Doc said, her underlying tone signaling to Garner her dissatisfaction with his decision.

"Copy that," Gelly replied. "One male captive."

"Maybe we could get some information out of the man," Wonderboy said.

The gollums drew closer. In moments, they would be walking right by, unaware of the four trained weapons pointed at their heads.

Garner thought for a moment. The male captive was acting strangely. Hands unbound, he could be mistaken as the one leading them. The gollums weren't pushing or prodding him. Maybe, simply outnumbered, he'd surrendered instead of fought?

"Drop 'em," Garner said once the creatures were nearly on top of them.

A trio of soft pops broke the evening silence. All three bullets found their marks. The gollums toppled like bowling pins, leaving the man standing alone. When he realized what had happened, the man threw himself to the ground and covered his head. Gelly and Doc rushed to his aid.

"It's OK," Doc said, placing a calming hand on the man's shoulder.

"Oh God, oh God, oh God," the man repeated, then broke into tears.

"They can't hurt you anymore," Doc said.

The man, recognizing the military colors on the four soldiers surrounding him, shook his head in shock. "What have you done?"

Garner and his crew glanced at each other, puzzled.

"What's your name?" Doc asked gently.

The man wrapped his arms around his knees, pulling them against his chest, and started to rock back and forth on his behind. He took a few deep breaths, trying to compose himself. "Alex. They have my family."

"What's happening here, Alex?"

"They threatened to kill my family if I didn't turn myself in."

"Threatened? They're animals," Gelly barked.

Doc glared at Gelly, gesturing that she'd handle this.

Gelly shrugged and turned away.

"Start from the beginning, Alex," Doc said.

Alex roughed his hands over his bearded face and through his shaggy hair. "I don't have time for this. I need to show up by dawn or they're going to kill my wife and little girl. Just let me go, please." Tears dripped down his cheeks.

"Sure, Alex, I understand," Doc said. She consoled people easily by maintaining an air of caregiver that unguarded most. Garner normally stayed out of her business, but her answer was unexpected. They couldn't let him go.

Doc waved away Garner, who had taken a step closer, then helped Alex to his feet.

"Is there anything you can tell us?" she questioned.

"Are there more of you?" Alex asked instead. "Doesn't matter either way. You should leave or you're going to die here." He turned and ran away, continuing along the tracks.

"We're just letting him go?" Wonderboy questioned.

Garner side-glanced Doc. She was already posturing. "Yes."

The crew moved away from the quickly decomposing gollum bodies, the stench of ammonia and traces of sulfur gagging them.

Garner glanced at his watch. They had already burned three hours. "Let's get moving. Gelly, find us that high ground so we can see what the hell's going on here."

"Yes, sir," Gelly spat with a partial grin, knowing Wonderboy was listening.

They ran in the dark along the tracks and into a decimated commercial section of the city. The quakes had shaken this area hard;

few buildings remained standing, most leveled to the ground or partially collapsed. Since then, little effort had been made to clean up the city.

Gelly led them carefully and quietly through the deepest shadows and between piles of rubble, past overgrown landscaping and around abandoned cars. By midnight, the crew of four lay prone on the rooftop of the 99 Restaurant overlooking the Walmart Supercenter across the parking lot.

The sat images paled in comparison to the scene in front of them. A chain-link fence enclosed the entire Walmart parking lot, five acres of blacktop at least. Torch fires lined the perimeter, pushing the nighttime back. Wood and plastic burned in several steel barrels at various sites inside the fence, turning the air acrid. Groups of people hovered around the barrels, drawing warmth from the spiking flames. Outside the fence, several patrols of two and three armed gollums—*armed*—walked the enclosure. Half carried blunt weapons such as bats, hammers, and crude clubs. The other half carried more lethal arms such as spears, hand-forged swords, bows and arrows, daggers, and machetes. Inside the fence but cordoned off from the human captives stood dozens of animals—cattle, horses, sheep, pigs, and even a few bison.

The group observed several porta potties lined next to each other at one end, meal prep stations and running water at the other. Cots and bedding, also in their own separate area, held the sick and feeble.

"Give a count?" Garner asked.

"I stopped counting after six hundred," Doc replied.

"Seven hundred forty-two captives, a hundred eighty-five gollums," Wonderboy corrected. "From what I can tell."

"Christ."

"Christ had nothing to do with this," Gelly said.

"They're clothed," Garner realized. Over the last few months, units had reported more and more creatures organizing and showing signs of intelligence. Even though he was observing the creatures' evolvement for the first time, he was still having a hard time believing it.

"Pelts by the looks of them." Gelly scanned the gollums with his night binoculars. "Souvenirs too. Small animal skulls, some ears and fingers. Can't tell if those are human or not."

"They're building a platform on the west side," Doc reported.

"There's a crack in the earth near it," Wonderboy added. He turned to the rest of them. "Did you know a quarter-mile wide rift opened along the Illinois River and swallowed Peoria? It's one of the biggest fissures between Chicago and Kansas City. This is likely a branch off that same fault line."

"Assessment?" Garner asked his team.

"Hostages for protection and bargaining power," Wonderboy offered quickly.

Doc shrugged. "Insurance to maintain their numbers in case of an attack."

"They're certainly preparing for something," Gelly said, alarmed. "There's a ramp leading underground."

"But why?" Wonderboy asked, for once not contradicting Gelly.

Gelly put down his binoculars. "These people are in danger, sir."

Garner, nodding, pulled back from the edge of the rooftop. "We can't leave them like this. The outcome is death no matter what the creatures plan to do with some seven hundred people. I'm going down."

"What?!"

"That's suicide."

"Garner, that's batshit crazy. We have our orders to observe and report back to Central," Doc said, placing her hands on her hips.

"We've done that part of the mission. Wonderboy recorded and uploaded the file to Central," Garner responded.

"It's actually not uploading, sir," Wonderboy said timidly. "But I'll keep trying," he added under Garner's glare.

"Pavlov was clear. Reconnaissance, yes. But he also asked that we learn what's happening," Garner continued. "We're not learning anything up here."

"Pavlov said not to engage," Doc responded. "He knew you'd want to pull something like this."

"That's why I have no intention of engaging. In fact, I'll leave my weapons here," Garner said coolly.

Doc's brow furrowed and her teeth clenched. "You're going to get killed. Too many times you've put a mission at risk, and we're supposed to go along with your half-baked ideas? Fuck that! I won't watch you die, and that's what's going to happen. Our job here's done, so I'm done. I'll meet you back at the pick-up point. I'll assume if you're not there in time that there's no reason to come looking for you." She looked at Wonderboy and Gelly, seeing if they'd have her back. She sighed heavily when they said nothing. "That's great. You two keep following him. Get your death wish granted."

She spun on her heels.

"Doc, please stay," Garner called to her.

"Fuck you, Garner." Doc climbed over the edge of the rooftop and was gone.

"Damn it, man. She really likes you," Gelly said. Wonderboy was nodding.

Garner ignored their comments. "I won't fault either of you if you want to go with her."

Neither man said a word.

Garner explained his plan while shedding his gear and earpiece. He kept a small handgun strapped to one ankle and a knife concealed on the other. In moments, he'd climbed down the side of the restaurant. He hoped he might see Doc again, but no such luck. She had made her decision. He wished she hadn't left.

Garner dismissed his feelings and skirted around another ruined building. It wasn't long before a gollum patrol found him resting against an abandoned car pretending to be injured.

They poked him with their long sticks, and though they spoke unintelligible gibberish, their intentions were clear. Garner slowly rose to his feet, faking leg pain. He limped the distance to the fence, the creatures following at a safe distance in case the prisoner decided to do something foolish.

He met two more creatures guarding the entrance to the Walmart parking lot, each holding swords that looked forged by a child but with edges unmistakably cut-worthy—something Garner didn't want to test.

The gate swung open, and he was pushed forcefully inside. Garner stumbled and fell to the ground, the model of weakness, as his captors closed the gate behind him and marched back into the brush.

A man and woman quickly came to his aid.

"Come on, son. Let's get you off the ground," the man said, helping Garner to his feet. He appeared to be in his sixties. He had a thick mustache and stubble beard. His face and clothes were smeared with grime.

"Where are you hurt, hon?" the woman asked on his other side. She, too, looked about sixty or so. The grey roots of her hair had grown out. A cold sore at the corner of her mouth cracked when she smiled.

"My leg. I think my ankle's sprained. I just need to rest," Garner explained, deciding at that moment to keep up the charade.

The man and woman walked him to an empty cot and helped him sit.

"I'll bring you some tea and ask the doctor to take a look at you," the woman said, then disappeared behind the nosing crowd. She shooed a few of them away, telling them to quit their meddling as she went.

He sat among the cots and mattresses set up on the pavement. The cots were occupied mostly with the elderly, the mattresses filled with kids huddled together like litters of puppies. One of the barrel fires he'd spotted earlier burned nearby, shedding some of its heat over the sleeping children.

The platform being built stood on the opposite side of the fenced area. He couldn't see much from his vantage and desperately wanted a closer look. Instead he watched the few people going into and out of the store freely.

"Why not bring the people who are sick and sleeping under shelter?" Garner asked the older man, who watched him suspiciously. He reminded Garner of his former boss, Mr. Reynolds.

The man broke eye contact with him as the woman returned with a cup of tea.

"This should warm you a bit," the woman said smiling. "My name's Peggy. That's Arthur."

Garner took a few sips of the hot but flavorless tea. "What is this place?" he asked.

"We're safe as long as we stay inside the fence," Peggy answered obliquely, her smile slipping from her face. "We—"

Arthur cut her off. "That's enough, Peggy."

"Oh, don't be that way, Art. He's not the enemy—or have you already forgotten?" Peg fired back.

"The Chief will want to see him," Arthur said.

"Who's the Chief?"

"That freakshow can wait. This man needs our help," Peggy said firmly. She knelt in front of Garner and gently prodded his leg. "Tell me where it hurts the most," she said to Garner.

"The man doesn't need our help, Peggy." Arthur eyed Garner closely. "I spent ten years in the service including four tours in Afghanistan. I recognize a soldier when I see one. Why are you here?"

"Peggy, Arthur, introduce me to your new friend." A short, stocky man, smiling broadly, casually walked up behind them, swinging his arm around and draping it over Arthur's shoulder.

Arthur stiffened and shot Peggy a subtle glance. She bowed her head submissively.

Ah. The Chief, Garner presumed.

The man wore a police campaign hat, battered and scuffed, with the State of Illinois patch on the front. His face was oddly broad and lesioned, the skin there stretched alarmingly thin. His neck looked like bundled sausage links, his hands meaty and sweaty. A police uniform, minus the standard tie, was worn carelessly with the top button undone, exposing an overly hairy chest and skin pocked with sores. The shirt's untucked hem hung over a pair of pants two sizes too small. From what Garner could glean, he was the only one in the entire enclosure with two handguns hanging openly from his belt. Overall, the man's five-foot, two-hundred-pound portly frame was disturbingly distorted and abnormal.

"What's your name, soldier?" the Chief asked him. He leaned in close enough that Garner could smell rancid breath and the foul tang of uncleanliness.

Before the earthquakes, before Hell took a dump on the earth, Garner had been in and out of trouble most of his teenage years. Had ridden in the back of a police car far too often for a kid his age. He knew intimidation and scare tactics. When at a disadvantage, saying as little as possible or nothing at all was the best mode of defiance.

"Nothing? Maybe you'll change your mind in a short while," the man said, thumbing toward the Walmart.

"Please, Chief. He's injured. Let him rest," Peggy pleaded.

"What do you say, Arthur? Is this man in need of care?"

The glare Arthur gave Peggy spoke volumes. "No, Chief."

"See? We're all cooperating now. Bring 'im inside the 'Mart!"

Two dirty and wiry men flanked him like guardsmen. Each carried a baton and tapped the end in their opposite hand, sneering at Garner.

"Come in peace or leave in pieces," one of the men said with a lisp.

"Is there a t-shirt inside you ripped that from?" Garner's quick wit earned him a swift baton strike against his lower back. "Mother fuck!"

The two men swept elbows under Garner's arms and hauled him toward the store. Even though the front had been destroyed at one point, metal shelving and plywood inside formed a barricade. The Chief, it seemed, controlled everyone and everything moving in and out. They proceeded through the only gate.

The place smelled like a fraternity house after an all-night kegger. The men dropped him into a chair at a ten-foot-wide table. Spent food wrappers, empty beer bottles, high-energy drink cans, white powder, and wasted pill capsules littered its surface. On the opposite side, the Chief settled into a chair of his own. Drool dripped from one corner of his mouth as he grinned. His white-coated tongue licked back the seepage.

What was ailing this man?

The Chief watched him for a period. The two guards remained behind Garner. He was shocked he hadn't been searched.

"Is your plan to stop our event? If it is, it won't work," the Chief said, breaking the stalemate.

Garner's brow furrowed. "I was drifting through when the creatures captured me. I thought I was a goner."

"You still might be if I grant it." Chief grinned wider. "Or the Master will just do what he wants."

"Master?"

Chief slammed his beefy fist on the table. A couple bottles jumped and rolled off the end. "I ask the questions around here!"

"Keep going, then. I don't have all night," Garner said. The wise remark meant another strike from one of the men behind him, this time on the shoulder. Garner grimaced. "Do that again and I'll shove it up your ass."

Chief guffawed. "You got balls, soldier." Spittle flew out of his mouth as he tried to contain his laughter. "Well, whether you're here by chance or by purpose, you picked the perfect night. If you left any of your soldier friends outside the perimeter, our friends will find them."

"Traitor," Garner spat. He sensed one of the guards shuffle his feet as he prepared to bring down the baton on Garner's other shoulder. He caught the club, twisting it forcefully out of the man's grip. Garner spun out of the chair and flipped the man over his back onto the table knocking the wind out him.

"No, no," Chief said calmly, waving a revolver.

Garner threw the baton aside and raised his hands.

"Get your dumbass off my table!" Chief slapped and pushed the wiry man aside. "The Master will deal with the boy soldier here. Throw him in the pen."

Garner was ushered away into another area of the box store to a locked steel door with *Employees Only* stenciled on its face. The man with the lisp tinkered with a set of keys. The door opened onto a small room, dark and smelling of urine. The two men spun him around, and the man he had flipped clubbed Garner on the forehead. His last memory before blacking out was of falling backward into the room.

"He's coming around."

"Give him some water."

"He's not having mine."

"Give me that, Pete, you fucknut."

Warm water poured down Garner's throat. He gagged and coughed.

"Easy, friend. Little sips." The man's raspy voice spoke next to him in the dark. "You got quite the bump on the head."

"Sons of bitches," another man whispered.

Garner's reality sharpened. His head throbbed as he traced the egg-sized lump on the top of his forehead. He couldn't see a thing in front of his face. "Where am I?"

"You're in the tank," the raspy-voiced man said.

Garner sat up and immediately regretted it. Between his pounding head and the stench of waste, nausea churned his stomach. He covered his nose, certain he'd vomit otherwise. Slowly, his eyes adjusted to the darkness. A very small flickering glow came from underneath the only door. Five other male figures shared the holding cell with him. Garner slid across the floor on his butt to place his back against a wall. He casually scuffed his lower legs together and breathed a quiet sigh of relief. Neither the handgun nor the knife had been discovered.

"I know this asshole," someone spoke from the shadows. "I'm in here because of him and his soldier buddies. Chief blamed me for killing the smurfs."

"Can it, Alex. I'm Robert," raspy voice said. "Across from you is Pete and Troy. Alex you've met, apparently. Next to you is Hector."

Garner offered nothing in return.

"And you," Robert said, "can get us out of here." It was a statement, not a question. One Garner ignored for now.

"The gollums. Why haven't they slaughtered you?" he asked instead.

"Gollums?"

"Like in *The Hobbit*?" another asked.

"Think that's what he's meaning, Pete."

"Yeah. Yeah, they do look like hobbits."

"Not hobbits, you idiot. Gollum, *my precious*." The imitation was way off.

"Shut the hell up, you two, before I put your heads in the piss bucket," Robert berated Troy and Pete, then addressed Garner. "That fat ass used to be our police chief, Jack Stuart. An unsung hero from the start, really. He organized the people of this city and fought off the smurfs—the creatures. Then four months ago, Chief, he changed, like something got inside him, yeah? Well, you saw him. He started insisting the creatures were friendly. He let the smurfs raise the fence. Let them herd us all in like cattle."

"Talks about the Master like some Second Coming all the time," Alex added.

"We don't know who that is," Robert said.

"Or what it is," Hector clarified. He had the deepest voice of the men.

The bump on Garner's forehead throbbed, but only dully. "There's a platform on the west end and a ramp leading inside the fault," he offered, feeling he could trust these men.

"Down below the earth? Are you sure?"

"Yes."

Robert, sounding perplexed, mumbled, "What's he doing?"

"Sacrifice?" Pete or Troy guessed. "Throw people into the fault, give thanks to his Master. It's deep, you know."

"The virgins will go first, I bet," the other replied. "'Cause their blood is untainted."

"You said taint."

They chuckled.

"I swear you two will drink every drop from the bucket."

"Shh!"

Footsteps echoed outside the room and shadows shifted underneath the door. Keys jingled and the door flew open. Three bright flashlights illuminated the dungy room, blinding the men inside.

"On your feet. All of ya."

"I think we're about to find out about this Master," Garner said to Robert.

"No talking!"

They were escorted by three of the Chief's men, each with a baton itching to use it. They were walked past a row of cash registers, then single file through the gate. Outside, the sky remained dark. Garner glanced at his watch. Dawn would arrive in another hour. He got shoved from behind.

"Keep it moving or I'll match that knot on your head," the wiry man said.

The Chief's men steered them across the parking lot. Many people lined the route, watching them pass, expressions grave. A woman jumped out from the pack and threw her arms around Alex. The Chief's men quickly separated him from the hysterical woman, serving both a brisk beating.

Torches burned around the platform. Gollums gathered the rest of the humans, then closed around them all, chanting and swaying. Some carried torches, others clapped wooden sticks together. The sounds lacked rhythm or coordination, as if each gollum acted of its own whim.

The platform, a collage of scavenged wood planks, stood higher than the surrounding fence. At its center, wide treads led down inside the fault below ground level, disappearing into the deep crevasse. The Chief stood on the platform holding a leash tied to a goat. He couldn't be heard over the noise from the gollums and waved the crowd of humans closer. Garner and the other five men were directed to climb onto the platform. As Garner took the steps, he thankfully noticed Wonderboy and Gelly among the undulating crowd. Nothing good could possibly come of this.

The sky was unusually clear as the sun inched toward the horizon. Suddenly, the chanting stopped.

"My friends and smurf guests!" Chief raised a fat hand high in the air like a preacher. "The time has come to welcome a new master, a savior, who will save us from damnation."

His paper-thin skin split where it stretched tightest, like the casing on an overcooked hot dog. Wounds gaped, oozing yellow pus.

"The Master will lead us to salvation and deliver us from evil."

As the Chief continued to spew unholy creeds, a guttural growl issued from underground. Garner looked to Robert, who stood next to him gaping at the crack in the earth. He'd heard it too.

The platform vibrated with a pounding that strengthened and became distinct. Something was coming. Coming from the fault.

The Chief increased his religious rhetoric to a feverish pitch. "Have mercy on your souls! Praise the Master!"

The gollums dropped to their knees and bowed. The crowd fell deathly quiet, the only sound Hector whispering the Hail Mary over and over.

From the darkness below the earth, a pair of silver round orbs appeared as if floating in midair, rising and drawing closer, wild and hateful.

Eyes. Garner would never forget the eyes for as long as he lived.

A beast of unimaginable proportions and grotesque features scaled the platform at the same moment the sun breached the horizon, a spotlight on the immense being. Nothing about it resembled any human characteristic. It stood seven feet tall on two gnarled legs, looking like a mad genetic experiment gone wrong. Like a wolf, it had a long snout and a maw full of flesh-rending teeth but lacked the pointed ears. Like a horse, its large feet were hooved but blackened at the bottom as though it had walked in fire and ash. The skin, blotchy white as if unacquainted with the sun, stretched taut around sinewy muscle and bony protrusions. Except for a patch across its upper back and long sparse hairs on its lengthy forearms, it was hairless.

The gollums raised and lowered their arms, bowing ceaselessly.

Visibly shaken, the Chief shuffled forward, towing the frightened goat by its leash. The animal bleated and pulled away, trying to escape. Managing a broad smile, he gestured toward the thrashing goat as a gift.

The beast glowered. Was it annoyance or disappointment or anger? Whatever it was, the beast showed no mercy. It snatched the wheezing goat and wrenched its head off like a bottle cap. The head sailed into the screaming crowd. The beast leaned back and tilted the body above its mouth, pouring the blood from its neck down its own throat. It squeezed the body, crushing organs and bones, to get every last drop.

It tossed away the pulverized goat and, taking no pause, tore into the Chief like a grizzly bear, splitting his face and throat with one swipe and disemboweling him with another. It rammed its clawed hand under the Chief's ribcage and ripped out his heart to devour it as though a delicacy.

Screams and panic scattered the crowd; many froze in fear, others climbed the fences only to get shoved back by armed gollums.

Garner's knees locked. He unconsciously retrieved his handgun, which shook uncontrollably in his hand. As the beast sucked down the Chief's guts, he fired in succession, emptying the gun. He missed every shot.

Still, the sound of the handgun put the other men in motion. Robert yanked Garner by the arm, and the hard landing off the platform got him moving.     He joined the rush of civilians running for the gate. The fence gave under the weight of the crowd and collapsed. Gollums caught between the fleeing masses and the gate fell underfoot, trampled. Garner pushed and shoved, a primal dread like he'd never before felt flooding his veins. Adrenaline mixed with the fear of looming death, spiking his flight response. He'd escape at all costs and never dare look back.

As soon as he stepped outside the confines of the fence, he bolted. Everything he'd ever feared in his life flashed in his mind, a horror film from which he couldn't turn away. The neighbor's vicious dog that once chased him home from the bus stop. The first time his father beat him and Avery, and every time after that. How he broke Mrs. Murphy's window and spent the night in jail after she called the police. The day he awaited his sentencing in front of a judge for assault, certain he'd see prison next. The night he and Becky discovered the gollum in his backyard. The moment he lost Avery.

Miles later, he collapsed on the steps of a bank branch, drenched in sweat and in the middle of a panic attack. His heart ripped at his chest. His lungs strained to suck in any air. His mouth turned to cotton. He had blood on his hands, certain it was not his own. He gagged and vomited everything he had left in his stomach. Breathing heavily, he leaned back against a granite pillar.

"Garner!"

His head swam as he tried to dispense with the horror enough to see who was running at him. Seeing a familiar face, he lost it and burst into tears.

"Gelly! Oh fuck, man!"

Gelly dropped the three gear packs he held, took a knee, and placed a hand on Garner's shoulder. "It's OK, brother. I got you."

"I never . . . oh, Christ!"

"Take a breath," Gelly consoled.

Garner held his breath for a moment and then let it out slowly. His sobs subsided as he regained some control. "What the hell are we doing out here, Gelly?"

"Saving lives," Gelly answered emphatically.

"Saving lives? Is that what just happened?"

"You're in shock. Let's get you warmed up." Gelly went to the packs and retrieved a field jacket and water. "Put this on and drink this. Wait here."

Gelly entered the bank alone, its lock long ago smashed to pieces. After a few moments, he returned. "There's a place where you can rest inside."

The lobby, teller counter, and offices had been vandalized. Gelly led Garner into one of the corner suites. Garner collapsed onto the floor, noting how the rug smelled of mold as his exhausted body took over.

The school bus lurched forward, bouncing over the railroad crossing and picking up speed. Two dozen elementary school children rocked along with the spring of the bus, chatting or laughing or teasing. The driver hunched grumpily over the steering wheel and glanced at the brats from time to time through the wide rearview mirror, ready to scold any one of them for misbehaving.

Kane sat a few rows from the back, watching out the window across the aisle as the neighborhood houses slipped lazily by like a slideshow. He adjusted his blue and green camouflaged bookbag on his right shoulder and clutched his paper bag lunch in his lap. Avery, his Transformers bookbag between his legs, sat closest to the window, face glued to the glass. Today, Avery had beaten his older brother in their daily race and snatched the window seat for himself. A rare occasion.

The bus rolled through an adjacent neighborhood for its last stop. A brother and sister boarded. The boy carried a baseball bat and glove.

"He's not supposed to bring a bat to school," Avery whispered.

Back on the main road, a straight shot to school, the bus bucked and backfired. A billow of black smoke puffed from the tailpipe. The driver shifted down a gear and revved the engine.

Outside, the morning glow dimmed as if dark clouds had rolled in.     Kane looked across the aisle. Moments later, he couldn't see any of the houses on either side of the street. Avery's eyes went wide as he watched his older brother's frigid response. The chatter on the bus quieted as the rest of the children registered that morning had suddenly become night.

The driver grinded every gear, swearing repeatedly. The bus lost momentum, crawling along the country road.

Something slapped the outside of the bus and everyone jumped, including Kane. Another slap. The children craned their necks. Kane stood, looking for the source.

"Sit down!" the driver yelled.

"I see people," Avery said, pointing.

Kane moved his brother out of the way to see out the window for himself. A crowd of people was keeping pace with the struggling bus as if in a parade, but something felt off. It was too dark to be certain, but Kane thought they weren't acting much like people.

The bus backfired one last time. The driver fought the steering wheel as he lost all power, the bus coming to a final rest. Kane caught the driver's stare as he glanced in the rearview mirror—caught his fear. Kane's heart beat a few paces faster.

"What's wrong?" Avery asked instinctively, tuned in to his brother's every mood.

"It's nothing. Engine trouble," Kane assured him.

But Avery wasn't buying it. He started to breathe heavily. "I want to go home."

More bangs up and down the sides of the bus sent it rocking. Low groans and hisses echoed from outside.

The driver stood, facing the children. "Everything will be fine. Stay in your seats. Another bus will be along shortly to get you to school. There's nothing to worry—"

The bus door exploded. A shower of glass flew into the small stairwell, spraying the driver. The man dove for cover too slowly, getting a face full of tiny shards that sank into his soft flesh. He cupped his eyes. As blood seeped between his fingers, he screamed, the pain only now reaching his brain.

Long, pale, bony arms emerged from the darkness and snatched the driver's legs. Children in the front rows screeched and ran for the back of the bus. The driver grabbed the boarding pole for dear life, but his bloody hands slipped. He clawed for any hold as the skeletal arms dragged him off the bus. The man's shrieks soon faded into the darkness.

Every child pushed to the back, each trying to hide behind the other. Kane found himself in front of his peers as the bus springs creaked and sagged under the weight of the creature climbing inside. The beast stepped to the head of the aisle and pointed a slender finger at Kane.

Like an invisible force had punched him square in the chest, Kane fell backward into the packed children cowering behind him. His mind filled with everything about this creature, but it also meant the creature knew everything about him.

Tears rolled down his face. His lower lip quivered.

He knew.

Garner exploded out of a deep sleep, punching and grabbing at the air until reality sobered him. Fear wrestled him for control.

Walmart. The platform. The crowd. Running. The bank. The molding rug.

"You needed the rest," Gelly said, setting aside his MRE.

"Wendigo," Garner said, staring blankly.

"What?"

"It's called a wendigo. It's driven by an insatiable hunger for flesh. Animal, human. Makes no difference. It feeds, then returns to the hellhole it came from. The people behind the fence were its buffet."

"How do you know this?" Gelly said quizzingly.

"I just . . . *know*," Garner replied, shaking his head ever so slightly.

"A lot of people did escape," Gelly said.

"It won't matter. The wendigo doesn't stop for anything. It'll sniff them out one by one until . . ."

"Until what?"

"Until it's time to return."

Gelly knelt next to Garner and shook him by the shoulders. "Hey, brother, we need you!"

Garner pressed his palms into his eyes as if trying to unscrew them. He took a gasp of air as if emerging from underwater. "I'm stuck in a nightmare."

"Yeah, the worst kind. The one you wake up from and realize was real." Gelly handed him a water.

Garner guzzled it down. "Where's Wonderboy?"

Gelly dropped his head.

"Please no."

"He could be out there. He went stir-crazy like everyone else when that whatzitgo appeared. I'm sorry, sir. I couldn't keep up with both of you."

"We'll find him, Corporal," Garner said, then hesitated a moment. "We have to stop this thing."

"At all costs, sir."

Garner and Gelly exited the bank after redistributing packs and reloading their weapons. Clouds had rolled under the sun, obscuring the precise time of day. His watch showed he had slept six hours. Pickup was less than nine hours away.

"Any idea which direction Wonderboy went?"

"After that kind of fear, there's only one place to run. Home."

"Home home? As in Aurora? That's a hundred miles from here," Garner said.

"Hundred and fifty miles to be exact," Gelly corrected.

"Damn!" Garner brushed a hand through his hair. "We need some wheels."

It didn't take long to find a functioning vehicle. They had hiked into a nearby neighborhood and, after three break-ins, found a pickup that had air in the tires, fuel in the tank, and started on the first crank. Garner drove while Gelly narrowed down their search area to a twenty-mile section of Route 55 North.

"He couldn't have gotten even halfway there in seven hours. He'll be exhausted by now," Gelly said while swiping his fingers over a map on the field tablet.

The double lane highway was broken, and forced Garner to keep his speed at a crawl so as not to blow a tire or snap an axle. He welcomed the distraction but couldn't get the wendigo out of his head, the horrors it had shown him, the bus from his dream and the one from the gollum attack.

As luck would have it, they found Wonderboy unconscious and curled against a guardrail, covered in sweat and dirt. Garner observed open sores on his hands and knees as they lifted Wonderboy into the backseat. "Did he crawl?"

The men drove back in silence. Gelly's head stayed in the tablet. Garner replayed the waking nightmare of the wendigo again and again. Those eyes! The beast had seen into his soul and surfaced his every insecurity, his every fear, his every weakness. Past, present, future—didn't matter. The beast thirsted for them all.

"What are you doing?" Garner asked Gelly, trying to divert his thoughts.

"Looking up how to kill the fucker."

"And?"

"It depends on which source you prefer: a *Dungeons & Dragons* manual or a video game user guide," Gelly said.

"What do they say?" Garner asked.

"You're serious?"

Garner shrugged.

Gelly raised his brow. "This is all myth and legend. But it's a freak of nature. It can blend into its surroundings, mimic any animal as a lure. Anything silver—bullets, an axe—or a stake through the heart will kill it. And if you kill it, you risk the spirits that keep it alive entering your body and becoming a wendigo yourself. Best bet is fire. It leaves no bone or tissue to waste. Otherwise, it can regenerate and hunt another day."

"Anything else?"

"Fast, strong, heightened senses, agile, stamina," Gelly read.

"Dog-ugly and evil as shit."

"Roll the dice correctly and you might be able to kill it," Gelly said. "This is highly speculative, sir."

"What choice do we have, Gelly?"

"Rendezvous with the Harpy and fly the fuck out of here."

"You don't mean that."

Gelly turned away, watching out his window. "Maybe I do."

"The beast will slaughter everyone, and the gollums will finish the rest," Garner said. "You're the one who said we're here to save people."

"They were already dead when we arrived. Bunch of trapped sheep calling it living."

"We have the means to do something about it."

"We might die trying."

Garner noticed the radio/CD-player in the dash. "Any CDs in the glovebox?"

Gelly opened it and pulled out a stack of cases. He leafed through and pulled one out, showing the title to Garner: Steppenwolf's *16 Greatest Hits.*

"Play it!" Garner turned up the volume to "Magic Carpet Ride" as they drove back into town. They turned into the Home Depot parking lot three blocks from the Walmart. The store's wide entrance had been damaged, either by the earthquake or looters. Garner backed the pickup truck inside the building and killed the engine.

"What are we doing here?" Gelly asked.

"We need to MacGyver some shit if we're going to beat this thing. I have some ideas, and I know you could make them."

Gelly's eyes lit up. He smiled broadly.

"That's it. Now let's get to work."

"What about Wonderboy?" Gelly asked.

"Let him rest," Garner said.

Gelly spent the afternoon cutting, bolting, building, and reinforcing several tools. The Home Depot had been looted of the more popular items, but there was plenty of remaining supplies they could reconfigure. The man smiled the whole time as he fashioned the weapons Garner had described.

Garner searched for fuel, gas, oil, accelerants—anything that could help generate a lot of heat in a short amount of time. The home improvement store had been stripped bare of such things, but he struck gold in adjacent stores and neighboring homes, finding enough to power Gelly's creations.

After some time, Gelly showed Garner how the equipment worked as they formed their plan. They walked through the aisles, discussing contingencies and risks.

Gelly shook his head. "Too many ways to escape."

"Could we shift some of the racks by the exits?" Garner pressed.

"Not enough charge on the forklifts. We'll need that juice if we draw the creature inside."

Garner sighed. "We have to go with what we have and hope the creature isn't intelligent enough."

"We have to assume the creature is intelligent. It'll either escape or kill both of us if we don't block off the garden warehouse."

"I'll do it," a voice said from behind them.

Both men turned to see Wonderboy walking toward them, a pack hanging off one shoulder and an automatic rifle strapped to the other. Hair disheveled and eyes bloodshot, he walked stiffly as if he had dismounted a horse.

Gelly met him and hugged the young man. "I thought I lost you, bro."

Wonderboy buried his face in Gelly's shoulder. "I'm sorry."

"Damn right you are," Gelly joked, slapping him on the back.

Wonderboy wiped tears away.

"Glad you're back," Garner said.

"I don't know if I am back, sir. When that thing looked at me? I never felt fear like that in my whole life. I swear I separated from my body and watched from the backseat, someone else driving. I ran until I couldn't anymore, then crawled on my hands and knees for a while." Wonderboy showed the raw cuts Garner had seen earlier, then stared off into the distance for a moment. He blinked several times as if pushing himself to return to the present. "I need to change my clothes."

Gelly wrinkled his nose. "You shit yourself, didn't you?"

"Meet us back in ten," Garner said, glancing at his watch. "If you want to sit this one out . . ."

"Not a chance," Wonderboy quickly replied. "I mean, I can't promise what I'll do if I see it again, but I won't sit on the sidelines."

Garner nodded approvingly.

The men separated. Wonderboy went straight to the restroom. Gelly hurried up an aisle to complete final preparations. Garner stood at the store entrance checking the lead wires from a disassembled security gate console, attached now with duct tape to a powerpack from a wireless drill.

*We have one shot at this.* If the myths held truth, the wendigo was ancient—a creature present at the dawn of humankind that had stalked people over centuries. Its continued existence meant no one had succeeded at stopping the beast over history. Maybe in the past, they were simply unprepared. *This time, it's different.*

In a couple of hours, evening would be upon them. Gelly and Wonderboy regrouped with Garner. The three reviewed the plan one last time.

At a location he'd been calling the Last Stand, Gelly pointed to a collection of shovels, a pitchfork, and blunt force tools. "All else fails, we go out swinging."

"How do we get the creature to come to us?" Wonderboy asked.

Garner jutted his chin toward the truck. "We go after it."

"We go after it?"

"Yeah! Coax it, shoot it, yell at it, whatever it takes to get it to follow us here."

"We don't even know where it is."

"Yes we do."

Wonderboy nodded, then stared off distantly again.

"You don't have to go," Garner said gently.

"I'm driving," Wonderboy snapped.

A few moments later, Wonderboy waited behind the wheel, gripping it until his knuckles turned white. Gelly placed the rifles in the pickup bed and hopped in the back. Garner threw open the passenger door and quickly rummaged through the glovebox.

"What are you looking for?" Wonderboy asked Garner.

Garner tossed one jewel case after another onto the floorboard. "Whoever owned this truck had lousy taste in music. Ah! Play this when we get close. First song." Garner handed the CD over to Wonderboy.

Wonderboy rolled his eyes. "The guy with the white glove?"

Garner shook his head. "Different guy. Never mind, just play the song when I say." He shut the passenger door, leaped in the back with Gelly, and slapped the side panel. "Let's go."

The trip to Walmart was a straight drive down a main road. Garner's hands slid around the grips of his rifle. He wiped his sweating palms on his pants. He checked the magazine clip one more time when the store came into view. Gelly sat across from him, fidgeting with a lighter. The two men locked eyes.

Gelly grinned. "I found a little surprise that might get their attention." He brandished several bottle rockets.

Garner knocked on the back window to alert Wonderboy. "Play the music!" Then, to Gelly, "Light 'em up."

Prince *whooped* over the truck's speakers. Bright keys and the slam of bass notes vibrated metal. Wonderboy jogged the truck at a steady speed parallel to the repaired fence as "Let's Go Crazy" blared from verse to chorus. Gelly lit fuses and aimed, sending bottle rockets over the chain-link divide. They exploded, some on route, some after bouncing on the pavement. Between the screaming music and the deafening blasts, a hornet's nest had been kicked.

The gollums had rounded up hundreds of escapees. The people gawked with looks of desperation and hope from inside the enclosure as the cacophony caught their attention. The gollums, confused and disoriented, took a minute to spot the truck. They scrambled in a chaotic mass and gave chase.

After lighting the last of the rockets, Gelly helped Garner dispose of the closest gollums with headshots that fueled the mob's ire. The men took their shots in tandem with the beat of the music.

"I didn't see it, did you?" Garner yelled to Gelly.

Gelly shook his head, eyes wide with the same panic mounting in Garner.

Garner knocked on the back window, gesturing the same question to Wonderboy. He mouthed "No" over the music.

Panic formed a lump in his throat. Their plan was already off the rails. "We have to circle back," he said, unnerved, as he and Gelly dropped another pair of gollums.

"No. We stick to the plan. If we run out of gas here, we're done." Gelly aimed and shot twice, hitting one mark and clipping another's shoulder. "Shit!"

Garner scowled, then slapped the side of the truck. Wonderboy killed the music and floored the gas, driving back toward the Home Depot and distancing themselves from the amassing creatures.

The tires screeched loudly across pavement as the vehicle skidded to a sudden stop, throwing Garner and Gelly forward in the truck bed with a thud. Dazed, both men looked for the reason Wonderboy had stopped.

Standing in the middle of the road ahead of the truck, the wendigo glared.

Garner's throat constricted and his every muscle froze. Once thin, pasty, and wolf-like, the creature was now twice its original size. Coarse hair so thick it looked like tree bark had filled in across its chest, arms, and legs. A ragged fur shawl draped loosely off its shoulders. Over its head it wore a buffalo skull, the two horns blackened and starkly contrasting the pale white plane of the facial bone. A rope sash crossed its chest, and woven through it, three human skulls dangled like trophies at one hip.

Gelly slapped the top of the cab. "Get us out of here!"

The truck revved and catapulted forward, casting Garner off balance. He caught himself before pitching over the side.

Wonderboy aimed the truck directly at the creature. Gelly fired off several shots over the top of the cab.

One half of Garner's brain told him to grip his gun and shoot. The other half of his brain fought to even recognize his limbs. He finally understood why so many people had remained behind the fence. They had been paralyzed with fear.

"Back to the depot!" Gelly yelled and slapped the cab again.

At the last moment, Wonderboy swerved around the wendigo. The creature reached and dragged its long claws along the side of the truck with an awful grating squeal. Gelly spun around and spent a few more rounds that barely nicked the creature's hide.

Unfazed, the wendigo chased them.

No amount of lead slowed the oncoming creature, not even when Garner found himself able to use his gun and aim. Clipping a curb, they bounded into the Home Depot parking lot and barreled straight for the entrance.

"We get one shot at this," Garner said to Gelly.

As the truck whipped through the entrance, Gelly reached with the end of his rifle and clipped the security gate latch. The massive gate started to lower.

Wonderboy jammed the brakes and weaved the truck down to the end of one aisle. Behind them, the wendigo ducked beneath the falling gate, then hesitated inside the store, observing its new surroundings. A moment later, the gate closed, trapping the creature inside with Garner's crew.

*Or*, Garner thought with a sinking stomach, *trapping us with it.*

The creature leaned on the gate as if testing its strength, but the metal was designed to stop things wielding far more force than what it could deliver.

At the back of the aisle, the men leaped out of the truck and took their positions behind a pallet of cement bags. Gelly handed Garner and Wonderboy nail guns while picking up a third for himself. The three hoses connected to the nail guns snaked around their feet and led to a large air tank Gelly had pressurized earlier. Each man had several coils of nails at the ready.

The wendigo lifted its head, sniffing the air, then settled its sights on its prey. Its eyes hid within the shadows of the buffalo skull.

Garner's leg pumped like a jackhammer. He clenched his teeth and fought off every urge to retreat, sure that those evil eyes burrowed even now straight into his soul.

"Come on! Come get some!" Garner beckoned. He released his sidearm and shot the wendigo. The bullet struck one of the buffalo horns and shattered it.

The wendigo growled, a rough roar like a lion aggrieved, and then it pounced.

"Wait until it's closer," Gelly warned.

The creature vaulted onto the racks and swung from one side of the aisle to the other. Shelves creaked under the strain as they were rocked back and forth. It closed half the distance with an unnatural agility and strength.

"Now!"

The men squeezed their triggers, a volley of nails following puffs of compressed air. Many of them sank into the arms and torso of the creature. The wendigo dropped from an upper rack, landing in the aisle's center. It lifted one arm, briefly interested in the nails embedded there.

"I didn't think this would work," Garner said, looking at the nail coils. Each tip had been coated in a reddish-brown substance.

"Copper." Gelly shrugged. "It's all I could find."

The wendigo growled once more, now trying to deflect nails as it continued its flight toward the men. It caromed down the aisle, turning itself into a target too hard to hit accurately. The men continued their volley until the pressure tank waned.

"I'm out!" Wonderboy said, throwing down his nail gun.

"Me too!" Gelly said.

"Go!" Garner said. "I'll draw it in."

Gelly and Wonderboy broke from cover and disappeared down the adjacent aisle.

Garner stepped out from behind the pallets and met the creature in the middle of the aisle. Man faced beast, barely as many paces separating them as the wendigo was tall.

A roaring yell founds its way of Garner's throat as he squeezed the trigger as quickly as possible, aiming for the soft spots along the wendigo's abdomen, chest, and neck. The coated nails penetrated, lodging deep. Greyish ichor ran down its front from dozens of puncture wounds. The creature slipped in its own blood and fell to one knee. One gnarled claw went to its chest and plucked the nails there free.

With a bubbling splatter, the small circles of torn flesh sealed shut, leaving behind only whitish scars.

Garner threw the empty nail gun, a frail attempt that missed the creature, then took a couple wasted shots with his handgun. "Follow me, you son of a bitch!"

He ran at full tilt down the adjoining aisle. Blood pulsed in his ears as his heart readied to explode out of his chest. His legs pumped, adrenaline dulling the muscle fatigue as he picked up speed. He could keep on running. He could run straight out of the building, down the street, as far as his legs would carry him out of town. He gritted his teeth angrily, hating himself for the thought, hating his cowardice. A quick glance over his shoulder showed that the wendigo was fast on his tail. Just as they had planned. A glimmer of hope renewed his resolve.

In the aisle ahead, two modified forklifts idled—Gelly in one, Wonderboy in the other. The lifts, angled toward each other, formed with their raised forks a narrow V-shaped opening. Along each fork, circular saw blades, tack welded in place, waited for the creature.

Garner ducked below the forks. Gelly and Wonderboy gassed the lifts, closing the gap between them. The wendigo pushed through the tightening opening. The now-serrated forks ripped deep into the creature's thighs. It screeched like a screaming coyote and thrashed between the lifts, deepening its injuries.

The wendigo shoved one of the forklifts away, freeing its injured legs and tipping the vehicle. Wonderboy dove for safety. Not wasting a moment, Gelly raised his forks and spun his lift to catch the creature in the midsection; it leaped clear, landing in the storage racks above. Hanging from the upper shelves, the wendigo protested like a keening hawk. It shrieked at the men one more time, then slipped into the shadows.

"It's trying to get out," Gelly called.

"I'm on it! Get the tank ready." Garner sprinted down the aisle. He checked his handgun; only a few bullets remained. Not like they would do any good. Perhaps enough to get its attention if necessary. He holstered his handgun and snatched a hatchet and a pitchfork from the Last Stand.

He couldn't see the creature, but he heard the stress of metal as it clambered through the higher shelving, saw the racks swaying.

Garner reached the checkout counters, the gated exit at his back. A large shadow moved lithely above. A howl echoed throughout the warehouse.

Garner swore under his breath. He held the hatchet and pitchfork firmly in each hand while thinking how absurd and ineffective they'd be against a supernatural creature. Gelly had insisted that piercing weapons could be as effective as a round of bullets, but out in the open, the tools his only defense, Garner thought he might as well have been naked. Their whole plan was based on a fictious monster manual.

The gate behind him rattled and hammered; Garner jumped.

*Gollums!*

The howl. A homing beacon.

"Shit!"

From aside, a large mass sprung at Garner, claws poised to kill.

Garner dove. A lethal claw swept over him, missing by a fraction of an inch. He slid into the square bay of the checkout counter, his shoulder slamming the underside of the wood hard.

The creature leaned over the register, snarling like a black bear. Its glare from behind the broken skull mask burrowed deep into Garner's very being.

He was trapped. He balled tighter in the small bay, wishing he could shrink into the tiniest hole. His mind separated from his body.


Kane stood in the aisle of the broken-down school bus. Frightened and crying children huddled behind him in the back. Avery cowered behind an empty seat.

The wendigo's imposing height and girth filled the entire width and height of the aisle ahead. And those eyes!

The eyes.

Kane knew something about its eyes. He recognized them. The same look of disappointment and anger he'd seen countless times.

His father's eyes.

No one and nothing could ever match his father's rage and abuse.

He wasn't feeling so afraid anymore.

Remembering the boy with the baseball bat, Kane searched among the students and found the boy and his sister clutching one another, the wooden bat at their feet. Kane claimed it and twisted his hands around the grip as if getting ready for a home-run pitch.

He skipped—no one would fault him for it—down the aisle and pulled back the bat, putting his entire body into the swing.

Wood met wendigo with a *crack*. The beast's head snapped back; the bat snapped in half. Kane, seeing the broken handle's dagger-sharp end, adjusted his grip and jammed the point between the wendigo's ribs. The beast yowled like a wounded wolf.

Garner opened his eyes, body and mind merging as one again. Before him stood the creature, the pitchfork piercing it between the ribs. Grinding his teeth, Garner drove the points deeper, pushing while climbing over the counter toward it.

The wendigo wailed again. Its hand swiped down and snapped the wooden handle in half, separating it from Garner's grip.

He was struck, blindsided, on the side of his head. Garner spun like a top tumbling. He landed hard on his back, head bouncing off the concrete floor. A taste like pennies filled his mouth as his vision blurred and his ears rang. For a moment, it felt as though his head had been dislodged from his body, a complete numbness settling upon him from the neck down.

The wendigo stood in a pool of its own blood shrieking in agony and working the pitchfork out from between its ribs. The crowd of gollums slammed themselves fiercely against the gate, unable to aid their master.

Garner spat a wad of fresh blood. He tongued his split lower lip and a gash inside his cheek. His legs wobbled as he struggled to his feet.

The pitchfork clanged to the cement floor.

Garner ran.

He beelined it toward the lumber section. A long pile of scrap wood, pallets, plywood, and planks sat in the middle of the floor. The smell of kerosene hung in the air. Garner jumped on top of the pile. One, two, three, four steps. A loose board shifted and he tumbled hard, his legs and shoulder taking the brunt of the fall, one foot driving deep into the pile and lodging itself between two boards. He fought with the wood and twisted his leg every which way. He couldn't get his boot free.

The wendigo trailed him, demonstrating inhuman balance as it navigated the quaking pile of wood.

It was nearly on top of him.

Garner unlaced his boot, yanked his foot free, and rolled.

"Do it!" he yelled. He couldn't spot Gelly or Wonderboy but knew they were near.

At the sound of his voice, Wonderboy stepped out of hiding at the other end of the aisle holding a butane torch. "Get out of there!" He waved at Garner.

"Do it now!"

Wonderboy touched the torch to the oily liquid that coated the floor and seeped under the wood pile. With an echoing *whoomp*, an orange blast of light erupted.

Garner dove through the flames, charring his clothing, and landed inside an adjacent bay.

An unearthly shriek sounded as fire engulfed the wendigo.

The metal around Garner shook as Gelly raised the forklift on the other side. Metal screeched and snapped and collapsed. Garner ducked and raised both arms around his head as the entire unit above him toppled like a house of cards onto the burning wood pile, trapping the still screaming creature. The upper stacks crashed into the next, downing the rest of the racks like dominoes.

The fire continued to burn and spread.

Garner crawled out from under the wreckage missing only a boot. His clothes smoldered.

"Garner!" Gelly called through the blinding smoke.

"I'm here," he said, exhausted, and lay back down on the floor. He coughed and choked on blood.

A hand wrapped around his wrist, and he grabbed hold, letting himself get hoisted up.

"Thanks."

Wonderboy nodded. "Sir."

"We got one more task," Garner said, his words mumbles. His lip and cheek were swollen, and he had certainly bitten his tongue.

The three men hurried toward the front of the store, Wonderboy torching everything as they went. A metal door nearby with *Exit in Emergency* stamped on it was their way out.

The gollums frantically slammed against the main entrance gate ahead, growing more agitated with every fresh contact of flesh on metal.

The fire was spreading fast, the warehouse already full of smoke.

"Gelly," Garner said, raising his handgun, "open the main entrance." Wonderboy raised his torch.

Gelly, a hatchet in hand, popped the locking latch. The large entrance gate started to open. The gollums shrieked and hissed. Like a flood dam had opened, they rushed into the burning building.

The gollums, bent on finding their endangered master, heeded the men no attention as the three escaped through the emergency exit.

Garner and Wonderboy stayed behind and barricaded the door while Gelly ran around to the large entrance and reversed the gate after the last of the gollums had gone through. Then the three men watched from the parking lot. Black smoke billowed out of the warehouse, yet the flames seemed less violent than before.

"Is it possible they can put the fire out?" Wonderboy asked.

Garner quietly wondered the same thing.

Several gollums appeared at the gate covered in soot and burns. They didn't pound frantically at the metal in any attempt to escape even though the smoke and fire were surely unbearable. Instead, they stood patiently, watching and waiting.

The wendigo emerged from the smoke and rested its long claws through the small openings. Its buffalo skull mask was gone, its clothing burned away.

The gate started to rise.

Garner and his men were defenseless. Everything was spent. The fire hadn't been enough to stop the supernatural creature. They wouldn't stand a chance.

A few gollums scooted under the gate and raced straight for them.

*Run!*

Dirt and dust swirled around them, a mini tornado. A spotlight illuminated the parking lot, tracking the fleeing men. The Harpy hovered silently. A stream of bullets erupted from the mounted machine gun, cutting down the oncoming gollums.

"It's Doc!" Gelly said excitedly. Though they'd lost their earpieces in the mayhem of the last several hours, a series of hand signals gave all the direction Doc needed to relay to the pilots.

As the men ran for cover, the Harpy glided away to align itself with the Home Depot entrance. Four missiles blasted from underneath the helicopter, striking the main gate. Explosions enveloped the entire front of the store, sending a plume of fire and smoke high in the air like an over-the-top fireworks display. The unseated orange letters of the store's name shot like rockets every which way. The machine gun unleashed a hail of bullets upon all movement as the Harpy floated up over the roof. From it fell two drum canisters that dropped into the center of the warehouse. The entire building disappeared in the ensuing flames.

A high-pitched shriek rose above the explosion and failing metal. The wendigo burst from the destruction, its entire hide aflame. It dashed across the parking lot, a racing fireball.

"We can't let it return to the fault!" Garner yelled, motioning to the helicopter.

Doc signaled OK and the pilots tore after it. The creature was fast, the machine gun faster.

The weakened wendigo stumbled under the first round of heavy shells. It darted under the cover of trees, through a small parking lot, and beneath a cafe awning, working to eliminate the pilot's line of sight.

The Harpy was undeterred with its proximity targeting system. Its pilots maneuvered the agile bird of prey, finding their shots.

The flames on the wendigo's hide diminished but stayed bright enough to spot. Another round of shells finally dropped the creature. It careened into the side of a hulled sedan, wasted.

The pilots of the Harpy shredded the wendigo and made Swiss cheese of the car. The heavy artillery ripped flesh, shattered bone, and pulverized everything else remaining.

Moments later, with the Harpy settled a road away, Garner, Gelly, and Wonderboy, banged, bruised, and cut but otherwise in good spirits, met Doc.

"You came back," Garner said gratefully, his mouth sore.

"I was wrong to leave." Doc stood straight with shoulders back, prepared for backlash and punishment for abandoning the mission.

Garner only smiled. "You're here now."

"I'm perfectly fine with you reporting my inexcusable actions to Central," Doc persisted.

"The only action I'm reporting is the success of this mission and whatever they make of this thing," Garner said, motioning to the pile of gore pasted on the vehicle and street.

"Sir—"

"Doc, it's OK."

Doc's striking blue eyes met his. A glimmer of something new passed between them. They both felt it, he knew, but the timing . . .

"Um, there's people who need medical attention," Garner redirected her.

"We need to burn the rest of it first," Gelly said, standing over the creature's remains.

"Let me take a few samples," Doc said. "Maybe we can learn something."

"I'll do it, Doc," Wonderboy volunteered.

"What? Are you sure?" Garner asked.

"I got this." Wonderboy took the four plastic vials, long tweezers, and rubber gloves from Doc. He squatted down on his haunches over the remains of the beast as he snapped on the rubber gloves. He probed the gore with the tweezers. Collected a few samples. Garner shrugged.

It wouldn't be so long into the future that he'd regret dismissing Wonderboy's odd behavior.


The chaos at Walmart more than rivaled that of Black Friday. The encampment lay in ruins as though crushed by heavy equipment. Small fires burned. The food area was upended, its tables overturned or broken, every chair bent out of shape. The sleeping quarters were scattered. Tarps smoldered in the sleeping area, stinking of burning plastic, and the splinters of smashed cots were strewn across the destroyed clothing and personal effects scattered everywhere.

The remaining survivors were in equal disarray. Garner's team triaged the injured. More people were going to die before dawn from all the bites and scratches inflicted. They had no choice but to separate this group from the rest.

Opportunists loaded carts full with food from the Chief's reserves; Garner stopped the looting quickly. Wonderboy returned soon after, handing Doc three full vials. "Sorry, one slipped out of my hands," he explained, flushed.

Doc, frowning, lowered the vials into her medical bag.

"You OK?" Garner asked Wonderboy.

"Yeah, yeah. Just, ya know, rough day."

"I need you on food detail. Inventory what's left."

Wonderboy nodded and hurried away. The rest of Garner's team had their jobs.

Garner, monitoring the survivors, noticed Peggy kneeling over Arthur, who lay lifeless on a broken cot. She adjusted the blankets under his chin and smoothed out the wrinkles as if trying to keep the deceased man warm. Streaks of tears had cleared paths down her dirty cheeks.

She noticed his presence. "You returned." Peggy reached and held Garner's arm tightly, a lifeline.

"This is not a good place to stay ..." Garner started softheartedly to the woman.

She grinned shamelessly, tightening her grip. "He's not done yet."

Garner frowned and gently pried Peggy's hands from his arm.

The shaken woman shrank back and resumed smoothing the blanket.

The late evening hours transitioned into early morning. The Harpy remained on standby a block from the encampment. Doc had been communicating with Central throughout the evening.

"How long do you think it'll take Central to bring in supplies?" Garner asked Doc.

"Garner?" Doc motioned to speak with him privately. She looked over her shoulder to ensure they wouldn't be overheard. "Central isn't coming. There won't be any rescue or supplies for these people."

Garner grinded his teeth. "We can't leave them like this."

"I didn't say we should," Doc said. "Understand, the Harpy has strict orders to leave by dawn."

Garner nodded. "Is there anything else we can do?"

"Broken bones have been set or at least stabilized. Lacerations stitched and bandaged. Many people, they're simply in shock. That's going to take time. I mean, aren't you?"

"I'm fine."

"You don't look fine. Come," Doc said, taking him by the arm and settling him in a chair. "You look like you got your ass beat."

"I did."

Garner gave into her care, powerless to resist. He was cut, scraped, and burned in places he hadn't noticed. Her touch, gentle but sure as she cleaned and bandaged the more worrisome wounds, grounded him. Her sweet breath brushed the back of his neck. He watched her bright blue eyes as she closed a cut on his arm, a hint of lavender coming over him as she leaned close to press the closure strip down.

"You're staring."

"Oh. Um . . . I didn't mean to upset you," Garner started. "Earlier. I'm a little impulsive. I realize how that impacts the team."

"Kane Garner? Impulsive? I never knew."

Garner grinned. "I know about your transfer. I completely understand and won't get in your way. It's just—I don't want any harm to come to you."

She placed a hand on his arm, her gaze softening. "You might need my protection more than I need yours."

"Clearly. Anyway, I was wrong. I wanted you to know that."

Doc grinned. "I knew that. Wait, are you trying to apologize?" She slapped him on the shoulder.

"Ouch!" Garner winced at one of the more sensitive wounds.

"I'm so sorry," she said, but laughed.


Before dawn, a few more people had passed. The living moved carefully under shelter inside the store. Garner sought to make himself more useful. A cookfire and the distribution of the Chief's remaining food and water had everyone realizing how hungry they were.

The Harpy was scheduled to depart soon. Garner gathered his crew.

"Gelly, Wonderboy, you return to Central. Doc and I will stay," Garner decided. "Corporal, report to Pavlov only. He'll send the aid we need. If he declines, then find another way."

"Yes, sir!" Gelly saluted out of habit. Garner rolled his eyes at the continued formality.

The crew broke for final preparations. Doc radioed the chopper pilots that two would be returning with them.

A slight vibration shook the ground beneath their feet. Aftershocks still sometimes happened these days, but this one felt different. The vibration strengthened, quickly sounding like rolling thunder. Buildings down the road teetered, then collapsed.

"Take cover!"

As if the day's myriad explosions had released some massive pressure underground, the fault line, dormant for two years, opened wider, swallowing the parking lot and splitting the Walmart in two.

Doc screamed. Garner grabbed her and ran from the breaking earth and crumpling building. Dirt and debris billowed.

After several rattling moments, the ground stilled and the sound of thunder faded. Tthe dust started to settle.

Garner's eyes stung. He spat dirt and blew his nose. Doc was on her knees with her face in her hands. Tears cut clear lines down her cheeks. He spotted Gelly and Wonderboy, coughing and hacking and covered in white dust, a few meters away.

A sinking feeling grew in the pit of Garner's stomach as he turned to face the destruction. The fault had consumed the store and everyone inside.

In the quiet, he and his crew froze, facing the emptiness before them.

A fiendish shriek pierced the stillness, echoing from below ground.

Gelly was first on his feet. "We have to go," he said to Garner, pulling Wonderboy while aiding Doc to her feet.

Garner's crew leaned on each other in a collective limp back to the waiting Harpy. The helicopter had faired the quake, blades already turning. One of the pilots motioned frantically for them to hurry, pointing back over their heads.

Garner didn't want to turn.

He knew.

He turned his head anyway.

Behind them, crawling out from the cover of dust and smoke, gollums, hundreds of them, fresh from their nests buried deep behind the Gates of Hell, rushed toward them like a wave of locusts.

*Run!*

Garner's crew poured into the cabin. The Harpy lifted, airborne as the first surge of gollums grazed the landing skid.

Garner strapped into his seat, jaw tense. He pounded his knee with a clenched fist. He punched the cabin roof until his knuckles split and blood smeared. He snatched a headset hanging off the bulkhead and snapped it in half. He grabbed another and slapped it onto his head. "Take us around. Low."

The copilot turned to regard him. "Sir, I advise we—"

"Do it!" Garner said. "Switch on the recorder. I want Central to see this."

The Harpy entered a wide arc and followed the newly expanded fault line. The dust cloud parted as the helicopter traveled low. Thousands upon thousands of Hell's spawn crawled from the darkest depths of the chasm and spread across the land, a disease.

"Their skin is pink," Wonderboy observed.

"They're smaller," Gelly added.

Wonderboy shook his head. "What does this mean?"

"Second wave," Gelly said.

Garner's neck and face burned hot as he boiled with rage. He took deep breaths, processing the number of lost lives and the implications of a new enemy surge. The wendigo had risen to lead a new army of gollums, to organize and march them unmatched across Earth. Nothing would have stopped them. Garner's team had halted the enemy's plan, stopping it dead in its tracks. He faced his team, noting their expressions of shock and despair. A team torn, fragile, on the precipice of defeat.

Garner drank some water and cleared his dry throat.

"You're questioning your purpose, perhaps wondering if I might get you killed. I don't blame you. I won't get in your way either. War takes a toll.

"We have our reasons why we stay in this fight. I thought I was saving my brother. Whatever the reason, today, we did something incredible, the four of us. We proved the enemy can be beaten no matter what it throws at us.

"I won't ask you to stay. This is an individual choice. Yours to make. But I know I can't do it alone. I don't fight for humankind but for the people nearest to me. Yet I'll be damned if I won't help as many people as I can along the way."

"I'm in," Gelly said without hesitation.

"I'm in. Gelly needs me to check his facts." Wonderboy smiled. Gelly hissed.

"I'm in too," Doc said. "Who else will stitch up you idiots?"

He sighed with relief, a strong sense of belonging giving him hope.

Garner signaled the pilots to return home.

Declassified by order of the
Governor of the West North Central Territory
Declass No.: 1073

# TRANSCRIPT

## SUBJECT
Case File D-1652: Open investigation of Major
Daniel Edward Hunt; Satellite Telephone
Correspondence

## PARTICIPANTS
Major Daniel Edward Hunt and Police 'Chief' Jack
Stuart of Springfield, Illinois

## DATE, TIME, PLACE
12-01-2036, 0326, National Guard Central
Operations, Kansas City, Missouri


[BEGIN AUDIO]

HUNT:   I thought I was perfectly clear that there
        was no contact until our business had
        concluded.

CHIEF:  Then explain why one of your boys is snoopin'
        around my establishment. No doubt a full unit
        is hidin' outside my perimeter.

HUNT:   What? I didn't authorize—

CHIEF:  You assured me no interference, Hunt. I'm
        startin' to think you might be renegin' on
        our deal.

HUNT:   Our deal remains unchanged. You have my word.

CHIEF: That still doesn't explain the man in my holdin' cell. He stinks like one of yours.

HUNT: The unit shouldn't be there, but I have my suspicions.

CHIEF: So, there is a unit in my vicinity. Ya know, one man can create a lot of problems for me. A fully geared unit could make it much worse for both of us.

HUNT: If the unit dispatched from here, I'll take care of it on my end.

CHIEF: What exactly does *take care of it* mean, Hunt?

HUNT: Severed from communications, nothing in or out. Recordings will fail to upload into our database. As far as I'm concerned, they disobeyed orders. If they disappeared, no one will come looking.

CHIEF: Oh, you're gettin' me excited, Hunt.

HUNT: I don't care much for your perverted charades or playing Jesus to those vile creatures. If you think you have one of my men in custody, then consider it an offering. A sacrifice, if you will.

CHIEF: *(giggles)* A *sacrifice*. Nice sentiment.

HUNT: Whatever floats your ass. I want what's been promised. Are we good?

CHIEF: *(giggles)*

HUNT: Jack, are we good?

CHIEF: Aw, come on now, Hunt. You know better than that. Ask me again.

HUNT: *(sighs)* Chief, are we good?

CHIEF: There you go. No more interference, Colonel, or the gold will disappear too.

[End Audio]


*INVESTIGATOR'S NOTE: Flight logs recorded a HX Harpy had departed on the morning of December 1 and returned December 3. Its cargo and route were not registered. An interview with Sergeant First Class Benjamin Pavlov under oath revealed that he had disobeyed orders and secretly sanctioned the flight with Omega Unit to Springfield, Illinois to survey unusual radar readings. The members of Omega Unit are permanently sealed.*

# WEAK POINT

*Four Years Later*


*[Emergency broadcast tone.]*

*We interrupt our programming. This is a national emergency message from the acting President of the United States. Please remain tuned for further information. Repeat, this is a national emergency message. Please stay tuned for updates.*

*"My fellow Americans, it brings me tremendous grief to share that this morning, at 8:06 a.m., the President of the United States succumbed to injuries sustained after the collision of his motorcade along Route 25 from Colorado Springs to Denver, and died. Our thoughts and prayers are with the First Lady and her children, Noah and Charlotte. The details leading up to this deeply unsettling tragedy are under investigation by local authorities in cooperation with Homeland Security and Secret Service officials, and we ask for the full cooperation of citizens in observing decorum by avoiding the scene.*

*"Although our Constitution provides for the situation our great Republic finds itself in, no vice president wishes to or takes pleasure in invoking the 25th Amendment. As it is my duty, one which I perform with the gravest severity, I am committing to a smooth transition on behalf of the American people and our allies.*

*"These are challenging times, for our nation and for the world, locked in a conflict like no other before it, thrust into a war against dark forces so unnatural, so foul, that our humanity is on the line.*

*"We are a resilient nation, a united nation, an enduring nation. In these drastic circumstances, I call for your support in responding equally for our survival, for our victory, and for our future. We must*

*excise like a cancer the irreparable, and redirect efforts toward healthy cells.*

*"To this endeavor, effective Immediately, I am ordering the temporary evacuation of every state east of the Mississippi River. We will concentrate our resources along a united front, from north to south, linking the cities of Houston, Dallas, Oklahoma City, Kansas City, Des Moines, Minneapolis, and Duluth.*

*"For our citizens east of the Mississippi, organize among your communities and in accordance with the efforts of local authorities to travel west by any means reasonable. Your nation supports you as we mobilize FEMA to establish pick-up zones in thousands of locations across your region. I implore you to tune into local broadcasts for further instructions."*

*[A long pause.]*

*"My fellow Americans, we will not be defeated. We will fight back. And we will win. This is the beginning of the end for our enemy. May God bless you all, and may God bless the United States of America."*

*[Emergency broadcast tone.]*

*We interrupt our programming. This is a national emergency message from the acting President of the United States. Please remain tuned for further information. Repeat, this is a national emergency message. Please stay tuned . . .*

"You're really going to listen to that again?" Angelina 'Doc' Dorsey rolled over in bed, the sheets sliding off her bare shoulder.

Kane Garner glimpsed the soft curve of her back where it met her hip, following it down her thigh and calf to her wiggling toes.

She knowingly pulled up the sheets, poorly covering up, and peeked over her shoulder, clearly hoping Garner would take the hint.

He didn't need much of a hint. He shut off the nighttime broadcast, tossed the handset to the nightstand, and missed. Ignoring the fumbled device, he wrapped an arm around Doc and pulled her close.

"It just proves that no one is safe," Garner reflected momentarily.

"He died in a car accident," Doc said.

"Not a chance. It doesn't make much sense to lie to people. They could put coded messages in broadcasts that relay the truth. It's the only reliable communication people listen to these days," Garner said.

"How do you know they're not doing that already?" Doc asked.

"You think so?"

Doc laughed. "I'm teasing. How should I know?"

"You work in Central Ops," Garner pointed out.

"As a research medic." Doc rolled over to face him, throwing an arm around his neck, and proceeded to twirl her fingers through his long hair.

"Come with us," he tried, not for the first time. "We could use you in the field."

She frowned. "I'm under orders, remember? Not everyone gets to come and go freely."

"Free? There are more restrictions every day. I'm left out of debriefs, I rarely speak with Ben, all assignments pass through Gelly . . ."

"Poor thing. Stay here, then. Join me in the lab."

"I'd love to, but we're redeployed tomorrow."

"Tomorrow?" She leaned back a bit. "I thought you were staying for the weekend."

"The border wall changed the rotations—deployed a little longer, at base a little less," Garner said. "When I get back?"

Doc nodded. "I need to work anyway. We're doing another battery of tests on the wendigo samples. I've been asked to report on the results."

Garner cringed, and Doc frowned again.

"Sorry," Garner said. "I love it when you're passionate about your work. It's the nightmares," Garner said, trailing off. A dark shadow eclipsed the depths of his mind like a closet door slowly opened by an unseen force creaking in the dead of night. Something watched him from that abyss. He shook the darkness aside.

"No, I'm sorry, Kane. I forget how much it affected you and the boys." A broad smile crossed Doc's face. "Where does it hurt the most?"

Garner played along. "The pain starts at my neck."

Doc kissed softly, a flutter of a butterfly's wing on his neck. Her hair hinted at strawberries in summer.

"Then here next." He pointed to his temple.

She kissed him on the temple.

"That does it." Garner grabbed her. Doc screeched spiritedly as they rolled together between the bedsheets, wrapping arms and legs around one another.

Early the next morning, Garner kissed Doc on the cheek as she slept. She groggily waved goodbye. He quietly left the dormitory and headed straight for the hangar bay where his truck was being serviced among a dozen or more Hummers and military tactical vehicles. The shop was a 24/7 operation abuzz with air tools, grinders, welders, and high-voltage rock-and-roll blasting over the loudspeakers. His Nissan Titan XD balanced on the lift, its armor plating and oversized front wheels removed, looking like an open maw.

"What's the damage, Walt?" Garner asked from across the hangar bay.

A bearded man with greasy hands, smears on his nose and brow, and stains across his navy overalls waved with his wrench. "She needed brakes." He leaned into the Titan and turned the tool. "Tires. Alignment. Mods are done too. She'll be ready in twenty minutes."

Garner pinched his brow together. "Mods? What mods?"

Walt pointed with his wrench. "Stripped the armor plating, installed a second fuel tank, and added balancer. It'll triple fuel efficiency."

"Who told you—"

"I did." Corporal Tyrone 'Gelly' Gelloti approached the two men, dressed in standard-issue green camouflage, sporting a recent crew cut just the way the senior ranks liked it, and carrying a shatterproof tablet.

Garner unwrinkled his forehead. "New assignment?"

"Received last night. I didn't want to bother you, so I took some liberties with the truck," Gelly said. He respectfully hesitated a few seconds to let Garner disagree in some manner. When no argument came, he opened the tablet. The blank screen came alive with the tap of his finger. "You'll understand in a moment."

A formal digital document displayed on the screen with the TOP SECRET watermark angled across the background. A document issued by Sergeant First Class Benjamin Pavlov.

Garner was . . . what? Angry, jealous, envious? More like irritated. It was just another example of feeling out of the loop. Ever since Central Ops relocated from Kansas City to Denver several months ago, the organization had changed from an informal structure with decentralized decision-making to something far more rigid and hierarchical. The military communicated only with those who had sworn the oath of enlistment, followed orders, and respected the chain of command. Everyone else remained merely personnel or contractor, outside the lines of communication and on a need-to-know basis regardless of contribution. Since Garner had never enlisted, and quite frankly had no interest, he wasn't supposed to be seeing this document. His jaw clenched. He hated authority.

Still, Garner noticed his name alongside Gelly's as a recipient of the document even though he wasn't cleared to view it. The hypocrisy. Certainly, Ben's doing. He saw the nonsense firsthand, no doubt.

This was no way to win a war.

He set aside his frustration and finished surveying the document. "I've read enough, Corporal. It says your orders were to notify me immediately; thank you for giving me the evening. I approve of the truck mods, but do we really need a second fuel tank? I figure there's several depots along the way."

"There are, sir, and we'll need to refuel a few times along the way. The extra tank is insurance," Gelly said.

"Insurance?"

"Our assignments often . . . deviate from the objective. I'd like to make sure we get home. The extra tank is long overdue. Sir."

Garner chuckled.

"You'll be carrying eco-fuel in the reserve tank," he said waving the wrench. Garner had forgotten he stood nearby, overhearing their conversation. "Take you a thousand miles without needing refilling but volatile as hell. Fire or stray bullet? Boom." Walt motioned with exploding hands.

The two men stepped outside, away from prying ears.

"This is our third assignment either transporting or providing security detail." Garner rubbed his beard. "Where is our passenger?"

"With Wonderboy. You know the Major has a tight rein on things. The border wall is a big deal around here. Nothing moves under, over, across, or through without his approval," Gelly explained. "A lot of hurry up and wait."

"It's times like these I'd rather venture on my own," Garner contemplated.

"What's up, bitches?!" Casie 'Wonderboy' Edwards joined the two men.

"Specialist Casie Edwards, attention." Gelly saluted. "Congratulations on your promotion."

"Thank you, sir," Wonderboy said, returning the salute.

"You're still a douche, Wonderboy. Don't expect me to actually call you Specialist from here out," Gelly said.

"About that, I was going to change my nickname," Wonderboy retorted.

"Forget that shit!"

Garner ignored both of them. "You were supposed to accompany our guest."

"He insisted on breakfast. I told him we'd pick him up outside the mess hall," Wonderboy said.

"One day into your promotion and already screwing up orders," Gelly said jokingly.

"Oh, fuck off!"

"Are you two done?" Garner asked. It was delivered jokingly, but he was still feeling irritated. He couldn't wait to get off base and back on the road. "We leave in thirty minutes whether the professor is done with his milk or not."

"Where are we taking him?" Wonderboy asked.

"Des Moines."

Wonderboy groaned. "Nine hours sitting in a cramped, smelly truck with you assholes?"

"More like eleven hours," Garner corrected. "I'm planning several stops to refuel, and we should expect multiple encounters with Middle Earthers. We each take a shift. I want to arrive before dark."

"Speaking of which, we have a new prototype over at R&D to test in the field," Gelly revealed.

"When were you going to tell us?" Wonderboy asked sharply.

"I just did," Gelly replied. "Don't be a smart-mouth."

"I am a smart-mouth." Wonderboy folded his arms. "I was a teen champion on *Jeopardy!*"

"You came in last," Gelly said.

Wonderboy grinned from ear to ear. "So you did watch."

"I want to see it," said Garner. Then, suddenly realizing what he'd said, clarified, "Not *Jeopardy!* Sorry, Wonderboy. Gelly, I'll meet you at the R&D building. Wonderboy, get the professor."

Wonderboy sighed and trotted off.

"Casie!"

The specialist stopped in his tracks and looked back at Garner.

Garner caught up with him, extending his hand. "Congratulations."

A lopsided smile slid onto the specialist's face. He nodded and went to his task.

Garner met Gelly behind the R&D building. One of the delivery doors was raised. Gelly stood next to a large red camping cooler. A thin man in uniform quickly approached Gelly and handed him a clipboard, the attached papers fluttering.

Garner parked and jumped out of his truck as the uniformed man disappeared into the depths of the R&D building, clipboard in hand.

"There it is," Garner said, grinning as if it were Christmas Day. Once at the cooler, he eagerly popped the lid, nearly causing the whole thing to tip over.

"Easy. I just signed my life away, you know," Gelly said, wincing.

Garner remained silent, focusing intently on the device lying safely packed inside. Even down to the dull grey color, it looked exactly like Reynolds Sr.'s gauntlet prototype that Garner had turned over to the government in the early days of the War. It had the form of an arm, articulated at the elbow and wrist, and was twice as long as a human arm, spanning two feet at its widest point. To operate it, a person's entire arm slid inside one end. The other end of the device was where gollums met their doom.

"Where's the power?" Garner asked.

"For now, your truck's backup battery," Gelly said, pointing to a couple of ports where a power supply could be connected.

Garner started to reach inside the cooler.

"No, no," Gelly said, stopping Garner from touching it. "Military personnel only."

Garner scowled.

"I mean we should wait until we're off base, sir," Gelly said in a low tone, ensuring he wouldn't be overheard.

Garner slapped the lid shut. "Load it up, Corporal."

Moments later, Garner and Gelly idled in front of the mess hall. Wonderboy immediately appeared, trotting toward Garner's truck. A smaller man in his early sixties—balding, white goatee, and carrying an oversized leather briefcase—followed paces behind.

"We might have a problem," Wonderboy stated, gesturing to the man behind him as Garner exited the truck.

"Are you in charge?" the small man asked Garner while nudging Wonderboy aside.

"Depends on who you ask," Garner replied. "Kane Garner." He extended his hand, but the man didn't correspond. Instead, he hugged the briefcase a little tighter.

"I was told I would be traveling by helicopter. I am expected at the university today," the man said hastily.

"Well, Andrew—" Garner began.

"I prefer Dr. Bia or just Doctor, Mr. Garner," Dr. Bia corrected. "I have advanced degrees in medicine and genetics. I think I've earned the respected title. Don't you think?"

"You don't want to hear what I think. *Doctor.*"

"Perhaps not, as I can't imagine it's anything of significant substance that would occupy my attention for more than a minute," Dr. Bia agreed. "In the interim, we're wasting valuable time conducting this boorish pissing match."

Garner looked at Gelly and Wonderboy. Both men rolled their eyes.

"You're going to be fun company," Garner said. "All flights have been grounded today. Too much smoke in the air, low fuel—hell, maybe it's because the president was killed yesterday. Who knows? Our orders are to drive you safely to the university, and we currently plan to have you there before dark. You can either get in the truck, or we leave your smartass behind."

Dr. Bia pursed his lips, probably not used to being spoken to like that. "It seems I don't have much choice."

Garner opened the rear passenger door and motioned for the doctor to get in. "I can place your briefcase in the back."

"The case stays with me," Dr. Bia said abruptly.

"Suit yourself, Doctor," Garner said, then to Gelly and Wonderboy, "Let's move."

Gelly drove. Garner sat in the front while Wonderboy and the doctor shared the backseat. As they exited Central Ops, Garner plugged their destination into the truck's navigation system. The display map highlighted Routes 76 and 80—northeast through Colorado, east across Nebraska. They'd detour around the cities of Lincoln and Omaha, and arrive in Des Moines from the south within ten hours. Red pins dotting the map marked several locations for fuel along their route.

"The dashes," Dr. Bia said.

Garner had tilted his side mirror earlier so he could see Dr. Bia without turning around. The doctor was observing everything the men were doing without being too obvious but seemed unaware of Garner watching him back. The doctor continued to hug the briefcase tightly with no intention of relaxing his grip.

"Pardon?" Garner glanced over his shoulder, pretending to not give a shit. It wasn't hard.

"On the navigator. What are the dashes?"

Garner tapped the navigation screen and zoomed in on an area surrounded by irregular dancing dotted lines. "War, Dr. Bia. These areas here and here are active zones."

"Our route goes through them." Dr. Bia's concern rose.

"This vehicle can handle any terrain, and you have the best shooters escorting you," Garner said.

"Your assurance brings me little comfort," Dr. Bia said discontentedly.

Garner glared at the man. "You should try to get some rest, Doctor. We have a long way to go."

Three hours later, they crossed into Nebraska and reached their first fuel stop. The fuel depot offered little else except a restroom. Garner pumped the gas while Gelly and Wonderboy stretched their legs. Dr. Bia opted to stay in the truck.

Wonderboy pressed the palms of his hands into his temples, then fished through his pockets and retrieved an unmarked bottle of white tablets. He threw back three pills followed by a long chug of water.

"Headaches again?" Garner asked.

"Like you wouldn't believe," Wonderboy said. "Ever since Springfield. It's like that wendigo is in my head with an icepick, stabbing away."

Garner swallowed hard.

"That creature . . . it's all you talk about, man," Gelly interjected.

Wonderboy's eyes narrowed accusingly. "Doesn't it seem weird it doesn't bother you at all?"

"Who said it didn't?" Gelly replied flatly.

"Yeah? Maybe it showed you something," Wonderboy pressed.

"Get lost," Gelly said, waving him off.

A shade crossed Wonderboy's vision. "I want to know what that fucking thing showed you."

Gelly squared off with him. "Careful, Specialist Edwards, with how you address a superior officer."

Wonderboy clenched his fists. "Pulling rank already? I thought you weren't going to call me Specialist."

"Stand down, Wonderboy." Garner pulled the young man by the shoulder. "What the fuck's gotten into you?"

Wonderboy shrugged Garner off and stomped away toward the restroom. Garner and Gelly exchanged puzzled looks with one another.

Garner drove. Gelly settled comfortably in the passenger seat with a foot propped on the dash, and Wonderboy rejoined the doctor in the back. After twenty minutes back on the road, Dr. Bia was rocked to sleep by the drone of the tires scratching pavement and the boring, flat view along Route 80. Wonderboy wasn't looking so good, white as a sheet and clammy. He fought fatigue. Each time he closed his eyes, they shot back open.

"You OK?" Garner asked.

Wonderboy nodded, resting his head against the window glass, watching the unbroken prairie.

"The wendigo did show me something," Gelly offered quietly from the front seat. "But I already faced my demons long ago 'cause I killed the sons-of-bitches who were the source of my fears."

A long quiet followed. Then, from the back, "What happened to you?"

"In Chicago, me and my younger brother lived in the backseat of my mother's car. We made ourselves scarce when she was high or hooking or both. You learn fast about life on the streets. We fell in with a group of boys like us. Runaways, homeless, troubled in school and at home.

"At first it was cool. The gang. We watched out for each other, stole petty stuff, shared everything. We even gave ourselves a name. Night Raiders." Gelly spread his hands as if the name hovered in air before him.

"Later, a new member joined. Older, had done some time in prison and had all the ink to show for it. Fuzz. A real badass. Just like that?" Gelly snapped his fingers. "He took over the gang, and we let him. Because we were afraid of him. We did more stealing. Bigger shit: cars, trucks, break-ins. Ran guns and drugs too, all kinds. Collected protection money. We worked as messengers, delivering threats and sometimes pain to people who didn't pay. Then boys were being pimped. Some returned beaten, bruised, bloody. A few never came back at all. It was in the news that a body washed ashore. One of our own.

"One day, Fuzz sent my brother on a run up the Gold Coast, a delivery to this rich prick, stock trader. But the run was more than drugs. Fuzz had offered my brother. Two days. Two days, he was missing. When he finally showed up, he had been raped and mutilated. He needed a doctor, but Fuzz wouldn't allow it. My brother died in my arms that night. He was twelve. The next day, Fuzz went missing and the stock trader met the other end of a hatchet.

"You want to know what the wendigo showed me? That. It made me relive that all over again. And I welcomed it. I welcomed it because I got a chance to see my brother again. I welcomed it because there's nothing on Earth or in Hell that could top the horrors I have seen."

"Christ, Gelly, I'm sorry. That's horrible," Garner said sadly.

"How did you avoid jail?" Wonderboy asked.

Gelly shrugged. "I was finally caught for other crimes. Spent a few years in juvie. I paired with a parole officer who believed in second chances. A judge approved time served under terms that I join the army and keep my record clean."

"Gentlemen, I apologize for eavesdropping," Dr. Bia joined. "I am saddened to hear about your experiences, Corporal. Your capacity to persevere suggests a strong will and upstanding character. You are an honorable man."

Gelly thumbed back toward him. "How can you not like this guy?"

Garner grunted.

"I was not informed that you were the team that took down the wendigo," Dr. Bia said, perhaps his version of an apology.

"The government keeps its secrets," Garner said plainly.

"Dr. Angelina Dorsey and her team have been accomplishing amazing work that has resulted in several promising breakthroughs," Dr. Bia said.

Gelly laughed. "When did Doc become a doc?"

"By the time breakthroughs are weapons-ready," Wonderboy interjected, "this war will be over and humanity extinct."

"I understand your concern, Specialist. In the work of both labs, I assure you speed is a top priority," Dr. Bia said.

"Your assurance brings me little comfort," Garner said through the rearview mirror.

Dr. Bia nodded—a silent *touché*—but before Garner could enjoy it, something caught his eye in the mirror. He spun around in the driver's seat. "Did you see that!?" He quickly glanced in the side mirrors, then punched the center display screen to call up the rear camera.

Gelly and Wonderboy, fully alert, rolled down their windows. Gelly slipped into his window and sat on the door to look behind them. "I have visual!"

"Hold on!" Garner hit the brakes and cut the wheel hard into a U-turn.

"I see them!" Wonderboy confirmed. "How did they get this far outside the hot zone?"

Garner accelerated the truck, closing the distance between them and the two figures confirmed by his team. Both creatures walked through the middle of a crop field some distance from the highway. Garner stopped the truck across from them. The three of them jumped out of the cab.

"Give me some eyes."

Wonderboy jogged to him and placed a pair of binoculars in his hand. Gelly was already lining up the shot.

Two gollums paraded along the open field, one wearing an orange life preserver around its neck, the other carrying a long pole. In tow, a large dog tethered to a leash, trying to escape.

Dr. Bia stuck his head out the rear window. "My schedule doesn't permit for this, Mr. Garner."

The men ignored him.

"Target in sights," Gelly said, one eye looking through the scope of his rifle.

Garner handed Wonderboy the binoculars and went straight to the back of the pickup. "Wait. I want to field-test our new toy."

"Is this wise, sir?" Gelly asked, not budging. "I have them in my crosshairs."

"I'd rather know now than when it might matter most," Garner said.

As if on cue, the dog barked.

"We've been spotted," Gelly announced. "They're coming."

Garner threw back the top of the crate and lifted the device. It was lighter than he remembered and had only one power cable hanging. He threw off his jacket and rolled up a shirt sleeve. He slipped his arm into the device. The mesh sleeve hugged his hand like a glove and nestled his forearm and upper arm, thus ensuring contact with its tiny electric sensors. The power jack, he plugged into the outlet inside the pickup bed. Thin LED lines of blue and white illuminated the gauntlet in a useless stylistic design that R&D hadn't bothered to remove from the original.

"Hundred yards," Gelly reported.

Garner lifted his arm and aimed the lethal end at the oncoming gollums. They screeched and screamed, thirsty for new prey. He squeezed his index finger, imitating pulling a trigger. The end of the device heated instantly and released a charged bolt. It struck the shoulder of the gollum with the life preserver, vaporizing flesh and bone and sending foam bits puffing into the air. The injured gollum stumbled, crying and flailing in pain, its arm hanging on by a strand of charred skin.

He fired the device again. A searing bolt punched the second gollum through the ribs, opening the entire chest cavity and cauterizing the massive wound at the same time. Its boiled guts dropped onto the field and the gollum collapsed on top of them.

Garner cursed, wriggling his arm out of the device and dropping it on the ground. The firing end of the appendage had heated the metal white-hot. Sparks snapped out of the other end as it lay cooling on the ground. Red burns pocked Garner's arm like tiny polka dots.

"Garner!"

"The thing burned me." More sparks danced, and a tendril of smoke rose from the power jack connected to the truck. Garner yanked the cord free and nearly got shocked in the process. "How's that for a field test?"

The dog barked and leaped through the field toward them.

Gelly aimed his rifle.

"Hold your fire!" Garner raised his arm.

The large dog, a mastiff mix, ran right up to Garner. He snatched the dog's leash, holding the canine at bay while he checked it for any bites, scratches, or signs of infection. A little thin, and very matted, but . . .

"He's—nope—she's clean."

The dog proceeded to lick and sniff his hand, and he scratched her head and ears. She groaned and panted happily.

"What the hell were they doing with a dog?" Wonderboy asked.

"Food, I'm guessing." Movement across the field. "Feel free to finish that one off, Gelly."

"On it." Gelly fired his rifle, dropping the gollum with the loose arm. Both bodies steamed as the dying flesh broke down, melting and pooling on the ground.

"Let's get you some water," Garner said to the dog. He retrieved a water bottle from the cooler in the back of the truck. He twisted the cap and poured out a little, which the dog slopped up eagerly.

"Mr. Garner, must you be reminded of your orders? It is paramount I return to the university as quickly as possible," Dr. Bia said exasperatedly from inside the vehicle. "And don't think for one moment that mangy dog is coming. I'm allergic, you should know."

Garner grinned.

Moments later, they were loaded and cruising down the road. The dog shared the front seat with Gelly as Garner drove and fed her bits of jerky beef. In the backseat beside Wonderboy, Dr. Bia sniffled and sneezed occasionally.

The rest of the trip passed uneventfully.

Garner drove Wonderboy's shift, as he looked no less pale or feverish. The specialist rested, occasionally groaning and whispering in his sleep.

After passing checkpoints through two active zones, a couple more refuels, and an unplanned bio stop for the professor, they rolled into Des Moines shortly after dark.

The city had been miraculously spared from the earthquakes and the onslaught of Hell's spawn. The residents had responded quickly, preparing for a future no one had thought possible by fortifying the city limits. Since then, barriers and outposts had been extended to include Cedar Rapids, Davenport, and Dubuque, creating the largest safe haven in the upper Midwest and a model for the new president's vision.

The city was a beacon for tens of thousands of displaced people around the region. Many took life-threatening risks by traveling across the country to seek refuge behind its gates. Long lines stretched for miles along Interstate 35.

"Grubbers," Dr. Bia muttered, belittling the people camping on the side of the road. They had likely been waiting days to enter the city.

"They're Americans, just like you and me," Garner corrected sharply.

"Humanity must seek unification around a single purpose if we enjoy any chance of winning this war, Mr. Garner. The people of Des Moines understand that. No one gets in unless you have a purpose. Grubbers haven't learned." Dr. Bia made eye contact though Garner's rearview mirror. "Why else are you able to drive to the head of the line, to be provided food, shelter, and the defenses you need? Because you have a purpose, a usefulness. Sadly, these people do not."

"The sooner we drop you off, the better," Garner said, wanting to throw the entitled doctor out onto the street and let the *grubbers* handle him.

Was the War already at that point of discarding the indefensible, the weak, the vulnerable? Was it really survival of the fittest? Survival of those who had purpose?

The doctor's point was sadly proven when they were given clearance at their last checkpoint and instructed not to slow or stop for anyone even if they jumped in front of their vehicle. People young, old, and in between had settled along the roadsides. Entire families huddled together with few possessions beyond the clothes on their backs. Many craned their necks, watching the truck rush past. Thankfully, no one leaped in their path.

The gates to Des Moines lifted. Armed guards waved them through quickly while keeping a group of angry and desperate grubbers at bay.

Once beyond the gates, a white compact car with a sheriff's emblem on the side and yellow flashing lights escorted them through the deserted streets of the city.

"Where is everyone?" Wonderboy asked.

"Curfew, Specialist. Strictly enforced," Dr. Bia said.

They rolled through the abandoned streets, noticing more white cars with yellow lights parked or patrolling the city.

"Law enforcement is well-staffed and trained," Dr. Bia volunteered. "There hasn't been a felony in years. Anyone who breaks the law is swiftly processed through the toughest judicial system. No second chances, no plea bargains. In words you can better understand, do not fuck with the police."

"Lawyers?" Wonderboy asked.

"No need for lawyers. The rule of law has been simplified so that even a child can understand."

"Punishment?"

"We lack the resources to waste on prisons. Eviction is the only sentence."

"Sounds like communism," Garner said.

Dr. Bia scoffed. "The residents voted for these changes. It's what they wanted to feel safe."

Garner bristled. "Safe or controlled?"

"Does it make a difference?"

Spotlights lit a thick block of polished granite with *Drake University* etched into the tough stone. The campus occupied several blocks. Dr. Bia guided them across the grounds and had them stop in front of a three-story brick administration building with a curved entrance. A bank of windows dressed the front.

A young woman, tall, thin, and wearing a white lab coat and glasses, her dark hair tied in a neat bun, stood expectantly on the curb. She opened the doctor's door as Garner brought the truck to a stop.

"Thank you, Wen," Dr. Bia said as he exited. He wiped his nose and stuffed the handkerchief into a pocket.

"You are late," she said abruptly to the doctor in an Asian accent. She took the briefcase from him, the first time he'd allowed it to leave his possession.

"Yes, so it seems. Did you get the samples I sent?"

The woman nodded once. "Everything is prepped and ready."

"Very good." Dr. Bia turned to Garner and his men with a slight bow. "Thank you for your service, gentlemen."

The dog stuck her head out the window beside Garner and barked.

Both Dr. Bia and Wen flinched in disgust.

"Have a nice life, Andy," Garner said smirkingly while rubbing the dog's head and watching the doctor and his assistant disappear into the building.

"Garner," Gelly said, motioning to the police escort still parked in front of them. A wide-shouldered man in his forties exited from the driver's side, his white uniform tailored to fit his frame. He placed on his head a black cowboy hat that bore the same emblem displayed on the car, and adjusted the two handguns hanging from his belt. He puffed his chest as he approached Garner's truck.

"Here we go," Garner said softly. He recognized the stroll of flexing authority from his youth.

The dog barked. Garner pushed the mutt back into the rear of the vehicle with Wonderboy.

"Evenin'," the sheriff said, smiling broadly, black mustache stretching across his lip. "The name's Sheriff Rosco. You boys done good bringin' the professor all this way. Much appreciated."

Garner tipped his head.

"Seen much on the way up?" the sheriff asked, meaning any action.

"Picked up a stray," Garner said, thumbing at the dog.

He peeked through the window. "I see. Infected?"

"You and I wouldn't be speaking right now if she were," Garner said.

"Well, I suppose not. Listen, we got a place for you boys to stay the night over at Royal Motel, just off Route 163. We could use your help in Davenport tomorrow, border wall construction along the Mississ'. Grubbers to the south disrupting workers, greenbacks trying every which way to get their disgusting selves across. All a big cluster, if you get me."

"Our orders are to join forces southwest of here, Sheriff," Garner tried.

Rosco leaned in, grinning. His eyes were bloodshot. "Those orders were voided as soon as you crossed into my city."

"Figured as much," Garner muttered, noticing Gelly tapping on the navigation screen.

"Sheriff, there's a motel the next block over. Why are you sending us near city limits?" Gelly asked.

"I don't want our residents catchin' nerves unnecessarily, if you catch my drift," Rosco said.

"We leave tonight. Problem solved," Garner said, heat rising up his neck.

"Is that what you are, soldier? A problem?"

"Well, Sheriff, that depends on who you're asking."

A second white police car pulled up slowly behind Garner's truck, yellow lights pulsing. The dog barked in the backseat.

Sheriff Rosco's brow furrowed and he narrowed his eyes at Garner. "The deputy will escort you to the Royal. Help us, and we'll send you on your way in no time."

Garner gritted his teeth. "We already helped deliver the doctor, and even—"

"Even so, thank you, Sheriff." Gelly waved appreciatively. "We're a little tired and could use the rest."

Garner's blood boiled. He watched Gelly from the corner of his eye. Gelly often noticed things that the rest of the team didn't. He'd be foolish not to trust Gelly's instincts even if the reason wasn't yet apparent.

"You boys have a good night now, and thank you for your service." Rosco rapped on the truck. As he stepped away, he waved the deputy's car ahead.

Garner shifted the truck into drive, quietly stewing over the treatment from Dr. Bia and Sheriff Rosco. *Thank you for your service. Horseshit!* He'd be lying if he said he didn't feel a little resentment toward Gelly for cutting him off. Honestly, he was irritated with Wonderboy curled up in the backseat too. He took a few breaths to calm his thoughts.

"Was he high?" Garner asked, clearheaded enough now to realize what Gelly might have observed.

"Something like that. This town's wound tighter than a coiled spring," Gelly explained. "Security is over the top, but this region was untouched during the initial outbreak and the second wave."

"And why did we have to rush Dr. Charming up here? They're hiding something," Garner concluded.

"Perhaps."

The conversation trailed off, and the men traveled in silence. The deputy's car escorted them outside the city and soon turned into an empty Royal Motel parking lot. The deputy didn't bother himself to do more than stick his head out his window to say, "The manager will direct you from here, gentlemen." Then he drove away.

The dog barked. Garner grinned and rubbed her head and ears. "I couldn't agree more. Come on, girl."

The motel manager shuffled out of the office dressed in a dirty, lengthy tank top, loose boxer briefs, and mismatched slippers. "Room One is open," he mumbled.

"We'll each take a room," Gelly said.

"Hey, you can't—"

Garner's crew stared him down. "Is that a problem?" Garner asked tightly.

"No pets," the manager said, grumbling powerlessly.

"Therapy dog." Garner started unloading their gear.

The manager mumbled something Garner couldn't hear, then turned back toward his office.

Garner called to him. "The garage across the street. Is that yours?"

"Opens in the morning," the manager said.

"I need repairs tonight."

"Opens in the morning," the manager repeated, a little more firmly.

Garner jumped into the bed of his truck, retrieved a three-pack of warm beer, and extended it to the manager. "For your trouble."

The manager's eyes widened and his lips cracked into a brief smile. He snatched the beer from Garner's hands. "Key's above the door."

"That was my beer," Wonderboy complained after the manager had gone.

"And it's the last thing you need. You look like shit. Get some rest," Garner said. "Same goes for you, Gelly. That's an order."

"What are you going to do?" Gelly asked.

Garner lifted the crate that contained the gauntlet. "Find out what's wrong with the power supply to this thing." What he needed more than that was time alone. He didn't think he could sleep right now regardless.

It was after midnight. Garner was settled in at a long workbench with plenty of task lighting. The bench stood against the wall of the two-bay auto garage. It was clean and organized. Mechanical tools hung from evenly spaced pegs on the walls or were stashed neatly in a few dented red mobile tool chests. Neither the garage nor the dirt lot held a single car. Either the manager ran a quick-repair shop, or he had no customers. Garner figured it was the latter.

Earlier, he had found the makings for hot coffee sitting in the garage's small office, including a large stash of ground beans more than likely a forbidden horde rather than a tendered payment. Even better, in the top drawer of a metal desk, he'd discovered a mini music player loaded with a hundred or more country songs. Not his style, but music nonetheless. With a little ingenuity, he'd wired the old MP3 player to a single car speaker he'd yanked free from a junk bin.

He sipped his third cup of steaming black coffee, tapped his foot to the music, and again examined the metal arm, separated into peeled-open pieces spread across the workbench.

At Garner's feet, the mastiff woke from a noisy sleep as the office door opened and Wonderboy entered the garage. She growled and backed away slowly, watching the specialist the whole time.

Garner glanced up from his work. "Feeling any better?"

Wonderboy shrugged as he shuffled into the bay area. He dropped onto a short stack of worn tires piled next to the workbench. "I've never felt like this before." His hair was pasted to his scalp, his pale face shining with sweat.

"Bed rest," Garner said, returning to his work.

"Is that coffee?

Garner motioned toward the office. "Might have to drink it out of a hubcap."

A few moments later, Wonderboy returned, sipping loudly from a spray can cap. "What's wrong with it?" He nodded at the gauntlet.

Garner shrugged. "I can't tell if this was innate to the original design or something our engineers wired. My old boss, Reynolds, was a brilliant engineer. I find it hard to believe he would have used this design.

"The truck battery sends too much power into the converter. The exchange amplifies the power source instead of adjusting it. It's causing the converter to get too hot. A couple double-A batteries would be more than effective.

"The cycles per second, which indicates how much power it consumes, are too fast. Apparently, though, there's only one speed."

"I have no idea what that all means," Wonderboy said.

"Simple. A specific amount of power needs to align with the specific output, not too much, not too little. It's a horrible design. This thing could have fried my entire arm."

Wonderboy bent over. "I can't do this anymore."

Garner paused. "It's just the flu."

"No, I'm a liability."

Garner watched him for a moment. "You just got promoted. What are you saying?"

Wonderboy pressed a palm against his forehead and took a deep breath. The dog growled again. Garner nudged her with his foot.

"Look, I get it—"

"No, you don't!" Wonderboy raised his voice. Sweat rolled down his temple. "I can't get it out of my head. It never leaves me alone."

"The wendigo." Saying it left Garner's tongue dry.

"It tells me things," Wonderboy said softly.

Garner's heart rate rose. His immediate thought was that he had left his sidearm in the truck. Across the workbench was an assortment of mechanical hand tools. He slowly wrapped his hand around a screwdriver and hid it in his lap.

"What kinds of things, Casie?"

"Derek Stevens."

"I don't . . ."

"Sniper. Had the highest number of kills. Bragged about it all the time. He wanted to join our unit."

"He challenged Doc in a shooting match, didn't he? He died," Garner said, worrying over where this was going.

Wonderboy wiped his running nose. "It told me . . . everything. How to do it. When. I resisted the nightmares and pain until I couldn't anymore. I entered his barrack one night and swapped his long barrel for a defective one. The next day, his rifle exploded. Tore off his face."

Garner took a breath. Another. "What's it telling you now?"

Wonderboy dried tears and snot with his sleeve.

"Casie, what's it telling you to do?"

"I'm so tired," Wonderboy said, his shoulders slumping. "I can't do it myself. It won't let me."

"Angelina has been studying this thing since we took it down. Even Dr. Bia could have some insight."

"Yeah, maybe you're right."

"Gelly and I will handle Davenport to see what's doing. I'll leave you the med pack and the sat phone. Take what you need to get some sleep. Will you call Angelina?"

Wonderboy nodded, laboriously rising to his feet as if devoid of energy.

Garner stood with him, concealing the screwdriver by his side.

Onto the workbench, Wonderboy threw down Garner's handgun that he'd been hiding behind his back. "I can't be trusted."

Garner frowned as he watched him leave.

At first light, Garner exited his truck and stretched. The dog leaped out with him and did her business in the middle of the parking lot. After reassembling the gauntlet, he'd sat in the motel parking lot and remained on watch throughout the night, too worried about Wonderboy and what he might do. Gelly was coming out of his room now, ready and geared.

"Where's the kid?" Gelly asked.

"Sick. Gonna let him rest. It's just us. And her," Garner said. The dog padded over to Gelly, wagging her tail.

Gelly scratched her head. "She should have a name."

"Mutt?"

Gelly scoffed. "Anything else but that. Whatever you decide, she's a lucky lady. She could be roasting over a fire by now."

"Lady. I like it."

"Better that Mutt."

The two men and Lady departed the motel. Sheriff Rosco met them at the eastern gate, standing outside his car with his thumbs hinged inside his gun belt. His shirt was wrinkled and pulled loose from his pants.

"Long night, Sheriff?" Garner said jokingly, bringing the truck to a stop next to him.

"You're down a man," Rosco observed.

Garner clenched his teeth, already feeling the tension. "The flu. Needs a day off."

The sheriff glowered. "I spoke to your commanding officer, Major Hunt, this morning. He and I have an understanding. You're on loan until I see fit, yes? I trust you can find your way to Davenport."

"Yes, sir," Gelly said from across the cab.

"Well, alright. That's what I like to hear."

"Get on with it," Garner said, and abruptly swirled his hand.

"Listen here. Ask for Lieutenant Wayland when you arrive. He'll assign your duties. You'll report to him at the end of every shift. Are we clear?" The sheriff looked to Garner, who he'd watched the whole time he spoke.

"Should I even answer that?" Garner said.

"What you should do is mind some manners like your friend there," Sheriff Rosco scolded.

"You're not telling me anything I haven't heard my whole life," Garner said bitterly. He shifted the truck into gear, squealing the tires through the gated checkpoint.

The entire three-hour drive east along Interstate 80 rushed by without any incidents. There were no other vehicles on the road except armed Humvees parked at varying intervals, no doubt reporting to Rosco. Garner decided to keep quiet about last night's conversation with Wonderboy for now. They switched driving midway, which allowed Garner much needed rest.

"Lieutenant Wayland," Gelly said to the guard at the Davenport gate.

The guardsman, a day older than eighteen, radioed into dispatch. They were cleared immediately. "South on 61 until you reach the river. You'll find the lieutenant stationed by the Centennial Bridge."

Darker clouds had rolled in from the south, threatening rain. Davenport was a surprisingly bustling town. Businesses sold a variety of goods and services. People walked, shopped, and dined as if holy hell was someone else's problem. The streets were congested with cars going here and there, many not heeding basic traffic rules. Gelly was forced to brake hard at several intersections.

"A florist?" Gelly craned his neck.

"What delusion is this town suffering?"

They spotted the Mississippi River and the Centennial Bridge, or at least what remained of it. The National Guard's base of operations occupied a large parking lot and a former baseball field. A soldier directed them to where they should park. On foot, they found Lieutenant Wayland—fatigues, clean cut—standing rigidly with his hands resting behind the small of his back. He stared across the murky brown water. Air smelling of waste wafted. A light, cool sprinkle started to fall.

Wayland saluted respectfully as Garner and Gelly approached. "I was told you were coming," he said, grimly shaking both men's hands. "That son of a bitch Rosco called me at four in the morning. He and his little fuck-troop of badges think we're screwing things up over here. I'm assuming that's why he sent you." He hesitated a moment, trying to read them, his cool green eyes assessing. "Well, I hate to admit it, but that asshat might be right. We seriously can use any help we can get.

"You're Kane Garner," Wayland continued. "I've heard about you."

"Good things, I hope," Garner said, not having expected this kind of blunt reception.

"You saw the circus." Wayland swung his arm toward the town of Davenport behind him. "We detonated the bridge last week. President's order. You'd think people would get a fucking clue. This town worries me more than the terror across the water. Can you see them?" He jabbed a finger at the charred remains of Rock Island, Illinois, on the opposite side of the Mississippi River.

"Holy geez!" Gelly ran his hands across the top of his buzzed head, raindrops splattering. "There must be hundreds of them."

"Shy of a thousand, Corporal. Goblins. Greenbacks. Gollums. Whatever. I call them boogers, just like the snot rocket that shoots out your nose." Wayland spat. "More arrive every day. They're planning. I know it in my bones.

"Anyway, we got a couple things going for us. They don't like the water. Can't swim, or perhaps the water hurts them. Second, every bridge up and down the Mississ' has been blown off its pillars.

"On the downside, if they figure out how to cross—and I'll be damned if that's not what they're trying to do—we don't have enough firepower to stop their numbers. And I don't have enough able folks ready to fight. Half the town lives like a bunch of hippies. Peace and love and all that shit. The other half has their heads in the sand like Sheriff Rosco, believing themselves safe as long as they don't look across the water. Sheriff's got more resources keeping people out of Des Moines than pointed at the shitstorm brewing across the river."

"Grubbers," Gelly said.

Wayland frowned. "No way to treat fellow Americans if you ask me." He spat again and watched his spit hit the water far below the blown bridge.

"They want to build a wall a hundred fifty miles from here splitting the country in two. Dumbest goddamn fucking idea of the century. Here's your wall." Wayland gestured grandly to the Mississippi River. "A wall of water. They can't fly over it. Can't tunnel under it. All we'd have to do is keep 'em from crossing it."

"Lieutenant, how can we help you?" Garner asked.

Wayland held his breath and puffed his cheeks. "Any day we're expecting a shipment of supplies by barge. The drop takes every soldier on base to unload, meaning we take our eyes off the creatures.

Puts us at our most vulnerable. During the last shipment, the boogers got a little excited, don't ask me why. Several tried crossing on a makeshift raft and nearly boarded the barge. A floating highway if overrun. We need lookouts watching our backs, stopping any trying to cross. I got a stash of beer and can promise one per headshot. Of course, feel free to practice your long shot at will."

Garner squinted against the misty rain to look again at Rock Island. The horde packed along the riverbank was the largest gathering he'd seen. He had an uneasy feeling, as if the creatures were staring back at him, biding their time. Garner looked away. "Anything else until the barge arrives?"

"Some of our boys could use a break. Patrols are 'round the clock, five miles up and down the Mississ'. Report to base and get on the schedule. Welcome to use your own vehicle or one of our own. Watch for people crossing the river. Help if you can even though standing orders say otherwise. Whether people know it or not, we're going to need everyone to finish this war. Glad to have you here, gentlemen."

Wayland saluted, spun on his heels, and left the two men alone.

Garner watched the cloud-covered sky. The sprinkling rain had trailed off. The wind picked up from the northwest, keeping the air cool and the stink at bay.

"What are you thinking, sir?" Gelly asked.

"That we're right where I don't want to be." Garner rubbed his stubbly chin. "Boxed in. Been fighting a long time, and still have this kind of horseshit happening. When are people going to wake up?"

"Before this," Gelly said, "I served eight years overseas. Three tours. If the fight was somewhere else, people didn't care. Soldiers came back stateside feeling like heroes, but no one gave a shit."

"This fight is on their doorstep, for God's sake," Garner said.

"Depends on your point of view," Gelly replied. "You got the sheriff telling everyone they're safe, plus Wayland and his men show a strong presence."

"False sense of security."

"I don't disagree."

"Any ideas?" Garner asked.

"We're not changing anyone's mind here if that's what you're thinking. We should provide coverage when the barge arrives and bug out when it's done. Wayland won't force us to stay."

"He's a good man. Wayland."

"High morals," Gelly agreed.

"Do you think he'd leave Davenport?" Garner asked.

"Join with us? Hard to tell. He seems quite loyal even if he hates it. Could call in a favor from Major Hunt."

Garner nodded, pondering the idea some more. "Let me check in with Wonderboy. Can you find out where the barge docks and who's been in touch with its captain?"

"On it." Gelly jogged away from the bridge and was soon lost among the bustle at base camp.

'how u feeling,' Garner sent to Wonderboy.

'just woke up hungry thirsty,' Wonderboy texted. 'feels like a bad hangover'

'glad u havent lost appetite'

'what's the assignment there'

'supervision, muscle'

'waste of skills,' Wonderboy replied. 'do u think bia had anything to do with it? he didnt like us much'

'king shit cop flexing on us'

'roger that'

'join us tomorrow?'

'absolutely. wish I was there now'

'anything else I should know'

'unable to reach Doc. deputy in white car parked across the street'

'keep trying. lmk when you do'

[thumbs-up]

Garner returned to his truck to find Lady stretched comfortably on her back and snoring loudly in the pickup bed. She stirred with a snort as soon as Garner opened his door. She propped her head on the side rail, praying for a treat. Smiling, Garner dug into his pocket and fed her his last strip of jerky. She gobbled it up, not bothering to chew her food.

Wayland's base of operations and communications comprised a former strip mall and several adjacent mobile trailers segregating functions, with one reserved as the lieutenant's living quarters. Spread about the roofs, cables looped between them and satellite dishes stood high. A former Japanese restaurant, repurposed as the food pantry and mess hall, occupied the next block to the north, its neon red sign shining bright. To the south was a parking lot with military vehicles and equipment crowded together. A former Boys & Girls Club, now serving as the main barracks, medical, and training facilities, stood beyond that. The entire base was scaled to support over three hundred soldiers and personnel, yet it looked like Wayland led two-thirds that number. Probably he was losing to desertions faster than he could recruit.

Garner had been to Davenport once before in his life. It used to be a popular city of roughly a hundred thousand residents, one ranked as a great place to live by some polling agency for its good schools, progressive job market, and diverse businesses and restaurants. A place where people didn't have to lock their front doors. Today, the population was thirty thousand at best. The schools, businesses, and restaurants functioned, barely, and only naive residents left their homes unlocked every night. A wide river was all that separated them from a mass of creatures. If the city had to be evacuated, it was a hundred and fifty miles to Des Moines. Garner wasn't so sure Rosco would be welcoming either. Davenport was a pressure cooker with the ingredients for something bad to happen. He shook his head, hating every bit of the circumstances.

Garner leashed Lady, and they walked at a good pace northeast, past the base and the mess hall, finding a bike path that trailed parallel to the river. Lady stopped abruptly and growled. Her nose, high in the air, searched for the source. Her eyes leveled on the evil mass across the water. She growled again, squatted, showed them what she thought.

"Come on, girl," Garner urged, pulling gently on the leash after she finished. "You'll be a good early warning, that's for sure."

They walked for a half mile and discovered where the barges docked. A former yacht club, devoid of the typical maze of docks and expensive boats, had a wide concrete boat ramp that extended into the water. They spotted Gelly there, speaking with a woman outside the clubhouse. Gelly introduced them when they approached.

"Kane Garner, this is Major Amber Phillips."

They shook hands. Late twenties, short dark hair, brown eyes that hadn't seen a good night's sleep in an age, but alert and a firm handshake.

Lady joined the introductions and licked Major Phillips's hand.

"Oh, you're such a pretty girl." Phillips rubbed Lady's head and ears.

"Major Phillips oversees supplies coming into the city by river," Gelly continued.

"Mostly materials for the border wall," Major Phillips added. "Unfortunately, a lot of the things we need here get deprioritized."

Garner understood. "Major, when is the next shipment due to arrive?"

"Today, in fact. The barge made a brief stop in Muscatine yesterday, so it should have been here by now," Phillips said, looking downriver as though she should see it at any moment.

"Is that normal? The Muscatine stop?"

"It depends on what they're hauling. I'm guessing it's packed to the rims."

"How often do you get a delivery?" Garner asked.

"Varies, but every seven to ten days."

"You got that look on your face," Gelly said.

Major Phillips frowned, not following.

"When did the gollums start arriving?" Garner asked.

Phillips looked across the river. "An encampment formed two months ago, a dozen at the time. Their numbers rose rapidly after that, and doubled in the last week after the bridges were blown."

"Same time as the last shipment?"

Phillips nodded. "Sounds about right."

"Wayland said a band of gollums tried to board the barge," Garner continued. "Did you see them?"

"Yes. Four of them crossed the river on a raft of driftwood using long sticks to steer it. We didn't see them until they'd nearly boarded the barge," Phillips said, then paused. "Why do you ask?"

Garner rubbed his stubbly chin. "They might be smarter than we know."

"The barge," Gelly said, reading Garner's mind.

"Have you been in contact with the captain?" Garner asked Phillips.

"We've been trying all day though the silence isn't entirely unusual."

"Major, I think the barge has been overrun. Pray that I'm wrong," Garner said. "We should prepare for the worst."

Major Phillips stiffened. "I'm not sure what rank you hold, Mr. Garner. None by the looks of it. A contractor, yes? You're not uncovering anything that we haven't already considered ourselves. I have men stationed at Davenport's southernmost point ready to report on first sight. But beyond that, Lieutenant Wayland gives orders around here."

Garner grimaced. "We're on the same team against a common enemy, Major, and those gollums, if they haven't already, will try to cross the river again. Do you have eyes upriver?"

"I don't have the manpower," Phillips said. "What would I be looking for?"

"A bigger raft."

Phillips's eyes narrowed as she hesitated. She unclipped a small walkie-talkie from her hip. "Boyd, copy."

*"Boyd for Major, over."*

"I need eyes at Eagle's Landing."

*"Seriously? I'm the only one on patrol on Interstate 80, over."*

"Where's Carter?"

*"Sick."*

"Get Carter to pack a barf bag and report to duty, then get over there. Report anything out of the ordinary, over."

*"We'll be exposed up here—"*

"Do it, Boyd! And hurry."

*"Copy that."*

Major Phillips turned back to Garner and Gelly. "I hope you're right. My pants are down, and my ass is hanging in the wind."

"If I'm wrong, I'll take the heat. But if I'm right, this town is doomed if we don't pay attention," Garner warned. "Let's go, Lady."

"Where're you going?" Phillips asked.

Garner spoke over his shoulder. "I need to inform Wayland. We need a defense."


Two armed soldiers guarded the closed doors inside a ready room. Wayland and Garner, joined by Gelly, Major Phillips, and a slight man named Markus, stood around a square table with a large-scale digital map of Davenport and its adjoining towns hovering a centimeter over the smooth, white surface.

Wayland threw down a dry-erase marker after circling areas of vulnerability and drawing arrows showing defensive options. "It's not me you need to convince. There's a select committee that runs things here, and they answer to Sheriff Rosco. They don't do anything without his approval."

"You're shitting me," Garner reacted. "So in the event of an imminent attack, you need approval to warn everyone in town."

"The real problem," said Markus, "is that there's no proof of what you're suggesting, Mr. Garner. Our people have been through a lot. We don't want to cause premature panic over these things."

Garner glared at the smug prick. "Who are you?"

"I am the liaison to the select committee. We have laws and order here. It's what keeps our people safe."

Garner leaned across the table. "Well, liaison, your laws and order are going to get a lot of people killed."

Wayland cleared his throat. "Markus has been a valuable advocate voicing our needs. I'd much rather deal with Markus than with the twelve-member committee in their ivory tower."

Markus grinned. "Thank you, Lieutenant."

"That wasn't a compliment."

"Rosco sent us to help," Garner interrupted. "His standing order shouldn't need committee approval."

"He meant help with patrol rotations and cleaning the latrine, not sounding unfounded alarms," Markus said.

"Unbelievable!" Garner pounded his fist on the table, bouncing the markers. Heat rose under his collar.

Gelly placed a hand on Garner's shoulder, a gesture that said he wasn't helping matters. The room fell silent.

Garner stepped back, sighing. He wanted to throttle everyone in the room—especially Markus. Why couldn't they see the looming danger?

"I could petition the committee," Markus offered. "There's no harm in the request."

"How long will that take?"

"I'll file it after this meeting, and the committee meets in two days—"

"Two days!" Garner's temperature shot higher. "You have no fucking idea what's coming. Your false sense of security will get half of your population killed. The other half will be picking over their bones with the rest of the horde by the time your committee gets their asses at their roundtable."

"Mr. Garner, I don't appreciate your tone—"

"Tone? Would you prefer my foot up your ass?"

"How dare you!"

The room erupted.

Garner grabbed Markus by the collar. Major Phillips wrapped an arm around Graner's throat. The soldiers guarding the door clicked off their safeties.

Gelly unholstered his sidearm. "Careful now."

"Enough!" Wayland slammed the table. "Stand down!"

Garner released Markus and shrugged off Phillips, the soldiers resumed their post, and Gelly secured his gun.

"Rosco said you were hotheaded," Wayland said to Garner. "However, if rumors about you and your team carry even a bucket of water, I'd be a fool not to seriously take your advisement."

Markus balked. "Lieutenant—"

"Major, sound the civil defense alarm," Wayland said. "Instruct our residents to shelter in place until further notice. Inform me as soon as that barge appears. I want updates from upriver too."

"Yes, sir!" Phillips saluted, then departed from the ready room.

"A word, Lieutenant," Markus insisted.

Wayland turned to Markus. "It better be useful."

"Privately."

"Say it here," Wayland said, placing his hands on his hips.

Markus glanced disapprovingly at Garner and Gelly. "Sounding the alarm might cause a panic, don't you think? Think of the repercussions if the barge arrives without incident."

Wayland's face bunched. "Gentlemen, escort Markus off the premises," he said to the armed guards.

The soldiers swept Markus out forcefully, against his protests.

"The committee will not approve," Markus called out from the doorway. "Expect a call very soon, Lieutenant. I advise you answer it."

Wayland released a breath of air as soon as Markus was gone. "I haven't felt this good in a while. If this is what it's like in the field, then I'm missing out." He swallowed the last drop from a cup of coffee. As he gripped the edge of the table, he leaned forward, appraising Garner and Gelly. "I want a plan from you two. None of these boogers enter my town."

As dusk faded to nightfall, the supply barge was spotted motoring steadily up the Mississippi.

Unfortunately, the civil defense siren hadn't been sounded. The electric mechanism that ran the siren had been damaged beyond repair. Wayland vowed to find out how it'd happened when this was over. Instead, his men had improvised by spreading news of the order through word of mouth. They canvassed the town one block after another, hoping the residents would do the rest.

Wayland's direct phone had rung before dark. His brow furrowed as he listened. After another moment, the conversation ended abruptly.

"Everything alright?" Garner had asked.

"Rosco approved everything without question. That never happens. He said they had their hands full over there too. Then the call cut off."

It had sounded strange. Wonderboy entered Garner's thoughts. He'd been about to check in with the specialist when the barge arrived.

Garner secured Lady in his truck with a leftover bone from the kitchen. He joined Gelly on the Centennial Bridge as the barge appeared around the bend. Four sets of green and red running lights blinked intermittently, marking the corners of the barge. Gelly lay prone next to him, lining up his rifle shot, as Garner took up his night vision binoculars.

"Steel beams, aluminum plating, crates, sheets of wood, *damn* this thing is loaded. The deck is inches from the waterline," Garner observed.

"*Anyone see the captain?*" someone asked over comms.

The wheelhouse was positioned at the front of the barge. Garner saw movement from within but couldn't discern any details through its filthy window. The barge remained on course and continued up the river, traveling toward the Centennial Bridge.

"*I see him,*" someone else said.

A man stepped outside the wheelhouse. The barge whistle blew nine times, then the man disappeared as the barge passed base operations.

"Did you see that?" Garner asked. "It looked like the captain got yanked back into the wheelhouse. The door just closed. Something isn't right." Garner thought for a moment. "Major Phillips, over," he said into his comm unit.

"*Go for Major,*" she replied.

"How many whistles does the captain blow each time there's a delivery? Over."

"*Never—*"

Garner reacted. "This is not a drill! Nine whistles, that's SOS. I repeat, SOS. Stop the barge at all costs!"

Comms lit up. People started talking at once until Wayland imposed his authority and regained control.

*"Garner, repeat,"* Wayland said.

"Yes, sir. SOS. The barge has been compromised."

Weapons fire pummeled the wheelhouse. Red tracers ricocheted off the hull plating. The barge didn't slow or alter its course upriver.

"Garner." Gelly pointed across the river.

Garner peered through the binoculars again, adjusting the focus. The entire crowd of gollums that had been camped for weeks across the river was gone.

"Where they'd go?"

"I need eyes on that barge," Garner said over comms, grabbing Gelly by the shoulder. The two men left the bridge's overhang and sprinted across the parking lot.

"Major Phillips, do you read?" Garner said over comms.

*"Phillips here."*

"Do you see the barge?"

*"Coming around the bend now,"* she said.

"Wayland," Garner said.

*"In position,"* Wayland returned.

Garner and Gelly raced northeast along the bike trail, chasing after the barge. The clubhouse came into sight. Wayland's men were hammering the barge with automatic fire that the steel hull repelled, suffering nothing more than burn marks and chipped paint.

They joined Wayland, Phillips, and more than thirty soldiers standing on the concrete ramp that dipped into the river. The barge didn't stop; it continued upriver. Wayland ordered a ceasefire.

"Where's it going?" Wayland asked, as confused as everyone else.

*"Ah, Major? Boyd here."* The man's voice sounded shaky over comms.

Major Phillips frowned. "What do you got, Boyd?"

*"Sir,"* Boyd's voice quivered. *"About a thousand or more gollums gathered across the water. Um . . . what should I do?"*

Phillips pointed at four of the soldiers standing nearby and motioned for them to hustle to Eagle's Landing. "Boyd, do you see anything else?"

*"The barge is about to land on the opposite shore. All of its lights cut out."*

Phillips cursed. "Stay on comms, Boyd. Hang tight. A unit is coming to you."

"Don't send the full unit," Gelly advised Wayland and Phillips. "Half should remain here as a fallback—and in case this is a diversion."

"Are they even capable of such a tactic?" Major Phillips asked.

"Major, the creatures are far more resourceful than most people believe," Garner replied. "I agree a diversion is possible, but based on the numbers I do think it's a direct assault. They have the means and the organization to cross. If only a few escape into the town, this place will be overrun by morning."

Wayland nodded and turned to Phillips. "Major, order up your best units to join Garner and the corporal at Eagle's Landing."

"On it," Major Phillips said.

Wayland nodded. "If there's a fight tonight, we may be outnumbered but we'll make every bullet count."

A half-smile crossed Garner's face. "I brought something that might give us an advantage."

Garner and Gelly hustled back to his truck. Garner had it started, gas pressed to floor and rear tires spinning, by the time Gelly climbed into the passenger side. Lady circled the backseat, thrilled to see them, barking and happily slobbering faces. A convoy of hummers, pickup trucks, and vans sprayed gravel in their single formation race northeast along State Street. After a few miles, they turned onto an overgrown side street, tall grass and brush narrowing the decayed road. Abandoned commercial buildings appeared like block shadows on either side. As the buildings faded behind them, the Mississippi River appeared ahead.

Comms crackled with too many voices at once as soon as the vehicles arrived at Eagle's Landing and its small craft boat ramp. The sound of rapid gunfire echoed in the night. Sparks flew and crashed against a dark mass floating in the middle of the river.

"Cease fire! Cease fire!" Garner yelled over comms. He and Gelly leaped out of the truck. Lady barked, upset she'd miss the action again. Garner turned back and opened the rear door. "Come, girl. You deserve a spot in this fight as much as the rest of us."

"Boyd?" Gelly called.

"Here, sir." A young man, surely no older than twenty years, blond, sweaty, and wide-eyed, raised his shaky hand.

"Report," Gelly said.

"They're coming across!" Boyd said, pointing out the obvious. "They have plating protecting the front and sides of the barge. Our bullets keep bouncing off."

"Stop wasting bullets, then," Gelly said.

Boyd stood with his mouth open, looking to Garner and then back to Gelly. "I . . . I . . ."

"You what!?"

"Hold a minute," Garner interrupted. He waited for the soldiers and volunteers who had followed them to Eagle's Landing to run up and waved them close. "Does anyone have anything more powerful than automatics?"

"Six grenades."

"Flame thrower."

"Dozen Molotovs."

"Sir." Boyd raised his hand. "The riverbed."

"What about it?"

"The water is shallow on this side. If the barge doesn't land on the boat ramp, it'll run aground ten yards from shore," Boyd said.

The barge was slowly getting closer. They had to act fast. Garner's thoughts reeled.

"You think the creatures know that, don't you?" Gelly probed.

Garner nodded. "Major Phillips said the creatures used sticks to pole the river. They might have been testing the water's depth."

Gelly slipped a hand across his head. "Unbelievable."

Garner picked his head up to address a group of frightened and anxious faces. "Listen up! We can't let the barge reach shore. It's game over if they do. If one gollum escapes us, the entire town will be infected by morning. Your families, your neighbors, your friends, they have little chance of surviving the night. Our best option is to ground them and pick them off with everything we got. Choose your targets carefully. Every bullet must count when the shit hits the fan. We are in this together, and we will win. Are you with me?"

Some voices shouted in agreement. Some.

"Get your fucking head in this fight! I said, *Are you with me?*" Garner raised his fist.

Unanimous cheers responded. The crowd quickly dissipated to prepare for the fight.

"Boyd!"

"Yes, sir." Boyd saluted.

"Find two cars and drive them down the ramp into the water. Make sure they sink up to the roof. Form a kill box at the top of the ramp. Three vehicles on each side and three across. Hurry. We don't have much time," Garner ordered.

Boyd saluted, spun on his heels, and started shouting orders.

Garner sighed as the barge drew closer. The motor churned as it pushed the craft through the water. "What do you think?"

Gelly stood next to him, sighting the barge through night vision binoculars. "It's a good plan, sir."

"Oh, fuck that. Don't yes me, Gelly."

Gelly continued looking through the binoculars. "It has risks."

"Go on."

"The barge is heavy-duty," Gelly said. "It may roll right over the cars you have in the water. No guarantee it means to dock here either. We've got miles of shoreline between here and the yacht club. It could change course at any moment."

"Can your rifle put some holes in that plating?"

"Without a doubt, but they would be blind shots, fifty-fifty."

"Then we need to guarantee the creatures come to us."

"Some kind of bait."

Garner straightened while taking in a deep breath. He slapped Gelly on the shoulder. "Genius."

Garner returned to his truck. Lady trotted by his side. He dropped the tailgate and opened the crate containing the gauntlet. He threw off his jacket and slid his entire right arm into the appendage. A bar of blue light pulsed, then turned solid after a moment. Full power.

"Come, Lady. Let's make some noise."

Garner approached the boat ramp. The last few vehicles rolled up to the ramp, forming the kill box as he had ordered. Soldiers took positions behind parked vehicles.

He looked to the river and swore under his breath. The barge had made a slight turn south. Based on the angle, it wasn't going to land where Garner wanted.

He leaped over the hood of a vehicle. Lady executed the jump far more gracefully. He stood at the end of the ramp on the edge of the river. He whistled and waved his arms at the barge. Lady immediately barked, announcing her presence.

Garner yelled again and again. "Over here!"

Slowly, the barge shifted against the flowing river and motored straight toward Eagle's Landing. Thirty yards from shore and closing.

The front of the barge floated over the submerged cars. Metal scraped on metal, a spine-tingling noise worse than a fork squealing on a plate. Then, at once, the barge halted. It was high-centered, teetering on top of the cars. The outboard engine revved, spitting water. It couldn't forward or reverse. It was stuck.

Lady barked viciously. Garner pulled her back from the river's edge.

"Light 'em up."

Three men ran down the ramp, brandishing large wine bottles stuffed with flaming rags. They launched the Molotovs. Each arched over the armored plating like bottle rockets on the 4th of July and smashed onto the deck of the barge with bursts of fire. Flames flared. Shrieks and screams echoed in an instant panic.

"Again!"

Three more fiery bottles found their targets. Creatures covered in flames leaped off the barge.

"Take 'em!"

Bullets tore into the gollums thrashing in the water until they stopped moving altogether, each body floating lifelessly. The remaining Molotovs doused the barge in gasoline and fueled the growing inferno. Screams and shrieks escalated into a frenzy.

"Be ready!"

An aluminum panel detached from the barge. A funnel of creatures frantically poured out of the opening, escaping the blaze only to eat a volley of bullets. They fell like dead wood; others contorted wildly in the water, easy pickings.

Lady's barking turned ferocious. A wave of creatures was thundering across the floating dead toward land. The dog twisted out of Garner's hands and charged into the approaching gollums. There was no use calling her back; Lady had fixed her own revenge to wage.

At last, Garner fired. The gauntlet's electrified bolt punched through three gollums, liquifying flesh and bone. With no time to admire his handiwork, he put the weapon to further good use. An oversized gollum leaped from the back of the closest downed creature and charged up the boat ramp, directly toward Garner. Bullets grazed the advancing behemoth, hardly slowing it. Garner stumbled backward and fired a wild shot at the creature. The creature stumbled. Garner cursed, thinking he'd missed. Then it face-planted. The bolt had bored through its head.

Numerous creatures successfully crossed onto the boat ramp, but none escaped the kill box. Their numbers dwindled fast. Bodies piled. Lady did her part by tearing the throats of those that dared come near her.

Garner pushed the gauntlet to its limit and fired one bolt after another, draining the power fast. Creatures fell two and three at a time, but with only a few bolts remaining and the fight nearly over, he retreated behind the kill box.

"We've got soldiers searching the shoreline to ensure none got past us," Gelly said, joining him as the rest of the team picked off the last of the nearby gollums. Blood dripped down the corporal's cheek.

"What happened to you?" Garner, concerned.

"Bullet fragment. Nothing serious. A couple men got hit in the crossfire."

"Get them back to base," Garner said, fumbling to get the device charging in the pickup bed.

"Already on it."

He nodded toward the smoking barge. "What do you think—how many kills?"

"Maybe a few hundred."

"Exactly. Where's the rest of them?"

Their answer came a little too late.

Comms crackled. "*—under attack—*"

Weapons fire echoed distantly.

"The yacht club!"

Garner pressed his earpiece. "Wayland! Come in!" Static sizzled loudly through his earpiece. "I can't get through. Boyd!"

"Here, sir!"

"Select ten men to stay here with you to clean up. Comb through the bodies. Make sure every creature is dead. Everyone else, back to the club! Go!"

Their forces sprang to their vehicles and hightailed it out of Eagle's Landing. Garner, Gelly, and Lady followed. Dangerous speeds on the highway, followed by a series of hard turns down side streets, deposited them into the parking lot of the yacht club. High-mast lights illuminated the boat ramp and the extensive battle underway there.

A mass of the missing horde had reached shore on a variety of rafts cobbled from building materials. The rest, crowded on other rafts, stabbed long poles into the bottom of the river, propelling the overloaded rafts toward the club.

Wayland's men fired everything they had. Some gollums fell but many escaped injury, swarming the boat and crossing the firing line. A few of Wayland's men went down, bitten or scratched before their attackers met their doom.

A large raft packed with thirty or more creatures threatened landfall.

"Hold on!" Garner said. He leaned on his horn. Soldiers scurried out of the way as his truck broke the line, powered down the boat ramp, and struck the raft head on in a few feet of water. The raft broke apart on impact, dispersing its occupants.

Gelly leaned out the passenger window, claiming every creature that climbed onto the truck. They tumbled off the hood, slipping under the river's current as quickly as Gelly could pull the trigger.

Garner reversed, leaped out of the cab and into the bed, and sleeved the gauntlet again. With the power fully restored, he fired at the flailing creatures. Electric bolts burned flesh and evaporated water to steam.

Across the ramp, another raft landed. Ten more creatures leaped onto shore, followed by another fully loaded raft. Major Phillips and her team met them head-on. The creatures scrambled up the ramp. The soldiers panicked and fired shots wildly. Nearly overcome, Phillips ordered the soldiers to pull back.

Gelly, eyes on Phillips, dropped two creatures—both headshots exploding bone and brain. Garner made quick work of the next four, which never saw their deaths coming.

It wasn't enough. Three overtook Phillips and her men. Thrown on her back, Phillips fought against one that had pounced on her. Claws raked the air inches from her face. She punched and kicked.

Shots rang out. The creature was suddenly flung aside. Wayland stepped over Phillips and emptied his handgun into the creature.

"Get up, Major!" he yelled. "We're not done yet." He gave her a helping hand.

"They're drifting away," someone yelled.

Dozens of rafts indeed continued downriver, their foul occupants impossible to count in the darkness, impossible to neutralize effectively.

Garner gritted his teeth. They could land on shore anywhere.

"Garner. Corporal. With me." Wayland waved over both men.

Wayland led them to a beached marine patrol boat. The three men shoved it into the water, jumped in, and entered the cabin. The engine started with a roar, jetting water from the back.

"Let's end this," he said.

Wayland engaged the throttle forward. The boat reared and skimmed over the river's surface. Two bright spotlights, one positioned on the bow and the other atop the wheelhouse, illuminated the murky river through the dark night.

They spotted the first raft, a small one with five creatures watching the boat approach. Gelly raised his rifle for the first shot.

"Save your ammo, Corporal," Wayland said.

Wayland kept the boat at a constant rate of speed, aiming directly for the raft.

"You better hold on to something," he said to the two men.

Within feet of the gollums, Wayland spun the wheel hard left, then hard right. The patrol boat circled the raft twice before straightening out. The resulting cascade of turbulent waves swamped the raft, tossing the five gollums overboard.

Wayland repeated the maneuver with several other small crafts. Garner and Gelly aided by slugging any of the gollums that surfaced. The larger crafts posed no challenge either; Gelly targeted the creatures working the long poles while Garner disintegrated the ropes keeping the rafts tied together. One after another, gollums plunged into the freezing river, surfacing as motionless, putrid blobs.

The men cruised the riverbanks searching for lingering threats until morning. By the crack of dawn, Wayland had swept five miles of the Mississippi.

They reconvened at the yacht club. Lady paced and barked in the truck, overjoyed to spot Garner. A serviceman freed her, and she jumped into Garner's arms as he was climbing out of the boat, knocking him back into it.

Garner rubbed her head and neck. She licked his face and pawed his arm as he clambered free of the boat. "Good girl."

One of Wayland's men, wide-eyed and pale, met the group at the top of the boat ramp. "Sir, it's Major Phillips."

The serviceman leashed Lady and they all rushed into the clubhouse and down a flight of stairs to the basement. Armed soldiers stood guard at the landing. Several more guarded a chain-link cage at the center of the basement. Inside were three people, all in a similar stage of transformation.

"Amber," Wayland whispered. He staggered toward the cage but was intercepted by two soldiers. He scowled. "Let me pass!"

"It's not safe, sir," one of the soldiers said. "Your orders."

"Jesus Christ!" Wayland rubbed a hand through his hair.

From behind the chain-link, Major Phillips turned her head at the sound of Wayland's voice. Her eyes were severely bloodshot, snot ran out of her flattening nose, and dark veins surfaced through her thin grey skin.

"Lieu . . . ten . . . ant . . ." Dark drool oozed from lips turned black and blue. She turned toward her arm and pulled back her sleeve, revealing a deep scratch from wrist to mid-forearm, swollen and ablaze with infection. She shivered.

Wayland dropped his head. Keeping his distance, he knelt, dropping eye to eye with Phillips. "What can I do?" he pleaded, wiping away tears.

"H-h-hurts," Phillips said, slightly above a whisper. She scratched the top of her head and came away with a large clump of hair. As she absentmindedly set her hair aside, her blackening eyes settled on Wayland's waist.

"Please," she said softly. A single tear rolled down her cheek.

Wayland looked down at his sidearm and shook his head. "Dear God, no." He rocked back on his haunches, sniffing back tears.

Garner stepped forward beside Wayland. "Sir, you don't have to be the one to do this."

Wayland threw back his shoulders with a deep breath and stood abruptly. "No! It is . . . my duty."

Garner and Gelly left Wayland and returned to the first floor. Three shots sounded like pops. After a few moments, Wayland trudged up the stairs, his head hung low.

"Garner, Corporal, see to the clean-up efforts, mind you? I'll be in my quarters," he said, and walked out of the clubhouse.


The barge captain had perished; otherwise, they counted no additional human causalities. The rotten egg stench of liquified gollums spoiling on the boat ramp soured what should have felt a more victorious atmosphere. Power washers wielded by silent soldiers blasted away blood and goo. The rest of the day was spent freeing the barge, towing it to the yacht club, and unloading what remained of the raw building materials that were its intended cargo.

Garner was riding on empty. He hadn't slept or eaten in over twenty-four hours. Frequent cups of coffee and the determination of the brave soldiers and personnel helping with ongoing tasks at Eagle's Landing and the yacht club kept him going.

With Major Phillips gone, Gelly pulled rank over Wayland's men. He dismissed half of the soldiers to eat and rest; the other half he organized into a rotation of guard duty, food, and showers. He ordered one soldier to escort Garner to a private room with a shower, and to deliver him a fresh change of clothes and a meal.

"He's not to be disturbed until morning," Gelly added.

"It's a little much, don't you think?" Garner argued.

"Private, shoot him if he doesn't comply with my orders," Gelly said.

Garner raised his hands, surrendering.

The soldier drove Garner and Lady down the riverside trail straight to the Boys & Girls Club. Training and medical took up the first floor, barracks the second, and private quarters and a lounge the third.

Garner was led to his promised private room with an attached bathroom. It had a twin bed with fresh linens and a comfortable pillow, a writing desk, and a solid dresser. His ready bag waited for him at the foot of the bed.

He tested the shower and grinned when the water turned hot. Though eager for the shower, a soft knock at the door stopped him. A cart stood outside his door with a sandwich, soup, corn, soda, and a dish of dog food. Lady gobbled her food and settled under the bed.

Garner marveled at the Coca-Cola in his hand. When was the last time he'd had one of these? He popped the tab. The sizzle of carbonation sounded so much like . . . *normal*. He guzzled the bubbly drink, following it up with the loudest belch he could muster.

He showered, letting the steam develop into a dense fog. The hot water cascaded soothingly over his head, easing the tight muscles of his neck and back, dirt and grime swirling around the drain. He dressed into fresh clothes and collapsed onto the bed. He slept soundly through the rest of the day and into the night.

He startled awake in the early morning when frantic pounding rattled his door.

"Des Moines is under attack!"

Garner flew out of bed, and Lady whimpered. He sprung open the door, but no one was there. He laced his boots and shouldered his ready bag.

"Come, Lady," he called.

He had a pending text from Gelly requesting his presence. A meeting was in progress in the ready room. Garner informed Gelly he was on his way.

Within minutes, he'd joined Gelly, Wayland, Markus, and a new face and the tallest man in the room. Garner beelined it for the fresh pot of coffee as Wayland introduced Lieutenant Commander Jackson. Lady made the rounds, sniffing everyone's ankles before finding a spot in the corner of the room and lying down.

"Lieutenant Commander Jackson is my newly appointed second-in-command, taking Major Phillips's place," Wayland said matter-of-factly. He presided over the meeting, looking cooly over the men around the table. He had a fresh shave, neat hair, and a clean uniform pressed crisp. Any hint of sadness from the prior day was gone.

"We received a distress call from Des Moines early this morning," Wayland said. He pressed a small remote in his hand, aiming it an electronic panel across the room.

Audio began. A man's voice, panicked.

"*Bird Nest to Goldfinch, do you copy? Goldfinch, this is Bird Nest. Do you copy? Fuck! Is this thing working? Do you read? Mother fucker! We're under attack. Repeat, under attack. The mother fuckers got out . . .*" [Shots fired.] "*They're in the building.*" [Scream.] "*Shut the fuck up! They can hear you, dumbass! Goldfinch, assistance required. Send everyone you got. Ah, fuck! Get back!*" [Shots fired; guttural cry.] "*Go! Get out—*" [Static.]

Wayland's lips firmed. "From dispatch. There's an emergency line to the police station accessible via our telecoms. We haven't been able raise anyone there since."

Garner glanced at Gelly.

"Specialist Edwards isn't answering either," Gelly said.

"The committee has authorized us to send every able citizen, Lieutenant, to assist Des Moines," Markus spoke, favoring a swollen lower lip and a bruised jaw.

"Now we have authorization," Garner said. "Nice job, liaison."

"I don't need to be taunted," Markus pushed back.

Wayland slammed a fist down, silencing them.

"We have no idea what's happening over there," Gelly interrupted. "Sending troops would leave Davenport completely exposed and, if the city has fallen already, waste our meager resources."

Lieutenant Commander Jackson nodded. "Losing one city is better than losing two."

"The corporal and I will go. We have one of our own already there," Garner said. "We'll regroup with him and report on the city's status. If it can't hold until backup joins us, it's likely not possible to save it anyway."

"I'm coming," Wayland said.

"The committee will not agree," Markus objected.

Wayland turned to Jackson. "Lieutenant Commander, I place you in charge and relieve myself from duty."

"Sir?"

"Base operations and personnel are yours to command. Fresh leadership is needed more than ever."

"Thank you, sir." Lieutenant Commander Jackson looked as shocked as everyone else in the room, but he quickly composed himself and saluted.

"Only the committee can approve such decisions," Markus objected, voice raised.

"Would the committee perhaps show more interest in hearing the story behind the civil defense alarm's vandalization?" Wayland asked. "No doubt the reason your face looks so pretty today."

Markus turned red. He snarled at the men around the table and, finding no supporters, appealed to Jackson. "Arrest him!"

Jackson laughed. "Leave, Markus, or I'll have *you* arrested."

"How dare you! On what grounds?"

"On the grounds that you're an ass. Leave now."

Markus huffed. His face twisted as he stormed out.

Garner nodded at Jackson.

"Every moment counts, gentlemen," Wayland said.


The three-hour drive to Des Moines commenced with quiet anticipation. Gelly slept with Lady's head draped across his lap. Wayland occupied the passenger side, alert and ready. He offered to share the driving, but Garner refused.

Halfway through the trip, with only static coming out of Des Moines, Garner broke the silence. "Why'd you do that back there?"

Wayland raised his eyebrows. "It wasn't so spontaneous. Major Phillips and I talked on many occasions about succession when the opportunity came. Defending a city isn't easy. In this war, every attack requires our victory. The enemy wins only a single time? Game over. I've been here since the beginning. Yesterday brought the worst. We got lucky. That, to me, meant the time had come to step aside and give the reins to someone else.

"I'll be honest, the night on the boat energized me. I'm forty years old. I don't want to sit back waiting anymore. I'd rather spend the days ahead of me taking the fight to the enemy."

Garner nodded. "Major Phillips was special to you. I'm very sorry."

"If it's OK with you, Kane Garner, I'd rather not talk about it."

Garner shrugged and focused instead on the barren road ahead, but it didn't stay deserted for very long. They spotted a few evacuees pushing e-scooters down the middle of the road. Three teenagers, dirty, sweaty, and each carrying a bulging backpack, waved them down.

"Don't go dat way, mister," one of the teens, wearing a blue shirt, warned.

"What happened?" Garner asked.

"Sprites are back," said another teen, this one wearing a grey and orange camouflage jacket.

"We heard sprite screams last night. Fuzz flyin' up and down da streets. We ain't hanging around," the third teen said. He wore an oversized SWIFTIE sweatshirt.

"Yeah, fuzz wouldn't let us leave. Closed da gates, dey did," said blue shirt.

"Den more people had da same idea," camouflage teen said.

"We were da first though," SWIFTIE said, tapping his head. "Street smart."

"Dat sounds douchey," camouflage teen said.

"Fuck off with you," SWIFTIE teen said.

"Any idea how many? Did they come from inside or outside the city?" Garner asked.

"People or fuzz?"

Blue shirt teen swatted camouflage teen. "Da sprites, dumbass."

"Oh, look! Hi, doggie!" SWIFTIE teen waved to Lady, who poked her head excitedly out the back window and whined.

"I ain't seen no dog in a long time," camouflage teen said.

"Cut it!" blue shirt teen interrupted the two from jabbering on, then turned back to Garner. "We ain't seen any sprites, only heard dem."

Wayland leaned toward Garner. "We're not getting anywhere."

"Get yourselves to Davenport," Garner said, waving them away.

"Hey mister, can we bum a charge?" blue shirt asked.

Garner nodded. "Make it quick."

The teens took turns boosting their e-scooters from the truck's power reserve and rode away, continuing east.

After several miles, they spotted more people fleeing Des Moines, some with just the clothes on their backs, others carrying children and choice belongings, and several pushing overburdened carts, wagons, and wheelbarrows. Garner spotted one man pushing a wheelchair loaded with bottled water, canned food, and a suitcase burst partway open to show clothes and shoes and tools. Soon after, he saw another man tackle him from behind and take ownership of the haul. Not minutes after that, he was overcome by two others.

Many shouted warnings as Garner drove by. He knew better than to stop and risk someone trying to hijack his truck.

They approached the city's first checkpoint. The gates hung open and the station stood abandoned when at least two guards should have occupied it. The grubbers usually camped along the road were gone.

Garner rolled slowly through the checkpoint. "Stay alert."

Gelly stirred awake in the backseat. He checked the two shotguns he had brought. Wayland prepared his two handguns, cocking one and placing the other on the dashboard.

"Nothing from Wonderboy," Gelly reported, looking at his tablet.

"I can't raise the sheriff or dispatch either," Wayland said, disgustedly tossing his mobile into the center console.

"We'll swing by the motel first," Garner said.

Lady licked his cheek and tried to climb into the front seat. Garner rubbed her neck, assuring the nervous dog.

The sight of the empty streets hit Garner harder than he'd expected, an effect he knew traced back to how unchanged Des Moines had seemed despite the War. A siren wailed in the distance—

the city, apparently, still had power—and the caustic odor of burning plastic and charred wood hung in the air.

"People are hiding in their homes," Gelly said, pointing subtly to a few disturbed window shades.

The truck bounced into the Royal Motel's parking lot. The three men exited the truck, but Wayland stood beside it in case they needed cover. Gelly hoofed it to the manager's office. Garner hurried to Wonderboy's room and pounded on the door.

"Wonderboy!"

No answer.

Garner bashed the doorknob with the butt of his rifle, then kicked in the door. He rapidly assessed the room: a pillow on the floor, the bedsheets tossed aside, dead mobile on the nightstand, gear piled in the corner, no weapon in sight. The specialist had left in a hurry.

"Garner!"

A dried crimson handprint on the office's glass door welcomed Garner as he joined Gelly. The stale air stank of iron. Behind the counter, blood saturated the rug, an overturned chair, a coil of tattered rope, and shredded clothing. More covered the rear wall.

"What do you think?" Garner asked, his throat suddenly dry.

Gelly used the barrel of the shotgun to pick up a long, blood-stained tank top. "Manager's."

Garner had a sinking feeling. "Where the hell is Wonderboy?"

Gelly and Garner exited the manager's office as a loud screech echoed from blocks away. Lady barked and clawed wildly at the window from inside the truck.

Wayland pointed west, toward the heart of the city, as all three of them climbed back into the truck. "Let's check the police station."

"There!" Gelly pointed after they'd traveled slowly a few blocks.

A white police car had barreled over the sidewalk and crashed into a telephone pole. The driver's door had been left wide open, and the light bar on top pulsed weakly in blue and red. A smudge of blood marred the driver's window.

"Let's keep moving," Garner said.

They spotted the first body face down in the middle of the street, a shirtless man soaking in his own blood, his entire back peeled open and exposing his broken ribs and spine.

"Jesus."

Garner steered slowly around the body. He followed Wayland's directions to the police station, stopping at a four-way intersection though not a soul braved the streets. The traffic lights flashed yellow.

Directly ahead, the station had taken a beating. Something had smashed the entrance doors. Bits of tempered glass sparkled on the steps and sidewalk like diamonds. An office chair hung partially through one of the windows.

*Pop! Pop!*

"Over there!" Wayland gestured to the right, pinpointing the fired shots.

Garner gassed the truck toward the source. They found no one, no evidence of a gun. Several blocks later, thickening smoke flowed through the deserted streets, the chemical fumes now more concentrated. The polished granite etched with *Drake University* appeared on their left. Garner drove onto campus, remembering how Dr. Bia spoke so arrogantly of the city's security as if they could never fail. The irony.

"What are we doing here?" Gelly asked.

"Hoping for answers," Garner replied. "Have you ever met Dr. Bia, Lieutenant?"

Wayland shook his head.

"He's a hoot."

Garner weaved through the narrow campus roads. Something horrible had happened here. Shredded and stained clothing dotted one of the manicured lawns. Tire tracks crisscrossed the grounds. One set led to a green van crumpled against a large dumpster, the second to a campus vehicle that had sideswiped a tree from the looks of it and vaulted over a short stone staircase before rolling onto its side.

Gelly jumped out of the truck to check for survivors, a shotgun tight against his shoulder. He reported both van and car empty as he climbed into the pickup bed. "And blood everywhere," he also told them.

As they rounded one of the residence buildings, the dining hall came into view. It had been hollowed out by fire. The roof had collapsed, likely squashing the fire and stopping its spread, but the damage had been thorough. Several bodies, blackened and burned beyond recognition, lay near the entrance. How many more had been trapped inside?

A gunshot sent the men for cover. The truck's bulletproof rear window deflected the bullet that narrowly missed Gelly.

"Hold on!" Garner floored the truck across the grassy common. The back wheels ate into the earth, spitting soft soil. He didn't slow until they'd driven long enough to outrange whoever had shot at them. Shortly, they idled toward the college's administration building where they had dropped off Dr. Bia a few days ago. They did not expect the chaos that had occurred here.

Five police cars, parked hastily, sat in front of the building, flashers running and doors ajar. Bullet shells littered the ground. Pockmarks dimpled the cars and the building's brick face. Several windows were blown out on the first floor, and black smoke rose from the third story.

Lady whimpered and shook in the backseat.

"You stay here, girl." Garner rubbed her head and chest, then turned to Wayland. "Ready?"

Feeling too exposed in the open, they geared quickly and headed straight for the administration entrance, weaving single file through the police vehicles. Gelly led, one shotgun pointed, the other strapped to his back, plenty of shells for both. Garner covered their flank with an automatic rifle. Extra magazines and the gauntlet waited their turn in his pack. Wayland watched their rear, grasping his handgun in both hands, his second holstered on his hip. Before entering the building, Gelly pointed to the spent shells around the entrance and inside the door.

"Military grade," Gelly said.

"Wonderboy?"

Gelly shrugged. "If it was him, I can't tell if he was fighting with the police or against them."

Garner's brow furrowed. "Let's keep going."

They filed carefully into a dim lobby with no power, its auxiliary-illuminated exits and stairwell foreboding. Their boots crunched over bits of shattered glass in what sounded like miniature explosions against the tiled floor.

At the reception desk, a slumped body. Gelly touched the end of his shotgun to the person's head. A little nudge, and the chair rolled back with a clatter, the young man's dead body flopping to the floor like a rag doll. His throat had been ripped out.

"Booger?" Wayland asked.

"Haven't seen anything like this before," Gelly explained. "They bite and scratch to drive their numbers. When hungry, they don't leave leftovers."

Slowly, Garner lifted a lanyard with a security card from around the man's neck. "Guess we're letting ourselves in today."

"This way." Gelly led the men over to the stairwell, following the damage and spent shells. Bullet holes peppered the metal door, now Swiss cheese, and gouged the tile.

The men rushed through the door, crowding the landing, and paused as the metal door latched closed behind them with a resounding thud. Auxiliary lights buzzed in the confined space.

"Up or down?" Wayland asked. Sweat rolled down his brow.

"Down." Gelly led them swiftly and quietly. At the next landing, one of Rosco's men lay crumpled, his neck turned unnaturally.

Garner examined the young officer. "No bite marks or wounds. I'm guessing he tripped or got pushed down the stairs."

"Poor bastard."

Several spots of blood splattered on the second subfloor landing along with a bloody handprint on the railing drew them farther down. The stairs ended on the third subfloor at a metal door, magnetically locked.

Garner produced the security card and held it against the black square pad next to the door. Inside the doorjamb, a bolt clicked. Garner grabbed the handle and motioned *Ready* at both men. He swung it open swiftly and rushed inside after Gelly and Wayland.

The basement looked to rely on a separate power supply. They entered a brightly lit hallway that branched in three directions. The area smelled of death. Bullet shells covered the floor, skipping across the concrete as the men stepped through them. Two more of Rosco's men lay dead a few paces from the door, jaws dislocated and throats gone. A short distance away, a third body, face down, had its spine pulled out through the back of his neck.

"This is no way to die." After a closer examination of the bodies, Gelly rose to his feet. "Still think these are gollums?" he questioned with a scowl on his face.

"Could it be . . .?" Garner asked fearfully. He couldn't spit out the beast's name that stirred deep, the disturbing nightmares.

*Wendigo.*

"No," Gelly said quickly, preventing Garner from completing his thought. "We put that terror down for good."

"Should we split up, each take a hallway?" Wayland asked.

"No," both Garner and Gelly said simultaneously.

"We're up against something new, maybe an experiment gone wrong," Gelly said. "We stay together."

"Which way?"

"Center," Gelly pointed.

The hallway took a slight bend. Bullet marks scarred the wall, proving Gelly's choice correct, and ended at a set of locked double doors with a bank of elevators on the right. Garner swiped the security card. The magnetic bolt clicked and an entry buzzer sounded.

The men filed through the double doors silently. They entered an elaborate lab laid out in a grid pattern. Square task rooms grouped by fours were separated by thick plexiglass walls and passages in between. Each room was white and airtight, and each held an examining table, sink, white cabinets, articulating task lamps, monitors, microscopes, beakers, and vials. Tubes connected vents to transparent tanks of varying sizes, and blue and red rubber hoses hung from pressure valves. The chlorine pungency of bleach stung Garner's nose.

A few of the ceiling lights were blown; others hummed annoyingly as they flickered. One panel of plexiglass from the nearest lab had shattered. Inside, a corpse on the examining table dripped blood.

"Oh shit! That's Rosco," Wayland said.

The lab's steel and glass door rested askew on its hinges. The men walked inside cautiously.

Sheriff Rosco's torso had been stripped bare. Four jagged lacerations crossed his chest, the flesh and muscle split and exposing his ribs. Large blood-soaked bandages clung to the body while several more sat discarded on the bloody floor. Red fingerprints coated every surface in the room.

"They tried saving his life," Wayland said sadly.

Garner searched the room trying to not step in blood—or anything else for that matter. A white countertop rested against one wall, cabinets below and above, a discarded syringe. Multiple rolls of gauze on the floor remained in their packaging. Another one, opened in a hurry, trailed across the lab, unraveled. A built-in desk contained a monitor, keyboard, and a handheld tablet.

He knuckled the tablet. The screen awoke. It took him a moment to realize he was watching a real-time video feed from above Rosco's body. He could see Gelly and Wayland standing on both sides of the table.

"Look at this," Garner said.

The men huddled around.

Garner swiped the screen. A digitized console appeared, including a dial. Garner turned the dial counterclockwise with his finger, skipping backward eight hours. The video showed an empty lab.

"Too far?"

He turned the dial clockwise, skipping ahead to about four hours ago when the feed showed movement. Two people rushed Sheriff Rosco, injured and bleeding, onto the examining table.

"That's Bia and Wonderboy," Gelly said.

"Any audio?"

"No."

Dr. Bia handed Wonderboy a pair of scissors, mouth moving with instructions. Wonderboy cut apart the sheriff's stained and shredded shirt, exposing the man's fresh wounds. Blood pulsed from the massive cuts, weakening him every passing moment. Bia stepped off-camera. Boxed bandages flew into view like Frisbees. Wonderboy frantically opened the bandages and placed them on open wounds. Bia reentered view, opening bandages as well. Both men's hands turned red as they tried to plug the wounds. Bia grabbed Wonderboy's hands and relocated them to the worst gash. The doctor injected something into Rosco's arm; his eyes snapped opened wide, his chest heaved, and his body convulsed. Blood spewed from his mouth and nose, coating his face. At once, the convulsing stopped. Rosco's entire body relaxed. Dr. Bia climbed onto the examining table and started compressions. After several moments, he stopped.

Using the stock of his rifle, Wonderboy butted Dr. Bia off the table, knocking him to the floor. Bia spoke rapidly, bloody hands raised in defense. Wonderboy pointed his rifle at the doctor, yelling. It was impossible to know what either of them said. A flash! Glass exploded into the room. Wonderboy fell forward into the examining table. Dr. Bia cowered, covering his head and face. Wonderboy turned and fired his rifle at something off-camera, then ran out of the room. After a few moments, Dr. Bia peered cautiously in that direction. He, too, then left the room in a hurry.

"Christ."

"We need to find both of them," Garner said, throwing down the tablet.

The first lab ended up the lesser of the tragedies the men discovered that afternoon. The adjacent lab was in complete ruin, equipment smashed and scattered across the floor, cabinet doors ripped off their hinges, blood smeared on the glass and walls. A coed in a blood-stained lab coat stared lifeless from the floor, a bite mark on her leg and a bullet wound through her head.

"Someone did her a favor," Gelly noted. The men moved on.

The next three labs, though in order, held a different horror. On their examining tables, abandoned mid-procedure, autopsy patients waited. All humans, all in the early stages of transforming into the vile creatures. Flayed skin exposed muscle and bone. Cracked open abdominal cavities yawned wide. One subject had the top section of his skull removed. Scalpels, bone cutters, and other implements had been dropped on the floor or left carelessly beside the bodies. Clear glass jars on carts near the examining tables held extracted organs and tissues. A personal device on one countertop played music. Even though the doors were closed, the rotten egg stench hit strong.

Across the hall, more labs contained infected humans in the later stages of transformation and in various phases of dissection. One didn't seem to have been cut open yet at all. This one, the men inspected.

"I—I don't see a bite or scratch mark," Wayland observed.

Garner nodded. He'd already suspected, and this body confirmed it. "They were purposely infecting people."

Wayland scowled in disgust. "You really think—why would they—"

"How else would you get this many test subjects? One captured gollum tears itself apart. Two captured gollums, very risky."

"Grubbers." Gelly cursed. "Dr. Bia said no one gets into the city unless they have a purpose."

"I can't wait to meet this asshole," Wayland said.

"The sheriff had a role too," Garner surmised. "His men controlled who entered. He trafficked the victims."

Another trail of rifle shells led them to a lab at the end of the aisle. Beyond the shot-out glass slumped two technicians, dead from multiple bullet wounds. Liquid goo coated the examining table and the floor underneath it, the ammonia odor prevalent.

"Is there video?" Wayland asked.

Gelly ducked through the destroyed glass wall, careful not to step in creature goo or blood pools. He returned with the tablet and searched the footage. This one had captured audio.

*A man, strapped down, naked, and sedated, was wheeled into the room by the two technicians.*

*"Case 23. Subject: male, 45 years, 1.7 meters tall, approximately 88 kilos," said the first technician.*

*"I thought he was a hundred kilos. Fuck. The dosage is wrong," the second technician said.*

*"I'm not bringing this fat-ass back to the Bay. Adjust the dosage here," the first said.*

*"I told Dr. Bia one hundred kilos."*

*"Shoot some of it out. Let's get on with it. I'd like to eat sometime today."*

*The second technician held the syringe up to the light. "Dumping two units." He walked over to the small sink, then returned to stand over the patient. "Injecting wendigo toxin."*

*Making no attempt to clean or swab the site, the technician stabbed the syringe into the man's arm and emptied its contents.*

*The two technicians turned at the sound of gunfire.*

*"What was that?"*

*More guns fired.*

*"What should we do?"*

*The technicians ducked behind the examining table.*

*The man on the table twitched, fingers and toes now rigid. The injection site swelled red. His eyes opened and rolled back, showing only the whites. Sweat covered the surface of his skin. His chest heaved, then fell into an irregular breathing pattern. The man groaned, alerting the technicians.*

*"It was too much," the second technician said. "Terminate the subject. We're getting out of here."*

*The first technician flung open one of the cabinets, then proceeded to the next one, then the next. "It's not here!"*

*The man on the table underwent a rapid and extreme transformation. His skin stretched. The veins beneath rose to the surface as if under suction. Each rib bulged up and pressed against skin thin as tissue. Both cheeks sank into the contours of his skull, now elongated and thickened. The man thrashed, struggling against the straps. One across his chest snapped.*

*The technicians saw something or someone outside the lab and leaped back against the cabinets in fear, forgetting the monstrosity on the table.*

*Gunshot! Glass sprayed into the room.*

*The creature grunted and fought for freedom. It rolled its head in agony, the nose and jaw disproportionately stretched, one eye now shrunken down to a small black orb while the other, clouded, moved without seeing.*

*Several more gunshots followed in rapid succession. The creature flopped and died, and its flesh started dissolving immediately. Both technicians, struck by stray bullets, collapsed to the ground, dead.*

Garner and Gelly looked at each other.

Heat rose up Garner's neck. "Angelina had Wonderboy collect samples from the wendigo."

"We don't know Doc was involved," Gelly said.

"I can't think about this right now." Garner said, gritting his teeth. "We find Wonderboy and get out. I'm going to burn this place to the ground."

They left the labs behind and entered another section of the basement. The rank smell of sewage and excrement struck them before they found two holding cells. An old man and a young boy sat in one, two women, forties, in the other. A couple of five-gallon buckets were the extent of their amenities.

"What in God's name is going on?" the old man asked, rushing to the bars as soon as he saw the men.

"How long have you been here?" Gelly asked.

"Three days, we think. We were promised food and shelter," the old man said, indicating the boy and two women were with him. "We would have never entered the city if we knew it meant sitting in a jail cell."

Gelly shook his head. "It's not jail."

"Have you seen anyone else?"

The old man shook his head at Garner's question. "Have you? We heard gunshots and screaming hours ago, and they took my son Rand for an exam this morning."

"It's not safe here," Garner said, avoiding the question and thinking of the man in the video. He swiped the security badge across a square pad, opening both cells. "Past the labs, up the stairs. You're not going to like what you see, so best to move as fast as you can."

The old man left quickly, the boy and both women jogging alongside him.

A dull explosion from the upper floors vibrated the foundation. The lights flickered.

"Let's double back," Garner said to Gelly and Wayland.

The three men returned to the labs and turned down an unexplored aisle. Partway down it, a splash of blood on the floor. They followed a trail of bloody footprints to an automatic rifle.

"Wonderboy's," Gelly said. He picked it up and checked the magazine. "It's loaded." He ejected the round in the chamber, then slung the rifle over his shoulder.

"There!" Wayland said.

A line of private offices. A foot stuck out of one.

"Stay alert," Garner said as they advanced.

"G-Garner?"

"Casie!" Garner ran.

There Casie was, on his back fighting for every breath. He coughed blood.

Garner shouldered out of his gear and knelt next to him. A quick assessment revealed a large wound along the side of his head where his ear should have been. Two puncture wounds in his chest seeped blood.

Wonderboy's eyes fluttered, taking too long to focus on Garner. He smiled weakly. "I knew . . . you'd come."

Garner swallowed the lump in his throat. "Who did this?"

Wonderboy shook his head. "The pain . . . voices . . ." He coughed, wincing. "I . . . I tried to stop it."

"You did what you were trained to do."

"P-pocket," Wonderboy said, fingers flicking up to indicate his jacket.

Garner gently patted Wonderboy's jacket. From inside the liner, Garner retrieved a vial containing a black substance.

"I'm sorry . . ." Wonderboy struggled to keep his eyes open. "So tired . . ."

"Casie! Stay with me," Garner said, shaking him softly.

Wonderboy's eyes went wide, and he grabbed Garner's arm like a vise. "When is . . . people . . . not what see . . . see . . . *seem.*" He released Garner's arm, gasped for air. Then the tension left his body.

Garner wiped his nose across his sleeve. He blinked back the pools forming in his eyes. "He's coming with us," he said stoically after gathering the courage to face his team.

"I'll carry him, sir," Gelly volunteered, no hesitation.

Their job wasn't done. Here, in Dr. Bia's office, the briefcase he'd held so dearly during their trip from Denver to Des Moines sat open on the desk. Several official papers stuck up from the upper pocket, a stamp with the presidential seal visible.

Garner lifted them free to see the signature of acting President Landon Barnes.

"What is it?" Wayland asked, looking over Garner's shoulder.

"I think this place was sanctioned by the president. Look. Inventory requests, shipments, budget approval. Some project called Cerberus."

"The three-headed dog."

"This one's dated from before the former president died," Garner realized.

Gelly unzipped a separate compartment and handed Garner a journal filled with scrawl. He flipped through some of the more recent entries.

"Listen to what Bia wrote. *Patient Zero continues to show remarkable adaptation to the wendigo toxin, exhibiting heightened senses, intelligence, and agility. Replication in subsequent subjects has resulted in disastrous results, with the last possible synthetic permutations exhausted. The source material partitioned to us runs low. Developing the specified amino structures will require additional testing. Request meeting with Landon to cease all weapons development in Denver and ship remaining source material to Des Moines. Request helicopter transport!*"

"That's fucked up," Wayland said.

"Help!" A woman, screaming from down the hall.

Garner gathered up papers, the journal, and a laptop, and stuffed them in the briefcase. He led the men out of the office and into the hallway, where smoke now drifted lazily.

"Quickly."

Down the hall, a right turn, a left turn into a cafe lounge.

There. Two gollums, cornering a young woman.

"Lieutenant," Garner said.

From behind and in quick succession, Wayland shot the first and Garner the second. Both dropped, not knowing what'd hit them.

"Are you hurt?" Garner asked the woman.

"No," she said, nearly in tears, her lab coat ripped and stained with blood. "Please help Dr. Bia."

"You're Wen, yes?"

She nodded, adjusting her frames.

"Where is he?"

She pointed to the doctor on the other side of the cafe. He'd fallen behind an overturned table and strewn chairs, unconscious and in a feverish sweat. Scratches and bites covered his body, signaling his inevitable, irreversible transformation. Veins bulged beneath his pale, clammy skin, already black near his wounds, the color spreading like a spiderweb.

"I'm sorry, Wen," Garner said helplessly.

She wiped the tears rolling down her cheeks, wrapping her arms around herself.

"We have to go." Garner guided Wen and the others out of the cafe.

As soon as Wen noticed Gelly shouldering Wonderboy's body, she pulled back angrily. "He did this. He killed them."

Smoke continued to smother the breathable air.

"Focus," Garner urged. "Is there another way out?"

Wen, perhaps realizing their dire situation, nodded. "Follow me."

Through a set of double doors, Wen called for the freight elevator and pressed for the first floor once they'd piled inside. The elevator deposited them in a shipping and receiving area. An emergency exit led them outside.

The fire, which had consumed the entire third floor, spread now to the second. Fine by Garner. They rounded the building, avoiding falling embers, and returned safely to the truck. Lady was in a fuss, scratching and crying inside the cab. Garner let her out. She froze, growling at Wen for a moment, then trotted to Wonderboy's body, sniffing and whining.

Garner retrieved a spare gas tank from the back of the truck and filled it with the highly volatile eco-fuel. He tore a piece of cloth and stuffed it into the spout. He returned to the freight elevator, placed the gas tank inside, and lit the cloth. He reached in to press the button for the basement and tossed the vial of wendigo tissue from Wonderboy in as the door closed.

He bolted for the truck, waving for everyone to take cover. A second later, the unstable fuel exploded. The foundation cracked and shook. The building heaved. Every window blew out.

Glass rained down. Garner shielded his head. Then something struck him from behind and pinned him to the ground. Rough hands clamped around his neck.

Lady reacted. She charged toward Garner, leaped over his head, and attacked. At the same time, a gunshot blasted and blood sprayed Garner's face. Lady and the extra weight flew off his back.

"No!"

When he rolled over, Lady had Wen by the arm. A fatal bullet wound gaped in the woman's head.

"Lady, leave it."

Wayland walked over to them, extending an arm to Garner.

Garner let himself be pulled up. His ears rang. "What the fuck?"

"It's what the specialist said. Your dog sensed it too." Wayland squatted next to Wen's body. Both her eyes were black as night. Her teeth had grown long in their sockets, each hand into a lethal claw.

"Bia's notes," Gelly said. "She was Patient Zero."

Wayland nodded. "The specialist said, *When is people not what seem*. The brain gets scrambled in the last moments of life. Doesn't make any sense sometimes. He meant to say, *Wen is not what she seems*. She killed those officers. Your man was trying to stop her."

"Christ, Wayland, maybe a heads-up next time," Garner said.

The lieutenant shrugged. "I figured she might attack you first. A calculated risk," Wayland said.

"Bia was a fucking madman," Gelly said.

"He didn't act alone," Garner said.

They turned to face the administration building. Flames licked and dark smoke billowed. A great deal of satisfaction washed over Garner to see millions of dollars of equipment burned to ash, putting an end to the human experimentation. Yet anger and bitterness clouded his thoughts. Government secrets still undermined this war, he knew this.

Worse, he wasn't sure what he'd do if Angelina played a part.


They remained in Des Moines for a few days, shoring up its borders. Witnesses reported several gollums roaming the city leaving carnage in their wake. Under Wayland's command, a dispatch of volunteer fighters ended their killing spree, bringing a fractured sense of calm to the once confident city. No longer would they think the War a distant worry.

Communications with Davenport reestablished, Wayland's team contacted Lieutenant Commander Jackson, who agreed to send a couple units as reinforcements and aid patrols.

On their last day, Garner and Gelly buried Wonderboy in the veterans cemetery. Lady whimpered from time to time, her head resting on her front paws.

Standing over the specialist's grave, Gelly shook his head. "He kept that vial for years."

"The creature haunted him from the start. The headaches, short disappearances, it explains a lot about Casie's behavior. He fought a private war, too proud to say anything," Garner replied.

Gelly bowed his head.

Garner looked across the cemetery. The uniformity of the white headstones issued a sense of peace, but it reminded him of how war takes its toll. The burden of Wonderboy's death rocked his world. He should have known.

                    Declassified by order of the
        Governor of the West North Central Territory
                            Declass No.: 3549


# TRANSCRIPT



**SUBJECT**
Des Moines, Iowa Incident

**DATE, TIME, PLACE**
07-11-2040, time as indicated, locations as
                    indicated


*[The following is a chronology of Specialist Casie
Edwards' known actions leading to the Des Moines
Incident collected from several CCTV videos or
surveillance otherwise noted. Footage location is
noted.]*


**TIME:** 2:14 a.m.
**LOCATION:** D.G. Auto Repair, 921 Cycle Drive
Three goblins walk along Cycle Drive in front of
Royal Motel. One minute later, Deputy Roger Wilkinson
speeds into the Royal Motel parking lot. He exits
his squad car and knocks on Room #1. Specialist Casie
Edwards answers the door. They have a brief
conversation. Edwards disappears into his room and
returns armed. Both Wilkinson and Edwards leave Royal
Motel together.

**TIME:** 2:28 a.m.
**LOCATION:** Easton Boulevard and East 40th Street
Deputy Wilkinson's car veers off the road and crashes
into a utility pole. A green van speeds away. The
driver cannot be discerned. A moment later, Edwards
is running westbound on Easton Boulevard.

**TIME:** 2:45 a.m.
**LOCATION:** Des Moines Police Outpost, Easton Boulevard and Ford Street; CCTV video in black and white.
A van drives along Easton Boulevard at increasing speeds, and crashes through the front entrance of the police outpost. A figure exits the driver's side and attacks officers drawn to the accident. Weapons fire at the attacker.

**TIME:** 2:51 a.m.
**LOCATION:** Des Moines Police Outpost, Easton Boulevard and Ford Street
Specialist Casie Edwards arrives at the police station. He fires his weapon while entering the building. He walks off-camera. Four minutes later, he walks backward into the frame firing his weapon in short bursts. A figure rushes him and knocks him down. The van backs out of the lobby and disappears off-camera. Edwards fires his weapon at the fleeing vehicle. Three squad cars arrive. The officers surround Edwards. Edwards surrenders to the officers.

**TIME:** 4:23 a.m.
**LOCATION:** Des Moines Police Station, Court Avenue
Edwards leaves the police station from a side entrance. He takes a squad car and drives north. *[Note: Number 8 is marked on the side of the squad car.]*

**TIME:** 4:46 a.m.
**LOCATION:** Corner of University Avenue and 13th Street
Squad car 8 driving westbound at a high speed. Two squad cars pursuing.

**TIME:** 5:09 a.m.
**LOCATION:** Food pantry on University Avenue
Squad car 8 and green van driving eastbound at high speeds.

**TIME:** 5:15 a.m.
**LOCATION:** Private residence on Carpenter Avenue

Green van driving westbound with squad car 8 tailgating.

**TIME:** 5:19 a.m.
**LOCATION:** Drake University campus
Green van speeding through campus nearly collides head-on with a campus vehicle. Green van crashes into a dumpster. The campus vehicle bounces off a tree, careens over a staircase, and rolls onto its side. Staff arrive at the accident. A figure exits the green van moving swiftly and attacks the nearest person. The figure chases other staff off-camera. Squad car 8 enters frame and stops moment at the accident scene for less than one minute, then proceeds off-camera.

**TIME:** 5:33 a.m.
**LOCATION:** Drake University campus, 3rd floor residence; footage collected from personal recording device of [REDACTED]. *[Note: Footage handed over on condition of anonymity. The identity of the owner has been redacted.]*
A figure enters the dining hall. Squad car 8 arrives. Edwards exits the vehicle and enters the dining hall. Several flashes (presumed gunfire) are seen through the windows. Black smoke emits from the entrance doors. Edwards stumbles out of the entrance. He falls on his hands and knees, gagging. He rises to his feet, re-enters the squad car, and drives off beyond the handheld device's frame. A moment later, four squad cars follow. Several people burst out of the dining hall, each on fire. *[Video cuts off.]*

**TIME:** 5:44am
**LOCATION:** Drake University, Administration Building
A dark figure moves swiftly across campus grounds toward the administration building. A squad car chases with an automatic gun outside the driver's window firing at the figure. The figure enters the building. Edwards parks the squad car and exits firing his weapon. Four squad cars arrive. Edwards runs to the entrance and fires his weapon, blowing out windows. The officers fire at Edwards. Edwards

dives into the building. A moment later, the police pursue Edwards into the building.


*INVESTIGATOR'S NOTE: Any events that transpired after what has been captured in the above recorded footage are unclear. The bodies of three officers, Sheriff Rosco, Dr. Andrew Bia, and several members of his staff were recovered. An eyewitness account reported a unit of three soldiers entering the administration building sometime later that morning. A power outage prevented the recovery of any additional footage. These soldiers are presumed members of Edwards's unit. Their identities have been withheld under the declaration of war and laws of armed conflict. The whereabouts of Specialist Casie Edwards remain unknown at the time of this summarization.*

# ABOUT THE AUTHOR

Michael and his family live in western Massachusetts with their two pugs, Maggie and Murphy, who act like they run the place.

Growing up in the 70s and 80s, Michael was glued to everything science fiction and strange from the Six Million Dollar Man, The Incredible Hulk, and Knight Rider to Star Wars, Star Trek, and The Terminator to Bigfoot, the Loch Ness monster, and the supernatural.

When Dungeons & Dragons worried every mother that her boys were acting out a melee in the backyard, new worlds opened with limitless possibilities and his creativity expanded. Trying his hand at writing felt like a natural progression.

When Michael is not writing, you'll find him restoring an 1961 Willys Jeep.

# AUTHOR'S REQUEST

Thank you for reading CRACK of DAWN Part One.  If you enjoyed reading this book as much as I enjoyed writing it, please post a review. I would love to hear from my readers.  A sentence or a few words would be greatly appreciated.

# More Titles by Michael Glenzel

FARMER
Watershed
World Fusion
Ole Buried Grounds
Friday Night Fights No.1 (a short story of monster fiction)
Friday Night Fights No.2: Wild Men of the Black Hills
Zombie High
Dogs of War: Unfinished Business


For more information about Michael's books, visit AlienAlmanac.com.

www.ingramcontent.com/pod-product-compliance
Lightning Source LLC
Chambersburg PA
CBHW060301310726
48976CB00007B/2156